THE DEATH SEASON

By Kate Ellis

Wesley Peterson series:
The Merchant's House
The Armada Boy
An Unhallowed Grave
The Funeral Boat
The Bone Garden
A Painted Doom
The Skeleton Room
The Plague Maiden
A Cursed Inheritance
The Marriage Hearse
The Shining Skull
The Blood Pit
A Perfect Death
The Flesh Tailor
The Jackal Man
The Cadaver Game
The Shadow Collector
The Shroud Maker
The Death Season

Joe Plantagenet series:
Seeking the Dead
Playing With Bones

For more information regarding Kate Ellis
log on to Kate's website: www.kateellis.co.uk

THE DEATH SEASON

Kate Ellis

piatkus

PIATKUS

First published in Great Britain in 2015 by Piatkus

Copyright © 2015 by Kate Ellis

The moral right of the author has been asserted.

*All characters and events in this publication, other than those
clearly in the public domain, are fictitious and any resemblance
to real persons, living or dead, is purely coincidental.*

All rights reserved.
No part of this publication may be reproduced, stored in a
retrieval system, or transmitted in any form or by any means, without
the prior permission in writing of the publisher, nor be otherwise circulated
in any form of binding or cover other than that in which it is published
and without a similar condition including this condition being
imposed on the subsequent purchaser.

A CIP catalogue record for this book
is available from the British Library.

ISBN 978-0-349-40313-7

Typeset in Baskerville by M Rules
Printed and bound in Great Britain by
Clays Ltd, St Ives plc.

Papers used by Piatkus are from well-managed forests
and other responsible sources.

MIX
Paper from
responsible sources
FSC® C104740

Piatkus
An imprint of
Little, Brown Book Group
100 Victoria Embankment
London EC4Y 0DY

An Hachette UK Company
www.hachette.co.uk

www.piatkus.co.uk

With thanks to Laura Pullin,
who allowed her name to be used
for a good cause.

South Lanarkshire Library Service	
CG	
C70174172+	
Askews & Holts	
C	£19.99
4542537	

Prologue

May 1980

He gasps for every breath, bobbing to the surface of the salty water like a cork then sinking again, towed under by an unseen force. Death is close. He can almost hear it whispering: 'I want you. You can't escape me now.'

This is the end. His head is on some violent fairground ride and he tastes vomit in his mouth, vomit and salt. He tries to cry out. He tries to pray. He tries to save himself by paddling his weakening limbs in a semblance of swimming but every effort makes it worse. He shouldn't have gone into the sea after drinking in the bar but he's always been one to follow stronger and more determined natures.

He closes his eyes, tempted to yield to the inevitable. Now he's losing the fight he feels strangely peaceful. He wants it to be over. Drifting towards oblivion, he feels a sudden pain. Somebody is grabbing him roughly, bruising his flesh, yanking his neck. Another body is beneath him, moving strongly and rhythmically. He gasps for breath as a bright light dazzles his eyes and he realises his head is now above the water, supported by something or someone unseen.

He feels himself being hauled onto the hot, gritty sand and he's half aware of people crowding round him. Like a large fish landed by some boastful fisherman, he is the centre of attention.

He groans, closing his eyes tightly against the brilliant sun, and when he opens them again he is cocooned in a towel. Then he hears a voice, familiar yet unfamiliar.

'Are you OK now?'

It is a voice he recognises. An English voice. It belongs to the boy he was drinking with earlier, sharing a beer in the taverna beside the beach.

'What happened?' Chris hears himself asking in a voice that doesn't seem to be his own.

'You got into trouble. Probably too much beer. I had to pull you out.'

Chris hauls himself into a sitting position and puts his head in his hands. He still feels sick but better . . . so much better.

'You could do with a drink. Hair of the dog.'

'I'll get it.' Chris tries to struggle to his feet but sinks back again. On the third attempt he succeeds and the other boy supports him as he staggers to the bar. They look like a pair of cartoon drunks but Chris senses that his companion is completely sober.

Chris's hands shake as he finds his waterproof wallet and gives his rescuer the money to buy the drinks.

'Did you know that if someone saves you from drowning you belong to them from then on?'

Chris looks at the boy and realises that he is deadly serious. From now on his life will no longer be his own.

1

19th July 1913

Cold. Whatever the season it is always cold in the little attic room I share with Daisy here at Sandton House. Even in this glorious summer weather the place has a chill about it, and whenever the wind blows it howls around the house like a creature in torment.

Daisy says a maid once hanged herself in here; tied a twisted sheet to the exposed beam, stood on the old wooden chair in the corner, and jumped. Daisy says that on a windy night you can still hear her body swinging to and fro but I know that it's only the creaking of the big oak tree outside the window. Daisy is a liar and I tell her so but she still wears that smug smirk on her face as if she has a secret known only to herself.

Only I am the one with a secret, a secret so momentous, so precious, that I have nursed it to myself. There have been times when I've longed to share it with somebody – even with Daisy; pinch-faced, spiteful little Daisy with her sharp, angular limbs and her chest flat as a boy's – but I know I must stay silent until the time is right. From now on, I must be careful not to undress in front of Daisy and I must always keep to

my side of the bed we share. I do not want her to see my growing belly,
not until all is settled and Alfred keeps his promise to me. Then I will
lord it over her. How I long to see her face when she realises that I am
going to be her mistress; that she will have to serve me and call me
madam.

Until then I do not want any whisper of my secret to reach the ears
of Mrs Stevens. I would not have the fat housekeeper with her pig face
and her watchful eyes know of my condition before Alfred does.

Alfred is away at present visiting his aunt at Paradise Court, her
fine estate near the town of Neston. The first time I missed that which
curses womankind each month, I did not tell him because I was unsure.
But now I am certain and I know I must break the news on his return.
When we lay together in the great oak bed in his chamber he swore to
make me his wife if I was good to him. I must not doubt his sincerity.
I must not doubt that he loves me in spite of the difference in our sta-
tions. He has been raised as a gentleman. A man of his word.

And so I keep my secret, cling to it as many cling to faith. What
grows within me shall raise me high. Alfred has sworn it.

October 2014

Paulette closed the lid of the old chest freezer in the outhouse and stood back to examine it. There was rust on the
base where it met the damp concrete floor and sometimes,
when she lay awake at night listening to the sounds of the
countryside, she worried that the seals were showing signs
of black mould. If the freezer stopped working at some
point she'd have to make other plans.

She heard a tap on the window and jumped. But when
she turned she could see it was only a branch of the apple
tree, laden with mummified fruit, brushing the filthy glass
like a skeletal hand. Tap, tap-tap. For a moment she'd

thought they'd found out and come for her. But how could they? She'd done nothing to make anybody suspicious.

She switched off the light – a single, cobwebbed bulb drooping forlornly from the bare rafters – and flicked on the torch. It was time to return to the cottage for a well-earned malt whisky, something she'd developed a taste for ever since she'd helped herself to some at one of the houses where she'd worked. The first time was out of curiosity – just to see what the fuss was about – then it became a habit. Of course she'd topped up the bottles with water to avoid detection. She'd always been careful about things like that.

After locking the outhouse door she made her way back to the cottage, hugging her long black cardigan around her body as she picked her way through the fallen apples that had rotted to pulp on the ground. The wind was getting up now, each gust seizing the half-bare branches of the surrounding trees and shaking them like a petulant child. But she hardly noticed because she had other things on her mind.

There was the freezer, of course: her own private dilemma; her box of secrets. And she had another secret: one so precious, so potentially lucrative, that it would soon solve all her problems.

She'd bided her time for a while and now she was collecting her payment. However, she had one big regret. She'd kept in contact with Merlin since their chance meeting and, eager to regain his attention, she'd yielded to the temptation to show off and shared her secret. Look what I can do. Look what I've become. How was she to know he'd come to claim a share?

*

5

Chief Superintendent Noreen Fitton was a determined woman. Tall and angular with fine brown hair cut severely short, she exuded an air of capability. DI Wesley Peterson suspected that his boss DCI Gerry Heffernan was scared of her, even though in private he called her 'Aunty Noreen' as if that homely title would render her harmless. It was the first time he'd known Gerry to be frightened of anybody who wasn't carrying a gun.

When she'd summoned Gerry to her well-appointed lair first thing that Thursday morning, he'd left the CID office with the reluctance of a schoolboy summoned to the headmaster's study for smoking behind the bike sheds. Things hadn't been easy for Gerry since he'd been shot during the arrest of a killer back in May and Wesley knew he was frustrated with his own frailty. Gerry Heffernan wasn't the type of man who took reminders of mortality well.

Wesley gazed out of the window at the view across the river. Tradmouth's tourist season was more or less over, leaving only a few hardy retired souls still bent on conquering the South West Coastal Path. But today the rain fell in horizontal sheets and the wind raged outside, setting the grey river churning and the brown palm fronds rustling on the waterfront. It wasn't a good day for walking – or much else for that matter – and Wesley was glad he was indoors.

Things had been unusually quiet for the past few weeks. Only a spate of break-ins at isolated dwellings had shattered Wesley's cherished illusion that all the local criminals had declared a strike or, better still, seen the error of their ways and decided to go straight. The burglar had so far targeted five empty second homes, leaving no clue to his identity. Gerry, the eternal optimist, reckoned his luck was bound to run out soon.

Wesley glanced at DS Rachel Tracey who was sitting, deep in paperwork, at her desk. Rachel's recent loss of weight had sharpened her features and her fine blond hair was now cut in a short bob. A few months ago she'd worn it long and Wesley had preferred it that way. But he knew it was none of his business. Because of the extra duties she'd taken on in Gerry's absence, her wedding had been postponed until the following spring but she hadn't spoken of it in his hearing recently and he hadn't dared to inquire. When he'd mentioned it tentatively to her house-mate, DC Trish Walton, she'd said that she knew as much as he did, raising her eyebrows as she spoke, as though there was something she wasn't telling him. Then she'd changed the subject.

Gerry's return interrupted his ruminations. There was a preoccupied look on the DCI's face as he walked in carrying an armful of files, as if he was contemplating some insurmountable problem. He too was looking thinner these days, although some might have said that was a good thing.

Wesley followed him into his glass-fronted office and as Gerry dumped the files on his desk Wesley saw him wince with pain. His face, once plump and round, topped by a thatch of grizzled hair, now looked drawn.

'How did you get on?'

Gerry harrumphed and slumped back in his seat. 'When she called me into her office like a naughty housemaid who'd been caught supping the master's best claret, I was convinced she wanted to put me out to grass using this shooting business as an excuse.'

Wesley opened his mouth to protest but Gerry carried on before he could get a word in.

'I know I haven't been pulling my weight recently.'

'Come on, Gerry, you've been doing as much as you can. It's no big deal being put on light duties after what you've been through.'

Gerry was a good copper who had a natural rapport with people, the law-abiding and the not-so-law-abiding. Besides, if he wasn't there, Wesley would miss his company and his wisdom. When he'd arrived in Tradmouth, the first black detective in the area freshly transferred from the Metropolitan Police's Art and Antiques Unit, Gerry had accepted and valued him right away. And although the two men came from very different backgrounds – Gerry from Liverpool and the Merchant Navy and Wesley from public school and university – they'd become good friends over the years.

'What exactly did CS Fitton say?'

Gerry gave a sad smile, showing the gap between his front teeth. He'd once told Wesley it was a sign of good luck; certainly he had been lucky to survive the shooting.

'Well, she didn't mention the words "early retirement", which came as a relief. In fact, as things are fairly quiet at the moment, she asked me to have a look at a few cold cases for her before she gives them to the team over at Neston. She said she'd value my opinion.'

'Paul says there's a new lead on these break-ins so if we clear that up, I might be able to give you a hand.'

Gerry raised his head, suddenly hopeful. 'What's the new lead?'

'A dark van was spotted at the scene of the last one.'

Gerry rolled his eyes. 'A dark van? Couldn't he do better than that? Like a registration number?'

'You can't have everything.'

Gerry stared at the files on his desk and frowned. 'I once

heard someone say that when you're given a cold case it means you aren't up to handling a hot one.'

Wesley knew the boss liked to overdramatise at times and this was one of them. 'That's nonsense and you know it.'

Gerry began to open the files, one after another, giving the contents a perfunctory examination before pushing it to one side. 'There's all sorts here. Unsolved murders. Armed robberies. I don't know where to start. Aunty Noreen said I was to go through them and choose a couple that interest me – see what I mean about her giving me something to keep me quiet?' He sighed. 'They're doing DNA reviews on them and all.'

'Well, that might produce something useful.'

'Mmm. Why don't you get on with searching for your dark van?'

Wesley left him to it, wishing there was something he could say that would cheer him up.

Magdalena parked the trolley and knocked on the door of room 352.

'Housekeeping.'

She stood quite still for a while and listened. Sometimes she would hear sounds of frantic activity and a breathless 'Just a minute,' but all she heard here was a heavy silence. She knocked again, just to be sure, and when there was no reply she took her pass key from her overall pocket and opened the door.

Magdalena had been brought up in her native Poland to remember her manners and her instinctive reaction was to apologise to the man in the chair by the window and tell him she'd come back later. But something about his absolute stillness wasn't right. She hovered by the door for a few moments and said a tentative, 'Excuse me.' When there was still no reaction she crept slowly towards the window where the man was sitting upright in a leather tub chair next to a low round table bearing an empty plate scattered with crumbs, probably the remains of a room-service sandwich. Next to the plate was a half-empty bottle of whisky and a tumbler stained with crusted amber liquid.

Magdalena forced herself to look at the man. He was probably in his sixties with thick, well-cut, steel-grey hair, suntanned flesh and slightly sagging jowls. A good-looking man for his age. A man who'd taken care of himself.

His striped shirt was open at the neck and there was a large dark patch on his pale chinos where his bladder had emptied. He wore no shoes and Magdalena noticed that one of his toes peeped out through a small hole in his left sock. She thought he looked slightly unreal, like a waxwork.

She stared at him for a while, willing him to wake up, watching anxiously for any movement of his chest that would tell her he was still breathing, even though she knew that life had left his body and he would never wake again.

She backed away nervously as if she half expected him to open his eyes, stand up and come after her. Then she went over to the bed, still made up neatly and obviously unslept in, and fumbled for the bedside telephone with trembling hands, unwilling to take her eyes off the dead man. Her heart was pounding as she connected with Reception and when a female voice answered she managed to gasp the words: 'The man in three five two. He's dead.'

2

1st September 1913

Mrs Stevens has found me out. She has been watching me for days now and this morning, after I'd finished mopping the tiled floor in the front hall, she caught me vomiting into the sluice. She called me to her parlour and sat watching like a great bombazine-clad spider while I stood captive in her web. I did not bow my head. I am not ashamed. There is no shame in love.

She asked me to name the father but I would not. Alfred is still with his aunt at Paradise Court, aiding her on some legal matter. His aunt has a daughter, his cousin; a girl around my own age, I understand. But I must not entertain envious thoughts. I am his and he is mine. And yet when I serve Alfred's mother at table and she treats me as a barely human automaton whose purpose is only to serve her needs, small doubts buzz into my heart like flies loose in a pantry. He has been absent three full weeks now but when I recall his sweet and loving words to me, I know that he will never betray me.

Mrs Stevens addresses me as Rose but I tell her I wish to be called by my real name of Martha. Mrs Toncliffe likes to give her maidservants the names of flowers but from now on I shall insist on Martha. I am no wilting flower. I am the mother of her grandchild.

The wind had died down overnight and the October sun was attempting to appear from behind the low white clouds.

'The weather forecast's good for today so I'd like to make a start,' said the director, a shaven-headed man in his forties whose slightly bulging eyes made him look permanently startled. He wore a Berghaus fleece and skin-tight jeans and he held a clipboard which he used to shield his eyes as he gazed up at the sky like someone expecting divine guidance.

Dr Neil Watson of the County Archaeological Unit stood a little way off with his colleagues. Ever since the filming of *Ultra Dig* had begun the previous day, there had been a lot of waiting around and very little digging. When he'd been asked to take part in the series as a visiting expert, he'd questioned the wisdom of choosing the lost village of Sandrock as the subject for the first programme. As politely as he could, he had pointed out to the producer that the site was downright dangerous, especially with the season of autumn gales approaching. In February 1918 many of the houses in the small fishing village perched on a cliff five miles along the coast from Tradmouth had toppled into the sea during a violent storm, leaving only a handful of structures still standing, including the remains of the small and ancient church that had once been the focus of the abandoned community.

The director had been undaunted by warnings that archaeologists and volunteers might be risking their lives clambering over precarious ruins barred from public access by prominent warning signs. He wanted jeopardy and seemed to use the word as a mantra. Jeopardy kept the viewers watching and that's why he'd chosen to film in October when the weather was unpredictable. Neil never thought he'd ever utter the words 'health and safety' but there was a first time for everything.

Eventually a compromise had been reached. The excavation would concentrate on the church, the building furthest away from the cliff edge. Everybody, apart from the director, had been relieved. 'Let's get going,' he said.

Neil looked at the archaeological team who'd started to drift off towards the church. There were fifteen in all, half of whom he'd worked with on past excavations, and several experienced volunteers, members of a local amateur archaeological society drafted in to provide extra manpower. He was scheduled to lead a dig at a Heritage Trust property near Neston in a couple of days' time so he hoped everything would run smoothly at Sandrock. The deal was that he would only be needed for filming once a day to dispense his wisdom and analyse the previous day's discoveries. He wouldn't even have to get his hands dirty if he didn't want to and the TV company was paying him more than he usually earned in a year. The director might be a pain who knew little or nothing about archaeology, but it was a temptation Neil hadn't been able to resist. And besides, the ruined church looked interesting.

The site had already been surveyed and the geophysics results had been examined. The actual dig was being led by a woman who'd done a great deal of work up in the Orkneys. Her name was Lucy Zinara and, although he'd never met her before, he knew her by reputation and wondered what had lured her down to Devon, away from

13

Orkney's brochs, cairns and prehistoric monuments. No doubt he'd find out in due course.

Now the weather had improved it was time to get started and Neil hoped that the demands of filming wouldn't interfere too much with the serious business of digging. He nodded to the director and began to make for the church, pushing open the gate that bore dire warnings of danger and was usually kept locked. The others had gone on ahead carrying their equipment – black buckets, kneeling pads, trowels, shovels and mattocks – with the camera crew bringing up the rear.

Neil was about to follow when the director grabbed his arm. 'I need you and Lucy to do a piece to camera to explain what's going on. We'll start as soon as she arrives.'

'Where is she?'

'She's been delayed.' The man sounded peeved but as soon as the words had left his lips, Neil heard a female voice, slightly breathless and genuinely apologetic.

'I'm so sorry. I got stuck behind a herd of cows.'

He looked round to see a woman hurrying towards him. She was in her early thirties, slightly built with short brown hair and a pleasant face devoid of make-up. She wore an old anorak and sturdy digging boots: appropriate clothing.

'Lucy. So glad you're here.' There was a hint of sarcasm in the director's voice and Neil saw Lucy's cheeks redden. 'I don't think you've met Dr Neil Watson from the County Archaeological Unit. He's acting as our archaeological consultant for the series.'

Lucy Zinara thrust out her hand. 'Pleased to meet you at last. I've heard of you, of course.' She smiled as though she was genuinely pleased to meet him.

'I've heard of you too. Interesting work you've been doing up in Orkney, I believe.'

He was pleased that he'd taken some trouble with his appearance that morning. He'd washed his shoulder-length mousy hair specially and scrubbed the soil from his finger nails. He was wearing the new combat jacket he'd bought to replace its disreputable predecessor and even his many-pocketed cargo pants were freshly laundered. He'd felt compelled to make an effort for the TV, and now Lucy was there he was glad he had.

'Where are you planning to put in the trenches?' he asked.

'I thought we'd have four initially. The geophys results have shown some interesting anomalies. Let's go and have a look.' She smiled again.

As they walked towards the shoulder-height remains of the small porch that was once the entrance to the church, she began to chat. 'I've been told that you'll only be here part of the time.'

'That's right. I'm supervising another dig for the Heritage Trust near Neston and I'll be flitting between the two sites.'

'It's Paradise Court, isn't it?'

He was surprised and rather gratified that she'd done her homework. 'That's right. Know it?'

'Actually I've got family links with the place.'

'So you're from round here?'

'Originally.'

He waited for her to say more but she didn't so Neil continued, filling the silence. 'According to records, there was an earlier house on the site of Paradise Court and it looks as though part of its foundations might be in the walled garden. We're also looking for an ice house we think is lost in the undergrowth. If you don't find much here at Sandrock, you're always welcome to give us a hand.'

'You're tempting me,' she said with a gleam in her eye.

'So what's brought you back to Devon?'

'My great-grandmother's ill and my mother needs support. Her parents died when she was young and Clara brought her up so they're close. Clara's in a nursing home about a mile and a half away.' She smiled. 'She's a tough old girl. She was a hundred in July.'

'It's a good age.'

She was about to answer when he heard the director's voice calling her name.

'Duty calls,' she said, as she turned to go.

The constable from Morbay police station who'd been summoned to the Morbay Palace Hotel expected it to be a routine visit. The police have to be called to every sudden death, and only rarely do they discover anything other than a natural death. Or occasionally a suicide.

According to the hotel, the deceased was called Alan Buchanan and he had given a London address. The constable thought the man looked quite peaceful sitting there in the tub chair, almost as though he was taking a nap and would wake up any moment. But the doctor had been called and would be arriving any moment to pronounce life extinct.

The constable anticipated that his duties would be confined to identifying the deceased and arranging for his next of kin to be informed, but the motions had to be gone through so he began to search the room. The bedside drawers contained nothing apart from a Bible and a guide to the hotel's facilities, and the wardrobe didn't reveal much inside, only a linen jacket hanging limply on a wooden hanger, a couple of pairs of trousers, three newish shirts and a selection of clean socks and underwear on a side shelf. The dead man had travelled light.

In the pockets of the jacket he came across a leather wallet. He had just discovered sixty-five pounds in cash and two credit cards, one in the name of Alan Buchanan and another in the name of Andrew Stedley, when he heard a knock on the door. The doctor had arrived.

Dr Susan Cramer had been shown up to room 352 by the manager, who was doing his best imitation of an undertaker on duty. The man hovered by the door as though he intended to hang around during her examination of the dead man, but luckily the young PC in attendance ushered him out, making reassuring noises: They'd take the body away as soon as possible. There'd be no disruption to the life of the hotel. The other guests would be blissfully unaware that anything as unpleasant as a sudden death had taken place on the premises.

Once the manager had left Dr Cramer knelt by the body, feeling for a pulse on the neck, just in case. But the flesh was marble-cold. The man had been dead some time, probably since the previous night.

Her hand brushed the thick grey hair and, unexpectedly, her fingers came into contact with something that felt harder and rougher than a human scalp. It was a couple of seconds before she realised that it was webbing.

'He's wearing a wig,' she said, lifting the hair then replacing it again quickly, reluctant to rob the dead man of his dignity.

17

'I noticed something a bit funny, Doctor,' the PC said nervously. He had a shock of fair hair and he reminded Dr Cramer of her younger son.

She stopped her examination and looked round. 'Funny ha-ha or funny peculiar?'

The PC gave a sheepish grin. 'Definitely peculiar. That drink on the table appears to have some sort of deposit in the bottom. And he had two credit cards on him, both in different names.'

'Sounds suspicious. You should tell the police.'

She didn't wait for him to think up an answer to her witticism before turning her attention to the glass. The lad was right: there was something peculiar.

She was wearing latex gloves so she had no hesitation in picking it up and sniffing it. All she could smell was whisky but there was certainly a crusted deposit at the bottom. There was no way she could dismiss this as a heart attack and send the body to the mortuary without further investigation.

After telling the PC to put a call in to CID, she looked up the number for the pathologist, Dr Colin Bowman. She wasn't happy with this one at all.

3

10th September 1913

Alfred is Mrs Toncliffe's only son, sole heir to his late father, Colonel Toncliffe, who passed from this life a year ago, shortly before I came to Sandton House, and now lies in the family vault of the parish church with his forebears. I never met the colonel but all the servants speak well of him. They do not, however, speak well of Alfred but that is because they do not know him as I do.

His mother, the lady I shall soon address as mother-in-law, is a tall, stately woman who reminds me of our gracious Queen Mary with her straight bearing and severe glances. Perhaps I shall be like that when I am mistress, all dignity and condescension. How my fortunes will rise when Alfred learns of our little joy, for I trust him to keep his word and marry me. He is a gentleman like his father before him.

I am not so big yet that I cannot conceal my condition with my apron. Mrs Stevens says that the moment my shame – for that is what she calls it – is obvious to all, I must leave the house and never return. That day will not be long in coming and I wait each day for news of my Alfred.

I have heard that his aunt will have need of him at Paradise Court for a while longer for there is some legal matter regarding her estate to untangle and Alfred is so wise in these matters in spite of his tender years. He is but twenty-two, some four years my senior. I think that is the perfect difference in age between man and wife. Meanwhile his mother rules here in her mourning black and her shiny jet jewels, and I think she has forgotten how to smile since the colonel's death. I wonder if her grandchild will make her smile again, for surely any child of Alfred's will be beautiful and will make her forget the lowly station of its mother once we are married.

Alfred has not sent word to me but I expect his aunt's affairs take all his attention. I had a letter from my mother in the morning post. How I long to tell her my secret, that I am to be married to a gentleman and that she will be the mother of a lady. I shall set her up in a house on Alfred's land and she will not be forced to endure the hardships of life in Sandrock much longer.

The excavation was going well so far and the watching cameras were so unobtrusive that Neil had almost forgotten they were there.

The director spent much of the time talking on the phone, ignoring the diggers, which suited Neil fine. Neil's piece to camera consisted of a conversation with Lucy about what they hoped to find in the trenches they were opening up. Lucy was a TV natural, he thought: warm and at her ease. He found himself responding to her relaxed manner, chatting unselfconsciously about the dig as if they weren't on public view. It looked as if this thing was going to work.

When his part of the filming was over he helped out in Lucy's trench for a while. As long as he was at Paradise Court by three thirty to catch up with what was going on, it would be fine. He had an experienced team there so didn't have to worry too much, as long as he showed his face every so often. It surprised him that he'd starting thinking like this – he'd expected to be anxious to escape from the interference and pretensions of the TV crew at every opportunity. But since he'd met Lucy Zinara, he found he really didn't mind hanging around at Sandrock at all.

Although the village had been destroyed in 1918 by the elements, its fate had been sealed years earlier when, in the late nineteenth century, the powers that be had dredged the sea shore to provide building materials for the dockyards in Plymouth. Over the years the waves eroded the foundations of the little fishing community until, on a fateful February night, the village collapsed into the sea with the loss of twenty souls. The wind and the weather had done the rest, leaving Sandrock as a collection of picturesque ruins. It had been chosen for the first programme in the series because of the drama of its destruction.

Most of the houses in the village that hadn't tumbled into the sea had been left as fragile shells, too hazardous to enter. However the little church dedicated to St Enroc, a sixth-century Celtic hermit, had been furthest away from the cliff edge and, although the storms and neglect of a century had reduced it to a roofless ruin, its walls still stood firm. It dated from the Middle Ages but possibly there had been an earlier structure on the site – the cell of St Enroc himself. Lucy said she hoped they'd find evidence of the elusive saint. So, he knew, did the TV company.

From the early nineteenth century to the abandonment of the village, St Enroc's had been used as a 'chapel of ease' so that the residents of Sandrock wouldn't have to walk the two miles to the nearest parish church each Sunday. There were no recorded burials there as the dead of Sandrock had been taken on a cart to the parish church for interment, which meant that the dig wouldn't be complicated by the discovery of human remains. Unless something earlier turned up; maybe even something from the days of St Enroc. Now that would be interesting, Neil thought.

Four trenches were now open within the walls of the church and the diggers had already uncovered a tiled floor a few inches below the surface. The tiles looked nineteenth-century, probably put down by some overenthusiastic Victorian restorers whose idea of caring for an ancient building was to destroy most of its original features and replace them with some new and shiny reproduction, their own romantic vision of medieval life.

In the car park three hundred yards inland, put there by the council years ago for the sightseers who came to gaze at the ruins of Sandrock from the nearby viewing platform, a small catering van was parked, providing bacon sandwiches and endless mugs of tea and coffee for the TV crew and diggers throughout the day. Neil was unaccustomed to such luxury and he said as much to Lucy as they walked up the hill to the van in search of refreshment.

'You said you had family links with Paradise Court,' he said, making conversation.

'Yes. I told you about my great-grandmother, didn't I?'

'Clara,' he said, pleased that he'd remembered the name.

'She grew up at Paradise Court and lived there until it was given to the Heritage Trust after World War Two. It had been used by the Army for something hush-hush and when she got it back she found she couldn't afford the upkeep.' She hesitated. 'Since she ... since she started getting confused, she's been mentioning Sandrock a lot and talking about houses crashing down around her. But as far as I know she's never been here. It's odd.'

'It might be something she's read, or she probably heard people talking about it when she was younger. Paradise Court's not that far away, is it.' He stopped and looked back. They had climbed the hill towards the car park and he could see the ruins of the village below him, the walls blending with the cliff and the calm sea beyond. It looked peaceful now with the sun-diamonds glinting on the waves and a pair of yachts skimming over the water with their white sails hoisted, but the sea could change from purring cat to angry tiger in an instant. It had been Sandrock's livelihood. Then one night it had turned on the village and become its destroyer.

Neil began to walk again. He suddenly felt hungry.

Dr Colin Bowman had been in the middle of a post-mortem when he received the call summoning him to the Morbay Palace Hotel to examine a dead man by the name of Alan Buchanan. It looked suspicious, he was told. The coroner and CID had been informed.

When he'd finished dealing with the corpse on the table, an unfortunate victim of a multiple collision on the Morbay bypass, Colin cleaned himself up and put on the tweed jacket he favoured on such occasions, casting a regretful glance at the kettle. He normally made himself a cup of Earl Grey after a postmortem – essential refreshment – but today there was no time.

The hotel was a rambling Edwardian edifice on the seafront, a mile from Morbay Hospital, so he took the car. Once he'd parked next to a pair of police patrol vehicles, he made for Reception where a young woman directed him to room 352 in a hushed voice, trying her best not to let any listening guests know that anything was amiss.

The case he was carrying contained all the equipment he needed and, because of its weight, he decided on the unhealthy option and took the lift. When he reached his destination the door was opened by a young constable. As he stepped into the room he saw a man in his thirties with dark brown skin, intelligent warm brown eyes and even, delicate features; he was wiry but not particularly tall. When he turned round he gave Colin a welcoming smile.

'Colin. Pleased to see you.' Wesley Peterson's words sounded sincere. 'How are you?'

'Not so bad, Wesley. Yourself? The family?'

Once Wesley replied that both he and his nearest and dearest were fine, Colin inquired about Wesley's sister, Maritia, who was a GP near Neston, married to the vicar of nearby Belsham. It was a routine they went through every time they met. Colin was a man who never forgot the social niceties, however grim the situation.

'Well, what have we got here, Wesley? Dr Cramer said it looks suspicious.'

'That's right.' He pointed to the table by the dead man's chair. 'She didn't like the look of the deposit in the glass he'd been drinking from. At first she thought it might have been suicide.'

Colin raised his eyebrows. 'Do I sense a "but"?'

'First of all he was in possession of two credit cards in different names and when I had a look round the room I noticed that the other glass on the refreshment tray had been rinsed but not dried. The man might have used the separate glass to have a drink of water but it's also possible that someone was in here with him and he cleaned up after himself.' He paused, as though saving the best until last. 'The dead man's wearing a wig and when Dr Cramer lifted it off she saw an unusual mark on the back of his neck. She thought it might be a neat incision of some kind.'

Wesley approached the dead man, who was still sitting in the tub chair like a host receiving guests, and gently, almost apologetically, placed a hand on the thick head of grey hair and lifted it carefully. It came off to reveal a scalp sparsely covered with wisps of white hair and immediately the man looked older, less distinguished.

'We all have our little vanities, I suppose,' said Colin, feeling a pang of pity for the stranger who was being robbed of all remnants of dignity in death. He stepped over and peered at the spot where Wesley was pointing. Sure enough there was a neat mark about a centimetre long on the nape of the man's neck, surrounded by a small amount of crusted blood.

'What do you think?' Wesley sounded eager for the verdict.

'I can't say anything definite until I've got him on the slab but you did right to bring it to my attention. I'll do a full postmortem in the morning and then, hopefully, we'll know exactly what we're dealing with.'

'Thanks, Colin. In the meantime I want this room treated as a crime scene until we know otherwise. A CSI team should be here soon and I've asked someone to have a look at the hotel's CCTV.'

'Is Gerry on his way over?'

Wesley shook his head. 'He's still not back at work full time.'

Colin looked surprised. 'I thought he was on the mend.

Last time I saw him he was looking much better, told me I wasn't going to see him professionally for a good few years yet.'

'It seems to be a slow business, Colin. He finds it frustrating but he's keeping himself busy looking into some of our unsolved cases.' He turned to look at the dead man. 'Although if this does turn out to be murder, I predict he'll find some way of getting involved. He's not a man who can be persuaded to take it easy.'

Colin guessed that Wesley was more worried about Gerry than he was saying. He touched his sleeve in a gesture of reassurance before struggling into his crime-scene suit and gloves to begin his examination of the corpse.

Clara was a hundred years old and therefore a star resident of the Sandton House Nursing Home, a mile and a half from Sandrock. On her birthday in July she had received a card from the Queen and a visit from the mayor and mayoress of Tradmouth who had shared her birthday cake and posed with her for the photographs that made the front page of the *Tradmouth Echo*. By virtue of her longevity, Clara had become a celebrity.

Brenda was on duty that evening. The shift fitted in with her family commitments and she quite liked the work, although she couldn't say she'd ever taken to Clara, who was too fond of ordering the carers about as though they were her servants. From what she'd gleaned from the other staff, Clara came from a wealthy family and nowadays her mind kept sliding back to the distant past. But Brenda still found herself resenting the way the old woman spoke to her, even though she had no choice but to smile and go along with it all if she was to keep her job. Since the last official inspection of the home, the manager came down heavily on anybody who put a foot wrong.

Clara, having been prepared for bed, was in her room and it was up to Brenda to take in her customary cup of hot chocolate. Clara was fond of chocolate. She'd received a lot of it for her birthday and it had played havoc with her bowels for days.

Brenda gave a token knock on the door and pushed it open. The old woman was lying in bed and her eyes were shut tight. She was already asleep so Brenda crept out of the room, switching off the light as the manager had instructed. Electricity was too expensive to waste.

She was on her way back to the kitchen when she heard a scream from Clara's room, a cry of desperation which almost made her drop the cup and its contents onto the new cord carpet. Clara was having another of her nightmares.

Brenda deposited the cup in the kitchen before hurrying back to the old woman's room. She didn't want her waking the other residents. Sometimes if one was restless it could set the others off and if that happened they were in for a hell of a night.

The screaming was louder now and, as Brenda burst into the room and flicked on the light, she saw that Clara was lying on her back with her watery blue eyes wide open, a look of sheer terror on her shrunken face as if she was seeing a vision of hell itself. Brenda hurried to the bed, grasped her claw-like hand and began to stroke it, forgetting for a moment her resentment of Clara's imperious manner.

'It's all right, Clara. You're just having a bad dream. Everything's OK. You're safe,' she crooned, her voice low and soothing.

27

But Clara was still trapped in her own terrifying world. 'Mummy. It's falling.'

As Brenda watched she curled her body into a foetal ball and covered her balding head with her skeletal arms. Brenda knelt by the bed. 'You're OK, Clara. I'm here.'

The old woman started to whimper. 'She won't move. Make her move.'

The sobs began to subside. For now, the nightmare was over.

As far as Jayden Ross was concerned they got what they deserved – the rich idiots who could afford to buy perfectly good houses just to use them for a few weeks a year. According to Jayden's code of morality, if he broke in while they were empty and helped himself to a few goodies, he was hardly doing anything wrong.. It was redistribution of wealth – and what was wrong with a bit of that?

He'd even made it into the papers: ANOTHER COTTAGE BREAK-IN – POLICE APPEAL FOR INFORMATION. Fame at last. His one regret was that it was usually cleaners who discovered his handiwork. He wished it could have been the owners. But there's collateral damage in every war.

He'd often passed the track leading to Woodside Cottage and a year ago he'd noticed a FOR SALE sign by the gate. The sign had soon vanished and recently he hadn't seen much sign of occupation there so he assumed it had been bought as a second home again. There were plenty around who didn't even have a first – his brother, his partner and the new baby included. They lived at his mum's. It was bloody crowded and the baby kept him awake at night with its continuous squawking.

Jayden's only transport was an ancient moped which

served him well day to day. But when he needed to do a job he had to borrow the van from his mate Lee. He'd known Lee since primary school and he didn't ask questions. The two of them had a lot in common, living on the Winterham Estate on the hinterland of Morbay with their respective mums, their dads having buggered off years ago. However Lee had a job working nights in a petrol station and Jayden had nothing apart from his benefits and what he'd gleaned from a spot of shoplifting before an overzealous store detective put a stop to that particular source of income. Now with his new enterprise he had stepped up a league. And he had the thrill of staying one step ahead of the baffled plods.

Because of Lee's working hours, Jayden could only borrow the van during the day, which didn't really matter because the places he chose were isolated. But before he acted he liked to see the lie of the land, so at ten thirty that evening he started the moped and left the Winterham Estate. Woodside Cottage lay down a network of tight, twisting lanes that branched off the main road to Tradmouth. If you didn't know it was there, you'd never find it.

When he was driving Lee's van he hated the narrow lanes, dreaded meeting a car, or worse still some agricultural vehicle, and having to manoeuvre backwards into a passing place. Things were easier on the moped and, besides, tonight the roads were virtually empty, probably because most of the tourists had gone home. Eventually he saw the painted sign in the beam of his headlight: WOODSIDE COTTAGE. When he'd passed it in the daylight he'd seen the house from the lane – small, whitewashed, thatched and surrounded by trees. Somebody's rural dream. But not for much longer.

He liked to watch the houses from the darkness before he struck. It gave him a feeling of power, the thrilling realisation that he could see them but they couldn't see him. When he'd come here a couple of nights ago he'd watched her through the open curtains – a woman alone, probably down here while her fat banker husband was up in London. They thought the countryside was peaceful, safe. He was about to shatter her smug, cosy world.

He stood near the trees, his eyes fixed on the downstairs window. It was lit up again and he wished he could get closer so that he could see inside but it wasn't worth the risk of discovery. She was there all right. He saw her leave the room and a few moments later she emerged from the side entrance and made for the outhouse that stood to the left of the house, her torch pointed at the door. It was the first time he'd had a good look at her. She was older than he'd imagined with a double chin and dyed blond hair scraped back into a ponytail. The long black cardigan she wore over her short skirt fell open to reveal a tight top which emphasised the rolls of fat around her middle. He'd expected a woman who had that sort of money to have looked after herself better.

He stayed hidden because the last thing he wanted was confrontation. He preferred to do his work by stealth when they were out during the day. She emerged from the outhouse and scurried back to the cottage like a frightened spider. The thought of her terror when she discovered that her home had been violated gave him a thrill of excitement.

In the meantime he'd wait. And watch. He liked watching them.

4

20th September 1913

Alfred returned earlier today and when I ask to meet him in private my request is granted at once, although his manner is serious and he does not kiss me. We avoid the drawing room where his mother spends the day and meet in the summerhouse.

The summer is gone now and the wind is cold. I wrap my thread-bare shawl around my shoulders and hurry outside. Mrs Stevens is upstairs so I do not have to explain myself. Daisy passes me in the servants' passage and catches my arm. She asks where I am going and I do not tell her. She looks as if she longs to slap my face. When I am mistress I will dismiss her without a character.

Alfred is waiting. I see him before he sees me and I think that he is so handsome in his country tweeds, every inch a gentleman. The moustache he has grown whilst at his aunt's suits him and gives him more authority, I think. There is certainly a new gravity about him, as though the responsibility he has assumed for his aunt's affairs has turned him suddenly from youth to man.

I let the shawl slip from my shoulders as it is not a garment fitting for a lady, and go towards him. I smile and my eyes are filled with longing. He has been away less than a month but it feels like an age.

As I approach to kiss his cheek he does not move. I wait for a smile, a sign of his affection, and after a few seconds he takes my hand.

'I cannot stay long,' he says. 'Mama wishes me to take tea with her.'

'Then we should both take tea with your mama,' I say. 'She will need to be told of our wedding.'

He frowns as if my words are outrageous and takes a step back, his mouth gaping. 'Wedding?' The word emerges in a gasp and I see that he does not understand.

I tell him my news. Our news. Ever since I realised for sure that I was carrying his child within me, I have anticipated this moment. I have lain in my bed imagining his delight that our love, our precious love, has borne fruit. But instead he stares at me, his eyes so cold that the blue I thought resembled the cornflowers in the fields is now the colour of ice.

Wesley's brain was too active for sleep. He propped himself up on his elbow and watched his wife Pam who was sleeping beside him, curled up on her side. In the moonlight seeping through the curtains he could see that a wisp of brown hair had fallen across her face and he felt an urge to push it back. But she was a light sleeper and he knew it would disturb her.

The glowing red numbers on the alarm clock told him it was one o'clock. If he didn't stop thinking about the dead man at the Morbay Palace Hotel soon, he'd be in no fit state tomorrow to co-ordinate the investigation into his death. He closed his eyes and tried to empty his mind but he kept seeing the man's lifeless face and the pathetic wig like a small dead animal in his hands, and when he finally fell asleep he dreamed about it.

When he next opened his eyes he saw that Pam had gone and that it was already quarter to eight. He'd intended to be in the office early to see what had come in overnight because he was supposed to be in charge now that Gerry was taking a back seat. He was annoyed with himself and annoyed with Pam for not waking him when she'd risen at seven to dress for work and get the children ready for school.

He arrived downstairs to find the children were eating their breakfast. Michael looked up from his cornflakes and grinned while Amelia leaped up from the table and gave him a hug. Pam was busy making coffee and when she heard him enter the room she turned, her face serious. 'You looked shattered so I didn't like waking you.'

'You should have done.'

Pam returned to what she was doing as Wesley dropped a couple of slices of bread into the toaster, almost tripping over Moriarty the cat who was licking her paws elegantly in a post-breakfast wash and brush-up.

When the toast was ready Pam sat down beside him. 'Make sure you're free on Saturday night. Yolanda's organised a social evening and charity auction to raise money for new playground equipment and all staff are expected to attend. No excuses for absence.'

Yolanda was the headmistress of the school where Pam taught, and so her boss. Wesley had met her just the once and he knew he'd rather spend the evening with a pack of hardened villains, but he said nothing.

'I've arranged for Michael and Amelia to stay the night with your sister so babysitters aren't a problem.'

Wesley saw Michael frown. 'I'm too old for babysitters,' he said.

'But you don't mind staying with Aunty Maritia and Uncle Mark, do you?'

Michael looked sheepish and shook his head.

'What time will you be back tonight?' Pam asked. The question sounded innocent, without reproach, but Wesley couldn't help feeling defensive as he told her that, thanks to the dead man at the hotel, he wasn't sure.

On leaving the house, he kissed her cheek and said he'd try and make it home as soon as he could. He thought she gave him a rueful look, as though he had let her down in some way. But it might have been his imagination – or his conscience.

He dashed out, deciding to take the car instead of walking down the steep hill into the town as he usually did. As soon as the fresh air hit him he shivered with the cold and from his front drive he could see that the town below was veiled in sea mist. He switched on his headlights before starting out and drove slowly down the steep main road into Tradmouth.

When he reached the police station he found the DCI's office empty. Gerry had often been late in the past, citing anything from a malfunctioning alarm clock to an attack by killer seagulls as an excuse. When Gerry said these things, everyone laughed but Wesley, the straight man of the duo, didn't have his boss's reputation for flippancy or his comic timing. Looking at Gerry's vacant chair, he knew he'd miss not working closely with him on this investigation. The thought was almost painful.

Wesley was about to sit down at his desk to find out whether anything useful had come in overnight when

Rachel hurried towards him. Her face looked strained and behind her make-up he could see the puffiness and the spider's web of fine lines around her eyes. He longed to ask her if something was wrong, but said nothing.

'When you've given your briefing we'd better get to Morbay for hotel-man's postmortem,' she said.

Wesley looked at his watch. 'Anything new come in?'

'Not yet. Nick Tarnaby's called in sick. Claims he has a bad back. He chooses his moments.'

Wesley sighed. Until yesterday they'd only had the break-ins to worry about. Now with this murder in Morbay, they'd be working at full stretch again and Gerry wouldn't be there to take charge. As well as that they were an officer short in Nick Tarnaby's absence, which meant he'd have to draft in more help. The first person who sprang to mind was the young constable who'd been called to the Morbay Palace Hotel. Rob Carter had shown initiative and he had ambitions to join CID so maybe, if he lived up to his promise, Wesley could accelerate matters for him. When he made the call to Morbay police station, asking for back-up and mentioning Rob's name, he felt as if he'd done his good deed for the day.

After giving his morning briefing he assigned three more officers to check on the man in the hotel. There had been two credit cards in his wallet, both in different names, so if he was involved in some sort of fraud then it was highly possible he had a criminal record. If they were to get anywhere with the investigation, they needed to discover everything they could about the victim's life.

By the time Wesley and Rachel set off for Morbay, Gerry still hadn't arrived and Wesley felt disappointed as he'd hoped to go over the case with him. However, it seemed that the DCI was obeying doctor's orders for a change and pacing himself.

As Wesley drove out of the station car park he felt momentarily overwhelmed, inundated by a wave of crime he felt unable to tackle. But he told himself that once the back-up arrived, everything would be fine and he began to feel excited about the challenge of being in charge. Then he remembered that Pam would return from work to an empty house that evening and many evenings to come, trying to deal with the children's demands while she wrote her reports and lesson plans. She needed him at the moment, but the team needed him too. He felt a nagging, restless frustration that he couldn't be in two places at once.

As they crossed the river on the car ferry Rachel leaned back and watched the river. Only a few months ago she'd confided in him that she wasn't sure about her forthcoming marriage to Nigel, a local farmer who was a good, reliable man, if possibly a little dull. At the same time she'd confessed her attraction to Wesley and he'd been so tempted to reciprocate that it had taken all his strength to resist. He'd reminded himself that he had Pam and the children. Besides, his strict but loving churchgoing parents, who'd come to England from Trinidad to train as doctors, would be devastated if he ever betrayed his family in that way. Some things were destructive, he'd told himself time and time again: some things wrecked families and caused untold pain. Some things were simply wrong. Each time he recalled his moment of temptation, he cringed with embarrassment. But now they were alone Wesley found the lure of discovering Rachel's wedding plans irresistible, like picking at a scab.

'How are the new wedding preparations going?'

Her wedding at St Margaret's church at the end of summer had been postponed when Gerry was shot, ostensibly because she'd taken on extra responsibilities at work. It had been bad timing but she'd promised that a new date would be set in due course.

She sniffed. 'OK, I think. My mum's enjoying herself.'

'You might have three brothers but you're her only daughter. It's a big thing for her.'

'Sometimes I wonder if I'm only going ahead with it to keep people happy,' she said, gazing out of the car window.

The words made his heart lurch. 'Pleasing other people is no reason to get married. You have to be sure.'

'I am,' she said, but the words sounded a little unconvincing.

'Nigel's a good man. He'll make you happy, I know he will.'

There was a long silence and for a moment Wesley feared that she was going to say something about what had happened between them, the relationship that Wesley had put a stop to before it had even begun. When she said nothing he was grateful.

For the rest of the journey they spoke only about the case, and on their arrival at Morbay Hospital's mortuary Colin greeted them effusively and offered them refreshment. Wesley said he'd have something later – he'd rather get the gruesome business out of the way first.

At least at Morbay's state-of-the-art mortuary there was a glass screen to separate the audience from the action. He watched as Colin went about his business and Rachel, standing beside him, was paying rapt attention, as if she considered it impolite to take her eyes off the proceedings.

'Any observations?' Wesley asked through the microphone in front of him.

'He's in his sixties at a guess. Not many distinguishing features, I'm afraid. Not much of his own hair left which, I presume, is why he resorted to a wig. No scars or tattoos. He's probably put on a few pounds in middle age but his muscle tone's not bad for his age. He looked after himself. And he has an impressive tan. Either he was a regular on the sun beds or he was used to a better climate than the Devon winter.'

Once Colin had finished his examination of the torso, he turned his attention to the head. Wesley averted his eyes as the pathologist peeled back the flesh and got to work with an electric saw. Seeing him make the Y-shaped incision in the chest was bad enough but this was the part that really disturbed him.

'Hello.' It was Colin's voice coming through the speakers behind the screen.

'What is it?' Wesley asked, forcing himself to look. To his horror Colin was holding up a brain, examining it carefully.

'I thought there was something odd about that mark on the back of his neck. Come and have a look at this.'

'I'd rather not if you don't mind, Colin. Just tell us what you've found.'

Colin placed the brain in a steel bowl held out for him by his assistant and beamed in Wesley's direction. 'It looks as if our friend here was stabbed in the back of the neck with a thin sharp object, probably something like a paperknife. Or a stiletto – not the heel, of course,' he added with a twinkle. 'It was rammed straight up into his brain. Very hard to detect at first, particularly with that wig he was wearing. Full marks to Dr Cramer for spotting it. I'm still awaiting the toxicology report but it's possible he was doped somehow and the killer was able to drive the weapon home without our victim putting up a fight.' He raised his hands and mimed the action, his expression uncharacteristically murderous.

'So it's definitely murder?'

'Oh yes. I'm sorry to add to your workload, Wesley. Any fingerprints found in the room where he died?'

'Lots. But it's a question of finding the killer's amongst all the others. Process of elimination. Both glasses and the bottle of whisky had been wiped clean so our killer probably wiped everything else he touched too. What about the time of death?'

'Well, he'd been dead a while when he was found but don't despair. His stomach contents included barely digested chicken, salad and white bread – a chicken sandwich at a guess, as well as a glass or two of whisky. He must have consumed all this shortly before he shuffled off this mortal coil so if you can find out when he ate the sandwich . . . '

Wesley allowed himself a small smile of triumph. 'We've already established from the hotel that he arrived back and collected his room key from Reception at five thirty and ordered a chicken sandwich and the bottle of whisky from room service at seven. If he ate it right away . . . '

'Estimated time of death between seven thirty and nine thirty then. You only get pinpoint accuracy on TV shows, I'm afraid.' Colin placed the steel bowl containing the dead man's brain on a trolley. 'Once I've finished here, I'll make us all a cup of tea. You look as though you could do with one.'

Wesley thanked him. But it would take more than Colin's tea and biscuits to bring whoever killed the man on the trolley to justice.

Neil had reached Sandrock at eight o'clock that Friday morning to get his filming done first thing so that he could arrive at Paradise Court at a reasonable time. Sandrock, he thought, was interesting but its demise was well documented, whereas Paradise Court, with its intriguing geophysics results, was a bit of a mystery.

He hoped that Lucy Zinara, with her family connection to Paradise Court, might come up with some useful information about the place. He liked Lucy. No, more than liked – he was attracted to her. But she'd worked in Orkney since she'd left university so who was to say that she wouldn't disappear back there once her family troubles had been sorted? he thought, allowing his inner pessimist to gain the ascendant.

The sea fret was drifting in from the water as he stood looking down on the mist-shrouded ruins. Life would have been tough for the inhabitants of Sandrock, even before the sea stole their homes. Once the seasons turned unkind it would have been a struggle to survive.

Neil's musings were interrupted by the director. 'We're ready to start filming now.' The words were pointed, as though he suspected Neil of slacking.

The man led the way to the church where the diggers were arriving, uncovering the trenches that they'd protected with tarpaulins the previous night. Lucy was with them sorting out the equipment and when she spotted Neil her face lit up with a smile. He smiled back.

There was a delay while the camera crew adjusted their

equipment. It was the sort of thing Neil usually found irritating but today it gave him a chance to talk to Lucy.

'I'm going to Paradise Court when I've finished here,' he said, sidling up to her. 'I'd like to talk to you about the place sometime if that's OK. Do you fancy meeting for a drink after you've finished for the evening?' He could hardly believe he'd had the courage to say it and hoped he'd managed to sound casual.

Lucy had been watching the camera crew's preparations but now she looked at him and for the first time he noticed that her eyes were grey flecked with green. It was hard to read her expression but he thought he detected a slight look of disapproval.

'Normally I'd say yes but Clara had a bad night last night and my mother wants me to go with her to the nursing home after we clear up this evening. I don't know how long I'll be. I'm sorry.' She fell silent for a few seconds before continuing, as if she thought some additional explanation was needed. 'My mum and I are her only living relatives, you see, and with me working down here I feel I should take on some of the responsibility.'

Neil was unsure what to say. It had crossed his mind that the old lady, who'd actually lived at Paradise Court before the war, might enjoy the chance to reminisce about her younger days as many elderly people did. Now though it seemed tactless to suggest it.

'Clara's been having vivid nightmares, almost like hallucinations,' Lucy went on. 'She wakes up screaming and shouting about walls collapsing around her.' Neil adopted what he hoped was an expression of sympathy, surprised and rather gratified that she was confiding in him. 'The manager of the home's quite concerned. She thinks she

41

might have been disturbed by these storms we've had recently. But I think it could be my fault. It's hard to know what to say when you visit so I've been rabbiting on about work, talking about Sandrock and the ruins.'

'I'm sure it can't have anything to do with you.'

'I hope you're right. I know it's all in her mind, but . . . '

Neil wasn't quite sure how to respond so he chose the unoriginal option and said how awful it must be for the old woman.

'Until recently she's been so sharp,' Lucy said as though she hadn't heard. 'I've always thought she was amazing for her age.'

'Do you think she remembers much about Paradise Court?'

Lucy smiled. 'She used to love to talk about the place.'

'Do you think there's a chance she'd talk about it to me? I always like to find out as much as I can about a site I'm investigating.'

Lucy looked a little uncertain. 'She's gone downhill so much over the past couple of weeks. I'm afraid you might not get much sense out of her. But she still has some good days. I'll have to see how she is.'

'Of course.'

'We're ready for you now.' The director's voice sounded a little peevish, as though he suspected they were shirking their duties.

While she was talking about Clara, Lucy's expression had softened; now Neil saw her take a deep breath and become the professional again. But before she walked away, she leaned towards him and spoke softly. 'I'll see what I can do about Clara, Neil. I just wish I knew what's frightening her.'

Neil didn't answer. He was no psychologist.

*

Alan Buchanan – or Andrew Stedley, whichever was his real name – was receiving the attention usually reserved for royalty or celebrities. His life was being probed into by Wesley's newly augmented team in the Tradmouth CID office, now transformed into a major incident room, and attempts were being made to trace his next of kin, so far without any luck.

When Wesley returned from Morbay Gerry beckoned him into his office and told him to shut the door behind him. As Wesley sat down he could see the cold case files on Gerry's desk had been pushed to one side and there was an eager look on the boss's face.

'Need a hand with this murder?'

Wesley hadn't seen Gerry so fired with enthusiasm since the shooting. 'Are you feeling up to it?'

'Mystery man found dead in suspicious circumstances in a hotel room? 'Course I'm up to it. What did Colin have to say?'

'He said the man might have been drugged – although he hasn't had the tox report back yet – then a thin, sharp instrument was thrust into the nape of his neck upwards into his brain. The cause of death wasn't immediately obvious and I suspect the killer hoped to get away with it; pass it off as natural ... or even suicide.'

'You'd have to be a contortionist to skewer yourself in the back of the neck,' Gerry said with a snort.

'So it looks as if it was premeditated, which means we've got a cool killer.'

'Any CCTV from the hotel?'

'Someone's running through it. The manager's being very co-operative.'

'He'll be worried about the hotel's reputation.' He

43

grinned. 'Don't suppose they'll be offering any Murder Mystery Weekends any time soon. What about prints?'

'None on the glass or the bottle and there was another glass that had just been washed so the killer might have had a drink with the victim before killing him.'

'The Judas kiss,' said Gerry. 'Which means the victim probably trusted his killer, maybe even thought of him as a friend.'

'You don't have to be a friend to share a drink with someone.'

'OK, maybe not a friend but at least on fairly good terms. And he can't have been afraid of him if he invited him into his hotel room.'

'True. Colin's put the time of death between seven thirty and nine thirty, by the way.'

'Good. What about the victim's dual identity?'

'His fingerprints aren't on our database under either name. He checked into the hotel in the name of Alan Buchanan, which matches one of the credit cards found in his wallet, and he gave a London address. That's being checked but the extra credit card's worrying me. Name of Andrew Stedley.'

'Maybe he's got a murky past which has caught up with him at last. Anything new on our burglaries?'

Wesley shook his head. 'The last one was ten days ago so let's hope he's having a rest. I've drafted in a few officers from Morbay but Nick Tarnaby's called in sick so I've got someone to cover for him too.'

'Whoever he is, he's got to be an improvement on Tarnaby, morose sod. I don't know how many times I've thought of returning him to uniform.'

'Why haven't you?' Wesley couldn't honestly say that he

liked Tarnaby, who rarely spoke unless he was spoken to first. At first he'd wondered whether the man's off-hand manner towards him was a result of racism, until he realised that he was like that with everyone. But Gerry had always stopped short of getting him transferred. There were many who said that, in spite of all his bluster, Gerry was too soft: his reluctance to blight Tarnaby's career was probably just another example.

'Well he's never actually made a serious balls-up, has he?'

Wesley had to admit that he'd always done just enough to stay on the right side of trouble but, in his opinion, that wasn't good enough.

'Who have you got to stand in for him?'

'A uniformed constable called Rob Carter. He was first on the scene at the hotel and he had the initiative to realise it wasn't straightforward and call in help. He told me he wants to transfer to CID. Even mentioned your name. He seems bright.'

'Must be if he mentioned me.'

Wesley nodded towards the discarded files on Gerry's desk. 'How are your cold cases going?'

'I've had a look through them and there are some new avenues I'd like to explore. But they've lain unsolved for so many years that a few more days won't make much difference. So if you could do with some help . . . ' He looked at Wesley eagerly.

'How are you feeling?' Wesley asked. The last thing he wanted was to overburden a convalescing man with work that would slow his recovery.

'Never better.' In an unconscious action, he touched the shoulder where the bullet had penetrated.

'What are you going to tell CS Fitton about the cold cases?'

'That I've examined them and can suggest some new lines of inquiry. The new cold case team set up at Neston nick can take on the legwork. She just wanted to give me something to keep me quiet. Occupational therapy, I think they call it.'

'She wanted to use your expertise, you mean.'

'If you want to put it like that, Wes.' He pushed a hand through his hair as though he was preening himself, a mischievous smile playing on his lips.

'What about your three-day week?'

'What about it?'

'Look, Gerry, it might be too much for you.'

Gerry stood up. 'Nonsense, Wes. Stop fussing. Mind if I address the troops?'

Wesley felt a glow of relief. Those terrible dark months when he feared Gerry's injuries would mean they'd never work together again were behind them. His old friend was back on form.

When Wesley looked at the clock on the office wall he saw that it was already five. All around him his colleagues were talking on phones or typing into computers. Sooner or later one of them would come up with something that might bring them closer to knowing who drugged the man in room 352 and drove a sharp instrument into the base of his skull.

The victim himself remained a mystery. Trish Walton had liaised with the Met and discovered that there was no Alan Buchanan living at the address he'd provided for the hotel. And when they did a check on the name Andrew

Stedley, things became even more confusing. Mr Stedley, who worked in an advertising agency, had had his wallet stolen on the Tube a week ago. His credit card had been in it along with three hundred pounds in cash. He'd reported the theft, of course, and he seemed to remember a tanned, grey-haired man bumping into him and apologising profusely. He hadn't thought about it at the time but he guessed that was when it must have happened. It had been a neat professional job.

Wesley suspected that both names might turn out to be false, which would make it hard to find out who the dead man really was, so while they were waiting for the bank that had issued Alan Buchanan's credit card to get back to them with an address, he ordered another fingerprint check. He found it hard to believe that such an expert thief could have escaped the attention of the police all these years and it was unlikely that a previously law-abiding person would suddenly decide to embark on a criminal career in middle age.

Colin had commented on the man's golden tan and toiletries found in his hotel bathroom had borne Spanish labels so Wesley reckoned he might have been living abroad. Gerry favoured that refuge of many British criminals on the run from the law – the Costa del Sol – or the Costa del Crime as it was sometimes known – and Wesley hoped the dead man's clothes or the wig would confirm the theory when Colin sent them over. He phoned to ask when they'd be arriving but Colin wasn't there so he left a message.

He hesitated before making his next call, the one to Pam to tell her he'd definitely be late home. It would come as no surprise to her, of course, but he felt the contact, however brief, might make up a little for his absence. When she didn't answer the phone he suddenly felt a pang of worry because she was normally home by this time. She might have taken the children out, or visited her mother, Della, or called round at his sister's. Nevertheless he couldn't help envisaging all sorts of disasters from a car accident to his family being held hostage by the burglar they were seeking – although so far he'd only targeted second homes. He knew he wouldn't be able to relax until he'd spoken to her.

He tried Pam's mobile but as it went to voicemail he saw Rachel watching him and he replaced the receiver, focusing his eyes on the large window that looked out onto the Memorial Gardens and the river beyond. The wind was getting up again and the boats on the river were starting to dance on the choppy water. He returned his attention to the report on his desk giving a list of all the dead man's possessions. There was nothing out of the ordinary among them, apart from the stolen credit card, but Wesley wanted to examine them himself, just to see whether he could find some clue to the man's life and true identity.

It was half past five when Gerry burst out of his office, a look of sheer joy on his face. Whatever news he had to impart, Wesley thought, had done wonders for his spirits. Apart from a diminished waistline, he looked like his old, ebullient self as he strode up to the noticeboard that filled the far wall of the room and called for attention. The chatter died down and those who'd been speaking on the phone murmured apologies and put their caller on hold.

'There's been a development,' Gerry said, catching Wesley's eye. 'Our hotel victim was involved in a murder back in 1979.' He paused, looking round his audience, then he held up a brown cardboard file as though he'd pulled off a particularly impressive conjuring trick, his face triumphant as a cup winner holding the trophy aloft. 'By coincidence, it's one of the unsolved cases the chief super asked me to have a look at.'

Wesley went to stand beside Gerry, who handed him the file.

'In 1979 a ten-year-old girl called Fiona Carp was found dead in woodland just outside the Bay View Holiday Camp in Morbay where she'd been staying with her parents,' Gerry continued. 'Cause of death asphyxiation. No signs of sexual interference but all the local child molesters were hauled in and everyone in the holiday camp was interviewed.'

'Any arrests?' Rachel asked.

'There was one but there wasn't enough evidence to proceed and after that every lead went cold. This was before the days of DNA, don't forget, so things were harder to prove. However, as part of a recent review some of the girl's clothing was sent to the lab to see if they could find any traces of DNA that couldn't be detected at the time. Every contact leaves a trace, as you all know, and our man left some skin cells on little Fiona's T-shirt. With these fancy new techniques nowadays they can find a match from the tiniest of samples.' He paused for effect. 'They've managed to get a profile – and it matches our dead man. And before anyone says it might have got there innocently, there was skin found under the girl's fingernails and samples taken at the time have been tested too with the same result.'

The stunned silence was broken by gasps and whispers

and after a few moments Rachel spoke again. 'So you're saying Alan Buchanan, the man from the hotel, killed this Fiona Carp?'

'That's exactly what I'm saying. Looks as if one of my cold cases has been solved,' said Gerry, resisting the urge to punch the air.

5

20th October 1913

False, perfidious Alfred. I feel I should hate him but I cannot.

I think of the maidservant in the story Daisy taunted me with when I first took up my position here. She hanged herself. She kicked away a chair and escaped her shame. For now I realise that Mrs Stevens is right. There will be no marriage, no elevation to that station in life to which I have always felt called in spite of the sneers of those around me.

When Mrs Stevens says I must learn to know my place, I do not answer. I sob when I lie in bed at night for I know that my place is beside Alfred and our baby. Daisy puts out her hand to comfort me but her clumsy kindness makes me hate her, just as I hate the world. Mrs Stevens says that as my condition can no longer be concealed, I must return to my mother in Sandrock, although the thought of that desolate village by the sea with its drying nets and its stench of fish fills me with such horror.

I stare at the beam in my bedroom and wonder if death is worse than being cast off like a piece of unwanted clothing by the man I loved, the man I trusted with my future.

*

On Saturday morning Wesley rose early, trying his best not to disturb Pam who was dozing beside him, and fed Moriarty who launched into her 'pathetic starving stray' act as soon as he opened the kitchen door.

He reached the CID office at eight to find Gerry had beaten him to it. He was sitting at his desk, going through an untidy heap of files and looking alert. The change in the DCI since he'd taken on the challenge of this new case was remarkable but Wesley, having rejoiced in the improvement at first, now feared that he might be overstretching himself. However, unlike Gerry, he was and always had been a natural worrier.

As soon as he walked in Gerry stood up and Wesley saw him wince with pain. Wesley hurried over to join him.

'You're in early, Gerry.'

'Couldn't sleep. I tried to call Jack Unsworth last night; he was the CIO on the Fiona Carp case. He's away for the weekend but we need to talk to him as soon as he gets back. I want to know how our dead man fitted into the picture at the time. There's no photograph of him in the files and no mention of an Alan Buchanan.'

'He could have been using another name.'

'Yeah. I was hoping Jack might be able to identify him. If he went in for nicking wallets, I'm surprised he's not on our database.'

'I think he's been living abroad.'

'Mmm. What brought him back to Morbay?'

'His killer?'

'Very possibly. By the way, Colin rang just before you arrived. He's sending over the dead man's things.'

'Good. I'll get someone to look through them.'

'Your protégé, Rob, seems to be settling in.'

Wesley saw Rob Carter, still in uniform, sitting at Nick Tarnaby's desk in the far corner of the room. His fair head was bowed in concentration. 'Tarnaby called in again.' Gerry rolled his eyes. 'Says his back's no better.'

When Wesley didn't reply, Gerry left it to him to allocate tasks. There would be a lot to get through.

There was no filming today. The director had gone off to London for the weekend and the TV people would return on Monday. Lucy had told her Sandrock team to take a weekend break too as the church dig was going well.

Neil had tried to ring his old university friend, Wesley Peterson, the previous evening but there'd been no reply. He'd been busy for the past few days so he hadn't caught the local news and this meant he wasn't sure whether Wesley was out investigating some crime somewhere. But Pam hadn't been at home either so perhaps they were out together, he thought, resolving to try again later.

Although Sandrock was unavailable that day, work was still continuing at Paradise Court. Neil never minded digging over the weekend – once he'd started he usually became so engrossed that any delay became a frustrating inconvenience – and today he seized the opportunity to open a new trench in the walled garden.

Earlier he'd summoned the courage to call Lucy Zinara to ask her if she wanted to come over and see what was going on, not really expecting a positive reply, but to his surprise she'd agreed. She was going with her mother to visit Clara at the nursing home but she would meet him at Paradise Court afterwards to see how the excavation there was progressing. It was her old family home so she was interested.

When Neil arrived at Paradise Court at ten thirty the digging had already started. The existing trenches in the walled gardens were getting deeper and the heaps of soil, resting on plastic sheets at the side, were growing in height, which was always a good sign.

After doing a round of the trenches, chatting to the diggers and examining the finds in the newspaper-lined plastic trays, he stood for a while looking at the main house some eighty feet away, taking in each architectural detail, imagining how it fitted in with his investigations. The house itself was an attractive white stucco building of pleasing, eighteenth-century proportions. According to old maps Neil had studied, it had been built on the foundations of an earlier house and the remains of one wing of the Paradise Court's larger Tudor predecessor still lay under the walled garden. Now the excavation was coming along well, remnants of the demolished Tudor brick walls were clearly visible in the ground. And some interesting finds were turning up: ancient nails, glass and building materials as well as a good selection of sixteenth- and seventeenth-century pottery. The remains of an oven had been discovered in what had probably been the kitchen along with a variety of smallish rooms which had once served essential domestic purposes.

He was examining a well-preserved section of an earthenware jug from one of the trenches near the house when he heard Lucy's voice. The sound made him jump and when he turned to face her his heart began to beat a little faster.

'Hello.' He returned the shard carefully to the safety of the finds tray and smiled at her. But she didn't return his smile.

'I've come from the nursing home,' she said after a couple of seconds.

'How's Clara?'

'Not good.'

Neil was about to say, 'Well, she's had a good innings,' or some similar platitude but he decided against it.

'The staff at the home seem to think that something's disturbed her and that's why she's up all night screaming the place down. They say it could be some traumatic memory she's been suppressing.'

'Is it something to do with the home? Something that's happened? You hear of these things and—'

'No,' she said emphatically. 'Sandton House is a good place and the staff are lovely.' She fell silent for a moment. 'Mum said it used to belong to relatives of ours many years ago before it was converted into a nursing home – a family called Toncliffe.'

'OK, no need to rub it in that you're descended from the gentry,' he said, trying to lighten the mood.

This raised a smile. 'Impoverished gentry. My parents never had two pennies to rub together.' Suddenly she looked more serious. 'Clara was particularly bad last night, shouting for her mother and going on about walls falling. And ice.'

'Ice?' Neil frowned, searching for something to say. The mention of ice triggered a connection in his mind, something that might distract Lucy from her problem. 'We're due to start work on a derelict ice house in the grounds. The Heritage Trust want to restore it but we'll have to be careful. The passage leading into it has caved in and the whole place is in a precarious state.'

'Can I have a look?'

'Of course.' She tucked her arm through his and he tried not to make optimistic assumptions as they walked away from the walled garden and down a rhododendron-shaded pathway, eventually arriving at a clearing containing what looked at first glance like a small Iron-Age burial mound. However at one side of this particular mound Neil could see a mass of fallen masonry, blocking what had once been the entrance.

'We're going to have to clear out all the rubble and see what condition it's in inside.'

Lucy stared at it for a while before she spoke. 'I wonder if this is what Clara's been going on about. She might have played here when she was little.'

Neil didn't know the answer to that one.

Colin Bowman had sent the dead man's clothes over from the mortuary. The pockets had been searched thoroughly at the scene but there hadn't been much to tell them about the man's life and death. A set of keys had been found but they were useless without an address to go with them and the one he'd given the hotel had turned out to be false. There was no mobile phone among his possessions, which meant that either he didn't have one or his killer had taken it with him. In this day and age, Wesley thought, the second option was the most likely. But he asked for a record of any calls made from the man's hotel room, just in case.

The clothing arrived packed neatly in the usual sturdy paper bags, never plastic as stained items from crime scenes tended to rot when sealed from the air. Wesley cleared a space on the table near the window before calling DC Trish Walton over. He pulled on a pair of crime-scene gloves before touching the packages and handed another pair to Trish. It wasn't a pleasant job but it had to be done.

He ignored the underwear – some things were too unsavoury for the CID office – and turned his attention to the package containing the trousers. When he opened it he caught a whiff of urine, wrinkled his nose and hastily dropped them back into the bag.

'What's the label?' he asked Trish, who was examining a shirt with minute concentration. His main fear was that the clothes had come from Marks and Spencer, in which case they were wasting their time.

'It's one I don't recognise. Looks Spanish to me.'

'Can you find out where the brand's sold? And can you check whether the bank that issued his credit card has got back to us yet?'

'Of course.' Trish looked relieved as she tore off her gloves and hurried back to her desk.

Wesley stood for a while staring at the bagged-up trousers, reminding himself that the dead man's DNA had been found on the clothes and under the fingernails of the child who'd been murdered in 1979, which meant he could well be a child killer. Now he himself was dead. Was it a case of vengeance for his past sins? Or was it something else entirely?

As he was resealing the bags so that they could be sent somewhere more appropriate, he heard someone calling his name. Rob Carter was standing at the door of the AV room, a darkened chamber off the main office where some hapless officer given the task of trawling through CCTV footage would sit isolated from his or her colleagues. It wasn't a popular job and Gerry usually arranged for everyone to take their turn, although Wesley noticed that Nick

Tarnaby seemed to be given more stints than most. That morning Rob had drawn the short straw.

'Sir, I think I've found something.'

Wesley followed Rob into the AV room and sat down while he rewound the footage, making the figures hurry backwards like people in an old silent film. He could see the time at the foot of the screen: six fifty-eight on the evening before the man's body was discovered.

Rob froze the image. 'There she is. Don't you think she looks out of place?'

Rob was right. The footage showed the hotel foyer where everyone seemed to be moving with a purpose, even if it was only waiting on a sofa or examining the menus at the entrance. They all looked like typical hotel visitors apart from one woman.

She was slightly overweight with a snub nose and dyed blond hair that curled around her shoulders. Her short fur jacket looked a little too small for her and her tight skirt revealed a pair of unattractive knees. Even from the black and white image, Wesley could tell that she was wearing too much make-up.

She hovered just inside the hotel entrance for a while as if she was trying to summon the courage to go further into the building. Then she took a slip of paper from her jacket pocket and examined it for a few seconds before hurrying, head down, into the reception area, as though she didn't want to draw attention to herself. She made for the stairs rather than the lift and disappeared from sight.

'What do you think, sir?' said Rob. 'Aging tart?'

Wesley didn't answer. 'Is there a camera on the dead man's corridor?'

'Yes, in the lift area, but that covers the stairs too.'

'So does our suspicious lady come out on the third floor?'

A look of triumph appeared on Rob's face. 'She certainly does. At four minutes past seven. Want to see?'

When Wesley nodded, Rob started up the frozen footage on a second screen. The lift doors opened and a portly man emerged then, a few seconds later the glass doors leading to the hotel staircase opened and the woman stood there for a moment, waiting for the man to disappear down the corridor, brandishing his room key. She looked around furtively, like someone who knew she wasn't supposed to be there, before shuffling down the corridor in the direction of the dead man's room.

'And do we have any sight of her leaving the building?'

'Yes. She appears again at seven thirty-five, hurrying with her head down. I'll find it for you.'

As Rob scrolled through, Wesley tried to get things straight in his mind. From Colin's estimation of the time of death, it was possible the woman on the screen was their killer. She didn't exactly look like a murderer but he'd met plenty who looked as innocent as a nun singing in the convent choir. And this woman definitely looked as though she had something to hide.

'Get onto the hotel, will you, Rob. Find out if anyone saw her ... or better still, whether anybody recognises her. And speak to room service. Was this woman in the man's room when the sandwich was delivered?'

He experienced a thrill of hope. Perhaps, after all these years, Gerry's positive nature was rubbing off on him.

On Gerry's return Wesley eagerly shared the latest news about the case. First of all there was the woman caught on the hotel's CCTV and they now knew that several calls had been made to a local number from the dead man's hotel room since his arrival. The number was being traced and the result would be in any minute. And then there was Trish's discovery that the labels in the dead man's clothes came from a chain store in Spain. News had also come in that the credit card in the name of Alan Buchanan had been issued by a Spanish branch of a British bank to an address in Marbella which, he was sure, explained why the man's DNA hadn't been on the British database. He'd been an ex-pat, possibly running from the terrible crime he'd committed in 1979. One of the team had contacted the Spanish police to find out whether their man was known to them and he was awaiting the answer.

After listening patiently to Wesley's account of these new developments, Gerry claimed he fancied some fresh air after being closeted in with the chief super for an hour and a trip over to Morbay to show the hotel staff and guests the CCTV stills would suit him fine. Wesley had planned to give the job to a couple of detective constables but he too was starting to find the atmosphere in the incident room oppressive so he agreed that was a good idea. They could consider the case on the way and, in their absence, Rachel was capable of dealing with anything that came in.

It was a fine day for late October with watery sunshine breaking through the gathering clouds, but the forecast Wesley had glimpsed on breakfast TV that morning hadn't been good with more wind and rain expected by the evening. As he drove to Morbay he remembered Pam's fundraising event that night. He didn't think he could face an evening of polite conversation with his wife's teaching colleagues, but if he was free he'd try and make it for Pam's sake.

As they neared Morbay, Gerry broke the amicable silence. 'What do you think, Wes? Is she some wronged ex-girlfriend from years ago who's heard he's back in town and decided to take her revenge?'

'We don't even know for sure that the woman on the CCTV footage went to his room. She might have been a guest or visiting someone else. We can't know until we've checked with the hotel.'

'She didn't look like a guest, Wes. The body language was all wrong. She knew she wasn't meant to be there.'

'Rob thought she looked like an aging tart.'

Gerry laughed. 'Maybe she was visiting a client who's not too fussy. Maybe our victim booked her and when she turned up he got the shock of his life and told her to get lost. Or maybe she wasn't a lady of the night. Maybe she just thought she was dressing to impress and she didn't have a mirror.'

'What about the Spanish connection?'

'If our man moved to the Costa del Sol it explains why he fell off our radar. But what made him come back?'

'Perhaps he thought that after all these years his sins wouldn't find him out, in which case he didn't know much about cold-case reviews and the latest developments in DNA technology.'

Gerry nodded. 'Take a left here, Wes.'

'Why?'

'Before we go to the hotel I want to revisit the scene of the crime.'

Wesley signalled left and took the road to the seafront. He drove to the outskirts of the resort and when they'd reached an area of fields and woodland Gerry spoke again.

'Here it is.'

Wesley saw a glossy sign bearing the words BAY VIEW HOLIDAY PARK in tasteful green and gold lettering. He stopped the car just inside the open gate and they got out.

'The place has been smartened up a bit,' Gerry observed as they strolled through the landscaped grounds dotted with new-looking log cabins. 'It used to be cheap and cheerful. Kiss-me-quick hats and bingo.' He pointed to a faux antique signpost. 'Now there's a Spa and an Outdoor Activities Centre.'

'People expect sophistication these days.'

'They've even taken down the barbed wire fence.'

'And ditched the name "holiday camp"' for "holiday park".'

'Times change, Wes.' He stopped and looked around. 'All the old chalets have long gone and I believe the place has changed hands a couple of times since the murder. We won't find anything here.'

Gerry retraced his steps, mildly disappointed, and Wesley drove on to their intended destination.

When they arrived at the car park of the Morbay Palace Hotel Wesley brought the car to a halt between a Jaguar and a large Lexus. They entered via the revolving door, a relic from the age when the hotel had been one of the principal establishments patronised by the smart set who flocked to Morbay at a time when a stay on the English Riviera was the height of fashion.

After negotiating the door just behind a middle-aged couple laden with luggage, they made for the long marble reception desk. The attractive Edwardian interior had been retained but the carpet was a little worn in places and some of the walls needed a fresh coat of paint.

A young woman stood behind the desk watching her

colleague attend to the couple with the luggage, apparently at a loose end. Her straight black hair was tied back in a glossy ponytail and her large brown eyes gave her the look of a startled pixie who'd suddenly found herself in an alien environment. The badge on the lapel of her navy-blue suit jacket proclaimed that her name was Francesca and when Wesley presented his warrant card to her, she looked at it and then at Wesley with that uncertainty people display when they're not quite sure if somebody's playing a trick on them. Then she assumed a helpful expression and asked how she could help them.

Wesley passed her a CCTV still. 'Do you recognise this woman? She was here in the hotel on Wednesday night, around the time we think the man in room three five two died.'

Her eyes widened in horror as she stared at the image. 'You think this woman . . . ?'

'We don't think anything at the moment, love,' Gerry said. 'We just need to know who she is and have a word with her.'

'I was on duty on Wednesday but I'm sure I've never seen her before. I don't think she's a guest.'

'Perhaps your colleagues could take a look at it,' said Wesley, suddenly feeling sorry for the girl.

The young man who was on Reception with her had finished checking in the newly arrived guests so Francesca called across to him. He too stared at the picture and shook his head. He hadn't been on duty on Wednesday evening but if they wanted to talk to the manager, he was sure he could help.

They waited in the foyer for ten minutes, sitting side by side on what was possibly the most comfortable sofa Wesley had ever encountered: squishy antique brown leather, easy to sink into but hard to get out of in a hurry. Noticing that Gerry had closed his eyes, he hoped that it wouldn't be too hard to rouse him once the manager was free. It would provide amusement for the staff and give a whole new meaning to the term sleeping policeman. Wesley watched as Francesca answered the phone, looked in his direction and signalled with a wave. The manager would see them now.

He tapped Gerry on the shoulder and he responded with a loud snort. In spite of his proclamations about feeling perfectly fit, work still tired him, but Wesley wasn't going to remind him of his body's weakness.

Gerry yawned and attempted to raise himself from the sofa but when he flopped back Wesley placed a discreet hand under his elbow and helped him up, hoping nobody was watching. Francesca must have seen but she gave no hint of it as she showed them into the office behind the Reception desk, separated from the action by an impressive mahogany door.

The manager's name was Denzil Stepwood and he was small and bald as a billiard ball, with the look of a man who lived on his nerves. Even when he sat back in his chair behind his large desk with his fingers arched like a doctor who was about to inquire what the trouble was, he looked restless.

After introductions and explanations were made Wesley pushed the picture of the mystery woman over the desk so that Stepwood could examine it.

Wesley had been expecting another negative reply and was surprised when Stepwood said the words, 'Yes, I know her.'

He caught Gerry's eye and saw that the DCI's lethargy had disappeared as soon as those four words were uttered.

'What's her name?'

'Paulette Reeves. She used to work here as a housekeeping assistant.'

'How long ago was this?' Gerry asked.

'She was working here five years ago when I took over then just before last Christmas her elderly mother fell ill and she left to look after her. She lived in so when she left she had to find somewhere to rent. I remember her particularly because she was having problems and we let her go with a little bonus, enough for her to put a rental deposit down on a house or flat for herself and her mother. The Morbay Palace is a family-run hotel and we believe in looking after our long-serving staff.'

'You've no idea why she came back on Wednesday?'

Stepwood looked slightly unsure of himself. 'No, but if she came in to see one of her old colleagues, it would hardly be surprising, would it? Although she looks rather ... er, dressed up for a casual visit.'

'Who were her particular friends here?' Wesley asked.

The manager suddenly looked awkward. 'To tell the truth, I think she kept herself very much to herself. She was a good worker, don't get me wrong, but she wasn't the most sociable of people.' He thought for a moment. 'Although I've heard that there was one topic of conversation that brought her out of her shell, so to speak. She used to go on about her holidays in Spain – apparently she loved her fortnight in the sun. Highlight of her year.'

At the mention of Spain, Wesley gave Gerry a nudge.

'Is it possible to speak to the staff who knew her?'

'Of course. Do you want to see them now?'

'No,' said Wesley. 'We'll send someone over later to have a word. You'll have an address for her?'

The manager shook his head. 'I'm sorry. I asked her to pass on a forwarding address when she got settled but she never did. And, as far as I know, nobody here has ever heard from her again.'

'We think she might have come here to visit the man who was found dead,' said Wesley. 'She entered the building just before seven and was filmed hurrying out thirty-five minutes later. Now if she wasn't visiting her old workmates . . .'

'I'll certainly check with them if anyone saw her but I'm sure they would have mentioned it if they had, Inspector.'

The thought that Stepwood might not know if his staff were skiving off work catching up on the gossip with an old colleague passed through Wesley's mind. But then he'd said that Paulette hadn't socialised much with her fellow workers – unless there was some other motive for her visit that they hadn't even thought of yet.

'Would someone be able to get up to the third floor without being caught on CCTV?' Wesley asked

Stepwood looked apologetic. 'Our security system's due to be upgraded but at the moment I'm afraid there's no camera on the staircase leading from the restaurant at the other end of the corridor.'

'In that case I'll need a list of restaurant bookings for that evening.'

'Of course. I'll see to it, although it is a public area so anybody can just walk through.'

They said their goodbyes and Gerry led the way out of the hotel.

It was now a question of finding Paulette Reeves and

asking her what she was doing near the dead man's room on Wednesday evening. And who knew, Wesley observed, once they'd found her they might discover who killed the man in room 352.

Pam Peterson felt obliged to make an effort, even though the Social Evening and Charity Auction at the Tradmouth Castle Hotel could be classified loosely as work. Wesley was supposed to go with her but she doubted he'd be back in time. The man who'd been inconsiderate enough to die in that Morbay hotel was claiming far more of her husband's attention than she was.

She'd driven the children over to Maritia's for their dinner and expressed her deep gratitude to Wesley's sister for helping her out. Maritia, like her and Wesley's mother, was one of those capable women who never seemed to run out of energy. There were times when Pam envied her.

Pam was just slipping on the Monsoon dress she'd had for ages but hadn't had much opportunity to wear when the phone rang. She hoped it would be Wesley telling her that he was on his way home but, to her disappointment, she heard her mother, Della's, voice instead. Della, unlike Wesley's mother, was a garrulous woman who'd been at the back of the queue when the common sense was being given out and sometimes Pam wished she'd just act her age and stop embarrassing her. This time she was calling to tell her about her latest venture into Internet dating but Pam said she couldn't talk as she was about to go out; she had her coat on and was at the front door. Luckily Della didn't detect the lie and rang off, allowing Pam to apply her make-up. Once she'd finished she stood back and looked at herself in the long bedroom mirror.

The dress suited her, she thought, and her shoulder-length brown hair was looking good since she had bought that new set of straighteners. However, there were times when she wondered whether Wesley was aware of her efforts. She took a deep breath and picked up her handbag, checking her mobile just in case Wesley had tried to call and she hadn't heard the phone. But there was nothing.

She drove down the hill to the town. Taking the car would mean she couldn't have a drink but she didn't fancy walking back home alone through the dark, winding streets.

She parked near the police station and looked up at the brightly lit first-floor windows, imagining Wesley inside, then took out her mobile. It would do no harm to call him, just to see whether he'd be able to join her at the hotel later on.

He answered after three rings.

'You'll never guess where I am,' she said in a voice she hoped was tantalising.

'Where?' She thought he sounded slightly impatient, as if he hadn't time to play games.

'I'm just outside the police station looking up at your office window and it's getting bloody windy out here.'

He came to the window and waved, silhouetted against the bright office lights. As she waved back she felt a thrill she hadn't experienced since their courting days at university. Then a second figure appeared. She'd half expected to see Gerry Heffernan's portly bulk but instead it was a slimly built woman she recognised as Rachel Tracey. The woman touched Wesley's arm and as he turned away from the window Pam experienced a pang of bitterness. She put the phone to her ear again. 'You still there?'

'Yes.'

'Any chance Gerry will allow you out to play? Can you get off in time to come to this do of mine?'

'I'll do my best but there's been a development today and we're busy following it up. I'm sorry, love.'

'Well, if you can, it's at the Tradmouth Castle – the Admiral Suite.' She hesitated. 'Please try and make it.' She wondered if she was beginning to sound too desperate but at that moment she needed him; and she needed Rachel Tracey not to be touching his arm.

'I'll do my best,' he repeated and the line went dead.

She felt desolate as she walked the hundred yards to the hotel. The wind was ruining her hair and the prospect of being on her best behaviour in front of her control-freak headmistress lay ahead of her. The other teachers would all be with their partners and she'd be forced to spend the evening smiling at strangers, many of them the parents of the children she taught. Suddenly she felt she needed a glass of wine or three to fortify her but even that little comfort was out of the question.

When she reached the hotel she passed the bustling bar and went up the sweeping wooden staircase to the Admiral Suite. The headmistress had thought the choice of venue would raise the tone of the event, dismissing the initial suggestion of the church hall as unambitious. Many of the staff had predicted financial disaster but, judging from the crowd she could see through the open doorway and buzz of conversation and laughter coming from within, this was unusually well attended for a school do.

She fixed a smile to her lips and stepped into the room. One of her colleagues spotted her and waved and she began to make her way over, wishing Wesley was there beside her.

After pushing her way through the crowd with mumbled excuse-me's she arrived at the round table. As she'd predicted her colleagues were with their partners and each seemed to have a glass of wine in front of them. She was about to make for the crowded bar in the corner when she heard a woman's voice.

'Hello. Pam, isn't it? Michael's mum?'

She turned and saw a woman with a sleek blond bob and a shift dress of elegant simplicity which made the dress that had so delighted Pam when she'd found it reduced in the sale seem cheap by comparison. The woman was slim, the sort of slim that results from living on one's nerves.

It took Pam a few seconds to place her. Then she remembered that this woman's son was in the same class as Michael and they'd chatted at the grammar school's open evening for new pupils. Her name escaped Pam but she remembered that the woman lived near her in an impressively large Edwardian villa halfway down the hill overlooking the town. She also remembered something about a brewery. That was it: her husband's family owned a local brewery.

'You remember my husband, don't you?'

The man was slightly smaller than his wife with well-cut dark hair greying at the temples. His once-athletic body had filled out a little in middle age but he had the sleek look of a man with few money worries. The handsome couple were smiling and Pam remembered that they'd been friendly at the open evening, even though their only son, Daniel, a pudgy, pasty-faced lad, didn't seem to be in Michael's chosen circle of friends. The man greeted her with a kiss on the cheek, as if they'd known each other for years.'

'It's good to see you again,' Pam said.

'You know my husband's been co-opted onto your school's board of governors,' the woman said.

Pam assumed an expression of polite interest. 'How come? You don't have a child at the school, do you?'

Pam's two children went to the primary school where Pam taught – or rather Amelia did, as Michael had now moved on – but she didn't remember seeing this couple at any parents' evenings. However the man was soon to enlighten her.

'I assume I was asked because I'm a local businessman,' he replied. 'Not that I'm much of an expert on schools – I'm happy to leave all that to you professionals – but I've recently handed over the day-to-day running of my business so now I have time on my hands for other things.' There was a self-effacing charm about him which made him immediately likeable and when he smiled Pam sensed a quiet authority, as though he was used to being in charge and knew how to get his own way without resorting to bullying or threats.

'Let Bradley get you a drink, Pam,' the woman said, putting a well-manicured hand on her arm.

Good, at least she now knew the man's name. If only she could remember the woman's. She thanked him and asked for a mineral water, sparkling.

'You will sit with us, won't you, Pam? We don't know a soul apart from Yolanda and she seems to be busy.'

Pam could see Yolanda, the headmistress, dashing around like a fury, organising things as usual. For a second Pam caught her eye and she half expected to be hauled off to help with some vital task or other, like selling raffle tickets or handing round canapés. But much to Pam's relief the woman commonly referred to in the staff room as 'the force of nature' disappeared from sight.

She glanced over at her colleagues who were deep in conversation and guessed that she'd hardly be missed. Besides, this friendly couple seemed to have taken pity on her because she was on her own and it would be churlish not to respond to their hospitable gesture. 'I'd be delighted to join you,' she said.

The woman whispered in Pam's ear, 'That's good because there's something I want to ask you.'

At that point Bradley returned with the drinks and Pam followed the couple to a free table, wondering what was coming. It was bound to be something unwelcome: perhaps a request for some private tutoring, or for help with some charitable enterprise. Pam had enough on her hands already but refusing any request that might involve work would require tact. She smiled and tried to make herself comfortable as the woman sat down beside her, leaning towards her anxiously, so close that Pam could smell her expensive perfume. If only she could remember her name, things might be easier, she thought, cursing herself for not paying more attention when they'd met before.

'Has Jennifer asked you about Michael?' Bradley said as he placed her mineral water in front of her.

Jennifer: good. 'Michael?' She waited for Bradley to continue but it was Jennifer who spoke, her voice slightly breathless, as though something was worrying her.

'Daniel says he always comes top in the tests they've been having. Poor Danny came second to bottom in his last one; maths, I think it was.'

'It's early in the term. And it takes some kids longer than others to settle into a new school,' Pam replied modestly. She couldn't stand parents who boasted about their children and didn't intend to become one, whatever the temptation.

Jennifer looked at her and Pam saw the strain on her face. 'To tell you the truth, we've been worried about Daniel. He doesn't seem to make friends easily and . . . '

'Do you think he's being bullied?' Pam's teacher's antennae picked up the mother's fear but Jennifer shook her head.

'I wouldn't go as far as that. It's just that I'd like him to have someone to walk down to the school bus with and as you live nearby . . . If Michael could call for Danny I'd really appreciate it. He was at Postan Grange and most of his classmates have gone on to boarding school. He knows nobody at the grammar.'

'I'll have a word with Michael. It should be fine,' Pam said, relieved that the task wasn't more onerous.

Jennifer took a sip of wine and Pam noticed that her hand was shaking a little. Her first thought was that Jennifer might have a drink problem, but she seemed to be drinking slowly so Pam dismissed the idea.

Then Jennifer spoke again. 'When we met your husband at Morbay Grammar that evening, he said he was a policeman.'

'A detective inspector,' Pam corrected. Jennifer's memory of their casual conversation a few weeks before was a lot better than hers.

'What kind of cases does he deal with?' Jennifer asked, fidgeting with the stem of her wine glass while her husband watched her serenely.

'Serious ones. Robbery and murder mostly.'

'Is that why he's not here tonight?'

'There was a murder in Morbay on Wednesday night

and when he has a case on, I hardly see him.' She tried hard to sound matter-of-fact about it. The sight of Jennifer's glass of wine renewed her longing for something stronger than water to help her through the evening.

'It can't be easy for you,' said Jennifer. Then she hesitated, glancing at Bradley who gave her an almost imperceptible nod. 'I don't suppose you and your husband would be free for Sunday lunch tomorrow?' The invitation sounded tentative, as though she was half expecting to be turned down. 'With the children, of course. It'd be nice for Michael and Daniel to get together.'

'That would be lovely,' Pam heard herself saying. 'Although I can't promise that Wesley will be available. It depends on this case.'

'I do hope he can make it.' Jennifer took a long drink of wine. 'You have a daughter too, I believe. Amelia, is it?'

Pam saw Bradley's fingers brush his wife's hand, a warning or a gesture of reassurance, she wasn't sure which.

'That's right.'

'How old is she?'

'Nine.'

Jennifer's eyes suddenly became bright with interest. 'You must bring her too,' she said and Pam was surprised to see a sudden spasm of pain pass across her face, like a cloud blotting out the sun. For a moment the three of them sat in silence and Pam had the strong feeling that whatever was wrong with Jennifer was connected somehow to her family life. She experienced a surge of curiosity but she suspected she'd need all her reserves of tact if she wasn't to put her foot in it.

Then Bradley broke the spell. 'Come on, drink up,' he said cheerfully. 'We're here to enjoy ourselves.'

Even if Pam had wanted to continue the conversation, it would have been impossible because Yolanda was banging a gavel on a table at the front of the room, calling for attention. Pam glanced at the door, hoping that Wesley would walk through it. But she hoped in vain.

Just before midnight Paulette Reeves visited the outhouse again. The wind was getting up and she could hear the trees creaking like ancient floorboards in a haunted house. Some people would be scared alone in that isolated place but she liked the loneliness; it was people who frightened her. People and her own foolishness.

When she left the outhouse she locked the door carefully behind her as she did every night, and hid the key in her special place behind the loose brick beside the outhouse window. As she hurried back to the house across the tiny yard the wind tugged at her hair. There'd be branches down before the night was out and her nearest neighbour on the other side of the wood would be out first thing in the morning with the chainsaw she could hear from a quarter of a mile away, bursting through the country peace. Not that she'd ever spoken to him. It would never do to get too close, not in the circumstances. She'd chosen this place for privacy and the last thing she wanted was an intruder.

After shutting the back door behind her she stood for a moment listening to the howling of the wind around the chimneys and the rattling of the windows. Sleep had been difficult since she'd invited the ghost from her past back into her life so she decided to settle for the night with a drink and watch one of the detective programmes she'd recorded. She'd always been careful to avoid the police in real life but she enjoyed watching their fictional counterparts from the safety of her armchair.

She returned to the small, low-ceilinged living room, kicked off her shoes and sat down in the shabby chintz armchair that embraced her sagging body like a lover, before picking up one of the travel brochures lying on the side table. She turned the bright glossy pages absent-mindedly, longing to take another of the trips that became impossible when she was landed with the responsibility of looking after her mother. Then she closed her eyes and was in Spain again, feeling the warm sun on her bare flesh. It was her special treat, her only indulgence, and if everything worked out she'd soon be back there. In the meantime she could pour herself a whisky.

Just as she reached for the bottle she heard a loud banging on the door; the iron knocker crashing down onto the wood. Somebody was out there. She froze for the few moments, wondering what to do. This was her home, her house of secrets.

For a moment she thought it might be the neighbour with the chainsaw, come on some benign mission, although he'd hardly visit at this time of night and even if he did, she didn't want to see him. She tiptoed into the small, narrow hallway with its bare pink walls, glad that she hadn't put on the light that would have made her visible through the frosted glass of the front door. But there was a light in the parlour so they'd know she was in.

After waiting a minute or so, statue-still, hoping whoever it was would go away, Paulette heard a car door slam and an engine start up. She was safe for the moment and so was her secret.

Five more minutes went by before she crept to the front

door, curious to see whether her visitor had left some clue to his or her identity. She put the door on the latch and stepped out into the darkness.

As soon as she'd left the shelter of the tiny porch, the wind seized her hair again and she raised her hands to her ears to protect them against the biting cold, looking around, alert as a small animal to waiting predators. She was about to scurry back inside when she spotted the dark bulk of a vehicle parked a little way off down the track leading to the cottage, half hidden in the shifting trees.

Suddenly she became aware of a movement to her right and as she turned her head there was an explosion of pain and she fell, stunned, onto the rough ground. Another blow came and she raised her arms to defend herself but her desperate fingers were knocked away by something hard and metallic that sent a sharp shock through her hand and rendered her helpless.

Her terrified scream emerged as a gasp when the instrument of death smashed down again on her skull.

Then she knew no more.

6

28th October 1913

He is to marry. A bottle of the late colonel's champagne is opened in the servants' hall so that the staff can celebrate the 'good news' while I remain in my room, my eyes sore with tears.

I return to Sandrock tomorrow. Even though it is less than two miles away, Mrs Stevens has asked the footman to take me in the dog cart most of the way and I know this is a kindness on her part. Yet my heart still seethes with anger.

I felt the child move in my belly this morning, a tiny butterfly's kick. Alfred avoids me but yesterday I saw him with his new fiancée. He met her while he was staying at his aunt's house, while he was away from me, and she is the daughter of a baronet. She is tall as a maypole with the face of a supercilious horse and he must have chosen her for her wealth rather than her beauty. May their union bring them no joy, only grief and pain. I curse them with all my heart.

Neil's accommodation was being paid for by the film company, which made a pleasant change. It wasn't often you got something for nothing in the cash-strapped world of archaeology. The guesthouse was a comfortable establishment, a former farmhouse half a mile from Sandrock, with crisp bedding, soft pillows and a breakfast that would last most people until teatime; although the archaeologists, their appetites increased by digging in the open air, only held out until lunch.

It was Sunday, another day of rest for all involved in the Sandrock dig, but Neil knew that work would have been delayed anyway because of the weather; not that he hadn't worked in worse during his time. As he dressed, anticipating the culinary treat awaiting him downstairs in the dining room, he could hear the wind outside even through the new double glazing. It was the season for gales on the south-west coast and the position of the Sandrock dig worried him so he hoped the director, in his quest for drama, wouldn't be tempted to place the team in any danger when they resumed work the next morning. But officially Lucy was in charge and he trusted her to be firm if necessary.

On his way down a tinny chime from his mobile phone announced that he had a text message. He was gratified to see that it was Lucy and she was asking if he was free for lunch. His fingers felt clumsy as he texted back. *Yes. Where and when?*

Apart from the obvious attraction of Lucy's company, their lunch might well provide him with much-needed background information about Paradise Court. He hadn't seen Wesley Peterson for a while and it would have been good to catch up with him and Pam, but there'd be other times and he was intrigued by the ice house. Lucy's great-grandmother had been raised at Paradise Court and had been rambling about ice. She'd been screaming, Lucy said, so perhaps some nasty memory about the ice house had emerged after many decades. On the other hand ice could mean anything – maybe someone had fallen through a frozen pond and drowned.

He caught a whiff of cooking bacon which drove all the questions out of his head.

Jayden Ross decided that he'd had enough of watching. The time had come to act and Sunday morning was as good a time as any. It was a while since he'd done the last job because he hadn't been able to get hold of Lee's van, but today Lee was planning to spend the day in bed so he'd said Jayden could help himself.

He'd done the last recce a couple of evenings ago, spying on the woman from the darkness, experiencing the thrill of being an unseen observer. Because it was a second home, he guessed she'd probably left yesterday, running back to the big city as soon as the weather turned hostile. The place was bound to be empty and if it wasn't he'd come back another time.

When he reached the cottage he parked the van and saw that she'd closed the curtains, as people often do when they're not at home, thinking it would fool the average thief. The cottage had that familiar unoccupied look. It was time to act.

He often thought of the women who owned the houses, of their nervousness at being alone in their isolated refuges during the week while their rich husbands were making money in London. And since his activities had made the local papers and the local news those nerves would have turned to fear. The thought gave him a feeling akin to power: he was famous at last.

After taking a hammer from the glove box, Jayden climbed out of the driver's seat. All quiet. That was good. He walked slowly to the front door and knocked, just to make doubly sure the place was empty. If she answered he'd pretend to be seeking odd jobs but he hoped the lie wouldn't be needed.

When there was no sign of life he raised the hammer to smash the glass. Then he waited a moment before putting his gloved hand through the gap and undoing the latch. Easy.

A swift exploration of the ground floor left him disappointed. These second homes were usually immaculate but this place was furnished with inexpensive modern furniture and had the unloved feeling of a cheap holiday let. In the kitchen dirty dishes teetered precariously in the sink and the bin by the back door was overflowing with rubbish. In the living room the daylight was blocked out by the closed curtains and a small TV chattered inanely to itself in the corner, giving the room a *Mary Celeste* feel, as though someone had left in a hurry.

He'd seen the woman going to and fro across the yard to the outhouse which suggested she kept something important in there, so he let himself out of the unlocked back door and saw a car parked at the back of the building, invisible from the drive. He went over to it and peered in. It was a small Toyota hatchback that had seen better days, not the sort of car he'd expected. They usually drove shiny SUVs, BMWs or Mercs. The sight of it made him more uneasy as he crossed the little yard and tried the door of the redbrick outhouse. It was locked so he peered through the cobwebbed window, but saw nothing in there except a large chest freezer, old and rusted at the base.

He returned to the house and helped himself to the radio he'd spotted in the kitchen. When he summoned the courage to creep upstairs he found evidence of recent occupation and all the signs were that he'd made a big mistake. In spite of his research, this was no second home. Second home owners tidied up when they left – or they hired cleaners to do the job for them. His mother was employed by an agency to clear up their mess, and the addresses had been printed out on the sheet he'd found in her bag just over a year ago, when he'd started making his plans.

He banished his misgivings – after all, this address had been on the list with the rest – and began to search the bedrooms, where he found a gold bracelet, an emerald brooch and two diamond rings in a cheap plastic jewellery box as well as a handbag thrust into the back of a wardrobe. The bag contained a bank card and two hundred pounds in cash, but he left the card because using it increased the risk of being caught and pocketed the cash with a feeling of deep satisfaction. His journey had been worthwhile after all.

As he left he didn't bother switching off the TV. If she wanted to waste electricity, that was her business. Neither did he lock the front door behind him. With the broken pane of glass the owner would realise soon enough that her refuge had been violated.

Job done.

That Sunday morning Wesley woke up with a nagging feeling of guilt, one that had become familiar over the years whenever he was forced to neglect his family in favour of work.

He hadn't made it to Pam's school charity do the night before. After a twelve-hour day at work he hadn't fancied spending an awkward evening in the company of people he wouldn't normally choose to mix with. Besides, there'd been a lot of work to get through: reported sightings of the dead man as well as interviews with the hotel staff and guests that needed to be trawled through for inconsistencies. In the end it had been ten o'clock by the time he and Gerry left the office and went their separate ways. Rachel had stayed on even though Gerry had told her to go and remind her fiancé, Nigel, what she looked like. She'd given him a sad smile and returned to her paperwork.

When he'd arrived back he'd expected to find Pam at home, having sneaked out of the semi-compulsory school social evening at the first opportunity. He'd been surprised to find the house empty and, just as he'd been about to call her, he'd heard a car draw up outside. He'd peeped through a gap in the curtains like a nosy neighbour and seen her getting out of a large sleek Mercedes SUV. Her own car hadn't been on the drive so he assumed she'd had a breakdown or flat tyre and that one of her colleagues had brought her home. However, when he opened the door he noticed her cheeks were flushed and she was smiling which, as she'd been dreading the event, he found surprising. He asked her how the evening was and she said it was better than she'd expected. She'd met a couple called Bradley and Jennifer Savernake who lived nearby and they'd offered her a lift home so she'd been free to have a drink and enjoy herself. Bradley was a school governor and their son, Daniel, was in Michael's class. And, better than that, they'd invited them all round for Sunday dinner at their place.

Wesley didn't tell her then that he probably wouldn't be able to make it: he was in no mood for recriminations. And after listening to her account of the evening for half an hour over a glass of wine, he'd felt so tired that he'd gone straight up to bed.

Pam had woken with a headache that morning and had taken a couple of painkillers before getting dressed and walking down the steep hill into Tradmouth with Wesley to pick up her car. On the way she pointed out Bradley and Jennifer's house, a large double-fronted villa, just visible through a pair of impressive wrought-iron gates, and set in a large, well-manicured garden with stunning views of the town and river below. Wesley must have passed the house each time he chose to walk to work but he'd never really noticed it before; now that he had, his first thought had been that it must be worth a fortune.

'Savernake,' he said. 'Any relation to Savernake's brewery?'

'Bradley was the managing director but the company's recently been taken over so he's stepped down. I think he's made a fortune out of the deal.'

Wesley had enjoyed the produce of Savernake's brewery many times, as had Gerry, so he was rather impressed with Pam's new friends, even before he'd met them. But the invitation to Sunday lunch with the Savernakes, however tempting, was one he wouldn't be able to accept. Pity.

When they parted, he gave Pam a kiss on the cheek and said that he'd give her a call if he was able to take a break for lunch, knowing that it was highly unlikely but not wanting to ruin her day. She seemed happy with the answer as she drove off with a wave.

Gerry had arrived in the CID office first and was addressing the team as Wesley walked in. Nick Tarnaby was still absent but Rob Carter, dressed in jeans and a striped shirt today rather than his uniform, was standing by the window listening with rapt attention.

As soon as Gerry finished, Wesley followed him into his office. 'Anything new?'

'Those phone calls the dead man made from his hotel phone – they've traced the number and it turns out it belongs to Paulette Reeves. We've now got an address for her. She lives near Whitely.'

'Great,' said Wesley. This was progress.

'We're still waiting for the Spanish police to get back to us about our mystery man.' Gerry's brow furrowed as it did when he was thinking.

There was a token knock on Gerry's office door and Wesley saw Rob Carter standing there like a border collie awaiting his shepherd's instructions.

'That address for Paulette Reeves, sir. According to the electoral roll she lives with a woman called Dorothy Jenkins.'

'Could be the elderly mother the people at the hotel mentioned,' said Wesley.

'Very likely.' Gerry looked down at a scrap of paper on his desk. 'Woodside Cottage, Deadman's Lane, Whitely. Let's go and have a word with her, Wes.'

As they left the police station Gerry began to speculate. 'I think she's an old flame of his. What if she went up to his room, they had a row and she ended up killing him.'

'Don't forget that Colin said he could have been drugged, although we're still waiting for the toxicology results for that glass and the stomach contents. And if she did kill him she probably took the weapon there with that intention.'

Gerry didn't answer. Wesley had shot his theory down in flames and his brain was working hard to come up with another one.

It wasn't far to Whitely; just two miles up the steep main road out of Tradmouth and a left turn down a network of narrow lanes. Wesley had visited the village many times before although he hadn't been aware of a Deadman's Lane, but then most of the rural lanes didn't bear signs proclaiming their official names as they would in a town. A quarter of a mile outside the village Gerry spotted a wooden sign with the name Woodside Cottage half hidden by an overgrown hedgerow. Wesley swung the car into the entrance and saw a small, thatched cottage at the end of the weed-infested tarmac track.

His first thought was that it was a pretty house, like something from a fairy tale, which represented every city dweller's idea of the perfect country retreat. Then he noticed that the window frames needed a coat of fresh paint, as did the cream-coloured cob walls. However, to Wesley, it was the lonely position that made it unattractive. The thought flashed into his mind that it would be a perfect refuge for someone who had something to hide.

As they parked in front of the cottage, Wesley realised why the place felt so oppressive. It was surrounded by trees, the classic cottage in the woods: the witch's house where children were kept caged awaiting a dreadful fate. He got out of the car, glad that Gerry was there with him, and when he reached the front door saw that it was standing slightly ajar and that one of its panes of glass had been smashed.

'Looks the same as the others,' said Wesley.

He put on a pair of crime-scene gloves and stepped into

the small hallway, calling Paulette's name, softly at first then louder. Then he heard the sound of human voices coming from behind the closed door to his right. When he pushed the door open he saw that the room was in semi-darkness and the only sign of life was a small TV chattering away in the corner. A half-empty glass of whisky and an untidy pile of holiday brochures stood on a side table beside a well-worn chintz armchair, as though their owner had abandoned them suddenly. Wesley fought an impulse to turn the TV off and walked through to the kitchen. Again it looked as though someone had left it in a hurry, with unwashed dishes and a tea bag sitting in a mug beside the kettle waiting to be doused with boiling water.

He turned to Gerry. 'Upstairs?'

As Wesley climbed the narrow stairs his heart began to beat faster. In his mind's eye he imagined some terrible scene of carnage up there – Paulette and the elderly mother lying with their throats cut on the floor, or strangled on the bed, their faces contorted in agony.

When he reached the landing he took a deep breath and pushed open one of the doors. It was a small bedroom and the bed was neatly made with an old quilted bedspread but the wardrobe and dressing table drawers were open, as if somebody had rifled through them. The clothes hanging in the wardrobe clearly belonged to somebody elderly and the top of the dressing table was cluttered with over-fussy orna-ments, probably the cherished souvenirs of a lifetime which were, apparently, undisturbed.

He went into the next room. This one was more spacious and boasted a new-looking floral quilt cover, a pack of teddy bears lounging against the frilly pillows on the bed and an assortment of floral prints on the plain white walls.

It was a feminine room – the room of a romantic teenage girl minus the boy band posters. A cheap plastic jewellery box lay open and discarded on the floor by the dressing table. Some of the dressing-table drawers were open too as if somebody had been rummaging for valuables.

Gerry popped his head round the door. 'I've looked in the bathroom. No sign.' He looked around the room. 'It's our man, wouldn't you agree?'

Wesley thought for a few moments. 'So far he's been choosing empty second homes but this place is occupied. There's an outhouse round the side. Let's have a look in there.' His instincts told him something was wrong. A householder who's been burgled calls the police or a neighbour. They don't just vanish.

They left the house by the back door and as they made for the redbrick outhouse Wesley spotted a small grey hatchback parked nearby. If the occupier had fled, it hadn't been by car, unless she had another; he put checking that out on his mental list of things to do. When they reached the outhouse Wesley tried the door and when it didn't budge he peered through the dusty window, but all he could see was an old chest freezer that had seen better days.

'It's locked.'

'I'll see if there's a key hanging in the kitchen,' said Gerry. 'It might be boringly predictable but that's where I'd keep it.'

As Gerry began to retrace his steps Wesley stood and surveyed the drive. Then something caught his eye. Some distance away to his left a large branch had fallen off one of the surrounding trees and now lay at a crazy angle on the ground.

He shielded his eyes against the glare of the grey sky and

called Gerry back, pointing to the site of devastation. 'It must have come down in the wind last night.' Then he spotted what looked like a bundle of cloth on the ground by the fallen branch, half hidden by the ferns that encroached on the drive. 'There's something lying next to it.'

'What is it?'

He left Gerry standing there and hurried over, coming to a sudden halt when he saw a tangle of dark clothing on the bare earth beneath the tree. He knew at once that it was a human body and that life had left it some time ago. He shouted to Gerry who trotted over to join him, arriving slightly breathless by his side.

'Is it Paulette Reeves?'

Wesley stared at the twisted thing that lay face down on the ground. It was obviously a woman but the rotten branch almost masked her head. 'Could be.'

'Accident? Our burglar breaks in and she flees the cottage and gets squashed by a falling branch.'

'If it was, she was unlucky.'

'We'd better get the team down here, just in case, and ask Colin nicely to pop over.'

Wesley suddenly remembered something. 'What about the mother? According to the electoral register she lived with a Dorothy Jenkins.'

'We'd better find her.'

Wesley returned to the car and took out his phone. There was no chance of him making it to lunch with Pam's new friends now. He just hoped he'd be forgiven.

Wesley's phone rang and when he looked at the caller display he saw that it was Neil. Much as he'd have liked to pass the time of day with his old friend and find out what was happening in the world of archaeology, he really hadn't time. Not with one woman dead and one missing.

He kept visualising the confused old lady wandering, lost and terrified, in the rolling countryside after fleeing the intruder; he saw her lying out there somewhere huddled behind some hedgerow suffering from hypothermia. Gerry said it was too early to organise a search but he wasn't so sure.

Then there was the problem of the man in the hotel. Now they knew that it was Paulette's number he'd been ringing from his room, it was more than likely she'd visited him that evening. But had she killed him? If the woman by the trees was indeed Paulette, it was frustrating that she'd died before they had a chance to question her and find out.

When he answered the call, Neil sounded unusually cheerful. Either he'd made some earth-shattering discovery at one of his digs, Wesley thought, or his love life was looking up.

'Will you be in this afternoon? I was thinking of coming round.'

'Sorry Neil, I'm working.'

There was a short silence at the other end of the line. 'What about Pam?'

'She's out for lunch. Sorry.'

'I was hoping to bring someone over.'

'Who?'

'Her name's Lucy Zinara. She's been working up in the Orkneys but now she's down here taking charge of the Sandrock dig – the one that's being filmed.'

'Sorry, Neil, I'll have to pass.' He couldn't resist asking the next question. 'Are you and this Lucy . . . ?'

'Too early to say,' Neil said quickly as though he found

the idea embarrassing. 'She's visiting her old great-grand-mother in a nursing home this morning but we're meeting up later. She's a hundred.'

'I didn't know you went for older women.'

'The great-granny, not Lucy.'

Neil sounded so serious that Wesley couldn't help smiling. Then he saw Colin Bowman's Range Rover making its stately way up the drive. 'Sorry, got to go. Good luck with Lucy.' It was about time Neil's romantic fortunes took a turn for the better. With a dead woman lying twenty yards away, it seemed like a bright thought in a dark world.

The crime-scene people had already assembled and the area around the trees was undergoing a painstaking search. The dead woman was now surrounded by CSIs and photographers who were recording the scene from every conceivable angle and as Colin emerged from his car he greeted Wesley and Gerry genially, as if he was at some social event.

They were given protective suits to put on and as Wesley struggled into his, Colin squatted beside the dead woman holding up a thermometer which he was examining closely. The pathologist claimed that he was never able to give an accurate time of death but that didn't stop him doing his best.

'We're keeping you busy, Colin,' Gerry said.

'If you keep going at this rate my mortuary will be full in no time.'

'Was it an accident?' Now the branch had been lifted out of the way Wesley could see the corpse properly. Her tight dark skirt had ridden up, showing an expanse of plump thigh, and a shapeless garment of indeterminate colour, probably a baggy cardigan, had draped itself around her body. Even though she wasn't dressed to kill this time, there was no doubt that this was the woman who'd been captured on the Morbay Palace Hotel's CCTV. They'd found Paulette Reeves.

As Colin examined the body in silence Wesley stood a few feet away listening to the hiss of the wind in the surrounding branches. Then the pathologist twisted round to face him. 'At first glance her injuries are consistent with a blow to the head.'

He pointed to the corpse's head. It was a mess with pieces of skull and brain exposed so Wesley didn't care to look too closely.

'You mean she was killed by the tree branch?'

'It's possible.'

Wesley detected a note of uncertainty in Colin's voice.

'Do I sense a "but"?' Gerry said, getting the question in first.

Colin touched the heavy branch lying beside the body with his gloved fingers. 'It didn't rain last night so I would have expected to see blood and hair on the wood and more blood underneath the head.'

'The earth around the body looks as if it's been disturbed,' Wesley observed. 'Think she was dragged over here?'

'Either that or she didn't die instantly and she tried to free herself from the branch,' said Colin. 'But I'll know more when I get her on the slab.'

Gerry thanked Colin and began to head towards the house. As Wesley followed, he heard a familiar voice.

'I understand you've found a woman's body. Is it Paulette Reeves?' He turned to see Rachel approaching. She was dressed appropriately in jeans and a hooded jacket and he saw that she had chosen green wellingtons as the footwear *du jour*, but then she had been raised on a local farm so she was only too aware of the hazards of rural life.

'Yes, it's her all right,' Wesley answered.

'Suspicious?'

'Not sure yet. Could be accidental.' He paused. 'But her cottage has been broken into.'

'Like the others?'

'Exactly the same.'

'Think she caught him in the act and he killed her?'

'It's possible. Paulette lived with her elderly mother but there's no sign of her. There's a team combing the woods and surrounding countryside. I'm hoping she hasn't gone far.'

'Unless the burglar's taken her.'

'Why would he do that?'

'Hostage. Or to make her reveal her debit card pin number. It happens.'

Rachel was right; human beings were capable of unimaginable evil. So far their burglar's MO hadn't hinted at violence. However, he'd always targeted empty properties before. What if this was the first time he'd found someone at home and the game had changed?

Rachel looked thoughtful. 'I know this cottage. A distant cousin of my mum's used to live here. Then some people from London bought it as a second home but I remember my mother saying they'd got rid of it.'

'When was this?'

'Must have been about a year ago. I think they sold it to some landlord so as far as I know it's rented out – a proper rental not a holiday let.'

'Know the landlord's name?'

'Sorry.'

'It shouldn't be hard to find out,' he said with confidence. 'I've already asked Rob to make inquiries.'

He could see Rob Carter standing beside the cottage door, his mobile phone to his ear. When he ended his call he strode over to them. Wesley could tell that he had news.

'The landlord's called Simon Corcoran and he lives in Morbay,' he said. 'I've just spoken to him. He wasn't pleased to be disturbed on a Sunday but he says he'll be over as soon as he can.'

'Did he say anything about his tenant?'

'First thing I asked him. He confirmed that she's a Mrs Paulette Reeves and she rents this place with her elderly mother. Says he's never had any trouble with her. Perfect tenant, according to him.'

'Any word on the mother yet?' Her absence was starting to worry him.

Rob shook his head.

'Get someone to contact the hospitals and nursing homes. Maybe she's been admitted somewhere and Paulette was here on her own.' He said the words confidently but there was dread at the back of his mind. Paulette had been lying out there in the trees so he didn't give much for the old woman's chances. 'Has the outhouse at the side of the cottage been searched yet?'

'It's locked,' said Rob apologetically, as though he was taking Wesley's question as a personal criticism. 'I shone a torch in the window and there's only an old freezer in there.'

'Better have a look anyway.'

Rachel caught Wesley's eye. 'There's not much more we can do here, is there. Are you going back to the station?'

'I'll come with Gerry as soon as Colin's finished.'

Wesley watched Rob hurry back to the outhouse where he fell into deep discussion with two uniformed officers. When he saw one of them squaring up to the door, preparing to burst it open by sheer force, Wesley hurried towards them. There were better ways.

'Any sign of the key in the house?'

There was a universal shaking of heads. 'Nothing that fits this door.'

'Well, it's hardly a complicated lock,' he said to Rob. 'It shouldn't be hard to deal with. Wait there.'

He went over to Gerry, who was chatting to Colin as he packed away his equipment. The mortuary van arrived and the pathologist gave them a brief wave as he scurried away.

'Got a minute, Gerry?'

Gerry swung round. 'What is it?'

'There's a door that needs opening.'

It was time for Gerry to do the party trick Wesley had seen many times before.

The DCI rolled his eyes. 'Am I the only one who can do anything around here? I hate to think how you lot got on while I was out of action.'

He delved into his coat pocket. He'd said once that he'd been given his set of skeleton keys by a grateful villain he'd arrested but in Wesley's experience villains were rarely grateful.

Once at the outhouse he watched as Gerry went about his work. By the end there was quite an audience as a group of uniformed officers who'd finished the preliminary search of the house gathered to watch.

Eventually the door opened smoothly, which surprised Wesley as he'd been expecting the groan of long-neglected hinges. As he stepped inside the bare, cobwebbed room, he could see glossy drips of oil on the concrete floor. Someone, possibly the landlord or even Paulette herself, had taken the trouble to oil the hinges recently.

As Rob had said, the only thing in the room was the chest freezer. It was plugged in and Wesley could hear the low hum of its motor. Gerry had come in behind him leaving the others loitering in the doorway, watching.

'Suppose we'd better have a look,' Wesley said before lifting the lid.

Expecting to see packets of frozen peas and oven chips, he was quite unprepared for the sight of a human face staring up at him behind a veil of clear plastic, like a drowning victim submerged in clear, shallow water.

The face was ice-pale, deeply lined and framed by wisps of snow-white hair. It looked as if Dorothy Jenkins had turned up at last.

7

29th October 1913

My mother looks up from the net she is mending as I approach. She sits on the sand, sleeves rolled to her elbows in the weak autumn sun, a rough cotton cap covering her grey-peppered hair. Her once-beautiful face is furrowed by the sea winds as she shields her eyes against the glare of the sky.

I shiver. The breeze blowing from the sea chills me to the bone and I wrinkle my nose at the stench of rotting fish. I pull my shawl around me and as I approach her I feel my baby move again inside me like some alien thing. I can only think of Alfred with loathing now. All the love I felt for him has died. His coldness has murdered it.

I know I will have to tell Mother what has happened and I utter the words as soon as I am close enough to speak. 'I have come home, Mother. I am with child. I am not the first girl in Sandrock to fall in this way and I will rise again, I swear it. Nobody shall pity me or call me a common slut.'

My mother is not impressed by my bold words. She calls me a fool and receives my news as if it has brought all the cares of this world down upon her shoulders. She says my brother, Nathan, will be angry when he returns with the day's catch and that I deserve a beating for my wickedness.

I keep my silence for I have a scheme that will save us all. As I sit in the cottage listening to the crash of the waves outside the window, my hands resting on my growing belly, I smile to myself. Alfred will pay for what he has done. My child shall not suffer for its father's betrayal.

Colin Bowman was an amiable man by nature. Some pathologists Gerry had worked with would have been irritated at the delay to their Sunday lunch that the discovery of a second body would inevitably cause, but Colin took it philosophically.

Floodlights had been brought into the gloomy outhouse so that he could examine the frozen corpse of the small, elderly woman, though he cautioned that it was impossible to give any sort of verdict before the body thawed out and he was able to examine her properly. When Wesley asked him how long she'd been in there, thinking the burglar might have been responsible, Colin estimated that the body had been frozen for a while.

As for time of death, that was far too much to ask. If you've murdered someone and you want to confuse the police investigation by making the time, or even the month, of death impossible to discover, put your victim in the deep freeze, Colin told Wesley as though he was dispensing invaluable advice.

Gerry and Wesley left the pathologist to his work and went outside. The wind was still strong but the feeble sun had warmed the air a little.

'What do you think, Wes?'

'I don't know what to think. We don't know whether the old woman in the freezer was murdered yet. She might have died from natural causes.'

'When someone dies you call the undertaker, you don't dump them in among the ice cream and frozen veg.'

Wesley took a deep breath. Gerry was right, of course. Unless ... 'What if Paulette wanted to delay the date of death for some reason. The terms of a will or something. It's just a thought.'

Gerry looked sceptical. 'Anything's possible, I suppose.'

Wesley began to make for the cottage. 'I'm going to ask the search team to look out for anything to link Paulette to our man at the hotel.'

'We're absolutely sure she killed him?'

Wesley hesitated. Was there a chance they were on the wrong track? 'Well, she was definitely near his room on the evening he died and he called her land line number several times. We need to find out what links her and Alan Buchanan – if that's his real name.'

'No word from Spain yet?'

'Still waiting.' Before Wesley could say any more they heard a vehicle approaching, and they saw a large black SUV with tinted windows that rendered the driver invisible. Wesley's first thought was that it was hardly suitable for the narrow, twisting Devon lanes. His second was that it looked like a criminal's car. But perhaps he was prejudiced.

The door opened and a man jumped out. He was well built, shaven-headed and dressed entirely in black, relieved only by the glint of gold jewellery. Wesley went to meet him, Gerry following. When he got closer he saw colourful tattoos peeping from the collar of the man's open-necked shirt and a tattooed snake slithering from his wrist onto his left hand.

'Simon Corcoran?'

'That's me.' There was something guarded about his reply. 'The cop who rang me said Paulette was dead. Has there been some sort of accident?'

Wesley chose not to answer the question. 'What can you tell me about her?'

'She was a good tenant. Didn't give me any trouble.'

'And her mother?'

'Why? Has something happened to her and all?'

'Can you tell us anything else about Ms Reeves?' said Gerry. 'What she did for a living, for instance. We know she used to work at a hotel in Morbay but she left that job a while ago.'

'She was a cleaner. She sometimes helps – helped – her niece out with her business.'

'Her niece?'

'Yeah, Laura. She runs the cleaning agency that services my holiday properties. That's how Paulette came to be living here. Laura said she'd left her job at the hotel and needed somewhere.'

'That's very generous of you, Mr Corcoran.'

'Not really. In six months I plan to tart this place up and turn it into another holiday let. With Laura's aunty installed I had some rent coming in for it for the time being. And it keeps Laura happy.'

Wesley glanced at Gerry. He suspected that Paulette might not have been aware of the temporary nature of the place she called home. 'And after that?'

He shrugged his large shoulders.

'What's Laura going to say when she finds out you were

planning to put her aunty and her gran out on the street?' said Gerry. From the look in his eyes, Wesley could tell he had taken a dislike to Simon Corcoran.

'I'm quite within my rights to do what I like once the lease runs out. So what's happened to Paulette?'

'It looks as if she was hit by a falling tree branch,' said Wesley.

'Accident then.'

Wesley didn't answer.

'Where's her old mum? In the house? I'd better get onto Laura . . . '

'We'll deal with all that. We need to speak to Laura ourselves. Can you give us her contact details?'

'Sure.' Corcoran found Laura's number on his phone and passed it to Wesley who entered it into his own phone.

'I presume she lives locally?'

'Morbay. Not far from me as a matter of fact.' A small smile played on his lips and Wesley thought Laura might be more to him than a business associate.

'Do you own many properties around here?' Wesley asked, trying to sound casual to avoid putting the man on his guard.

'About thirty. A mixture of holiday lets and rented accommodation. How long are you lot going to be hanging around here?'

'As long as it takes,' said Gerry.

'But if it's an accident surely—'

'We haven't finished our investigation yet. There's the question of the suspicious death of Dorothy Jenkins.'

Corcoran's mouth fell open. This was certainly news to him.

'What was your relationship with Paulette Reeves?'

The man looked confused, as if the news of Dorothy's death had shaken him. 'Relationship? I didn't have one. She was a tenant who sometimes cleaned my properties, that's all. How did Dorothy die? Was she murdered?'

'Sorry. I can't comment yet.' Wesley searched in his pocket for his picture of the man who'd died at the hotel. 'Do you know this man?'

The answer was a shake of Corcoran's hairless head. It had been a long shot but Wesley had thought it was worth asking.

Wesley went and made the call to Laura, careful to break the news as gently as he could. It was hard to gauge Laura's reaction over the phone but she didn't sound particularly distressed.

When she said she'd be free later that afternoon, Wesley told Gerry he was going home for half an hour. He'd meet up with him at the station later and they'd visit Laura in Morbay.

But Gerry suggested that he take Rachel with him instead, saying she was better with grieving relatives. Even though Wesley suspected he'd made the decision because he was tired, he knew that Gerry was right: Rachel was the proper person for the job.

When Wesley arrived home Pam greeted him in the hall, her eyes shining. She had the look of a woman who'd just enjoyed a good lunch, washed down with something stronger than a cup of tea.

She'd had a good time at Bradley and Jennifer's. Bradley was very charming, she said, as though he'd made quite an impression. Wesley felt a bat squeak of jealousy which he swiftly suppressed. Jennifer seemed a bit nervy but she was very sweet and she'd made a great fuss of Amelia. They were good people to be friendly with, she went on. Wesley wasn't sure how to interpret this last remark and he had a sneaking suspicion that Bradley's recent ownership of Savernake's Brewery was causing Pam to connect with her inner snob; his grandmother back in Trinidad had some-times displayed such tendencies but he'd never thought to see them in his wife.

The children were in their rooms, catching up with their homework for the following day, but Wesley experienced a strong desire to see them, to compensate for his earlier absence. He climbed the stairs wearily, fatigue hitting him like a sudden gust of wind, and when he looked into Amelia's room she greeted him with a hug and started chat-tering about her visit to Mum's new friends. At first she'd had nobody to play with because Michael had gone off to Daniel's bedroom. But then Jennifer had taken her upstairs to a beautiful room filled with toys: doll's houses; dolls of all kinds and dressing-up clothes. She wrinkled her nose as she proclaimed some of it was a bit babyish, but Wesley could tell that she'd secretly enjoyed herself. He said he hoped she'd been good and she gave him a mischievous grin as she assured him she'd behaved impeccably. He said he'd check with Pam later.

After a token knock on Michael's door, he entered his son's bedroom and found the boy wrestling with a mathe-matical problem. From his expression as he looked up, Wesley knew that he was relieved at the interruption.

'Did you have a good time at Bradley and Jennifer's?'

'It was OK,' he answered without enthusiasm.

'Their son's in your class, isn't he?'

'Yeah. He's got some good games,' he said before return-ing to his maths homework. But as Wesley was about to leave the room, he spoke again.

'Why couldn't you come, Dad?'

'I had to work.'

'You always have to work.' Michael picked up his pen and stared at the exercise book in front of him.

'I'm sorry,' Wesley said. 'It can't be helped. When this case is over . . . '

'There'll be another one. I need to get on with this. I have to give it in tomorrow.'

'Need any help?'

'No.'

The answer was blunt and Wesley stood there, feeling as if he'd been punched. He'd become an absent father. He tried his best but it wasn't good enough. He'd let his son down and if things went wrong it'd be his fault. An urgent desire to share his thoughts with Pam came over him but when he looked at his watch he saw that he didn't have much time. He had to get back to the station because he was due to visit Paulette Reeves' niece. Downstairs he found Pam in the living room, preparing her lessons for the next day.

'I've been talking to Michael. He says I'm never here. Made me feel really bad.'

'He's only telling it as he sees it,' she said, looking up from her work. 'He's at the age when he needs you.'

'I know.' He sat down on the sofa and put his head in his hands. He felt as though he was being torn in two and the feeling was painful.

'Jennifer's asked us to go round for a meal.'

'If I don't have time for my own son, socialising with

strangers is hardly top of my priority list.' The words came out sharper than he'd intended and he saw Pam turn away, as though the words had hurt her.

'Sorry, I didn't mean it to come out like that. I'd love to come but I've got a lot on at work.'

'I get the message.' She pressed her lips together in a stubborn line. At that moment she reminded him of her mother, another stubborn woman.

He looked at his watch. There was no more time to discuss the matter. Rachel would be waiting for him.

Paulette Reeves' niece, Laura Pullin, was an attractive woman. In her late thirties with streaked strawberry blonde hair, she had a figure most women would envy and her tight jeans and chiffon blouse looked designer rather than Primark. She was far removed from the old Mrs Mop image of a cleaner, but Simon Corcoran had said she ran an agency so she probably left the donkey work to others.

Her modern apartment was in an upmarket part of Morbay, halfway up a hill with a spectacular view of the sea. A collection of bright abstract canvases on the pristine white walls and a large orange rug on the pale wooden floor provided a splash of colour and the sleek, beechwood furniture, like its owner, looked expensive.

As Rachel entered the room Wesley saw her assess her surroundings before giving Laura a sympathetic smile. Once he'd made the introductions Laura invited them to sit down on a low sofa upholstered in pale oatmeal linen. This was no place for children or animals.

'We're sorry about your aunt,' said Wesley.

'Thanks,' said Laura, bowing her head as if in respect for the dead. Wesley could see shock on her face but there were no tears in her eyes. 'You said on the phone that Paulette's death was probably an accident. Does that mean you're not sure?'

'We'll know more after the postmortem,' said Rachel. 'Were you close?'

'We never used to be. Then about a year ago she asked me if I knew anywhere she could rent. She said her mother was ill so she was going to leave her job at the hotel to look after her.'

Wesley leaned forward. 'Tell us about Paulette.'

Laura looked up and gave him a small sad smile. 'She was always a bit of an individual. I believe she got up to all sorts when she was young.'

'What sort of things?'

'I don't really know. I was only little at the time. She was my mother's youngest sister, you see – her half-sister actually. All I know for sure is that she loved her holidays in the sun, until she had to give them up to look after Dorothy, that is.'

'Your grandmother lived with her?'

'She's not my grandmother. After my real gran died my granddad married again. Then him and Dorothy had Paulette.'

'You found her the cottage through Simon Corcoran?'

'That's right.' Wesley saw her cheeks flush.

'You said she liked her holidays in the sun,' said Wesley. 'Did she ever go to Spain?'

'Yes. Why?'

'Whereabouts?'

'Not sure.'

'Did she mention anyone she'd met there? A man called Alan Buchanan for instance?'

Laura shook her head.

'What else can you tell us about her?' said Rachel.

'Well, she was married once briefly but her husband died in some sort of accident. I think he worked on the oil rigs. I don't know what she did before she met him but my mother always said she'd had a bit of a past, if you know what I mean.'

'Can we speak to your mother?'

'Sorry. She passed away three years ago. You said Aunty Paulette's dead but you haven't mentioned Dorothy. Is she all right?'

'When did you last see her?'

Laura lowered her eyes. 'Not for ages. We really weren't that close. I did phone Paulette a couple of months ago but she said Dorothy wasn't well so she didn't want visitors. It must be at least three months since I last saw her. Time flies, doesn't it.'

Wesley's eyes met Rachel's. Someone had to break the news about the old woman in the freezer. He was relieved when Rachel spoke first.

'I'm sorry to have to tell you that the body of an elderly woman was found at the cottage.'

Wesley saw Laura's hand go up to her mouth.

'We don't know the cause of death yet, I'm afraid,' he said, visualising the body lying in that freezer, ice pale, eyes shut as if asleep. 'But we're treating it as suspicious.'

Laura became more agitated, as though the reality of the situation had just hit her. 'Were they both murdered? Was it someone who broke in?' The words came out in a rush.

'There were signs of a break-in but it's too early to say whether—'

Laura rose from her seat. 'Is it that burglar who's been in the papers? Did they disturb him?'

'We're following a number of leads at the moment.' Wesley realised that his words sounded frustratingly official, the language of obstructive authority, and wished he could have found a kinder, gentler way to express himself. 'Would you be willing to identify the bodies? I'm sorry to ask but it has to be done.'

Because of Rachel's past experience as a family liaison officer, she was usually the one landed with breaking bad news and asking this awkward question.

Laura took a deep breath and sank back into her seat. 'Do I have to?'

'Unless there are any other family members who'd be able to instead.'

'There's my cousin, Nick,' she said hopefully, as if she was eager to pass on the burden. 'You might know him. He's a copper.'

'What's his surname?'

'Tarnaby. Nick Tarnaby. Not that I see much of him.'

This was news. Wesley tried to hide his surprise and asked the next question.

'What relation is he to Paulette?' Rachel had shifted to the edge of the chair, listening intently.

'His mum was my mum's sister, Paulette's half-sister, although she was always much closer to Paulette than my mum was. I haven't seen much of Nick recently, not since his wife ran off. He lives his own life.'

'His wife's left him?'

Out of the corner of his eye he saw Rachel's surprised expression.

'Yes. Mind you, I didn't like her much. She was a flighty cow. He's well rid of her if you ask me.'

'Do you know when he last saw Paulette and Dorothy?'

Laura shook her head. 'Sorry. No idea. But I can give you his address if you like.'

'There's no need,' said Wesley quickly. 'We know how to contact him.' He paused. It was time to ask the next question. 'I was asking about a man called Alan Buchanan earlier. He was found dead at the Morbay Palace Hotel and we're treating his death as murder. We think he'd been in contact with Paulette and that she might have visited him on the evening he died. Are you sure you've never heard her mention him?'

When Laura gave him a blank look he went on to describe the man, hoping it would jog her memory. But she shook her head: she was absolutely certain she'd never heard the name before.

'Do you want us to ask Nick to make the formal ID?' Wesley asked gently, suddenly feeling sorry for the woman.

A shadow of anxiety suddenly passed across Laura's face. 'Yes please. I don't think I can face seeing them dead like that.'

'No problem,' said Wesley.

As they were on their way back to Tradmouth, Wesley received a call from Gerry. Paulette Reeves' fingerprints matched some that had been found in the murdered man's room at the Morbay Palace Hotel. They had been discovered on a coffee table that according to the chambermaid had been wiped over before the arrival of the dead guest so there was no chance of them having been left on an earlier occasion. This was proof positive that Paulette had gone there to see the man that evening. Now they needed to find out why. And whether she killed him.

Wesley had never really taken to Nick Tarnaby. There were times when he'd wondered about the private life he kept so closely guarded and this was the first he, or anybody else at work, knew about his wife leaving him. A benevolent angel whispered into his ear that the man's marital disharmony might explain his taciturn nature and that he should treat him with understanding. But some snide devil whispered louder in the other ear that it was more likely that the man's morose attitude had driven his wife away. Whatever the truth, Nick was about to receive a visit.

When Wesley returned to the office and broke the news, Gerry expressed a desire to come with him, his eyes shining with enthusiasm. For one thing, he was curious to see where Nick lived, and also to see whether his bad back would clear up miraculously as soon as they appeared on his doorstep.

As they were setting off, the phone on Wesley's desk rang and he rushed to answer it. The voice on the other end of the line had an unfamiliar accent and it took him several moments to place it as Spanish.

'Am I speaking to Detective Inspector Peterson?' the voice asked in impeccable English.

'Speaking.'

'This is Sergeant Javier Ximenes, Marbella police. We were sent details of a dead man found in your jurisdiction.'

Wesley sat down and picked up a pen, alert with hope. 'Any luck?'

'Yes. The man is known to us.' Wesley felt a thrill of triumph as he signalled to Gerry and waved him over, pressing the speakerphone key. He saw that the officers working around him had fallen silent and had begun to listen attentively.

'We think his name's Alan Buchanan – or at least that was the name he was using over here,' Wesley said, his pen poised over the pad next to his phone.

'That's the name we have for him. According to our records, he was born in the UK in 1952 and moved here in 1981. He gave his occupation as entertainer and he's worked in clubs over here. He has a financial stake in a couple of nightclubs that we think are linked with illegal activities, drugs and so on. We've also suspected him of dabbling in credit card fraud and blackmail, although we've never been able to prove anything. He has some dubious friends in the British ex-pat community here and he's been questioned on suspicion a number of times but there's never been enough evidence against him to prose-cute.'

Wesley had known several individuals like that in the course of his career and he couldn't help sympathising with his Spanish counterpart.

'I've never actually met the man but when you made your inquiry I spoke with some of my colleagues. Some of them remember him as a smooth talker ... even in Spanish.'

'Was he married? Cohabiting?'

'According to our records he was single but that doesn't mean there haven't been women. So he ended up dying in an English hotel room? What happened? Heart attack?'

'He was murdered. Someone drugged him and then thrust a sharp object into his brain.'

There was a short period of silence on the other end of the line then Wesley heard Ximenes say something under his breath in his native tongue. 'Perhaps he got on the wrong side of one of your local villains,' the officer continued. 'Maybe tried to muscle in on someone else's territory?'

'That's what we're trying to find out.' He paused, looking at Gerry. 'We've been examining one of our unsolved cases and we've reason to believe he was involved in the murder of a schoolgirl here back in 1979. The name Alan Buchanan didn't come up in the original investigation so we think he might have been using a different name in those days.'

'I see.' Wesley could hear the surprise in Ximenes's voice. 'There's no suggestion he's been involved in anything like that over here. Just shows you, you never can tell.' Wesley could almost see the man shaking his head in disbelief.

'Look, could you possibly arrange for someone to search his address and let us know if you find anything that might be relevant – anything that might tell us why he decided to come over here. Any correspondence, especially anything that might connect him to a woman called Paulette Reeves.'

'I'm sure I can arrange that and if I find anything, I'll give you another call.'

'Well, we were right about the Spanish connection,' said Gerry as he started to make for the door.

'But the reason for his murder must lie here. Something brought him back. We just have to find out what that something was.'

'He might have been homesick for Blighty. Can't be easy dealing with all that sunshine.'

They were halfway down the stairs and Gerry was walking ahead when Wesley saw him put his left hand on the wall to steady himself and wince with pain. He rushed forward and put a supporting hand under his elbow.

'You OK, Gerry?'

'I'm fine. Don't fuss. I have enough of that sort of thing at home with Joyce.'

'Joyce is right. You should be taking it easy.'

Gerry's wife, Kathy, had been killed in a hit and run

accident some years ago, long before Wesley had transferred to Tradmouth. He'd met Joyce, a plump, sensible woman who worked at the register office in Morbay, while he was investigating a case and they'd gradually become closer. Joyce had moved in to look after him as soon as he was released from hospital after the shooting; Wesley sensed that Gerry wasn't altogether happy with the arrangement now that he was feeling stronger. But Wesley thought Joyce was good for Gerry. The DCI wasn't a man who was suited to living alone and uncared for.

'It's just a twinge. I need a bit of fresh air, that's all.'

'It's pouring with rain. And I can't see that visiting Nick Tarnaby would be good for anyone's health.'

'You don't like him, do you, Wes?'

Wesley didn't answer.

'It's not like you to take a dislike to people.'

'Let's just get it over with.'

'At least he'll be able to make the formal ID on Paulette and her mum. Colin's fixed the PM for tomorrow, by the way. Paulette's that is. He says he's got to wait for her old mum to thaw out.'

The words conjured a surreal image. Gerry was looking better now but his wobble had unnerved Wesley a little.

Wesley was a naturally fast walker, striding ahead, impatient to reach his destination. But today he matched his pace to Gerry's. Gerry seemed to be dealing fine with the gentle exercise although Wesley couldn't help glancing at him from time to time to make sure all was well. They passed the marketplace and carried on up a road of Victorian terraced houses. Unlike most of the other roads leading out of town, this one had been built on reclaimed land in the nineteenth century so it was fairly flat.

Neither of the men had ever visited Nick Tarnaby's address before and they were surprised when they reached a scruffy brick-built terraced house tucked away down a small cul-de-sac. Many of the houses in Tradmouth were picturesque, pastel-painted cottages but this one wouldn't have looked out of place in a northern industrial town. There was a tiny patch of front garden containing nothing but a sad-looking shrub and a selection of weeds, and the two plastic doorbells at the side of the front door told them the house was divided into flats. Wesley pressed the one with the name Tarnaby beneath it and waited.

After a while the door opened a crack and Nick Tarnaby peered out. His eyes widened in horror when he saw who had come calling but he opened the door wider and ran a nervous hand through his thinning ginger hair. He was wearing tracksuit bottoms and a baggy T-shirt proclaiming the virtues of a well-known brand of lager. In his off-duty clothes he looked somehow younger and now, with the daylight on his face, Wesley could see bruising around his left eye as well as a cut on his lip. At a guess the man had been in some sort of fight.

Tarnaby opened his mouth to speak but it seemed that the shock of their arrival had robbed him of words so it was Wesley broke the silence. 'How are you feeling, Nick?'

Tarnaby's eyes darted from one man to the other. 'Bit better,' he said, the words packed with suspicion.

'Mind if we come in?' said Gerry.

Tarnaby hesitated. 'It's a bit of a mess.'

'We're not here to do an article for *Hello!* magazine about your beautiful home,' said Gerry, stepping over the threshold.

Tarnaby led the way into a small shabby sitting room,

cluttered with DVDs, empty beer cans and dirty dishes. It was a plain room with pale blue woodchip walls that needed a coat of paint. A cheap Roman blind hung limply askew at the window and the fireplace had long ago been replaced by a flaking radiator. There was no sign of a woman's influence so Wesley decided that the stories about Tarnaby's wife walking out on him were true. He'd never talked to the man about anything other than work; perhaps he should have taken more interest in his problems.

Gerry moved a heap of car magazines aside and sat down stiffly on the stained sofa. Tarnaby was watching him as he'd watch a prowling crocodile, preparing for it to spring with snapping jaws.

'So you've not been too well?' Gerry began with a dangerous smile on his face.

'I'll probably be OK to come back to work in a few days but–'

'How did you get that nasty bruise?' Wesley asked.

'I fell.'

'Well I don't want you back till it's cleared up,' Gerry said. 'The state you're in, you'll give CID a bad name. Your bad back seems to be better.'

Tarnaby didn't answer.

'I think you'd better sit down, Nick,' said Wesley.

Tarnaby obeyed, perching uneasily on the edge of an armchair.

'There's no easy way to tell you this but your Aunt Paulette's been found dead and we're treating her death as suspicious. I'm sorry.'

Tarnaby stared at him open-mouthed.

'We've already informed your cousin, Laura, and we

thought we'd come and tell you ourselves,' Wesley continued. From what he could judge, Tarnaby seemed surprised at the news but not unduly upset. 'We also found another body at the scene. It was your step-grandmother, Dorothy Jenkins. I'm sorry.'

'Yeah, sorry to have to break it like this but ...' Gerry's voice trailed off and Wesley knew he was attempting, in his clumsy way, to express his genuine sympathy.

'How?'

'We think Paulette's death might have been accidental but we're treating Dorothy's death as suspicious.'

Tarnaby shook his head in disbelief. 'But who'd want to kill her?'

'That's what we're trying to find out,' said Wesley.

'Was it this burglar? Did he break in and find her and ...' Nick's words sounded half-hearted, as though he was expressing outrage because it was expected of him.

'We don't know who was responsible yet,' said Gerry. 'And with your family connection, there's no question of you being on the investigation team. Sorry.'

Tarnaby slumped down into in his seat, staring ahead, fists clenched. Wesley noticed that his knuckles were grazed. He'd been in some sort of fight all right and doubtless that, rather than a bad back, was keeping him away from work. But it wasn't the time to inquire too deeply.

'You know the form, Nick. We need to know everything there is to know about the lives of your aunt and her mother,' Wesley said.

Nick seemed to relax a little. 'Sure.'

'Laura told us your mother's Paulette's half-sister. We'd like to speak to her.'

Tarnaby rolled his eyes. 'She's sunning herself in Australia.

Emigrated there with her partner ten years ago 'cause she couldn't stand the climate here. I've not spoken to her for ages.'

Nick's words surprised Wesley, but he'd discovered over the years that not all families were like his own. Some were distant and some were downright dysfunctional. The niggling fear that loomed into his mind on sleepless nights was that, with the pressures of his work, his own family could end up like that.

'I suppose I'd better call her to tell her the news,' Nick said as if this was an unwelcome chore. He paused. 'She was the only one who had any time for Dorothy, to tell you the truth.'

'Can we have her phone number?' Wesley asked.

When Nick had looked it up in his dog-eared address book Wesley wrote the number down.

Tarnaby went on to confirm everything they already knew. Paulette had lived in at the Morbay Palace Hotel until her mother needed care. She had given up her job at the hotel about a year ago, and Laura had got her some part-time cleaning work to keep the wolf from the door. Laura had also found her the rented cottage through Simon Corcoran. That was it really. He'd only visited her cottage a couple of times. But he hadn't been recently – hadn't had time what with one thing and another.

'I believe your aunt used to holiday in Spain.'

'She always said the Costa del Sol was her one little treat. Used to come back ... ' He searched for the right word. 'Glowing. Between you and me I think she had a bloke out there.'

'She didn't go to Marbella by any chance?'

'Yeah. Why?'

Wesley noted a satisfied look on Gerry's face.

Paulette's connection with the man in the Morbay Palace Hotel hadn't been mentioned. But there'd be time for that once they found out more about her.

'Do you know anything about her early life?'

'According to my mum she was a bit of a girl in her youth. Men and all that.'

'Any names?'

Tarnaby shook his head.

'Did she always work in hotels?'

'I remember my mum saying she used to work at a holiday camp.'

'Like a Butlin's red coat?' Gerry chipped in.

'Don't know.'

'Could it have been the Bay View in Morbay?' Wesley asked.

Tarnaby shook his head. 'No idea. She just said holiday camp.'

'What about Dorothy?' Wesley asked.

'She was granddad's second wife and I think she was working at a big house in Belsham when they met. Thought she was a cut above just because she'd worked for some posh family.' He sniffed. 'I can't say I liked her. She was a cold woman.'

Wesley caught Gerry's eye and saw his mouth twitch upwards. The description of her as a cold woman seemed grimly appropriate in the circumstances. But instantly Gerry rearranged his features into a suitably solemn expression.

'When did you last see Paulette?'

'Must be almost three months ago.'

'I suppose you've had your own worries,' said Wesley, looking around.

Tarnaby's frecked face flushed. 'OK I've had a hard time recently but it hasn't affected my work, has it.'

'If something's bothering you, it's always best to tell me, you know,' said Gerry. 'I don't bite.'

Nick Tarnaby looked sceptical about Gerry's last statement. 'Nothing's bothering me. I'm just upset about Dorothy and my aunty, that's all.' He paused. 'How did they die?'

'We think your aunt died of a head injury but we're not sure about Dorothy yet. The postmortem's being done tomorrow morning but we need someone to identify them. Are you willing to do it?'

Tarnaby looked unsure of himself. 'If I have to.'

'They're at Tradmouth Hospital,' said Wesley. 'I can call to say what time you'll arrive.'

He stood up. 'Might as well get it over and done with. If you give me time to get changed ... '

'We'll walk down with you,' said Gerry. 'It's not something I'd want anyone to do on their own.' All of a sudden his voice was full of sympathy. Nick Tarnaby might not be the sharpest of CID's human assets but he was a colleague who'd just lost two members of his family.

'If you think of anything at all that might help find whoever did this, let us know,' said Wesley.

'Sure.'

'And just for the record where were you on Saturday night?'

The colour drained from Tarnaby's face. 'I was here watching telly. Wasn't feeling too well.'

'When did you have your accident?' From the shade of

the bruising Wesley estimated it had been done within the last few days, probably around the time he'd rung in sick, but he waited for the answer.

'Friday night,' Tarnaby replied quickly before leaving the room to slip into something more respectful.

Wesley waited in silence, sitting beside Gerry on the sofa. Something about Nick Tarnaby's reaction to the news made him uneasy.

'So Paulette used to work at a holiday camp,' Wesley said, breaking the silence. 'If it was the Bay View, we've found a link to Alan Buchanan and Fiona Carp. We're seeing the SIO in charge of the Fiona Carp case tomorrow, aren't we?'

Gerry nodded but before Wesley could say anything else Nick Tarnaby appeared in the doorway wearing a fresh shirt and a pair of jeans.

'I'm ready,' he said like a man about to face the guillotine.

Jayden Ross had seen it on the TV that was permanently switched on in the lounge. It had been on the local news bulletin: the bodies of two women had been found at Woodside Cottage near Whitely. There were signs of a break-in and the police were treating it as suspicious.

He'd gone up to his room, shaking, and tried to relax by playing on his Xbox, but for the rest of the day he felt as if some alien force had drained the energy from his body. He put it down to nerves. His mother suffered from nerves and spent a lot of time lying on the sofa, especially when she'd been on the vodka the night before.

As soon as he'd got back from Woodside Cottage he'd parked his mate's van and hidden the stuff he'd nicked under an old tarpaulin in the lock-up garage round the back of the house. When he heard about the bodies on the news he wondered whether to dump it all but, after some thought, he reckoned it was too good. He could get quite a bit for the radio down the pub. As for the jewellery, he would keep hold of that for the time being.

He spent what was left of the day in bed listening to music, only rising at seven when his stomach began to crave food. When he got downstairs he found his mother sitting hunched on the settee near the window painting her fingernails bright red, her face a picture of concentration. She looked up as he came in and said she was making the most of the peace before his brother returned and the baby started howling again. His brother and his partner had taken it down to the shop to buy some nappies in a desperate attempt to get it to sleep. The baby was a girl but Jayden always thought of her as 'it' – the 'it' that never shut up; the 'it' that kept him awake every bloody night. The house was amazingly quiet when 'it' wasn't there.

She had put some newspaper down on the coffee table in case of accidents, which was lucky because he saw a drip of varnish, like a drop of blood, land on a picture of the mayor shaking hands with his counterpart from Morbay's twin town in France. Jayden said nothing and stood there for a while watching her. He supposed that she wore rubber gloves while she was working, otherwise the varnish would be bound to chip off. It was something he'd never bothered to ask but suddenly he was curious to know all about her work. In particular he wanted to know about the people who owned Woodside Cottage.

He sat in the armchair trying to focus on the massive flat

screen TV blaring out artificial laughter from the corner of the room but he found it impossible to concentrate.

He finally made a decision. 'Mum, you know that cottage near Whitely where they found those two women?'

She looked up at him blankly. 'What women?'

'It was on the local news. Two women were found dead there. Place called Woodside Cottage. Isn't that one of the places where you clean?'

His mother looked puzzled. 'Not any more. It was sold about a year ago. I think the bloke who bought it rents it out now and those women, whoever they are, obviously didn't need my services. Story of my life. Everyone's bloody cutting back. Used to clean for twelve people, I did, but now it's down to seven. Fucking recession,' she added with authority before returning to her nails, unperturbed by the mention of death.

'So you don't know who these women are?'

'Haven't a bloody clue.' She narrowed her eyes like a cat about to pounce on a helpless mouse. 'You'd be better off getting down to that Job Centre instead of asking stupid questions. We could do with a bit more money coming into this house.'

'Don't worry, I've got plans,' Jayden said with forced confidence, although he couldn't banish the dead women from his mind.

When his brother got in the baby was crying as usual so Jayden escaped upstairs to the boxroom, the only space he could call his own, and took the plastic box containing his haul of cash and jewellery from the back of his wardrobe. He had collected over six hundred pounds now and the jewellery was an investment he didn't intend to cash in until the fuss about the burglaries had died down. What with that, and the electrical stuff he could sell, he was doing nicely and he wasn't going to let two dead women spoil it.

He hurried downstairs and plucked his coat from the hook in the tiny hall. The bloody baby was howling from the living room. Once he could afford it, once he had collected enough, he'd find a place of his own.

He put on his coat and went out, shutting the front door carefully behind him. His mate was taking the night off and he'd said he could borrow his van.

He knew the target. A nice little place on the outskirts of Stokeworthy he'd had his eye on for some time.

8

4th January 1914

I have a daughter, a child of such beauty that I sit by the makeshift cot where she sleeps staring at the tiny fingers, the fine eyelashes and the fair, downy head. She is perfect and hardly ever cries, which is good because my brother, Nathan, says that if the little bastard disturbs his sleep he will throw her and me out into the cold.

Nathan has changed since my return. He says I have brought disgrace on him and that the men of the village snigger and make ribald comments about me. He is ashamed of his own sister now but when he knows my plans his shame will fade. We have always endured poverty, always been one step away from the workhouse, but soon this will change.

I smile as I write the letter that will change my fortunes. I will have Alfred trapped in my net just as my brother, and our father before him, trap the fish in the wild waters round about and bring them home to Sandrock, a gold and silver harvest.

*

On Monday morning Wesley felt irritated with the world.

When he'd left home Michael had been setting off to catch the school bus. Pam had told him to call for Daniel Savernake on the way and walk with him to the bus stop. Michael had pulled a face, much to Pam's annoyance, but Wesley had been more philosophical: at Michael's age they choose their own company and you can't force friendship. He'd told Pam he'd try and be back for dinner, failing to mention that he'd have to return to work afterwards. Making the effort to be there for an hour or two was the least he could do.

On his way into the office Trish Walton greeted him with the news that the only fingerprints found in the cottage belonged to the two dead women, Paulette's niece, Laura, and the landlord, Simon Corcoran. Paulette and her mother hadn't had many visitors, he thought. Even Nick Tarnaby, whose partial prints had also been found in the hall and living room, hadn't been there to see them in months.

Nick had made a positive identification of his aunt and step-grandmother the day before, apparently undaunted by the ordeal. But then he was a police officer who'd seen more unpleasant sights in the course of his work so his indifference meant nothing.

Neither Nick nor the police had been able to contact Nick's mother. The woman who might be able to confirm the holiday camp theory was away for a few days. Gerry seemed to take her absence almost as a personal affront.

Wesley gave the morning briefing to the team while Gerry went through the Fiona Carp files. They were both fairly sure that the answer to Alan Buchanan's death lay in the past. But if the man had fled to Spain after Fiona's death, why had he chosen now to return to the scene of his crime?

As Wesley assigned the tasks for the day, he could see the DCI scratching his head as he read. When the briefing was over, he joined Gerry. 'How's it going?' he asked.

Gerry exhaled with what sounded like a mournful sigh. 'I've been over and over this file and there's no mention of an Alan Buchanan, or Paulette for that matter. They don't seem to figure in the case at all. And of course there are no photographs of the people who were interviewed as witnesses so if Buchanan and Paulette were using different names back then we wouldn't be any the wiser.'

'Any suspects?'

'The main suspect was a lad called Stephen Newton who worked in the kitchens.'

'Could Buchanan be him?'

Gerry produced a photograph from the file of a young man with short brown hair and an open, freckled face. 'He was arrested so we've got his mugshot.' He studied the picture. 'I don't think he's Buchanan, do you?'

Wesley had to agree that there was no resemblance. 'So why was he suspected?'

'It seems Fiona took a real shine to him and she used to follow him around when he was off duty. He admitted she made a nuisance of herself but he denied seeing her on the evening she died.'

'Did he have an alibi for the time she disappeared?'

'He claimed he was playing cards with one of the chefs. Trouble is, the chef said he slipped out for half an hour. Enough time to do the deed and come back as if nothing had happened.'

'What did Newton say he was doing?'

'He said he was on the toilet. Upset stomach.'

'Was it true?'

'Who's to say? He must have been bad if he was in there half an hour but he never mentioned it to any of his work-mates. He was arrested on suspicion because he'd been heard telling Fiona to leave him alone, but nothing was ever proved.'

'And now, with Alan Buchanan's skin under the dead girl's fingernails, it looks as if Newton was innocent.' Wesley thought for a few moments. 'But we still need to speak to him.'

'If we can find him.' Gerry looked at his watch. 'Time we were on our way to the hospital for Paulette Reeves' postmortem. If we keep Colin waiting we might have to go without our tea and biscuits.'

Colin was waiting for them at the mortuary at Tradmouth Hospital which was only ten minutes' walk away. The autopsy on Alan Buchanan had been conducted at Morbay Hospital where the facilities were more up to date, but Wesley knew that Colin preferred the more low-tech atmosphere of Tradmouth and his office there had a positively homely feeling. As soon as they arrived Colin offered refreshment, switching on the electric kettle in the corner of the room and taking a trio of bone china mugs from his cupboard along with a selection of biscuits from an exclusive London store. As Gerry had commented so often, they knew how to live down at the mortuary.

Once the pleasantries were over Colin changed his clothes and led them into the postmortem room where the body of Paulette Reeves was lying on a stainless steel table.

'Where's the mum?' Gerry asked.

'Not completely thawed out yet, I'm afraid. We'll have to wait a little longer to find out how she died.'

Gerry grunted – he wasn't the world's most patient man – but then he turned his full attention to Paulette, watching every stage of the gruesome procedure while Wesley studied his feet.

'What's the verdict?' Gerry asked when Colin had finished.

'As I originally thought, she sustained devastating head injuries.'

'The fallen branch?'

'There are no wooden splinters in the wound so I think the scene was staged to fool us. I'd say she was battered to death with something smooth and rounded, possibly metal. Maybe a piece of piping or a tool of some kind. And I think the body was moved soon after death. Got the crime scene report yet?'

Wesley shook his head. 'I'll hurry them up but someone mentioned there were blood stains near the front door and tracks in the earth at the side of the drive as if something had been dragged along the ground.'

'That would fit.'

'There was nothing like the weapon you describe found at the scene so if the killer brought it with him, it suggests premeditation,' said Wesley.

'Or our burglar goes around armed, just in case,' said Gerry.

There was a pause while Wesley marshalled his thoughts. 'Did you know we've discovered a link between Paulette Reeves and Alan Buchanan?'

Colin stopped what he was doing. 'What kind of link?'

It was Gerry who answered. 'We think Buchanan made

several phone calls to Paulette here, and she visited his hotel room around the time he died.'

Colin stared at the corpse on the table in front of him, now being neatly sewn up by his assistant. 'Do you think she killed him?'

'That's what we're trying to find out.'

'Well it's something I can't help you with, I'm afraid. All I can tell you is that she was a fairly healthy specimen, apart from being a bit on the plump side.' He looked at Gerry meaningfully. 'And if someone hadn't smashed her skull in she might have lived to a ripe old age.' He began to take off his gloves. 'I'll send you my report in due course as usual.'

They thanked Colin and left the mortuary, relieved to be out of the place. While they were on their way out another body bag was arriving on a trolley. Wesley hurried past it and averted his eyes.

'Jack Unsworth's expecting us,' said Gerry as they walked back to the police station along the embankment.

The water was grey and choppy and all the pleasure boats which plied up and down the river during the summer months were tied up at their pontoons, bobbing on the waves as if they were trying to escape their moorings. Most of the smaller yachts had now been lifted onto dry land for safety in the various marinas lining the river. Only a few fishing boats chugging home to land their catches and the regular ferries had ventured out. Tradmouth out of season had a forlorn, abandoned look and soon the trees fringing the river would shed their leaves and raise their skeletal arms to the leaden sky. Wesley found himself yearning for summer again, even though it meant the town being overrun by tourists and a rise in the crime rate.

'Where does Unsworth live?' Wesley had never met the

retired DCI who'd been in charge of the Fiona Carp case but he knew him by reputation, which had been formidable. Gerry rated him and that was a recommendation in itself.

'Near Dukesbridge. He suggested a decent pub for lunch. No harm in mixing business and pleasure, is there?' he said with a knowing grin.

'You're still officially an invalid, Gerry, so I guess you're entitled.' Wesley just hoped that Unsworth would be able to shed some light on the case that he felt was beginning to slip out of his control.

Lucy Zinara wanted to look at the site from a distance so she stood on the wooden platform built to give tourists a clear view of the ruined village. There was nobody there today, which wasn't surprising as the wind had worsened. It wasn't a day for sightseeing.

She leaned against the rail and surveyed the ruins below. From where she stood she could see Neil Watson talking to one of the diggers, an earnest young man with a ponytail. She wished Neil could be there full-time, a buffer between herself and the director who was becoming more unbearable by the moment. She'd studied archaeology at York and since she'd left university ten years ago she'd worked up in Orkney on a series of Neolithic sites before being put in charge of the excavation of a Viking boat burial. For a while now she'd longed to take part in a TV archaeology programme and she knew she'd been lucky to land the Sandrock job. But sometimes she wondered whether the old warning 'be careful what you wish for' had some truth about it. She could deal with the frustration and disruption of filming but putting up with the director's unpredictable whims and bumptious attitude wasn't so easy.

When her phone rang she fumbled in her coat pocket and grasped the tiny instrument, worried that it might slip through her chilled fingers and fall through the gaps between the wooden planks into the churning sea below.

'Lucy, is that you?' Her mother, Sue, always asked this, as though she expected a stranger to answer. She replied patiently that she was at work and couldn't talk for long.

'Clara's had another bad night. They had to call the doctor.'

Sue Zinara had never had much sense of occasion. It hardly sounded like an emergency. 'I'm just about to do a piece to camera,' Lucy lied. 'I'll see you later. You can tell me all about it then. Sorry, I've got to go.'

Lucy felt guilty as she ended the call, but it was true that she was supposed to be working. As she made her way back to the site, she saw Neil walking towards her. His face was serious, as though he'd just received bad news.

'I've had a call from my colleague Dave at Paradise Court. He wants me to go over right away.'

'What's so urgent?'

Neil hesitated. 'I don't know yet.' He paused. 'But Dave sounded worried. There could be a problem.'

Jack Unsworth was in his late seventies and he'd been a big man in his time. But a lack of canteen dinners and a concerted effort by his wife to make him lose weight had left him a shadow of his former self. His mop of white hair and his face, furrowed through years of assiduous smoking, a pleasure long since denied him by his wife and doctor, gave him the look of a world-weary gnome who'd seen it all. He greeted Gerry heartily, taking his hand in both of his as if he'd rescued him from some dire situation. He'd heard about Gerry's injuries. Bad business.

When Wesley was introduced the handshake he received was less enthusiastic. The two men had never met before but Unsworth said he'd heard of him. Being the only black detective in the local CID, Wesley had encountered this guarded reaction before. It annoyed him as he'd hoped that by now the colour of his skin would no longer mark him out as a novelty or a trophy for someone in authority who wanted to prove their inclusive credentials. Even so, he shook Unsworth's hand and smiled. The man came from a different generation and he knew he had to make allowances.

They remained in the glass porch of the immaculate little bungalow on the outskirts of Dukesbridge. Wesley soon realised why. A female voice called out from some-where in the depths of the house.

'Who's that, Jack?'

'Just an old colleague, dear.' Unsworth's eyes darted in panic. Wesley recognised a hen-pecked husband when he saw one.

'Aren't you going to invite him in?'

'No, dear, we've got some business to discuss. I thought we'd go to the Lamb and Flag for lunch.'

'Why don't you have lunch here? I can make you some-thing.' She spoke in a voice that brooked no argument but Unsworth was poised for flight.

'No, dear. We don't want to put you to any trouble,' he said meekly.

He signalled to Gerry and Wesley, shooing them outside and closing the back door carefully before he shuffled round the side of the bungalow to a shed, looking around all the time to make sure he wasn't being watched from the sparkling windows. Wesley had never seen a man so cowed, especially a man who, during the course of his long career, had brought violent criminals to justice.

Unsworth unlocked the shed and disappeared inside, emerging after a few moments with an old box file. He tucked it under his arm and as they began to walk down the drive he fell in beside Gerry, asking after old colleagues and listening intently to Gerry's replies, devouring any morsels of station gossip like a starving man. Wesley walked a little behind, understanding how it must feel to be at the centre of activity, only to be cast suddenly out into the darkness of retirement, answering only to the authority of his wife. It was something his generation would probably never experience but it hit the likes of Jack Unsworth hard.

The Lamb and Flag was a pleasant-looking pub, pink-painted with hanging baskets outside swaying precariously in the biting breeze. As soon as Unsworth entered the barman greeted him like an old friend. The gloomy interior oozed comfort with its brass lamps, polished mahogany bar and worn leather benches. This was Jack Unsworth's home from home, his refuge, and where he chose to do business.

Unsworth led them to an empty table and placed the box file on the old oak surface in front of him. Gerry fetched the drinks; pints of Savernake's Best Bitter for himself and Unsworth and a mineral water for Wesley, who was driving. Wesley looked longingly at the pint glasses when they arrived. He would have liked to sample the produce of Pam's new friends' family brewery.

Gerry had brought some menus back from the bar and

handed them out. Wesley went to the bar to order three ploughman's lunches and when he returned he saw that the box file was open and the contents spread across the table. On top of the papers Gerry had placed a picture of the dead man from the Morbay Palace Hotel.

Unsworth picked up the photograph. 'That's him. I'd put money on it,' he said as Wesley sat down.

'You recognise him?'

'His girlfriend supplied an alibi so he wasn't a suspect at the time.'

'Put us out of our misery, Jack,' said Gerry. 'What do you know about him?'

'Well, he didn't call himself Alan Buchanan for a start. His name was Merlin Mitchell in those days and he was an entertainer; used to sing and do magic tricks, that sort of thing.'

Wesley felt a glow of satisfaction. The Spanish police had mentioned a show business connection.

Unsworth took a long drink from his glass and put it down. 'I remember he was a smooth talker. Thought a lot of himself. His girlfriend gave him a cast-iron alibi but I got the impression that he wouldn't have thought twice about ditching her if he had a better offer, if you know what I mean. She could hardly be described as a stunner but she was the faithful, clingy type, bordering on the obsessive in my opinion.'

'His DNA was found on Fiona Carp's clothing and under her fingernails.'

Unsworth took another drink. 'It did look as if she'd tried to defend herself but in those days we didn't have the benefit of modern science, more's the pity.'

'It looks like Mitchell's girlfriend was lying for him.'

'Their story checked out at the time.' Unsworth sounded defensive, as if he suspected Gerry of casting a slur on his abilities.

'Your main suspect was a Stephen Newton, I believe,' said Wesley.

'That's right. Fiona Carp had developed a bit of a crush on him – used to follow him round. Several people heard him telling her to get lost.'

'And his alibi wasn't up to much?'

'The upset stomach story's a bit hard to prove either way, especially as he said he went back to the staff chalet where he was staying to use the toilet and the lad he was sharing with was out for the evening so he had no witnesses to back him up. Also Newton had a nasty scratch on his arm. Said he'd done it on some brambles.'

'Why wasn't he charged?'

'All the evidence against him was circumstantial. But, with hindsight, that was a good thing now Merlin Mitchell's in the frame. Could have been a miscarriage of justice. Retrial; quashed conviction; my name being dragged through the mud; compensation; the lot.' He shuddered. 'Besides, the Newton lad was like a rabbit caught in the headlights when we interviewed him and the case against him didn't feel right somehow. My nose told me he wasn't capable of it.'

'Have you any idea why this Merlin Mitchell would want to strangle a young girl?' Gerry asked

Unsworth shook his head. 'As far as we knew he had no criminal record. Even in those days the holiday camp company always checked on anyone working near kiddies.'

'But if they used a false identity, they'd have no way of knowing.'

'You're right. Even today you can get past that sort of thing if you're clever and determined enough.'

'The girl hadn't been sexually assaulted so presumably that wasn't the motive,' said Wesley.

Jack Unsworth took yet another drink and put his glass back on the table. 'I didn't make a connection at the time but now I sometimes wonder whether the thefts had something to do with it.'

Gerry sat up straight. 'There's no mention of thefts in the files I've read.'

'There was nothing to link them with the kid's murder so it was treated as a separate case,' said Unsworth. 'Besides, the management wanted to hush them up. Bad for business.'

'Tell us about them,' said Wesley, leaning forward.

'Nothing much to tell. Some of the chalets were broken into and cash and jewellery stolen. A couple of uniforms were sent round, more as reassurance than anything else because the management didn't want the guests' chalets searched. They reckoned it would ruin people's holidays and I can see their point.'

'So the thefts were never solved?'

'No. And funnily enough they stopped soon after the murder so nothing more was said. I reckon it was probably one of the inmates.'

'Inmates?'

Unsworth gave a mischievous smile. 'It's all changed now but in those days the place was surrounded by a wire fence like a prison camp. Although it could just as easily have been one of the staff. I guess we'll never know.'

'Our dead man – the one you knew as Merlin Mitchell – moved to Spain in 1981,' said Wesley. 'And according to the police over there he had his finger in all sorts of dubious pies even though he was clever enough to avoid a conviction over the years. A stolen credit card was found in the hotel room where he died so it seems he just couldn't kick his bad habits. Is it possible he was responsible for the thefts at the holiday camp?'

'When you put it like that, it would explain a lot. But I can't see what it could have to do with little Fiona's death.'

'Unless she caught him at it and threatened to give the game away.' Gerry cleared his throat. 'Look, Jack, I've read the files but you actually talked to the people. What impression did you get of Fiona?'

'How do you mean?'

'What kind of kid was she?'

Wesley thought it was a good question. He took a sip of mineral water and awaited the answer.

'People described her as a live wire. Into everything. Curious. She used to follow people around. Her mum and dad said she liked mystery stories and playing at detectives.'

'So she might have stumbled on Merlin Mitchell's activities?' said Gerry.

'She was just a kid.'

'Kids can tell secrets,' said Wesley. 'He'd have been arrested, lost his job, his girlfriend. He was an entertainer. He probably had ambitions.'

'I think Wesley's right, Jack,' said Gerry. 'You can't argue with the DNA evidence.'

Jack gave Wesley a grudging nod.

'I'd like to speak to Fiona's family,' said Wesley.

'You think Merlin's murder could be revenge?' said Unsworth.

'If someone kills your child ... ' He didn't finish the

137

sentence. The very idea was too painful to express. 'On the other hand, how would they have known it was him? We didn't know until the cold-case review DNA results came through.'

Unsworth and Gerry sat in puzzled silence and Wesley was relieved when the barmaid brought their food over. Eating would give him time to think.

'By the way,' said Gerry when the lunch was almost finished. 'I couldn't find a name for Mitchell's girlfriend in the files I've read.'

'It should be in there somewhere, hidden in the list of also-rans, the routine statements that came to nothing.' Unsworth pushed his empty plate to one side and began to delve into the depths of his box file. He drew out a list and studied it. 'I think this is her – Susan Paulette Jenkins.'

Wesley saw Gerry put his head in his hands. He must have seen the name among all the others in the case file but he hadn't made the connection: Paulette's mother was Dorothy Jenkins so Paulette's surname had been Jenkins before her brief marriage to the tragic oil rig worker.

They now had their connection between Paulette and Merlin Mitchell. She had given him his alibi for Fiona Carp's murder – and now both of them were dead.

9

2nd February 1914

The letter was sent with the carrier a week ago and today I received a reply.

My words to Alfred had been subtle, the threat of exposure masked in velvet words. How pitiful if your beautiful daughter, your own flesh, suffered in poverty for the sins of her mother. How terrible it would be if your new marriage should be marred by the revelation of her existence. I asked for a modest sum on this occasion. The rest will come later. I will bide my time, play the fish until it has no will to resist.

I tear open his letter and two pound notes fall to the ground, fluttering and spinning like giant snowflakes. I smile to myself. He has bitten and this is the start of his bounty.

My daughter thrashes her plump limbs and gurgles in the old drawer that serves as her cradle. She shall have a crib fit for a princess before long.

Neil Watson experienced an unfamiliar tingle of nerves as he drove to Paradise Court. Dave had sounded shaken when he'd called and Neil was impatient to find out why.

After two miles he turned off the main road. The entrance to the long drive lay down a network of Devon lanes, thin, winding and lined with tall hedgerows. It was like finding one's way through a maze but over the years he'd worked for the Devon County Archaeological Unit he'd grown used to the terrain.

He spotted one of the familiar Heritage Trust signposts, tasteful green-grey with black lettering and the Trust's stylised castle logo, and was soon driving through the gateway towards the house. The plethora of freshly painted signs suggested that the Heritage Trust was spending quite a bit on the place: they'd certainly been generous with their funding for the excavation and the renovation of the ice house wouldn't come cheap either, not considering its ruined state. After parking the car he made for the walled garden.

He could hear the scraping of trowels on earth as he did the rounds of the trenches, chatting to the diggers, examining the finds trays and peering at what was left of the walls of the earlier house. It was no longer raining but there were puddles on the ground. Digging would be a dirty job and for once he was relieved that he didn't have to get his hands dirty with only a thin mat between his knees and the damp ground. He told himself he must be getting old.

A young women in trench five told him where Dave was and that he'd been at the ice house all morning. He thanked her and took the twisted, shady path to the ice house. As soon as he turned the corner he saw Dave, a portly figure with a real-ale gut and an Indiana Jones hat covering his long thinning hair. He was fidgeting with his mobile phone and wore a worried frown on his normally affable face.

'What's up?'

As Neil walked towards him, Dave looked as relieved as someone with a burning chip pan who's just heard the fire fighters arrive at the door. 'I need you to have a look at something.'

'What?'

Without replying Dave led the way to the ice house. When Neil had last seen it the entrance had been sealed with stone like the mouth of a cave blocked by a rock fall, but now it had been cleared and a brick-lined passage was visible, collapsed in places and looking downright dangerous.

'When's it being shored up?' he asked. 'I never thought I'd quote Health and Safety at anyone but we can't risk people working in here until it's safe.'

'It's being done this afternoon,' said Dave, handing Neil a hard hat and taking a torch from his pocket. 'When we were doing the initial clearing out, I shone my torch through a gap in the debris and ... Well, if you're up for going in there, come and see for yourself.'

In spite of the precarious appearance of the tunnel roof, Neil didn't need asking twice. The passage wasn't long, only eight feet or so, and the end was blocked by a wall of fallen masonry. If this was like other ice houses he'd seen, a domed, brick-lined chamber sunk deep into the ground would lie beyond the barrier. Ice would have been harvested from nearby ponds in the depths of winter and stored here for use in Paradise Court's kitchens. Servants would have been sent here to fetch it to the house. It can't have been a popular job.

As Dave stopped at the end of the passage Neil glanced upwards nervously. Trickles of soil had been cascading from the roof as they walked and in places the arch of bricks had disintegrated, leaving only earth above them.

The rotting odour of damp soil and vegetation filled the stale air. It smelled like a grave in there.

'Look at this,' said Dave, standing by the wall of fallen debris and holding his torch up to a small gap.

Cautiously Neil edged towards him, took the torch and peered through, shining the beam into the darkness. The brick-lined vault was still in fairly good condition but the floor was littered with debris.

Then Neil saw a glimpse of creamy white against the dust: a little dome that could have been the egg of some large and exotic bird. But this dome appeared to have two dark holes, two eye sockets peeping out of the rubble.

'Well?' Dave whispered.

'Let's talk about this outside,' Neil said, anxious to be out of there, away from the danger of being buried alive.

Dave didn't need any persuading. The two men hurried towards the daylight.

Wesley had put Rachel in charge of tracing Fiona Carp's relatives in case one of them might be in the vicinity, bent on vengeance. He'd also asked the team to trace Stephen Newton. He wanted to find out what had happened to the young chef who'd caught Fiona's eye. According to Jack Unsworth, she'd followed him about, possibly as a result of some pre-adolescent crush or maybe her nascent interest in mystery and detection. Stephen Newton might be able to throw light on the matter but so far they were having trouble finding out where he was.

Gerry had felt tired so he'd gone home, taking the files on Fiona Carp's murder with him. He wanted to read through them again, he said, in case there was something else he'd missed.

When six o'clock came, Wesley told Rachel he too was going home for an hour or so to see his family and grab something to eat instead of having a takeaway at his desk. As the others were still working, making calls, sifting through statements and awaiting developments, he knew he wouldn't be missed in that short space of time.

He arrived at six thirty, expecting to find the usual scene of domestic chaos with Pam trying to prepare her lessons for the next day while serving up dinner and making sure the children settled to their homework. Instead, when he opened the front door and called Pam's name, the house seemed unusually quiet, even though the lights were blazing and an appetising aroma of cooking was wafting from the kitchen.

Then he heard the sound of female voices and as he took off his coat he looked up and saw Amelia standing at the top of the stairs. As soon as she saw him, her glum expression vanished and she hurtled downstairs and launched herself into his arms.

'I'm glad you're here, Dad.' She didn't call him 'Daddy' any more, he noted with a twinge of sadness.

'Why's that?'

'Michael's got Daniel here and they won't let me in the room.'

'Want me to have a word?'

Amelia shook her dark curls vigorously. 'No way. It's bad enough you being a policeman without acting like one at home.'

Wesley didn't know whether to laugh or feel hurt. 'What do you mean, bad enough me being a policeman?'

The little girl frowned. This was obviously something she hadn't thought out which meant she'd probably heard someone else saying it. Pam maybe? Did she really moan about him in front of the children?

'Tell you what,' he said. 'When I've finished working on this case we'll go away somewhere for the weekend. How about going to Gran and Grandpa's in London? We could do the sights; go to the London Eye and Buckingham Palace.' He was sure this suggestion would satisfy everyone and felt rather pleased with himself.

Amelia regarded him solemnly. 'A girl in my class is going on a trip around the States next summer. And one of the boys is going to Africa on safari.'

'Good for them,' Wesley said quickly, trying to ignore the veiled criticism. So she thought her family was boring. Boring was sometimes good. 'What about London then?'

'OK. I'm hungry.'

He had assumed that they'd already eaten but it seemed he was wrong. 'Haven't you had dinner yet?'

'Jennifer's here. Her and mum are in the kitchen. Jennifer says she's going to take me to the aquarium in Plymouth.'

This was somewhere Wesley had been promising to take her but work had always got in the way. His daughter was becoming an expert in conscience-pricking.

'That's very kind of her.' He looked at his watch. 'I'll see whether our dinner's ready. I take it Michael hasn't eaten either?'

'We had biscuits when we got in,' she said mournfully, like some ragged orphan in the poorhouse forced to live on gruel.

He felt a pang of irritation. Perhaps this was Pam's way of telling him she'd finally had enough of his work demands and it might take a display of penitence worthy of a medieval pilgrim crawling on hands and knees to a distant sacred shrine.

144

He kissed his daughter on the forehead and made for the kitchen, sensing that he would need all his reserves of tact to deal with the situation. Pam was sitting there sipping from a glass of red wine. The woman who sat opposite her wore jeans and a pink sweater with a silk scarf tied elegantly around her neck. At first glance she had that look of effortless chic; the impression that everything about her appearance was right. But for a split second he saw her eyes widen like those of a nervous animal scenting danger.

Pam stood up unsteadily, pushing her chair back with a loud scraping sound that set his teeth on edge. 'Wes. Come and meet Jennifer.'

Wesley shook the woman's hand. He noticed that her handshake was limp and her palms were clammy.

'Good to meet you, Jennifer. Thanks for offering to take Amelia to the aquarium. She's been nagging to go there ever since they did a project on fish at school but I've had a lot on at work.'

'It's no problem, honestly,' she said breathlessly. Wesley thought he caught a hint of anxiety behind the words; perhaps a desire to make a good impression.

He saw Amelia standing in the doorway like an admonishing ghost so he beckoned her in and put his arm round her shoulders.

'When's dinner?' she asked, pulling away from his embrace.

Jennifer half rose, holding out her hand to Amelia, all social wariness gone, her eyes shining as if she'd been handed some wonderful treasure. 'I'll take you out to dinner, darling. Somewhere nice in Tradmouth. How about it?' She glanced at Pam for approval.

Pam looked at Wesley. 'Sorry. I've got something ready. Another time perhaps.'

Jennifer sank down into her seat again. 'Of course. Another time.' She smiled at Amelia, who looked mildly disappointed as her mother took out a casserole from the oven. Pam spooned some out on a plate and Amelia took it to the table and began to eat, watching the grown-ups with great interest.

The smell of the food was making Wesley's stomach rumble but it would have been rude to eat in the circumstances. He looked at Jennifer and saw that she was watching his daughter with something akin to adoration.

'Thanks for the invitation to Sunday dinner. I'm sorry I couldn't make it.'

Jennifer tore her eyes from Amelia. 'So am I. I thought it would be good to get together because Michael and Danny get on so well.' She lowered her voice. 'Danny was very withdrawn when he started at Morbay Grammar and I was afraid he was being bullied. So you can understand how relieved I was when he found a friend who lives nearby.'

'Of course.' She was still watching Amelia with hungry eyes as though she wanted to sweep the child up and smother her in kisses.

'Is Daniel your only child?' He caught Pam's eye. She was frowning and gave her head a small, almost imperceptible shake. He'd made a major faux pas. But there was no going back now.

Jennifer bowed her head. 'Danny's Bradley's son from his first marriage.' She hesitated. 'I had a daughter but she died. Meningitis. If she'd lived she would have been Amelia's age now.'

'I'm so sorry,' Wesley said. The shock of the revelation

had robbed him of the ability to come up with anything more original.

He knew he had to change the subject. 'Pam tells me your husband owns Savernake's Brewery.'

'Owned,' she corrected. 'He's just sold it to a larger company which was a difficult decision because the business was started by his great-grandfather.'

The words were awkward, as though she found the subject distasteful. Perhaps the sale of the company had resulted in redundancies, or she regretted the end of an era; or maybe her mind was still on her lost daughter.

'Pam told me you're a police inspector,' she said. 'You must be so busy with this awful murder – the man in Morbay. I read about it in the paper. And these burglaries. It said on the news that he killed a woman over in Whitely. Are you any nearer catching him? I mean our house isn't exactly isolated but it has extensive gardens and it's not overlooked. If anybody broke in when Bradley wasn't there . . . ' She didn't finish the sentence but then she didn't have to. The apprehension in her eyes told him more than a thousand words. Like most law-abiding citizens when a murderer was at large, she was worried.

'We're following a number of leads,' he said, knowing that he sounded like an official statement.

'But is the public in any danger?'

He said he thought not. In reality he didn't know the answer to that one.

Lucy Zinara held her mother's hand, clinging to it for comfort as they sat by the bed.

Clara lay there, her wispy grey hair, once so abundant and now so thin, surrounding her parchment skull like a

147

halo spread out on the pillow. Her flesh, covered with the brown spots of old age, looked as delicate as a cobweb.

'Should we try and speak to her?' Sue Zinara whispered. In the past few days it was as if her daughter was taking on the parent's role, providing a steady, calming presence while her mother let her emotions have free rein. Clara had brought her up, taking her parents' place after their deaths. To Sue she'd been everything: not only grandmother but mother and father too.

'I don't suppose it'd do any harm.' Lucy glanced at her watch. It was nine o'clock and dark outside. She hadn't seen Neil since he'd disappeared off to Paradise Court and she'd been disappointed when he hadn't returned to Sandrock before close of play that afternoon.

Clara gave a small, almost inaudible moan. Lucy sensed that she was still troubled, as though she didn't want to go to her Maker before she'd got whatever was bothering her out into the open.

Her lips were moving now, as if in silent prayer. Lucy bent over her, trying to make out what she was saying, but the muttered words didn't make any sense.

There was only one word she caught. It sounded like her own name, Clara, though she couldn't be sure.

Then the old woman opened her eyes wide, mouthed the word 'Mama' and gave a deep shuddering sigh.

She was staring at the ceiling with sightless eyes and Lucy noticed that her chest was no longer moving to the tentative rhythm of her laboured breathing.

Clara was dead.

10

23rd February 1914

Three weeks have passed since his last letter and the baby thrives. I have called her Edith after his mother. I wrote to tell him of my choice and today I received his reply.

He makes no mention of Edith's name; instead he has a proposition for me, one he claims will be to my advantage. He will meet me in the porch of St Enroc's church at the edge of our village to discuss the matter. Perhaps he wishes to acknowledge our daughter. Perhaps he is prepared to be generous.

I arrive early for our meeting, relieved that nobody is around to pry for the men in the village are out, braving the cold and the rough sea to bring the harvest of fish home, and the women are mending the nets with chilled and reddened fingers. I carry my child in my arms, ready to present her to her father, and I wait, shielded from the icy wind within the little porch. After half an hour I hear the beat of distant hooves and I see the trap approaching down the lane pulled by a grey horse. He sits atop, whip in hand, and he looks angry. At first I fear for the beast but it is an old horse, quiet and obedient and he makes no move to chivvy it along. When he sees me he does not smile.

I hold Edith up to show him as he walks towards me down the church path. He looks plumper than he did when I last saw him. He is a married man now, but he looks miserable. There is no joy in his eyes as he beholds little Edith, his flesh and blood. Instead he stands several feet away as though he cannot bear to be near me and wastes no time on pleasantries.

'I have given some thought to our situation,' he begins. He is business-like, as though he addresses some tenant farmer. 'The truth is that I cannot afford to pay any more for your daughter.'

'Our daughter,' I correct.

'There is no money.' An apologetic note creeps into his voice. 'I have always had a weakness for the racetrack as you know and now my creditors circle like vultures.'

'You have a new wife,' I say. 'I understand that she is wealthy.'

For the first time he smiles but there is bitterness in his eyes. 'I was deceived. Her father made some foolish investments. He is as broke as I am.'

I stare at him. My plans have come to nothing and I feel like sinking to my knees and railing against the cruelty of fate and the fickleness of horseflesh.

'However, I have a suggestion,' he says. I see fresh hope in his eyes and once more he looks like the boy I fell in love with.

Wesley could have done without Jennifer Savernake's visit the previous evening. She'd stayed for another half-hour and by the time she left he'd felt famished and guilty about leaving the others to deal with the workload. He'd bolted his dinner and had suffered from indigestion for the rest of the evening.

He knew he should be pleased that Pam was entertaining friends in his unavoidable absence and, in a way, he was. But there was something about Jennifer that made him uneasy, an intensity, a neediness perhaps. He told himself that he was being selfish. If Pam liked her, that should be good enough for him.

On Tuesday morning he set off early, walking down the steep streets into the town, his feet kicking up the falling leaves. It was the season when everything died. He'd always preferred spring to autumn.

Just as he reached the office his phone rang, the caller display telling him it was Neil.

'Hi Neil,' he said, keen to hear news that didn't involve theft, murder and an increase to his workload. 'Sorry about the other day, by the way, but with this case ...'

'I know, mate. Look, I just wanted to let you know that there may be human remains at one of the sites I'm working on.'

Wesley sank down into his chair. 'Have you let the coroner know?'

'Not yet because I'm not sure. I could only see it by shining a torch through a gap in the rubble blocking a passage. There might be some difficulty getting to the location. Health and Safety.'

'So what do you want me to do about it?'

'We're going to try and clear the passage out today – just thought I'd better warn you.'

Wesley knew the word 'thanks' might come out as sarcastic so he just told Neil to keep him posted, hoping that the bones glimpsed through that gap in the rubble would turn out to belong to an animal which had wandered in there and become trapped. He wondered why Neil had bothered telling him before he was sure, but he was soon to discover the real purpose of his call.

'Look, Wes, will you and Pam be free tonight because I was thinking of taking Lucy for a drink in Tradmouth. I thought we might call round; give you a chance to meet her.'

Wesley had to smile. 'I can't promise I'll be there but Pam should be in if you want her approval.'

'Wes, a word.' Wesley looked round. Gerry had just swept in. There was a glint in his eye, the anticipation of the thrill of the chase. As Wesley ended his call he saw that Rachel was watching him as though she had something to say.

'Any progress on Fiona Carp's family?' he asked her.

She shook her head. 'Not yet. But I've got some new leads to follow today. What's happening with Nick Tarnaby? Is he coming back to work?'

Wesley told her he didn't know, then followed the DCI into his lair and sat down. He knew the signs: Gerry wanted to go over the case to get things straight in his mind. In Wesley's experience, it always helped.

'Rachel's just asked about Nick,' Wesley began.

'I've told him to take some more time off. Even if he was here, I wouldn't want him working on the case. It's family. He's too involved.'

Wesley nodded. He'd have made the same decision himself.

'Jack Unsworth was a great help yesterday,' said Gerry. 'I'm as sure as I can be that these murders are connected with the death of Fiona Carp. The man who killed her is dead and so is the woman who gave him his alibi. Rach is trying to trace Fiona's family.'

'And Stephen Newton, the original suspect?'

'Haven't found him yet but it shouldn't take long.'

'So you think the burglar's out of the frame?'

Gerry paused. 'Not sure, Wes. By the way, Colin called me at home first thing to say that the old lady's thawed out at last so he can do the PM this morning. You up for that?'

The phone on his desk began to ring and he started to root through the heap of files and papers to get to it. Gerry had always subscribed to the theory that a tidy desk signified an unimaginative mind. By the time he answered he looked breathless.

'DCI Heffernan,' he barked. Then after a few moments he hit the speakerphone key so that Wesley could hear the conversation.

Wesley recognised the voice at once. It was Laura Pullin, Paulette Reeves' niece and Nick Tarnaby's cousin. 'There's something you need to know,' she said quietly as if she was afraid of being overheard. 'He was putting pressure on her, even messed up the central heating so she had no hot water. I dread to think what that place would have been like once winter really arrived.'

'Who are we talking about, Ms Pullin?'

'Simon Corcoran of course. He didn't want to wait until Paulette's lease ran out. He's going to do the place up and let it out as a luxury holiday cottage. He started off by asking but when she wouldn't budge, he started to get nasty.'

'Paulette told you this?'

There was a short silence on the other end of the line. 'No. I knew what was going on.'

'And you've only just decided to tell us.'

Wesley could hear the irritation in Gerry's voice. Laura

had withheld what could be important information and he wondered what had brought about her change of heart, but he was soon to find out.

'This is embarrassing . . . '

'I don't embarrass easily so you might as well come clean, love.'

Wesley heard her take a deep breath. 'Me and Simon. Well, we were . . . '

'You were having an affair?' said Gerry.

'Yes. But I never liked the way he treated Aunty. He did me a favour by letting her rent the place but once the arrangement didn't suit him anymore . . . We had a big row about it shortly before she . . . '

'So why didn't you tell Inspector Peterson when he came to see you?'

She didn't answer.

'Have you and Corcoran fallen out?'

It was a good guess; one Wesley had already made himself.

'Something like that.'

'We could get you for wasting police time, you know that?' He paused. 'But we won't if you come in and make a new statement. I want to know everything about Corcoran's dealings with your aunt. Don't leave anything out this time. And by the way, Dorothy Jenkins' postmortem is scheduled for later today. Just keeping you informed.'

Laura had no choice but to thank Gerry, sounding suitably grateful. He'd let her off lightly; Wesley knew he'd have done the same.

And it looked as if they now had a new suspect. Simon Corcoran had wanted Paulette and her mother out of that cottage; maybe he'd gone round that night and they'd argued and things had got out of hand. Maybe the break-in and Paulette's involvement in the Fiona Carp case had been coincidences. They did happen from time to time.

Neil had been told to be available for filming by ten thirty and as he left Paradise Court at nine thirty the ice-house passage was being made safe with props and planks. However, it would be some time before the ice chamber beyond the fallen debris could be accessed without the ever-present danger of being buried alive.

Perhaps he shouldn't have called Wesley before he had anything definite to report but he'd wanted the reassurance of sharing the problem that had kept him awake most of the night. Each time he'd closed his eyes he'd seen that white dome, so small and delicate. He'd excavated children's graves in the course of his career and this reminded him so much of those sad little remains.

The journey to Sandrock seemed to flash by fast, even though he wasn't breaking the speed limit, but when he arrived there was no sign of Lucy's SUV and this puzzled him. He walked round the trenches and learned that there had been a few decent finds that morning. A coin dating to the reign of Henry VIII and a piece of medieval stained glass from the little church which had been placed in a plastic bag with a small amount of water to save it from disintegrating.

He was examining a fragment of a glazed medieval floor tile when he heard the director's hectoring voice.

'Neil. Can I have a word.'

Neil returned the tile to the finds tray and followed the man out.

'Where's Lucy?' Neil asked as they stopped in what remained of the church porch.

'She rang to say she won't make it today. Something about her great-granny shuffling off this mortal coil.' He said the words with heavy irony and a callousness that made Neil feel like punching him, even though he wasn't normally a violent man. 'I ask you, the old girl was a hundred and twenty or something so it was hardly unexpected. I call it downright unprofessional.'

Neil felt obliged to leap to Lucy's defence. 'It's not easy when a relative dies,' he said, squaring up to the director, who pushed his cashmere scarf back over his shoulder and looked away.

'She was scheduled to do a piece to camera and an interview with you about today's finds.'

'I can do that with someone else. No problem.'

'It means rescheduling.'

'That's not the end of the world.' He paused, looking in the direction of the ruins of Sandrock. 'It hardly compares with a whole village being swept into the sea with twenty people killed, does it?'

The director didn't answer. He stalked away towards the waiting camera crew. In the mood he was in, Neil didn't envy them.

He took out his phone and keyed in Lucy's number. If nothing else he could offer her his sympathies.

She answered after three rings and sounded as though she'd been crying.

'Sorry to hear about Clara.'

'Hope things aren't too awkward there.'

'I'm sure everyone understands,' Neil lied.

'We were with her at the end.'

'That's good.' He wasn't quite sure what else to say.

'She seemed troubled.'

He was about to say that she was at peace now but it sounded like the worst kind of cliché. Instead he thought it best to change the subject.

'We're starting work on the ice house at Paradise Court today. Making it safe.'

'Is something the matter?'

'Why?'

'You sound worried.'

He was surprised that she'd picked up on the nuance of unease that must have crept into his voice. There was a long silence before he answered. 'We couldn't see properly because the passageway's collapsed but ... but I thought I saw some bones in there.'

He was surprised when Lucy abruptly ended the call.

Dorothy Jenkins' postmortem had been an inconclusive affair. Colin had hedged his professional bets and said that in all likelihood the old woman had died of natural causes. As to the time of death, it was impossible to say. Her time in the freezer had confused things, which, Colin said, might have been the intention of whoever put her in there.

Apart from the unusual circumstances of her discovery, he could find no indication of foul play. It was a mystery, he said; and he was glad it wasn't up to him to solve it.

Wesley returned to the police station, experiencing a nagging tug of frustration as he walked with Gerry along the embankment.

'What do you reckon, Wes? Did Paulette do her old mum in and dump her in the freezer? Is that why she was desperate not to leave the cottage? With her mum's body in the outhouse there was no way she could move out and that's why she told Corcoran she was staying put. Then he started putting the pressure on.'

'You think he killed her when his patience finally ran out?'

'Why not?'

'But where does our burglar fit in? Or Merlin Mitchell?'

Gerry didn't answer and they went on in silence for a while until he spoke again. 'How's your Pam?'

'OK. She seems to have made a new best friend – a woman with a kid in Michael's class whose husband's a governor of Pam's school. The husband was the MD of Savernake's Brewery.'

Gerry's eyes lit up. 'Let me know if he's giving out free samples.'

'He's just sold the company.'

Gerry pulled a face. 'Hope it won't affect the quality.'

They'd reached the station and as they entered the incident room Rachel stood up to greet them. Wesley's eyes were drawn to her left hand and he saw that the solitaire ring that had graced her third finger for the past months wasn't there. He opened his mouth to ask the question that leaped into his mind but decided against it.

'The crime scene report's come in,' she said. 'Those stains near the front door are definitely Paulette Reeves' blood. And there are traces of blood between the house and the trees too, as if the body was dragged to where it was found.'

'Anything else?'

'There's been another burglary in Stokeworthy. Holiday home belonging to a family from London. Cleaner went in as arranged and found a pane of glass broken. Same MO.'

'I presume the house was unoccupied?'

'Yes. Identical to the others – apart from Paulette's place that is. He certainly varied his pattern with that one. The crime scene team are over in Stokeworthy now.'

'Let's hope he's left something for us this time,' said Gerry.

Rachel smiled. 'Better than that. The owner installed CCTV. Rob's in the AV room going through the footage.'

They made for the AV room, Gerry rubbing his hands together in anticipation, and as they entered Rob Carter scrambled to his feet. He still reminded Wesley of an eager sheepdog, anxious to please, and he saw something else in his eyes too – the fervour of ambition. He wondered whether it would last once the novelty of being in CID wore off.

'You've found something?' Wesley asked.

'Yes, sir. There's a clear image of the burglar approaching the front door.'

Wesley peered at the screen. The figure was quite clear, a young man wearing dark clothes and a baseball cap. He was average height and wiry with a thin face that reminded Wesley of a weasel. As far as he could recall, he'd never seen him before in his life.

Gerry's face was screwed up in concentration, as if he was trying to remember some elusive fact. 'I don't recognise him so he can't be one of our regular customers here in Tradmouth.'

'See if you can find him on the computer, will you, Rob,' said Wesley. 'And while you're at it get a picture sent over to Morbay. Someone there might know who he is.'

Rob Carter scurried off and came back twenty minutes later with a name: Jayden Ross, aged twenty-three, already had three convictions for shoplifting. Now it looked as if he'd branched out.

The people who'd erected the web of planks and metal props appeared to know what they were doing, or at least Neil hoped they did. One of his recurring nightmares was being buried alive in some collapsed trench.

'Will it be OK in there? It won't crash down on our heads, will it?' he said to the man in charge, a hirsute structural engineer brought in by the Heritage Trust to deal with the problem.

He gave Neil an indulgent smile as if he was a child asking a particularly naïve question. 'The arch is the strongest structure known to man.'

'I had heard something,' said Neil, putting up a hand to check that his hard hat was firmly in place. He watched as the workmen cleared the final debris and took it out through the strengthened passage in wheelbarrows. When they'd finished the engineer prepared to make his examination of the domed circular chamber.

Neil watched as he stepped inside, flashing his powerful torch around the ceiling, checking for signs of danger. 'It's in remarkably good nick,' was the verdict. 'You can start in here whenever you're ready.'

When Neil had been there before, his torch beam had caught something white in the dust and fallen bricks to the right of the entrance. Now he entered and focused his torch on the spot.

'Something the matter?' the engineer asked.

Neil didn't answer. He was concentrating on the little white object half hidden beneath a layer of broken bricks and damp earth. At first he made no move to touch the

160

little skull with the small, perfect teeth and the hollow sockets where eyes had once been. Then he took his small leaf trowel from his pocket and gently teased the rubble away from where the base of the skull met the spine. He turned to the engineer who was peering over his shoulder, gaping in horror, breath held.

'I'll have to inform the police and the coroner,' Neil said softly.

11

28th February 1914

In other circumstances Alfred's suggestion might have been met with enthusiasm. The position of lady's maid is considerably more desirable than that of parlourmaid: it is almost the occupation of a lady.

The fact that our vicar took a special interest in me while I was growing up in Sandrock – singling me out along with the son of one of the tenant farmers for special tuition on account of our aptitude for learning – settled the matter. I can read, write and keep accounts as well as being a competent seamstress and knowing a little French and Latin. The vicar insisted that I was too good for a parlour maid but my family were in need of money so I had little choice in the matter. The vicar has said little to me since Edith's christening. He looks at me sadly, as though I have disappointed him.

Now I am decided. Alfred's aunt, Lady Berridge, is in need of a personal maid and since Alfred cannot support me and his child, I shall go to Paradise Court and leave Edith in my mother's care. Perhaps this will be to my advantage for they say Lady Berridge is a very wealthy woman.

*

As Wesley watched Jayden Ross through the two-way mirror he thought he looked quite at home in the interview room. He had been given a cup of what purported to be tea from the machine in the corridor and, now he'd drunk the contents, he proceeded to rip the flimsy vessel apart with the studied concentration of a boy tearing the wings off a captive insect.

He was an unprepossessing figure, his lean body draped in a grey tracksuit and a baseball cap perched on his shorn head. Wesley thought he looked a little pathetic; but then so many of the murderers he'd seen in the course of his careers looked the same.

'You ready?' Wesley asked Gerry, who was standing beside him.

'He's been in there fifteen minutes. Should be softened up nicely by now.'

'Rachel and Trish have already asked him about the burglaries but he claims he was at home on each occasion. Says his mum or his brother will back him up.'

'I'm sure they will. There's no forensic evidence or fingerprints to place him at the scenes. He's been clever so far – even though he doesn't look it.'

'Let's make a start,' Wesley said, impatient to get at the truth. If their luck was in they might have found Paulette Reeves' killer.

They entered the interview room, nodding to the uniformed PC guarding the door, and announced their arrival for the benefit of the tape Wesley had just set running.

It was Wesley who spoke first. 'You broke into an empty holiday home on Sunday night.'

'Prove it.'

Wesley had placed a blow-up of the image from the

CCTV footage face down on the battered Formica table between them. He now turned it over and pushed it towards Jayden who stared at it as if it was something unpleasant he'd found stuck to his expensive trainers.

'That's you, isn't it.'

'Don't know.'

'Come on, Jayden,' said Gerry. 'At the moment it doesn't look good for you at all. A woman was found dead at one of the houses you broke into. Woodside Cottage near Whitely. Remember it? We think whoever broke in must have killed her when she found him going through her things.'

Jayden eyes darted from one man to the other. He looked like a trapped beast which has realised that it has no choice but to give up the fight. 'I didn't. Honest. The telly was on but the place was empty. I swear.'

'Let's start at the beginning,' said Wesley. 'You admit you've been breaking into holiday cottages – second homes.'

'You might as well come clean, Jayden,' said Gerry at his most avuncular. 'What have you done with the stuff you nicked?'

'No comment.'

'You're only putting off the inevitable,' said Wesley. 'Your house is being searched as we speak.'

Jayden appeared to relax a little.

'Or if it's somewhere else, we'll find it. Your houses have lock-up garages at the end of the block, don't they?'

Jayden's eyes widened. He was a useless liar.

'One of our officers has just called in. Apparently there's a lot of interesting stuff in your mum's lock-up. We're matching it with our list of stolen items.'

Jayden pressed his lips together and said nothing.

164

'Your mum gave you your alibis,' said Wesley. 'She lied to us, didn't she?'

Jayden didn't answer.

'OK, we'll leave that for the moment. I can see you don't want to get her into trouble. Let's talk about the break-ins. The people who own those houses only use them a few times a year, don't they. They've got more money than sense, isn't that right? How did you know they were second homes?'

Jayden looked down at the table.

'We'll find out eventually so you might as well tell us now. Get it off your chest,' said Gerry putting his face close to Jayden's.

Jayden pondered his options for a while. Then he spoke. 'My mum cleans for them. She's got a list of addresses but she doesn't know I take a look at it from time to time. Look, she's got nothing to do with this.'

'Presumably your mum has keys to these places too?'

Jayden looked at Wesley as though the question had been a stupid one. 'Sure she does but if I'd used them it would have been too obvious, wouldn't it. Your lot would find out who had keys and come along asking questions.' He straightened his back, suddenly self-righteous. 'I never made much mess 'cause I knew they'd tell Mum to clear it up. They're rich. They could afford it.'

'You see yourself as a fighter for social justice, do you?' said Gerry. 'Robin Hood has a lot to answer for.'

'They didn't miss the stuff I nicked. It's all insured, isn't it?'

'Are you jealous of the people who own the houses? Is that why you do it?'

Wesley leaned forward, interrupting Gerry's attempt at

amateur psychology. He looked Jayden in the eye. 'Wood-side Cottage wasn't a holiday home. Paulette Reeves and her elderly mother rented it.'

Jayden flinched as though Wesley had struck him. 'I didn't know. It was on my mum's list, same as the others.'

'Old list is it?' Wesley asked.

'Don't know. I just found it.'

'The people your mother used to clean for moved out of Woodside Cottage a year ago. It was bought by a landlord who rented it out to Mrs Reeves.'

'How was I to know that?' Jayden sounded indignant. 'I'm not fucking psychic.'

'So when you broke into Woodside Cottage your luck ran out. Mrs Reeves disturbed you so you panicked and killed her.'

'That's not what happened. I went inside and took a few things but I didn't see nobody and that's God's honest truth. The place was empty.'

'Describe what you found in the house,' Wesley said.

Jayden thought for a few moments. 'It was weird. The curtains were shut and the telly was on. It was like that ship. The *Mary* whatsit.'

'The *Mary Celeste*.'

'That's the one. Anyway, I took some stuff and shot out quick. I swear on my mum's life I never killed anyone.' He looked from one man to the other, pleading with them to believe him. Somehow Wesley did.

'Do you recce the places before you burgle them?'

The answer was a tentative nod.

'While you were watching Woodside Cottage did you see anybody around apart from the woman who lived there?'

Jayden nodded eagerly and the peak of his baseball cap

166

bobbed up and down like a duck's bill. 'I went there a couple of times and the first time I saw a bloke arrive in a big four by four. Top of the range. Black. Tinted windows. Nice.'

'Can you describe him?'

'Big. Shaved head. I thought he must be the owner . . . the woman's husband.'

Wesley looked at Gerry. 'Sounds like the landlord.'

'Well if he's the landlord, they didn't get on. I could hear the shouting from where I was standing and when he left he slammed the door and drove off like a bloody racing driver.' He shook his head again in disbelief. 'If you're looking for who killed her, he'd be top of my list.'

Gerry announced for the tape that the interview was ended.

'Thanks for that, Jayden,' he said as he stood up. 'Have a nice day.'

Wesley was glad he couldn't quite make out Jayden's mumbled reply.

According to records the ice house had been in a state of ruin since 1918 when a storm had brought a tree down, crushing the passage leading to the entrance and rendering the structure unstable. The tree had been removed but nobody had bothered to repair the ice house. It had been constructed in the eighteenth century and by the time of its destruction hadn't been in use for quite a while. An anachronism at a time of technological innovation, it had lain there forgotten until the Heritage Trust had decided to restore it as a curiosity.

But before that falling tree had destroyed the entrance, somehow a child had got in there and died.

Neil had followed the usual procedure, informing the coroner and putting in a call to Wesley who'd sounded harassed, as though he had other things on his mind. Neil suggested that, as the remains were bound to be over seventy years old, he could send a uniform to complete the formalities, but Wesley hadn't wanted to miss out. He'd promised to come over as soon as he was free.

Neil turned his phone over and over in his hand, wondering whether to call Lucy again or if another call would seem like harassment. She had reacted strangely when he'd mentioned the possibility of bones before. Perhaps when he revealed what they'd actually found, he'd know why.

He selected her number and waited. When she answered she sounded as if she'd been crying.

'Sorry to bother you again, Lucy. How are things?'

'We've just been speaking to the funeral director. Then we'll have to clear out her room at the nursing home. Hope I've not upset the filming too much.'

'I don't know. I haven't been back to Sandrock since first thing this morning.' He paused. 'You know those bones I thought I saw in the ice house at Paradise Court? It's the skeleton of a young child.'

There was a long silence before Lucy spoke again. 'How long has it been there?'

'I've no idea but it must date from before the ice house was damaged in a storm. From what I've managed to gather from the historian up at the house that was in 1918. Mind you, it hadn't been in use for over ten years by then.'

'How old was this child?'

'Four or thereabouts. I've asked a bone specialist to come

and take a look so hopefully we'll know more after that. Your family lived here. Were there any stories about kids going missing? Wandering off and never seen again?'

'Not that I know of.' There were a few moments of silence and Neil sensed there was something she was holding back. 'I'll ask my mother if she knows anything.'

'Thanks. I'd like to give the kid a name ... whoever he or she is.' He wasn't usually the sentimental type but his professional armour had been pierced when he'd seen that little set of bones lying there; the child who'd never been given the chance to live out its life.

He was about to return to the ice house to see what was happening when he heard Wesley's voice.

'What's this about a skeleton?'

Neil swung round, relieved to see his old friend. 'It's the skeleton of a young kid. From the teeth I'd estimate that he or she was about four. If I had to hazard a guess about how the poor little blighter died, I'd say that it wandered into the ice house shortly before the entrance was sealed off by a falling tree in 1918 and got trapped. I've asked the estate historian to see if he can come up with a name for a kid who vanished around that time.'

'Should be straightforward then,' said Wesley with a grin. 'You won't need my services.'

Neil shook his head. 'It was probably a tragic accident.' He suddenly looked solemn. 'There's no sign of a head injury or anything like that so he or she was probably trapped in there and died of starvation. Horrible thought.'

Wesley suppressed a shudder as the image of a terrified child imprisoned in the darkness, shouting for help at first then, when no help arrived, lying down to die alone. It didn't bear thinking about. He looked at his watch. 'I've been holed up with a murder suspect all morning and I wanted some fresh air but I haven't got long.'

'You've got someone for your hotel murder? Or is it the woman in the cottage?'

'We're working on the theory that the man in the hotel was killed by the second victim who was then murdered by someone unrelated to the first crime.'

'I know I'm not an expert in the crime-fighting business but isn't that a bit of a coincidence?'

'Coincidences happen.'

Neil could tell he wasn't convinced.

'Are you going to show me round the dig now I'm here?'

'I thought you'd never ask,' Neil said, leading the way.

When Wesley returned Gerry rose slowly from his seat. 'What's this about a kid's body being found?' He was frowning, anticipating the worst.

'Don't worry, Gerry. All the evidence points to him having died in 1918. Accidental death. Not our problem.'

'It's a boy then?'

'It's impossible to tell the sex of such a young child from looking at the bones, I'm afraid. Anything come in while I've been out?'

'Laura Pullin came in to make a statement about Corcoran's dealings with her aunt, and she's not a happy lady. If you ask me, they've had some sort of bust-up. Someone went round to his house to bring him in for questioning but he's away for the night in Bristol. Apparently he has properties there as well.'

'Quite the entrepreneur.'

'Quite the crooked landlord,' said Gerry with a snort. 'I

bet he'd use any means possible to get rid of an inconvenient tenant.'

'Murder?'

'You heard what Jayden Ross said. Him and Paulette were arguing.'

'Believe him?'

'He might be a burglar and a nasty little toerag but I think he's telling the truth about that. What if Corcoran went back there on the night Paulette died and things got out of hand? She threatened to damage his precious car and he snatched a weapon and struck out. He had a body on his hands so he dragged her to the fallen tree in the hope it'd be taken for an accident.'

Wesley nodded in agreement. It was as feasible a scenario as any. Now all they had to do was to get Simon Corcoran to confess.

Gerry gave a heavy sigh and buried his head in his hands.

'You OK, Gerry?'

Gerry looked up. 'Bit tired, that's all.'

'You're still supposed to be on light duties.'

'You won't tell on me, will you?' he said like a naughty schoolboy.

'I will if you don't start taking it easy, pacing yourself. Why don't you get home early? Everything's under control and I can manage. Besides, I don't think it'll be long before the case is sewn up. We've cracked the burglaries already.'

Gerry went and began to flick through the cold case files which had been moved from his desk to the top of the filing cabinet. 'While we weren't busy I was supposed to be having a look through this lot. Little did I think that, thanks to good old DNA, we'd get one of them wrapped up so quickly.'

'There you are. The burglaries and the Fiona Carp case. That's not a bad clear-up rate.' Wesley knew that Gerry needed reassurance that his injuries hadn't weakened his abilities.

Gerry lowered his voice. 'One little mystery I'd like to solve is why Rach has stopped wearing her engagement ring. Is the wedding still on or what?'

'Don't ask me,' said Wesley quickly.

'You could ask her.'

'Trish shares a house with her – she should know.' But he had no intention of mentioning it to Trish. It was something he didn't want to think about.

It was as though the mention of Rachel had made her appear at the open door of Gerry's office. When she asked if she could have a word, Wesley felt the blood rushing to his face.

'I've just taken a call from a Sergeant Javier Ximenes of the Marbella police,' she said. 'The address they had for Alan Buchanan has been searched. They found Paulette Reeves' name in an address book and some rather gushing letters from her, the first one dating from two years ago saying she was glad they'd met again. He's e-mailing copies over. According to records Buchanan arrived at Heathrow ten days ago.' She placed a sheet of paper on Gerry's desk. 'The Spanish police also examined his phone records. Paulette's been calling him fairly regularly for the past couple of years. He received a lengthy call from her land line a few days before he travelled to England.'

'Why wasn't this picked up when we went through Paulette's phone records?'

'They haven't finished going that far back yet,' she said with a hint of defensiveness. 'So far they've been concentrating on local calls around the time of the murder.'

'OK,' said Wesley, raising his hands in appeasement. 'I wasn't having a go at you. I'm just a bit annoyed that an officer in another country has had to bring it to our attention, that's all.'

Rachel looked hurt. 'Sergeant Ximenes said he'll let us know if they find anything else.'

'Thanks, Rach,' said Gerry, lounging back in his chair. 'Has someone checked whether Nick Tarnaby's mum in Australia's back home yet?'

'She's still away. Won't be back for a few days. I called Nick but he hasn't spoken to her either.'

'I need someone to talk to her as soon as possible,' Wesley said. 'If she was closer to Dorothy and Paulette than Laura's mother was, she might be able to tell us more about them.'

Rachel didn't answer. She left the room, glancing at Wesley on her way out. He picked up the paper she'd just left and pretended to study it.

'What do you make of this new information from Spain?' Gerry asked, scratching his head.

'It looks like Paulette's kept in touch with her old flame and he came here to meet her.' Wesley turned the sheet of paper over in his fingers. 'She lied for Mitchell when he killed Fiona Carp.'

'Probably saw herself as Bonnie to his Clyde,' said Gerry. 'But if Fiona caught him stealing and he'd got away with killing her, why did he leave the holiday camp so suddenly before the end of the season?'

'Probably because the main suspect, Stephen Newton,

was released and he was afraid the police would start to ask awkward questions.'

'Then why didn't Paulette go off with him if they were that close? And what was Merlin doing between the time he left the holiday camp and 1981 when he turned up in Marbella?'

'I think something Paulette told him brought him back to Devon.'

'What?'

'That's what I want to find out.'

'And then she killed him when he got here. Think they quarrelled?'

'Do you?'

Gerry considered the question. 'Nobody at the hotel heard raised voices.'

'And the method of murder suggests premeditation rather than a loss of control in a fit of temper.'

'Perhaps we're reading too much into it, Wes. She was dressed up like a dog's dinner when she visited him at the hotel. Maybe she was hoping he'd come here to settle down with her at last. And she lost it when he let her down. A simple crime of passion.'

There was a knock and when Wesley looked round he saw Trish Walton standing there looking pleased with herself.

'I've traced Stephen Newton,' she said. 'He's working as a chef in Exeter. I've got his home address and the address of the bistro where he works.'

'Good.' Gerry lowered his voice. 'Close the door, will you Trish. I've got a question for you.'

She looked puzzled but did as she was asked, standing in front of Gerry's desk like a schoolgirl awaiting the teacher's verdict on work she'd just handed in. Gerry looked around as though he feared someone would overhear.

'I notice Rach isn't wearing her ring,' he said bluntly. 'Wedding still on, is it?'

Wesley could have buried his head in his hands. Gerry had always loved to be in on all the station gossip but he found subtlety a challenge.

'Nigel came round last night so I presume everything's OK. She's lost a bit of weight recently so she might have sent the ring to the jeweller's for the size to be changed. I'll ask her, shall I?'

Gerry nodded, positively conspiratorial. 'Good idea. I need to know if I've got to get my best suit out of mothballs for the wedding.' He gave Trish a theatrical wink. 'Don't tell her I've been asking, will you. Wouldn't do my reputation any good.'

'I'll be the soul of discretion, sir.' Trish grinned back. She was wearing her long dark hair loose today and she looked pretty when she smiled. Wesley noticed that her teeth were particularly white. She was going out with a dentist, which obviously had its advantages.

'Tell you what, Wes,' Gerry said when Trish had gone. 'Why don't you and Rach go up to Exeter and talk to this Stephen Newton. If you're lucky, he might let you sample his cooking.' He licked his lips. 'Come to think of it, I'm hungry.' He looked at his watch. 'Three o'clock. I could send that new lad, Rob, out for a cake. Fancy one?'

Wesley shook his head.

'I'll see if Rach is free.'

'You do that, Wes. Maybe you can do a bit of probing,'

Questioning Rachel about her private life was the last

thing he intended to do but he wasn't going to tell Gerry that.

Just over an hour later he was parking the car in the centre of Exeter, Rachel sitting beside him in the passenger seat. Neither of them had spoken much during the journey apart from occasional observations about the case. They had Stephen Newton's home address but Wesley thought they'd be more likely to catch him at work. He was head chef at a bistro on the cathedral close: a nice location. Newton had come up in the world since his days of holiday camp mass catering.

They could have spoken to the man over the telephone but Wesley always preferred to see the face of the person he was interviewing. He liked to watch their eyes, look for the flicker of recognition or evasion, know when he was being lied to.

He made his way down High Street with Rachel at his side, past shops that had risen from the bomb-damaged rubble of the ancient city after the Second World War. From time to time she slowed down to look in the shop windows, resisting the pull of temptation. He walked on, making for the historic cathedral yard dominated by the huge Gothic cathedral with its elaborate façade of carved saints, angels, kings and prophets. When he had been a student in the city, he had loved sitting on the grass in front of the cathedral talking with friends in the sunshine. But today there were no idling students or visitors and the outside tables of the cafés and restaurants nearby were empty. The sky was grey and a cutting wind blew around the close. He'd have to make do with memories.

'You were at university here, weren't you?' It was the first question Rachel had asked him since they had left Trad-mouth. 'There are times I regret not going myself.'

'You could still do it.'

She pulled a face. 'Easier said than done.'

'What would Nigel think?'

'I don't suppose he'd mind. He just goes along with any-thing I say.'

Her words came as a relief. Their moment of madness in Manchester back in May hadn't ruined things. 'How are the plans progressing?'

'OK. Next spring I'll be Mrs Haynes. Farmer's wife ... just like my mum.'

'That's good, isn't it?'

The smile she gave was flawed with sadness. 'It's the best on offer, at the moment.'

'Nigel's a good man. I like him.' He could have added that Nigel was solid, reliable and trustworthy but didn't think this would go down well. Rachel was in the market for a lover, not a sheepdog.

She said nothing until they reached the Cloisters Bistro, a bijou establishment on the ground floor of an old half-timbered building with bare wooden tables inside and an outside eating area which looked empty and windswept. There was a Closed sign on the door but Wesley ignored it and rapped loudly on the glass.

The door was opened by a tall young waiter in a red waistcoat who towered over both of them and looked mildly irritated. 'We're not open 'til five thirty,' he said as if he was addressing a pair of simple children.

Wesley produced his warrant card and made the intro-ductions. 'We're here to see Stephen Newton. Is he in?'

The waiter seemed to shrink before their eyes. He led the

way silently to the kitchens where a smallish man in his fifties was preparing a sauce. He had snow-white hair and bushy black eyebrows which gave him a look of permanent astonishment and, from the embroidered name on his chef's whites, Wesley knew they'd found their man.

'Someone to see you, Chef,' said the waiter. 'Police,' he added in an ominous whisper.

Stephen Newton looked up from his sauce. 'I won't be a moment. Take a seat.' He was trying his best to sound casual but Wesley could see that his hand had begun to shake a little. He was nervous and yet he had no criminal convictions, unless you counted two speeding offences, one distant and one fairly recent, that had showed up on the computer when they'd entered his name.

'Come into my office,' he said once he'd summoned a colleague to take over the sauce.

Wesley and Rachel followed him into a tiny, glass-fronted office, a bit like Gerry Heffernan's in miniature, but a good deal tidier. The chef indicated a pair of wooden stools and they took a seat.

'What's this about?' Newton asked as he sat down at his desk. Wesley noticed his right eye twitching nervously.

'When you worked at the Bay View Holiday Camp just outside Morbay in 1979 a young girl called Fiona Carp was murdered.'

The colour drained from Newton's face. 'Not that again.'

Wesley picked up on the man's despair, the fear that the worst part of his life was about to be resurrected like a rotting corpse. He felt a sudden need to reassure him. 'You've no need to worry. You're no longer under suspicion. We've had new DNA evidence that puts you in the clear.'

Wesley had rarely seen anybody so relieved. Newton buried his head in his hands and when he looked up again Wesley thought he could see the glint of tears in his eyes. 'Ever since 1979 I've been wondering if the police were going to turn up and start the whole nightmare again. When you arrived . . . '

'I'm sorry,' said Wesley. 'It can't have been easy.'

Newton looked him in the eye, pleading rather than aggressive. 'Do you know what it's like to be suspected of something like that? I was eighteen, just a kid myself. It was my first proper job and that bloody girl developed some kind of crush on me and kept following me around whenever I was off duty. All I did was tell her to get lost and even though she was a nuisance I'd never have harmed her. But that's not what the police thought. Someone heard me shouting at her to leave me alone so they thought I must have killed her. It was no use saying I've got no interest whatsoever in little girls. Or little boys either for that matter,' he added quickly in case his statement was misunderstood.

'We know the truth now,' Rachel said. 'You can relax.'

Newton turned to her. 'Relax. I've spent bloody years looking over my shoulder, jumping whenever the bloody phone rings. For a long time afterwards all the relationships I had came to nothing because I'd lost my ability to trust anyone. It was as though I had a big tattoo on my forehead saying "murderer". "Child killer".'

Rachel bowed her head and Wesley could think of nothing to say to comfort a man whose life had been blighted by suspicion. He sometimes thought that 'there's no smoke without fire' was one of the most destructive phrases in the English language.

But was it possible that he would want to take revenge on the man who'd really got away with Fiona Carp's murder? Even though they were fairly certain that Paulette had killed Merlin Mitchell, this was a possibility he couldn't rule out.

'We'd like to ask you a few questions about your time at the holiday camp, if that's OK,' said Wesley. 'A man was found murdered in a hotel in Morbay last week. He used to be known as Merlin Mitchell.'

Newton stood up, indignant. 'Well, I didn't do it.'

'We're not saying you did. However, those DNA results I mentioned suggest that Mitchell was Fiona Carp's killer.'

Newton sank down into his seat again as though the news had come as a shock.

'Do you remember Merlin Mitchell?' Wesley asked.

Newton nodded.

'When did you last see him?'

'In 1979 at the Bay View Holiday Camp. I didn't particularly like him. I steered clear.'

'There were thefts from the chalets.'

'That's right. The staff accommodation was searched but nothing was ever found.'

'We think Mitchell was the thief.'

'That doesn't surprise me.'

'Can you tell us anything about him?'

'Only that he could be charming. But there was a nasty side to him too.'

Wesley and Rachel exchanged looks.

'He had a girlfriend who gave him an alibi for the time of Fiona's murder.'

Newton frowned, as though he was trying hard to remember. 'So he did. One of these plain girls who thinks the best way to catch a man is to flash what assets she has.

Definitely the doormat type. She'd have said whatever he told her to say.'

'Her name was Paulette. You remember her well?'

'Not that well.'

'Was there anyone else?'

'There were a few from what I recall. Paulette didn't seem to mind his infidelities.'

'Can you remember the names of anyone else he was involved with?' Wesley asked.

'There was a chalet maid called Karen – a real looker and a few years younger than Paulette.' He wrinkled his brow, trying to remember. 'I heard he went off with her.'

'When?'

'About three weeks before the season ended. Not long after Fiona's murder.'

'He left Paulette?'

He suddenly looked unsure of himself. 'That's what everyone thought. And there was a lad who worked in the kitchens with me who hung round with him a lot. According to rumour, they were close. Very close.'

'Merlin was bisexual?'

Stephen shrugged. 'I'd say he got it where he could.'

'What was the lad's name?'

'John. And before you ask, I can't remember his surname.'

'What about Paulette?

'She stayed on until the end of the season then she left. That's what people did. It wasn't the kind of job you stayed in for long. You'd just do a season – maybe two. I'd had enough after one.'

'So as far as you know, Paulette and Merlin went their separate ways?'

'As far as I know.'

'Was she upset when Merlin left?'

'I don't know. I didn't have much to do with her.'

'And Karen definitely left at the same time as Merlin?'

'I think so but I can't be sure.'

'What about John?'

'I remember he left around then too 'cause he left us short-staffed in the kitchens. But there was a high turnover of staff in those days. People left all the time.'

'What can you tell us about Karen?' Wesley asked.

'She was about my age. Tallish, dark-haired, pretty. No idea what she saw in Merlin but she seemed to fall for him in a big way. Mind you, I suppose he had a certain brand of spurious glamour, strutting about on that stage every night.' He hesitated. 'I didn't think much about it at the time yet I'm sure the thefts stopped when Merlin left. Nobody said much though, because the management wanted to hush it up for the sake of the camp's reputation.'

'Is it possible that Fiona found out that Merlin was behind the thefts? Could that be why she was killed?'

'It wouldn't surprise me. Look, I know nothing about Merlin Mitchell's life after he left the holiday camp and I don't know what became of Paulette or Karen.'

'Or John?'

'No.'

'Paulette was murdered a few days after Mitchell's body was discovered. We have evidence to suggest that she killed him.'

Newton sat for a few moments, taking it in. 'Well, she was obsessed with him. If she'd harboured resentment all these years ... They say hell hath no fury like a woman scorned, don't they.' He turned to Wesley. 'I'm sorry, but I've told you everything I know.'

'Where were you last Wednesday night?'

'Here with about a hundred witnesses.'

'And Saturday night?'

'Ditto. It's our busiest night.'

Wesley consoled himself with the fact that their journey hadn't been entirely wasted. They now knew that there had been another woman in Merlin Mitchell's life, one who might have been Paulette Reeves' rival. And then there was the young man, John. Wesley wondered where he fitted in.

He caught Rachel's eye. It was time to go. 'Before we leave, Mr Newton, can you remember this Karen's surname?'

Newton pursed his lips, deep in thought. 'I can't be sure but I think it began with C.'

'Could it have been Corcoran?' Wesley asked.

'It's possible.'

They drove back through the rush hour traffic, delayed on the A38. As they turned on to the Neston road, Rachel asked Wesley what he thought.

'We need to find Karen.'

'If she is related to Corcoran this makes him more of a suspect.'

Wesley was too preoccupied to answer.

The light was fading by the time they were approaching Tradmouth and as Wesley steered the car down the winding road he caught sight of a swooping owl in the headlights: another killer in search of prey.

12

6th March 1914

Lady Berridge is not as I expected. She is fat with unruly hair, a vague manner and the face of a benevolent pig. She wears loose gowns without corsets and takes a great interest in art and literature.

I find myself liking her in spite of myself for she addresses me kindly and calls me Martha. I think my mother would not approve of a lady being so free and easy, entertaining artists and writers who resemble tramps and lounge at her feet like dogs – although they lap wine rather than water, as does she. She is never without a glass in her hand.

I find her daughter somewhat strange. There was a boy in Sandrock who was said to be simple and Jane Berridge wears the same vacant expression on her face. She is a little plump and wears loose gowns like her mama. She is pretty enough with fair curls and a turned-up nose but there is an emptiness behind those large blue eyes and her conversation is limited to trivialities. I have seen her mother watch her with a blend of love and despair and, despite her undoubted expectations,

phone call from uniform. Simon Corcoran had returned home from Bristol and he was being brought in as requested.

Gerry looked positively triumphant. 'Can't wait to hear what he's got to say for himself.'

'Before I went home last night I asked Trish to see what she could find out about him. Morbay told her there'd been several complaints about him but no charges have ever been brought. One woman claimed that he wanted her out of her flat because he was going to renovate the building and push the rents sky high. She reported that he sent a couple of heavies round to threaten her – he denied it all, of course but that wasn't the only case.'

'He wanted to renovate Paulette Reeves' cottage. Perhaps he made a habit of harassing tenants, threatening violence if they didn't do as they were told.'

Wesley thought for a few moments. 'You're right. Maybe her death isn't related to Merlin Mitchell's.'

'Is that what we're calling him or is it still Alan Buchanan?'

'I doubt if either belongs to him so I guess one is as good as another. I'm still hoping that his real identity is hidden away somewhere in some long-forgotten police file. It's hard to believe that he only began his criminal career while he was working at that holiday camp.'

Gerry stood up. 'Jayden Ross is up before the magistrates later. Are we going to have another word with him while he's still enjoying our hospitality?'

Wesley shook his head. 'I think he's told us everything he knows.'

'You don't think he panicked and knocked Paulette over the head?'

Before Wesley could reply, Rachel came in with a note-book in her hand. 'I think I've found out why Paulette

189

Reeves concealed her mother's death. Paulette was still drawing the old woman's pension and various other benefits. We don't know exactly when she died but ... Isolated place. No neighbours to stick their noses in and ask where Dorothy was.'

Gerry nodded slowly. 'So the old lady dies of natural causes, she sees the freezer standing there practically empty and gives in to temptation. You might be right, Rach.'

'It would explain a lot,' said Wesley. When Rachel had left he shut the door. 'Nick came in. I sent him home.'

'Good.'

'I told him to let us know if he speaks to his mum in Australia.'

'You think she might have something to tell us?'

Wesley didn't know the answer to that one.

The phone on Gerry's desk began to ring. After a brief conversation Gerry said with relish, 'Corcoran's arrived. Let's go and have a word.'

Corcoran was waiting for them in the interview room. He had brought his solicitor with him, which Wesley thought was the sign of a guilty conscience.

As they sat down they introduced themselves for the benefit of the tape.

'Have a good trip to Bristol, Mr Corcoran?' Gerry asked. Wesley knew he was at his most dangerous when he was being charming.

Corcoran glanced at his solicitor, a young woman with a long face and swept-back hair. She looked the horsey type, not the sort of woman Wesley imagined Corcoran would go for. 'Not bad.' There was a wariness in his voice.

'First of all I have to ask you where you were on Saturday night,' said Wesley.

'At home. Watching telly.'

'Anyone with you?'

'No.'

'What were you watching?' Wesley sounded genuinely interested.

'It was a film. James Bond.'

There was a time long ago, lost in the mists of time before the invention of video recorders, computer technology and a host of cable channels, when watching TV could be a provable alibi. The suspect had only to outline the plot of an episode broadcast the previous night and there was a strong likelihood that he'd watched it live. But this sort of alibi hadn't applied for many years now that people could watch anything at any time. Corcoran had to do much better than that.

'Did you go to Woodside Cottage that night?'

'No.'

'Our Traffic Division has cameras with number plate recognition. Maybe I should ask them if your car was in the Woodside Cottage area at the relevant time.'

Corcoran began to fidget. 'I might have gone out.'

'Where?'

Corcoran gave his solicitor a pleading look and she told him he didn't have to answer any questions he didn't want to. Wesley wished she hadn't; Corcoran wasn't the type to need any persuasion not to cooperate. He was rather surprised when the man answered.

'I went to the Wheatsheaf in Lower Whitely. I was meeting someone there.'

'Was this before or after your appointment with Mr Bond?' Gerry asked.

'After. I had some business to do.'

'Who with?' said Wesley. 'We'll need a name.'

'I'd rather not say. But you can ask anyone in the pub. There were lots of people there.'

'It would be better if you told us who you met.'

Corcoran considered the matter for a moment. 'OK, his name's Jimmy Wheasden. He's a business associate.'

Gerry snorted. 'Jimmy Wheasden. The only business I'd associate him with is dodgy business. GBH and threatening behaviour if I remember right.'

'That was when he was younger. He's a businessman now.'

'The follies of youth, eh,' Gerry said with an indulgent smile. 'Lower Whitely's not far from Woodside Cottage, is it.'

'About a mile.' Corcoran sounded wary.

Gerry's smile disappeared. 'Did you pop in there on the way to check on your investment? Or afterwards when you'd had a few?'

'I was drinking shandy,' Corcoran said self-righteously. 'I've been done once. I don't drive over the limit any more.'

'At least that's one sin we can cross off the list, then,' said Wesley. 'Unlike the minor matter of harassing tenants. And before you say anything, we have complaints on record and people who would testify if necessary.'

Wesley's words had irked Corcoran. He prodded a finger in the direction of his face. 'Nothing was ever proved. Some tenants try it on. They don't pay their rent, I ask them nicely to move out and they get their revenge. It's an occupational hazard.'

'My heart bleeds,' said Gerry. 'So you have to send a couple of nice gentlemen with large muscles and small morals round to teach them a lesson in manners, eh?'

'No comment.'

Wesley cleared his throat. 'You intended to renovate Woodside Cottage so that you could let it out to holiday-makers for an extortionate rent next season, so you needed Paulette and her mother out. We've spoken to Laura Pullin about it. You and Laura aren't together any more, I believe.'

'That's none of your business.'

'Nothing like a woman scorned to betray your innermost secrets,' said Gerry. 'Was Wheasden going to give you a hand? Maybe he did. Maybe you and him went to Woodside Cottage together after the pub and dealt with your little problem with a blunt instrument.'

'No way.'

Gerry sat back, looking smug. He was on the verge of making Corcoran lose his temper.

Wesley took over. 'So why did you meet Wheasden at the Wheatsheaf?'

'We can be discreet,' said Gerry. 'We've had years of practice, haven't we, Inspector Peterson.'

Wesley nodded obligingly, his eyes on Corcoran's face. He was the best suspect they had for Paulette Reeves' murder and he saw the scenario in his mind's eye: Corcoran coming straight from the pub in order to intimidate a woman who was getting in the way of his money-making scheme. The argument, the weapon brought to frighten the victim. The impulse. The woman lying dead or dying at his feet. The tree conveniently blown down in the storm, the perfect scapegoat. It fitted. But could they prove it?

'Was it about Woodside Cottage?' Wesley asked.

'It was just business, that's all.'

'More planning to throw old ladies out into the snow?' said Gerry.

'It isn't snowing.' The reply was swift and said with an impudent smile. Corcoran thought he'd got the better of them. 'You can't prove anything against me.' He glanced at his solicitor. 'I've done nothing illegal. Can I go now?'

Wesley saw Gerry hesitate. They'd both have liked to see Corcoran marched down to the cells to contemplate the error of his ways but they had no solid reason to hold him and his solicitor was studying her watch. However, they knew where to find him if necessary.

'Think he killed her?' Gerry said softly as they walked off down the corridor back to the CID office.

'I think it's more than possible,' Wesley replied.

'We'll contact Traffic to see if they can place him near the scene.'

'Trouble is those narrow country lanes don't have fancy number plate recognition cameras, do they.'

'Don't be defeatist, Wes. If he did it, we'll get him. I'll send someone over to talk to Jimmy Wheasden. As far as I can remember, he's never been able to keep his mouth shut.'

Wesley wished he could share Gerry's confidence.

'When did the ice-house passage collapse?'

Margaret, the forensic anthropologist, sat back on her heels and stared at the little skeleton on the ground. The scene was lit by a pair of arc lights Neil had managed to borrow, the beams focusing on the set of bones which now lay free of rubble.

'According to records it happened during a storm in 1918, possibly the same one that sent the village of Sandrock plunging into the sea.'

'You're working up at Sandrock, aren't you, Neil?'

'I've got to go and do my bit once a day if you can call that working, but I'm mainly here at Paradise Court.' He waved his hand towards the bones. 'I estimated he was about four? Would you agree?'

Margaret looked up. She was a plump, motherly woman in her fifties with grey-peppered hair. She was also the best forensic anthropologist Neil had ever worked with. 'I'm sure you know as much about the aging of children's skeletons as I do, Neil. From the eruption of the teeth, I'd say you've got it spot on.'

'What about cause of death? I thought he might have been playing in here and got trapped when the entrance collapsed.'

Margaret put out a gloved hand and touched the little skull tenderly, like a mother caressing a sleeping child. Then she shook her head. 'I don't think so. Someone laid him out here on his back with his arms crossed over his chest. If he'd been trapped in here I would have expected him to be curled up in the foetal position, as if he'd gone to sleep. I could be wrong, of course, but . . . '

'You think someone put him here?' There was shock in Neil's voice.

'I think he – or she – was killed then placed in here.'

'You say killed. Could it have been an accident – or natural causes?'

Margaret took her hand away from the skull. 'The bones are very small but this slight staining on the facial bones suggests asphyxiation. I could be wrong but . . . '

'You think this is a murder victim?'

Margaret struggled to her feet and peeled off her gloves. 'You say the entrance has been sealed since 1918. Any chance anyone could have got in since then?'

Neil shook his head.

'In that case there's no reason for a police investigation. It'll just be a case of giving the poor little thing a decent burial.'

'And finding out who he or she was.'

Margaret smiled. 'That as well.'

It was almost five o'clock when the toxicology report arrived on Wesley's desk.

Merlin Mitchell, alias Alan Buchanan, had been drugged with a common kind of sleeping pill. It had been a large dose which matched the residue found in the whisky glass in his hotel room and would have made him drowsy at first, then he would have lost consciousness.

Wesley raised his voice so that he could be heard over the buzz of conversation in the office. 'Has anyone got a list of medicines found at Paulette Reeves' cottage?'

Rachel began rifling through the papers on her desk. Eventually she pulled out a single sheet and brought it over to Wesley, perching herself on the edge of her desk, her skirt riding up to show a glimpse of thigh.

After studying the paper for a while he looked up. 'Merlin Mitchell was drugged with benzodiazepine. Paulette Reeves had some that had been prescribed to her in her medicine cupboard. He consumed far more than the proper dose and with the alcohol . . . '

'More evidence that Reeves did it, then,' said Rachel with some satisfaction.

'It's a common type prescribed for sleep disorders and anxiety.' Wesley thought he'd better point out that the evidence wasn't exactly conclusive.

'But with the CCTV and fingerprint evidence . . . ' Rachel sounded a little irritated.

'OK. I acknowledge that she probably did it. But why?'

'Revenge? He went off with another woman after she'd lied to give him an alibi for Fiona Carp's murder.'

'That was way back in 1979. Why wait until now?'

'I don't know. Maybe it was the first opportunity she had.'

'She'd obviously met him in Spain so she could have done it then. And why was she killed?'

'She found Jayden Ross breaking in and he killed her in panic. He claimed he didn't break in till the Sunday morning – twelve hours or so after she died – but we've only got his word for that.'

'You think it's as obvious as that?'

Rachel focused her eyes on his with a coquettish smile. 'Yes, don't you?'

'What about Simon Corcoran?'

'He's a possible too. Does Nick know that his aunty's probably a murderer yet?'

Wesley shook his head.

'Well, he can't be left in the dark for ever.'

Wesley took the list over to Gerry's office, aware that Rachel was watching him. As he entered he found the DCI flicking through one of the files that had been abandoned on his filing cabinet since the Morbay Palace Hotel business began. Gerry looked up but didn't smile.

'I had a call a few minutes ago,' Gerry began. 'We've got an address for Fiona Carp's parents. They're still living in Clevedon, just south of Bristol. I think we should pay them a visit tomorrow, if only out of courtesy. I'll ask Rach to warn them we're coming. They need to be told about the new developments in the case.'

Wesley agreed. Fiona's parents had a right to know what

was going on. Knowing wouldn't bring Fiona back, but it might help a little.

'Anything new to report?' Gerry asked.

When Wesley told him about the toxicology report and the pills found at Paulette's cottage, he looked satisfied, like a man who'd just enjoyed a good meal. 'That clinches it, don't you think, Wes?'

'Do you think a jury would convict her on the evidence we've got? It's all circumstantial.'

'We've got convictions on less,' said Gerry.

'And Paulette's murder?'

Gerry hesitated. 'I don't think Jayden Ross is our man.'

'You favour Corcoran?'

'Don't you?'

Wesley didn't answer.

Gerry looked at his watch. 'I'm getting off home and I suggest you do the same. We'll make a prompt start in the morning.'

It seemed a little early to be abandoning his post but he saw the wisdom of Gerry's suggestion. Everything was under control, routine matters were being dealt with and they couldn't really make any progress until the morning so it was a good opportunity to make amends to Pam and to see the children, however briefly.

He slipped out of the office, hoping nobody had noticed, and walked home up the steep streets to the top of the town, his feet sliding on the damp, fallen leaves. It had stopped raining but the wind was still strong so he pulled up the zip on his coat to shield his neck from the cutting air. His route took him past the Savernakes' gate and he couldn't resist peering through. The drawing-room lights were on so he could see the room quite clearly; inside, Jennifer

Savernake was standing with her back to the window talking on the telephone, twisting a strand of hair in her fingers. He hurried on. If she turned he didn't want her to see him watching.

When he arrived home Amelia rushed to greet him and Pam emerged from the kitchen.

'I wasn't expecting you back so early.'

'There wasn't much more I could do so I decided to leave them to it.' He kissed her cheek. 'And come home to see my lovely wife.'

Pam rolled her eyes. 'My mother warned me about flattery. I've got loads of marking to do so can you help Michael with his homework and see to the dinner? Then Amelia needs to go through her spellings for tomorrow.'

She vanished into the living room and he was left with Amelia looking up at him like a faithful puppy. He smiled at her and ruffled her hair which she promptly smoothed again in mock disgust.

'How about those spellings?' he said. 'And what do you fancy for supper?'

'Spaghetti,' she said. 'And will you take me to the haunted village?'

'What haunted village?'

'Where Uncle Neil's working. It's going to be on telly.'

Wesley smiled. 'It's a ruined village. As far as I know there aren't any ghosts.'

'Michael said there were.'

'Michael's teasing you.'

'Will you take me?'

'If I've got time.'

'You never have time.'

The words hit him like a hammer. He was a neglectful

father, something he'd never intended to be. But when the case was over he'd make it up to her; it was the least he could do.

'Jennifer'll take me if I ask her. She's going to take me to the aquarium as well.'

Before he could answer Pam emerged from the living room.

'You are still OK for Brad and Jennifer's party on Saturday?'

'Hopefully.'

'Jennifer's got some amazing toys at her house,' Amelia chipped in. 'And there's a lovely room she says is for a special little girl. She says I can sleep there next Saturday night.'

'That's nice,' said Wesley, slightly uneasy, recalling that Jennifer Savernake had lost a daughter in tragic circumstances. Perhaps she was becoming too attached to Amelia.

Pam spoke again. 'Jennifer's invited Mark and Maritia on Saturday.'

His heart lifted at the prospect of seeing his sister. 'Great. How does she know them?'

'Bradley's commissioned a memorial plaque in Mark's church in memory of their daughter who died. The Savernake family lived in the parish for a couple of centuries and Belsham church is full of their memorials.'

Wesley had been dreading having to make small talk with people he barely knew, but if Maritia and her husband were going to be there it would sugar the pill. Besides, because of work commitments, he hadn't seen them for a while.

He made for the kitchen with Amelia in tow and took a

couple of pans from the cupboard, eyeing the phone and willing it not to ring.

He wanted a peaceful night in with no interruptions.

Nights off from the hectic world of catering were rare and precious to Stephen Newton. He'd thought more than once of trying to get a job in Tradmouth to be nearer Eddie. They'd met when Eddie had been working in an Exeter bar but a few months ago he'd become bar manager at the Marina Hotel, an offer Eddie couldn't refuse, even though it meant that the pair were now an hour's drive apart.

The demands of work meant they often had to meet up in the daylight hours but today Stephen had a rare couple of days off, a break he'd been owed since before the summer.

As he drove into Tradmouth he felt a thrill of anticipation. He hadn't told Eddie about the time he'd been suspected of murdering a child and his fragile world had collapsed. His ordeal back then felt like an unexploded bomb in a cellar, always there, ticking away, ready to explode when he least expected. Talking to Eddie might just defuse that bomb and make his life safe again.

He drove to the car park next to the choppy waters of the river Trad, and as he was getting out of the car he could see the Marina Hotel, lit up like a warm beacon on a cold, windy night. Eddy was in there and they would soon be together. The thought gave him a warm glow inside.

As Stephen neared the hotel he saw a figure standing in the entrance, and when the face came into focus he realised that it was one he knew, changed with the years but still recognisable. He had always had a good memory for faces and even after all this time he was sure he was right.

He hesitated, wondering whether to approach the stranger and say hello; debating whether he should mention the visit he'd had from the police. But as the figure walked away from the hotel entrance Stephen looked at his watch and realised he was due to meet Eddie in five minutes, so he hadn't time to satisfy his curiosity. In any event perhaps it was best to do nothing. The past was the past and it was something he knew he should put behind him.

He thrust his hands into his pockets against the cold and walked towards the hotel.

13

10th March 1914

I spot Jane in the walled garden at the side of the house. She paces up and down as though she is waiting anxiously for some momentous event. I watch her from the window of her mother's bedroom. If Jane has a secret assignation she is foolish to keep it where she can be observed. But Jane is a fool, naïve beyond belief. She still plays with the dolls of her childhood with their waxen faces and their rosebud lips pursed in perpetual disapproval. She also spends hours crouched by the great doll's house in her room, locked in her private world where the dolls are her companions and she is the mistress of their destiny.

But now she paces between the well-tended rose beds and I see a second figure approaching. I recognise him as Stanley, the young under-gardener with the bold stare. I do not like him. He thinks himself handsome and so he is with his lithe body and his unruly black hair. But there is a self-satisfied sneer upon his thick lips and lust in his brown eyes. On one occasion he suggested we meet in secret. When I slapped his face he merely smiled.

I think this is not the first time he and Jane have met because when he beckons to her she follows him from the garden like a dog obeying its master.

Sleep didn't come easily to Wesley that night and as he lay awake he started to go over things in his head. His mind kept returning to 1979. As far as he could tell, the whole affair began when Fiona Carp's killer returned to the scene of his crime.

Eventually he slept and woke at seven thirty to find Pam warning him that he'd be late.

He grabbed a slice of toast to eat on the way down to the station. It was a bright autumn day and the russet leaves drifted lazily off the trees as he walked, fluttering gold in the sunshine. When he reached the CID office he could hear Gerry's voice issuing the orders for the day. The boss had arrived before him.

He had a quick word with Rachel then, as he followed Gerry into his office, his eyes were drawn to Nick Tarnaby's empty desk.

'Nick's done as he was told, I see.'

Gerry lowered his voice. 'There was a message on my desk when I got in. There's been a complaint from his wife. Seems he got those bruises in a fight with her new feller.'

Wesley said nothing for a few moments. He'd never particularly taken to Tarnaby but now he found himself feeling a sudden wave of sympathy for him. His wife had abandoned him, his step-grandmother had been found dead in bizarre circumstances and his aunt, herself a murder suspect, had been brutally murdered. And now with this new revelation about his private life, he realised that the man must have been under considerable strain.

'Do you think his wife's boyfriend'll bring charges?'

Gerry slumped down in his chair, exasperated. 'No idea. But Nick's career might be tainted – even finished – if he does.'

'Rachel said he was asking about Corcoran. You don't think there's a risk he'll do something stupid?'

'If he does they won't throw the book at him, they'll chuck the whole bloody library. He'll be out of the force quicker than you can say Police and Criminal Evidence Act.'

There was a long silence while Gerry rearranged some of the files on his desk – displacement activity, Wesley suspected. Then he looked up. 'Fiona Carp's family up in Clevedon are expecting a visit from us today.'

'Rachel's found an address for Karen Corden. She lives in Bristol so maybe we can visit her while we're up that way. Rachel's calling her so we'll soon know.'

'Good thinking, Wes,' was all Gerry had to say.

There was something about finding the bones of a young child that had always got to Neil Watson. After so many years in the archaeology game he felt he should have become hardened to such things, but he wasn't.

He hadn't slept well, drifting off into fitful oblivion then waking with a start and looking at the alarm clock, only to find that an hour had passed. And he had to drive to Paradise Court before going on to Sandrock to do his bit for the cameras.

At Paradise Court he avoided the ice house even though the bones had now been removed and the reconstruction work had begun. He concentrated instead on the walled garden, examining the finds before doing a little digging in a trench which had produced the foundations of a Tudor brick wall and some fragments of window glass, part of the high-status building which might once have housed Lucy's ancestors. The thought of Lucy made him realise that he was at risk of becoming distracted by Paradise Court's rich archaeology. If he didn't make a move, he'd be late and the director would throw one of his hissy fits. Besides, the TV company was paying him handsomely and, should one of their staff come knocking on his door again, he didn't want to be dismissed as being unprofessional. He told his colleagues he'd be back later and set off for Sandrock.

When he arrived Lucy was in deep conversation with the TV crew. He watched her for a while and saw that she was laughing; evidently her shock at her great-grandmother's death hadn't lasted long.

The director saw him and when he raised a hand in greeting Neil strolled over to join them.

'Because Lucy wasn't here on Tuesday we're going to film two days' worth of interviews today,' he announced. 'That OK by you?'

'Sure,' said Neil. Lucy looked happier today but he told himself it might not be wise to mention the violent end of the child in the ice house. On the other hand, it had been her family's home and he was curious to discover anything he could about the people who'd lived there in 1918. Besides, it would give him an excuse to take her to lunch.

It was Lucy who broached the subject first as they were walking towards the excavation. 'Any news on that skeleton?'

'Only that the child was definitely aged about four. As I told you, the ice house was disused and the entrance was blocked during that storm in 1918 so the bones must date from that time, or possibly before.'

'I've been thinking about what Clara said before she died. It was something that sounded like "ice". Could she have meant the ice house?'

'How old would Clara have been in 1918?'

'About four, I suppose.' Her eyes widened in alarm. 'Do you think she might have known this kid? They might have been playing together and she saw him get trapped and was too frightened to tell anyone.'

Neil could have told her what Margaret said about the likely cause of death but he decided against it for the moment. All he could think of was that there had been a possible eyewitness and now she was dead. If Lucy was right, she might have suppressed the traumatic memory for ninety-seven years.

'Who was living at Paradise Court at that time?'

'It might have been Clara's grandmother, Lady Berridge, but my mother might know more. I'll ask her.'

'If I get a chance I'll have a look through some old local newspapers to see if any children went missing around that time.'

'Good idea.' She straightened her back. 'Are you ready to do this interview?'

'As soon as I've spoken to the team and had a look at what they've found.'

She looked relaxed and eager to get down to work as they arrived at the excavation. But then she didn't know that her great-grandmother might have witnessed a murder.

When Rachel called Karen Corden, now Karen Beecham, she'd admitted that she'd known Merlin Mitchell and said that she'd be available that afternoon any time after three thirty if they wanted to speak to her.

There was a spark of excitement in Gerry's eyes when Wesley broke the news. But before they drove north, Wesley wanted to visit Jack Unsworth on the way. There was nothing in the files to suggest that Karen Corden had been of interest during the investigation into Fiona's Carp's murder but there was a chance that he might remember her.

Then there was the John Stephen Newton had mentioned. Jack Unsworth had been there, in charge of the investigation. Wesley was sure he'd have more to tell them. He suggested they arrange to meet Jack for an early lunch in the Lamb and Flag. Gerry shared Wesley's enthusiasm for the idea and made the call to Jack. Retired cops are usually eager to get back into harness, Gerry observed, and there was nothing like a challenge to relieve the long days of gardening and wife-pleasing.

As Gerry predicted, Jack was delighted to see them as they walked into the lounge bar and once they were settled with their food in front of them Wesley took the list from his pocket.

'We've spoken to Stephen Newton.'

Jack looked surprised. 'How is he?'

'He's a chef in Exeter. Doing well as far as I can see.'

Jack stared down into his beer. 'I think I was a bit hard on the lad at the time.'

'You had no choice, Jack. He was the chief suspect in a child murder,' said Gerry.

'But he didn't do it, did he?'

'We know that now but ... '

'He was the sensitive type. He didn't take the questioning well. Maybe I should have been more—'

'He's fine.' He didn't mention the years Stephen Newton had spent expecting to be hauled in again for questioning for something he hadn't done; his inability to trust anyone or form relationships for years afterwards. Jack had simply been doing his job and it wasn't worth making him feel bad about it now.

'He told us that as well as having a relationship with Paulette Jenkins, Mitchell was friendly with a younger woman called Karen Corden.'

Jack put down his knife and fork and shifted forward in his seat, his eyes aglow, savouring this morsel of gossip. 'He kept that bloody quiet. *Ménage à trois*, eh?'

'Can you see Paulette going along with that? Or is it more likely she didn't know?'

'Probably didn't know,' he said. 'But it was clear to me that Mitchell was one for the ladies.'

'And the gentlemen?' Wesley inquired.

'What makes you ask?'

'Stephen Newton said Mitchell wasn't fussy.'

'Well, Newton's homosexual himself so he would say that.'

Wesley could hear the disapproval in Jack's voice and wondered if this was the reason the man had come down so hard on the young chef.

'So you don't reckon it was true?' said Gerry.

'All I can say is that it never came to my attention.'

'Do you remember Karen Corden?' Wesley asked.

'Can't say I do.'

'Do you remember Mitchell being friendly with a lad called John who worked in the kitchens with Newton?'

'Can't say it rings a bell.'

Wesley tried to hide his disappointment as Gerry changed the subject and the rest of the meal was spent in pleasant small talk until they set out for Clevedon at one o'clock. Before they left the Lamb and Flag they told Jack they intended to visit Fiona Carp's parents on the way to Bristol and he wished them luck. It was something Wesley wasn't looking forward to.

'Jack's one of the old school,' Gerry said as they reached the M5.

'I gathered that.'

'But he's a good bloke really.'

'Giving Newton a hard time because he's gay?'

'The kid made a nuisance of herself and followed Newton round and on top of that he didn't have an alibi. Would you have done things differently?'

'I'd have considered other suspects. I might even have paid more attention to Merlin Mitchell.'

'Paulette gave him what seemed like a cast-iron alibi. Hindsight's a wonderful thing, Wes. You've got to think how it looked at the time.'

Wesley fell silent, trying to tell himself that perhaps he was being oversensitive.

The motorway was clear for once and the weather had improved by the time they arrived in Clevedon. Along the road that ran by the promenade of the genteel little resort, Wesley could see the murky brown waters of the Bristol Channel churning to his left. He drove on past the town's long Victorian pier before turning down a side road.

After a few more turns they reached the Carps' new address, a retiree's dream of a small bungalow near the sea. At the time of Fiona's murder the Carps had been living in Swindon, but Wesley wasn't surprised that they'd moved. The memories in their original family home must have been painful to live with.

Fiona Carp's father was a gaunt man in his seventies

with sparse white hair combed over a brown-speckled scalp and a grey complexion that suggested he was suffering from some underlying illness. When Gerry asked if they could come in the man led the way to a small living room furnished with an overlarge dark brown three-piece suite which gave the room a cramped, oppressive feel. There was a plain red carpet, office-style vertical blinds and few ornaments apart from a table in the corner bearing a vase of artificial flowers and half a dozen framed photographs of Fiona from babyhood to the time of her death. It had the look of a shrine.

'Is your wife in?' Gerry asked gently.

The man lowered himself painfully into an armchair by the window. 'My wife passed away ten years ago.'

'We're so sorry,' said Wesley. 'We weren't told.'

'Why should you be? The police where we lived dealt with it.'

'What was it?' Gerry's question was tentative, as though he was afraid of causing more upset.

'June killed herself. Fiona was our only child. They say time heals but it doesn't. It just got worse over the years. Every Christmas, every birthday reminded her and in the end she took some pills to stop the pain. The bastard who killed our Fiona killed June as well.' He said the words in a matter-of-fact way, without bitterness. He looked Gerry in the eye. 'Have you found him? Have you found who killed my girl?'

'We've reviewed the case and identified an individual through DNA found on Fiona's clothes and under her fingernails,' said Gerry.

'They said at the time they'd found traces of skin under her nails. They said she'd probably put up a fight,' he said almost proudly. 'You're sure he's the right one this time? You arrested a young lad but you let him go. Was it him after all?'

'No, it wasn't him,' said Wesley. 'It was someone who had an alibi at the time so he didn't come under suspicion.'

'Who was he?'

'He was known as Merlin Mitchell. He was an entertainer.'

Carp's eyes lit up with recognition. 'We used to go and watch his shows – he used to do all these magic tricks for the kiddies, we thought he was great. Are you sure it was him?'

'Yes.'

'But why would he kill our Fiona?' He sank back in his chair, shaking his head with disbelief. 'It doesn't make sense.'

Wesley recalled what Stephen Newton had said about Fiona. She was a curious kid, a bit of a nuisance.

'There were thefts from chalets. We think she might have seen something,' said Wesley.

'And this Merlin was the thief?'

'We think so.'

To his surprise a sad smile appeared on Carp's lips. 'That'd be just like our Fiona. She used to watch people – fancied herself as some sort of detective. It was just a phase though – she would have moved on to something else in a month or two. She was a cheeky little thing, always into everything.'

'I believe she had a crush on the young chef who was questioned.'

'He was a good-looking lad and she used to follow him round. It was like kids who have crushes on pop stars only with her it was that Steve. He told her to get lost but it didn't put her off. In a way I'm glad he didn't do it. He was only a kid himself.' He shook his head. 'Merlin Mitchell. I can't believe it.'

'Do you remember a woman called Paulette Reeves who worked as a chalet maid? She was friendly with Mitchell?'

'Can't say I do.'

'You told the police that Fiona was behaving as though she had a secret.'

'Everything was an adventure to our Fiona.' Without warning his face crumpled into a mask of grief and tears began to stream down his pale cheeks. Gerry went over to him, perching on the arm of his chair to place a comforting hand on his shoulder.

Wesley watched as Carp took a grubby handkerchief from his trouser pocket and blew his nose, apologising for making a show of himself.

'Nothing to apologise for, mate,' Gerry said, giving the man's shoulder a squeeze.

'Sometimes it hits me, you know how it is.'

Gerry nodded. He'd lost his wife, Kathy, so he knew.

'We'll leave you to it,' said Gerry, straightening himself up. 'Sorry to have bothered you. I know it can't be easy. Oh, by the way, sorry to ask this but it's just routine. We're asking everyone. Where were you last Wednesday?'

'Morbay. I'm a model railway enthusiast and there was a collectors' fair on at the Pavilion.'

'Did you stay overnight?'

Carp gave the address of a bed and breakfast establishment not far from the Morbay Palace Hotel.

Gerry didn't say a word as they returned to the car but Wesley knew what he was thinking. Carp had been in

Morbay at the time of Mitchell's murder with nobody to vouch for him. If by some means he'd found out who'd killed his daughter, he had to be a suspect. Even though everything pointed to Paulette Reeves' guilt, they still had to consider other possibilities such as Mitchell and Paulette having been killed by the same person.

From Clevedon it didn't take long to reach Karen Corden's address in Bristol. It was in the desirable Clifton area, a tall, pale stone Georgian house of pleasing proportions and a house Wesley could covet if he'd been the covetous type.

'I smell money,' said Gerry as they walked up the flight of steps leading to the front door.

Wesley rang the doorbell and waited, looking at his watch. It was four o'clock and she had said she'd be back by three thirty, but there was no answer.

'Oh I'm sorry, I was delayed at work.' The woman who'd come up behind them on the steps, brandishing her door key, was tall with unnaturally black hair and a long ethnic skirt. Only the lines on her face and the slight sagging of her chin belied her youthful manner. Stephen Newton had described her as a looker and she must have been stunning in her youth. 'Are you the policemen from Devon?'

'That's right.' Wesley made the introductions and she shook their hands before leading them inside into a drawing room painted in an exquisite shade of Georgian blue and inviting them to sit. There was a lot of art on the walls, mostly abstract. Karen saw Wesley looking round.

'They're mine. I teach art at the university. Part-time.'

Wesley knew he should have said something complimentary about the paintings but his natural honesty made it difficult so he was relieved when she started talking again.

214

'I must admit I was intrigued by that call from the police. Of course I was worried at first. I thought something had happened to one of the kids.'

She shuddered and Wesley felt a pang of sympathy. To many people an unexpected call from the police means news of a tragedy that will change their lives for ever.

'Were you told what we want to speak to you about?'

'They said it was something to do with a murder in Morbay. I haven't been to Morbay for years. Not since—'

'Not since you worked as a chalet maid at the holiday camp there,' said Gerry.

She looked at him as though he'd said something remarkably clever. 'That's right.'

'A man was found dead in the Morbay Palace Hotel last Thursday morning. He'd been murdered.'

'The officer asked me if I remembered Merlin Mitchell. Was it him?'

'He checked into the hotel under the name Alan Buchanan. He'd been living in Spain under that name for years.'

She looked genuinely puzzled. 'I don't understand what this has to do with me.'

'We're trying to find out everything we can about him and your name's come up in our inquiries.' Wesley felt bad about handing her the photograph of the dead man, arranged tastefully so as not to cause offence. 'Can you confirm that this is the man you knew as Merlin Mitchell.'

She stared at the picture for a while. 'Yes, I can see it's him,' she whispered after a period of stunned silence.

'You knew him when you were working at the Bay View Holiday Camp?'

'Yes.' She looked around as if she was afraid of being overheard.

'Was Merlin Mitchell his real name?'

'He didn't tell me otherwise.'

'Do you know anything about his background? Did he talk about any family? Or where he came from?'

'Never. He liked to be mysterious, if you know what I mean.'

'Do you remember a young chef called Stephen Newton?'

'Vaguely.'

'He told us you were friendly with Merlin Mitchell.'

She bowed her head for a few moments. 'He could charm the birds from the trees and I fell for it,' she said softly.

'A child called Fiona Carp was killed while you were working there. We now have evidence that Merlin Mitchell was responsible.'

'No ... no, that's wrong,' she said, her eyes wide with disbelief. 'He couldn't have done it. He was with someone at the time – another chalet maid.'

'Paulette Jenkins?'

'Yes.'

'What can you tell us about her?'

'She was older than me but she always dressed a bit ... tarty, if you know what I mean. She used to follow him round, really had the hots for him. He was definitely with her at the time. He told me he was telling her he wasn't interested but I'm not sure if that was true. I think I believed it at the time because I wanted to.'

'Did you know Merlin had been stealing from chalets?'

'No.' The word emerged like a yelp of pain. 'I don't know where you're getting all this from but it isn't true. OK, I had a fling with him and I know I wasn't the only one. He'd shag anything that moved but he wasn't a murderer.'

'Or a thief?'

'Not that I was aware of.' She sounded unsure of herself.

'But it doesn't surprise you that he was?'

'Lots of girls go through a phase when they fancy the bad boy. I was just going through that phase. I know better now and I'm not particularly proud of it but, honestly, I didn't know he was the thief. All I knew was that he was a laugh and he was ...' She searched for the appropriate word. 'Exciting.'

'You left Bay View around the same time as Merlin Mitchell. Did you go away with him?'

'No way. My sister was ill and my mum asked me to come home. I was seventeen at the time. Still a kid. Look, what makes you think he killed that child? Everyone always thought it was some pervert who'd got into the camp somehow.'

'Because of new developments in DNA technology, I'm afraid there's little doubt,' said Wesley. 'We're working on the theory that she stumbled on his thieving activities and he silenced her.'

Karen shook her head. 'I'm still finding it hard to believe. Have you any idea who killed him?'

'Our main suspect was found dead herself on Sunday. She was the chalet maid who gave him his alibi – Paulette Reeves, formerly Paulette Jenkins.'

She fell silent for a few moments, taking it in.

'I didn't like her. I think she was jealous of me. Merlin swore he didn't fancy her anymore and he wanted to finish it. I was naïve enough to believe it but, looking back, it was probably a load of bullshit. Do you think she killed him then committed suicide because she couldn't live with what she'd done?'

It was a reasonable assumption but Wesley had to tell her she was wrong. 'I'm afraid she was murdered too.' There was a long pause. 'Where were you last Wednesday evening?'

'Here with my husband and kids.'

'And Saturday night?'

'We had a party for my eldest's birthday. I've got about thirty witnesses.'

'OK, love,' said Gerry. 'But we would like to ask you what you can remember about the events of 1979.'

She bowed her head and sat for a while in silence. Then she raised her eyes to Wesley's. 'It was Merlin who made the first move. He was older than me. Around thirty and good-looking. All the boys I'd known before were really boring in comparison if that makes sense.'

Wesley nodded. Charisma was something you were born with, and sometimes in life it could be worth more than money.

'Other women were after him and somehow that made him more desirable. He chose to be with me when he could have anyone.'

'You say he wanted rid of Paulette Jenkins,' said Gerry.

'That's what he told me.'

'Were there other women too?'

Karen hesitated. 'I don't think it was just women. There was a boy who used to hang round with him. I didn't think much of it at the time but now ...'

Wesley and Gerry waited for her to continue.

'I was a bit innocent back then and I assumed they were just mates but with hindsight I think they may have been having some sort of relationship. They did seem very close.'

'What was the lad's name?'

218

'John. I can't remember his surname. He worked in the kitchens.'

Wesley saw Gerry's alert expression.

'What happened to him after Merlin left?'

'I'm not sure but I don't recall seeing him around.'

'So he might have left with Merlin?'

'It never occurred to me at the time but, now I come to think of it, he might have done.'

'You haven't any photographs of these people?'

She shook her head.

'What was this John like?' Wesley asked.

'Young; nice-looking; long dark hair. He wasn't the sort of person you'd remember really. I thought he just hung out with Merlin because he thought he was exciting – a bit like I did.' She thought for a moment. 'It was hard to know what John was thinking. He just sort of blended into the background but there was something about him. It was as if he was watching people.' She hesitated. 'I think he used to watch me.'

They got back to Tradmouth at five thirty and when they reached the police station Gerry went straight to his office, only to find a message saying that CS Fitton wanted to see him. However, Rob Carter had left a list of all the Johns, Jonathans and Jons employed at the holiday camp on his desk and he wanted to take a look before anything else came up to distract him.

Wesley followed him in and waited while Gerry hunched over the list, running his finger down the names.

'There are seven Johns, three Jonathans and two Jons. Why couldn't he be called Engelbert or Marmaduke?' Gerry muttered as if he was taking the surfeit of Johns as a personal affront. 'Rob's managed to trace and eliminate half of them but not the one we're after. We need to find this lad and speak to him.'

'Lad. He'll be in his fifties now.' As Wesley picked up the list, Gerry stood and sent the old files, balanced precariously on the corner of his desk, tumbling to the floor. They landed with a splat and the contents spilled out. Wesley bent to retrieve them, telling Gerry to get off to his meeting. He'd deal with it.

He began to place the papers back in their files, stopping every now and then to read: a missing child here, an elderly lady bludgeoned to death during a robbery there; a catalogue of human misery, all unsolved or unproved. Of course advances in science gave new hope, just as they had done in the Fiona Carp case.

He returned some files to the top of the cabinet and squatted down to pick up the rest. A couple lay open and, unexpectedly, a name at the head of a yellowing report caught his eye: Savernake. Curiosity made him flick through the papers and as he read he learned that in 1980 a Christopher Savernake had died at the age of twenty-one after sustaining head injuries in a lane near his home in Belsham.

Wesley wondered whether this Christopher was related to Bradley and Jennifer and whether it would be tactless to ask them.

'Sir.' He looked up and saw Trish Walton hovering at the door. 'There was a call from a Stephen Newton and he says can you ring him back.'

Wesley thanked her and after putting the Christopher Savernake file with the others, he rushed to his own desk and tried Newton's number. But all he heard was an automated voicemail message. Sometimes he hated technology.

As soon as he put the phone down it rang.

'Am I speaking to Chief Inspector Heffernan?' The voice was female, low-pitched and sensual with a slight London accent. He visualised her as young, attractive and sexy but he knew he could be wrong.

'DCI Heffernan's not here at the moment. This is Detective Inspector Peterson. Can I help you?'

There was a moment of hesitation, as if she was making up her mind. Then she spoke again. 'It's about the murder. The man at the hotel. I saw his name and picture in the newspaper and it said the police were appealing for anyone who knows him to come forward.' She hesitated. 'Well, I know him. He was staying with me. All his things are still at my flat.'

Wesley picked up a pen and scrabbled round his desk for a suitable scrap of paper. This could be the breakthrough they were waiting for.

14

15th March 1914

Lady Berridge confides in me. When we are alone in her room and I am brushing her hair, she twists round on her dressing stool and shares all manner of intimate details of her life and marriage.

Her husband, she tells me, was impotent after Jane's birth and, even though she longed for more children, it was not to be. She says I will understand all when I have children of my own. She does not know about Edith. I have said nothing and Alfred has kept the shameful secret to himself.

She confides her worries about Jane. She describes her as an innocent, too good for this world. I nod at this charitable opinion for I know mothers can only believe good of their offspring. I would be so myself with Edith who, according to my mother's letters, thrives in my absence.

I eat with my mistress now when she has no visitors. I think I am becoming indispensible to her, which is my intention. There are times when she treats me almost as a daughter. Almost but not quite.

I spend little time in the servants' hall. Being my lady's personal maid and confidante, the other servants consider me too lofty to share their meals and their banter and fall silent when I enter. How I am risen in the world.

Jane looks pale and is sick most days. Her mother thinks she is ill and intends to call the doctor.

The caller's name was Roxanne Smith and she'd known Alan, as she called him, for over a year. They'd met in Marbella where she'd been living but when she'd come to live in London six months ago, they'd lost touch. Then twelve days ago she'd arrived home from work to find him waiting outside the door of her Brixton flat, having charmed one of the neighbours into admitting him to the building. He'd ended up persuading her to let him stay but, after a couple of days, he'd announced out of the blue that he had business in Devon and would be back once everything was sorted out. He'd been vague about the nature of the business but he'd always been a difficult man to pin down.

When Roxanne asked what she should do with his things, Wesley asked her to keep them there because he wanted to look through them. He looked at his watch. It was Friday tomorrow, not the best day to travel to London, but it couldn't be helped. He needed to examine the dead man's possessions. Mitchell had obviously travelled light to Morbay but the contents of the luggage he'd brought to London might reveal more about what had brought him back to England.

When Gerry returned Wesley told him about Roxanne's call and that he planned to go to London to meet her. He was sure there was something they didn't yet know, something that would provide the key to the whole affair, and Roxanne might just be able to provide some answers. Trish interrupted before Gerry could reply.

'I've been going through Paulette Reeves' bank account and I've found something odd,' she said.

Wesley followed her to her desk, which was strewn with copies of bank statements. To Wesley they looked remarkably healthy considering their owner worked part-time as a cleaner, even taking into consideration the fact that she was illegally claiming her dead mother's pension.

'For the past six months there have been regular payments into her account. A thousand a month. Not a fortune but enough to make a difference to someone on her income.'

'Where do the payments come from?'

'They're made in cash via automatic paying-in machines in various branches. The first in Plymouth, then a few in Tradmouth, Morbay and Bloxham. Always within the first few days of the month.'

Wesley studied the statements. Trish was right. There was no clue to Paulette's benefactor's identity but one thing was certain: whoever it was had gone to great lengths to remain anonymous.

'Think it could be blackmail?'

'Paulette Reeves was a cleaner,' she said. 'She might have stumbled on something while she was working.'

'Have we got a list of places she cleaned?'

'Her niece, Laura, provided a list of addresses but she also did some work on an ad hoc basis, just through word of mouth, so it might not be complete.'

She delved beneath the bank statements and pulled out two sheets of paper: the first listed the names of the people Paulette had worked for most recently and the second a dozen or so addresses where she'd cleaned in the past. Both contained a few familiar names: neighbours; Pam's fellow teachers; even the Savernakes were there. Laura Pullin's agency was obviously doing well. However, one name on the second list stood out as though it had been printed in huge gold letters; a name that made his heart turn over.

A few months ago Paulette Reeves had cleaned for a Dr Maritia Fitzgerald of Belsham vicarage. She had worked for his own sister.

At lunchtime Neil and Lucy had eaten hurriedly before getting straight back to work. Neil found the whole process of filming irksome, especially when it interfered with the important business of archaeology.

It had taken courage to ask Lucy for a drink after she'd finished filming. He'd almost convinced himself that she wouldn't be in the mood following her recent bereavement and he was pleasantly surprised when she accepted the invitation, suggesting the Toncliffe Arms, the little thatched pub they passed every day, about a mile away among a hamlet of cottages on the road to Sandrock. It served food, she said. They could have dinner there.

They drove in convoy and parked on the small patch of waste ground that served as the pub's car park. Neil thought he could detect an air of suppressed excitement in Lucy's manner but he told himself he was imagining it. He never had that much luck with women.

Once they'd finished eating, Lucy went outside to fetch something from her car, leaving Neil alone. A local at the bar was staring at him and when their eyes met he gave him a nod and turned back to his conversation with the barman. Neil was used to being an object of curiosity in country pubs out of the tourist season but he was glad when Lucy returned carrying a battered briefcase.

'When my mother found out I was working at Sandrock she looked these out for me,' she said, taking a brown paper bag from the briefcase and passing it to Neil. 'They're pictures of Sandrock before it was destroyed: there are some interesting ones of the church.'

Neil took the sepia photographs out of the bag and flicked through them.

'You can borrow them if you like.'

As he thanked her, their hands almost touched and he resisted the temptation to take her hand in his, regretting his reticence a few seconds later. It had been a long time and he felt he'd almost forgotten how the subtle dance of courtship operates. 'Would you like another drink?'

'I'm driving. Better not.'

'A shandy? Orange juice?'

'I have to get back. Mum's been busy contacting everyone about Clara's funeral and ... ' She didn't move. 'I've asked her if she has any pictures of Clara when she was young to use in the service. The vicar said people sometimes project old photos of the person onto a screen.'

'That's a nice idea,' said Neil.

Lucy froze. 'But if Clara had bad memories ... ' She lowered her voice. 'I want to know what happened in her past to make her so terrified.' She took the briefcase and stood up. 'I have to go.'

As she bent over to kiss him on the cheek she stopped, still stooping towards him, and placed her hand gently behind his head. Their lips met, tentatively at first, then with more commitment.

'Stop that you two or I'll chuck a bucket of water over you,' said a loud Devon voice, followed by a gale of chuckles from the bar. Neil looked round and saw that the local and the barman were watching, craving entertainment.

When Lucy had gone he started to study the old photographs, eyes lowered, trying his best to be unobtrusive.

Wesley didn't see as much of his sister as he'd like. They both led busy lives. As well as returning to work part-time after giving birth to Dominic, Maritia's position as vicar's wife brought extra demands on her time: the Sunday School, parish meetings and keeping the peace among the flower arrangers – something that she joked qualified her for a senior position in the United Nations. Once the parish had got over the initial surprise that their vicar's new wife was black, something that made a few of the older residents treat her with polite caution, it hadn't taken her long to endear herself to Mark's congregation. Since childhood Maritia had always been unflappable, Wesley thought – sometimes irritatingly so.

He went alone to Belsham vicarage, a large Victorian edifice, sufficiently unattractive to have survived the church's tendency to sell off its more luscious treasures and place the incumbent clergyman or woman in an unappealing modern box. The vicarage was cold and draughty and had once been the scene of a murder but Mark and Maritia had no choice other than to make the best of it.

It was seven when Wesley rang his sister's doorbell and when Mark answered he greeted his brother-in-law, genuinely pleased to see him again. Mark, with his open features and shock of fair hair, had always reminded Wesley of an enthusiastic schoolboy; the captain of every sports team and top of the class. He had met Maritia when they were both studying at Oxford, her first serious boyfriend, and Wesley's parents, apart from a few initial qualms about both their children making mixed-race marriages, approved of her choice. However, it would be hard for anybody to object to Mark.

Wesley was invited in and offered tea. He suspected a lot of tea flowed in this house; gallons of it like a never-ending stream. As Mark handed him a steaming mug and hurried out saying he had to make some phone calls in his study, Maritia entered the room, carrying Dominic who was grizzling in her arms.

'Wasn't expecting to see you tonight,' she said as she sat down on the threadbare sofa, holding the baby against her shoulder. 'Everything OK? Pam all right?'

'Fine, thanks. Are you going to this do at the Savernakes' on Saturday?'

'I've just been arranging a babysitter. Pam says you've been invited too. I didn't realise you knew them.'

'Likewise.'

'I've only met Bradley a couple of times but Mark's had quite a bit to do with him. His parents used to own Belsham Manor – big Georgian place at the bottom of the road which is now the Belsham Manor Hotel. The church is full of Savernake family memorials.'

'So as well as owning the brewery they were lords of the manor?'

'Sounds positively feudal, doesn't it. I think the manor came before the brewery – that was just some Victorian ancestor's way of raking in extra cash.'

'What's Mark's connection with Bradley and Jennifer? Do they come to church here?'

'Not that I'm aware of. They had a daughter called Sally

who died a few years ago. She's buried in the churchyard and Bradley wants to erect a plaque in her memory in the church to go with the rest of the family memorials.'

'Nice of him.'

'I expect it's tax deductible.'

Wesley raised his eyebrows. 'You don't like him?'

'I'm the vicar's wife. I've got to like everyone,' she said lightly.

'But you think he has an ulterior motive?'

She held the baby in front of her, pulling a face that made him chuckle. For a few moments her attention seemed to be focused totally on her son. Then she turned to Wesley. 'No, Bradley's all right. I'm just being uncharitable. Take no notice.'

'He's run a successful business so he's probably no saint. He must have made a fortune from the takeover.'

'You've always had a suspicious mind, Wes. That's probably why you do what you do. In my position I'm supposed to think the best of everyone and sometimes it's not easy, believe me.'

'Actually I wanted to ask you a few questions in my professional capacity.'

The smile vanished from her lips and she arranged the baby on her knee, rubbing his little back. 'How do you mean?'

'You employed a cleaner called Paulette Reeves?'

'The agency sent someone called Paulette. I'd just had Dominic and I needed a bit of extra help around the place. She was only here a few days.'

'You've heard about the murder near Whitely?'

'There was something on the TV news but I wasn't taking much notice. That wasn't her?'

'Yes. Why didn't you let me know you'd employed her?' He sounded almost hurt.

'Because I didn't make the connection.'

'What can you tell me about her?'

Maritia's normally open expression became guarded, as though she wasn't comfortable with what she was about to say. 'I'm ashamed to say that I didn't like her. She seemed . . . ' She searched for the appropriate word. 'Sly. I'd just got Dominic off to sleep and when I came downstairs I found her searching through the drawers in the sideboard over there. She pushed the drawer shut and pretended she was dusting but I'd seen her.' Maritia grinned. 'Not that she'd find anything of interest here – only old bills, flat batteries and pens that have run out of ink.'

'You're sure about this?'

'Oh yes. To be honest I was relieved when they sent someone else the next day. We don't have anything scandalous to hide but it still leaves you with a nasty feeling if you find someone snooping through your things.'

Wesley wondered whether to mention that Paulette might have had a sideline in blackmail to supplement her income but he decided on discretion. He thanked his sister for the tea and stood up to leave.

'See you at the Savernakes' party,' she said.

It was then he remembered the other question he wanted to ask. 'Is there a memorial to a Christopher Savernake in the church? Someone who died in the early 1980s aged twenty-one?'

'A relative of Bradley's.'

'Could be.'

She put Dominic down carefully on the sofa, placing a cushion strategically to prevent him rolling off, and went over to the sideboard to fetch a bunch of keys which she gave to her brother. 'You can take a look if you like. I'd better give you the church alarm code too.' She scribbled some numbers on a sheet from a notepad and placed it in Wesley's hand. 'Bring the keys straight back, won't you.'

As he took them he experienced a pang of reluctance. He wanted to get home to his family instead of wandering around a cold, still church with a storm brewing outside. But he told himself it wouldn't take long to satisfy his curiosity.

Stephen Newton hadn't bothered calling Wesley Peterson back. It was now out of normal working hours and, besides, it was hardly urgent.

The previous evening when he'd seen that face from the past he hadn't had the opportunity to say anything. Perhaps that had been for the best; some people didn't want to be reminded of what they once were. He, of all people, understood that.

He hadn't mentioned it to Eddie when they'd met but now he felt a need to talk about those distant days to someone who'd been there; someone who'd known the people involved. It was one thing talking to the black DI with the sympathetic manner, but he hadn't known what it was like.

Eddie wasn't due to finish his shift that evening until half nine which meant he had some time to kill. Eddie had told him the Galleon Bar at the Tradmouth Castle Hotel was a good place for a quiet drink and that's exactly what Stephen felt he needed. He wanted to think things through.

Tradmouth wasn't a large town so he didn't know why

he should have been surprised to see his ghost from the past again when he walked into the bar. As Stephen watched the apparition standing with a laughing group in the corner, he became more and more sure that he was right and when the individual left the group and slipped out of the bar he decided to follow. If he was wrong, the worst that could happen was that he'd make a fool of himself.

His quarry was heading up the wide, thickly carpeted staircase, making for the toilets. Stephen took the stairs two at a time and it was only seconds before he caught up.

'Excuse me,' he said.

When the person turned to face him and looked into his eyes, he saw recognition there. He hadn't been mistaken.

'Long time no see,' he said, as he saw a shadow of horror pass across his new companion's face.

15

17th March 1914

Lady Berridge has sent her artistic young men away, claiming to be unwell. She weeps constantly and nothing I say comforts her.

The doctor has told her the worst possible news. Jane is pregnant and cannot or will not name the father of her child. I keep what I saw that day in the walled garden to myself. It does not suit my purpose to bring another into the matter.

My lady wrings her hands and says, 'What shall I do, Martha?' over and over again. I rest my hand on her silk-clad shoulder as she wonders who can have taken advantage of Jane's innocent nature. None of the young men of her acquaintance would be so wicked, she claims, and berates herself for her lack of vigilance.

When I make the suggestion that Jane's child, when it is born, can go to my own mother to be looked after in Sandrock, exaggerating the comfort of our situation there, she seizes upon the suggestion as the solution to all her woes. She will pay handsomely, of course and the child will want for nothing.

In her mind she sees the chubby infant playing upon the beach in endless sunshine. She knows nothing of the hardships of fisherfolk's lives. She does not know of the storms, the stench of rotting fish and the pain of the women with fingers chapped and bleeding from mending the nets. I smile and say nothing. Let her have her dreams.

The child is never to be spoken of. No one must know of its existence. Jane keeps to her room where she nurses her growing belly and weeps.

Wesley caught the London train from Neston around nine that Friday morning and spent the journey gazing out of the window, deep in thought, hardly aware of his fellow passengers. During the journey he tried Stephen Newton's number several times and when there was still no answer he started to feel uneasy. But he told himself that Newton had probably changed his mind about speaking to him. He might be worrying for nothing.

He was due to meet Roxanne Smith outside her place of work at twelve thirty and she'd promised to bring along Mitchell's suitcase. He'd told her he'd have picked it up if it was heavy but she'd insisted that she wanted it out of her flat. She didn't want to be reminded of him.

As the train sped on past nameless towns and flashing green countryside, he thought about what he'd seen in Belsham church the previous night.

After unlocking the door and dealing with the alarm in the porch, he'd opened the creaking oak inner door and stepped into the dark, silent medieval church. He'd stood in the doorway for a few seconds as his eyes adjusted to the darkness, listening to the wind outside. The sound of a branch tap-tapping on one of the north aisle windows had made him jump and he'd fumbled for the light switch, relieved when the lights had flickered on.

The place smelled vaguely of polish and lilies and it was typical of many Devon churches with its carved rood screen painted in subtle medieval shades. The serene faces of the saints lovingly portrayed in the bottom section by some pious fifteenth-century artist had been scratched out during the Reformation and the brutality of the destruction jarred with the beauty of what remained. As he'd wandered around the church, he'd felt as if a thousand eyes were watching him but those eyes hadn't been hostile. On the contrary, there was an atmosphere of deep peace wrought by the prayers and hopes of centuries.

Wesley had made a slow circuit of the building, studying every memorial and plaque fixed to the walls and floor. The Savernake family memorials were in the chancel, not far from the altar – the most honoured place. The first dated to the early years of the nineteenth century, the period when Jane Austen was penning her immortal stories of rural and small-town society. There they were, generation after generation: Archibald Savernake, Esquire; Colonel Ezekiel Savernake; Nathaniel Bradley Savernake, Esquire of Belsham Manor and his dear wife Susannah. Then there was a sad memorial to a Midshipman Thomas Bradley Savernake of the Royal Navy who had died serving his king and country in 1917 aged twenty. But it was the later Savernakes who'd interested Wesley most.

The memorial Wesley had been looking for was a small brass plaque half hidden behind a large Mothers' Union banner.

In loving memory of Christopher Savernake, beloved son of George and Mary Savernake of Belsham Manor, taken tragically aged twenty-one on 23rd August 1980.

It was the right one; the victim in Gerry's cold case. But the fact that Bradley Savernake had never mentioned it was hardly sinister. Losing a brother in distressing circumstances wasn't the sort of thing you'd mention to a mere acquaintance. He would have liked to return to the office and consult Gerry's file again but it was getting late so he'd gone home and helped Michael with his homework instead, his curiosity partially satisfied.

The journey to London passed swiftly and he arrived at Paddington Station at midday, leaving him just enough time to catch the Underground and walk the rest of the way to Roxanne's Bloomsbury office.

It was a couple of months since he'd visited London and then he'd travelled straight to his parents' house in Dulwich without venturing into the centre. As he strolled along the crowded pavements he found it hard to believe that he'd once felt at home in these streets when he'd served in the Met. Now he felt overwhelmed by the bustle and the tall buildings seemed to close in on him like the walls of a prison.

Roxanne worked at a recruitment agency on the ground floor of a Portland stone office block not far from Russell Square. Wesley arrived there slightly early and hung around outside, watching the passers-by – students, visitors seeking out the British Museum – all hurrying like worker ants. If he needed confirmation that moving to the West Country had been right, he had it now.

Realising that Roxanne would have no way of recognising him, he thought it best to call at her office and make himself known. It was an open-plan office and ten people, male and female, all young and smartly dressed, sat behind computer monitors set on identical pale wood desks. As he pushed open the glass door, they all looked up as one. Only one desk was unoccupied and he noticed an attractive young black woman at the far end of the room, putting on her coat.

When he announced that he was looking for Roxanne Smith, all heads turned towards the escapee.

She was tall and slim with long legs worthy of a model. Her straightened hair fell around her shoulders and even her business uniform of black skirt and jacket and white blouse didn't diminish her stunning beauty. Wesley couldn't help wondering why Merlin Mitchell had been staying at her flat. He'd been at least thirty years her senior and looked it, in spite of his best efforts with the wig.

She hurried over to him, a nervous smile on her glossy lips. 'Inspector Peterson?' she asked, lowering her voice so her colleagues wouldn't hear.

'That's right.'

'I've brought Alan's suitcase. It's in the stockroom.'

'I'll pick it up later if that's OK. I thought we might talk over lunch?'

For a moment she looked uncertain, as though she didn't know whether to trust him. Then she nodded. 'There's a café on the next block. They do a good sandwich.'

'Lead the way.'

Once they were seated in the café with their sandwiches in front of them, Wesley felt a little self-conscious, as though he was doing something slightly questionable. But he tried to sound business-like as he asked her how she'd come to meet the man she'd known as Alan Buchanan.

'I suppose you want the whole story,' she said, her dark brown eyes on him.

'That would be helpful.'

'I went to Marbella when I finished university. I didn't fancy settling down so I decided to get a job there for a while, just for the adventure, I guess. Anyway, the first week I was there I met Alan in a club and he said he had a friend who was looking for a receptionist. It turned out later that he knew the "friend" from a casino and the company was going bankrupt, but at the time I was impressed.' She pouted. 'You wouldn't believe how many lines I fell for.'

'You're not the first and you won't be the last. Tell me about Alan.'

'He was much older than me but he had something – the gift of the gab, charm, charisma, whatever you want to call it. He always seemed to have money and he used to sing in nightclubs. He knew a lot of people I thought were powerful.' She gave a derisive snort. 'Only now I know they were just cheap crooks. I moved into his apartment, which was a big mistake on my part.'

'What do you know about his background?'

'He told me he'd been brought up in England. He said he'd worked in show business over there and decided there were more opportunities on the Costa.'

'And you were star-struck.'

She smiled and touched his hand. 'I was dumb. At first he seemed so sophisticated – the experienced older man who could give me a good time. But it soon turned sour when I discovered what he was.' She lowered her eyes, as though she was ashamed. 'I tried to convince myself that the dubious men who came to the apartment were just business associates and that the money came from legitimate sources, but it's amazing how you can delude yourself.'

'So what happened?'

238

'I found a number of credit cards, all in different names. Eventually I couldn't fool myself any longer. That's when I got out.'

'What did you do?'

'I had a friend from university who worked in London and when she told me her company was looking for people I didn't hesitate. It was a chance to put my mistakes behind me. I didn't tell Alan I was going until the day before I was due to travel and I hoped I'd never see him again.'

'You must have had a hell of a shock when he turned up here.' It suddenly occurred to Wesley that Roxanne too had good reason to want Merlin Mitchell out of the way for good. 'How did he get hold of your address?'

'He'd made a note of my friend's address and contacted her. I'd never told her about him because I was too ashamed. He charmed my address out of her so maybe I should have warned her.'

'So he just turned up?'

'I found him waiting for me – gave me the shock of my life. He said he was going to Devon to meet someone but he needed a bed for a couple of nights.' She sniffed. 'I told him he wasn't having mine and I made him sleep on the settee but he still tried his luck, even though he didn't get very far. He said he'd be back to pick his things up.'

'Did he say who he was meeting in Devon?'

'All he said was that he'd been offered an unmissable business opportunity. Boy, was I relieved when he never came back.'

'Have you looked in his suitcase?'

'There's nothing much in there, only some clothes and his passport.' She snorted. 'It's not even in the name I knew him by.'

She took a UK passport from her bag and pushed it across the table as though it was contaminated. Wesley opened it. The name inside was Mervyn Mitchell, place of birth London. The Merlin must have been a small adjustment for show business purposes, something to add a little magic.

'There was this too.' Roxanne took a brown envelope out of the bag and placed it in front of Wesley. 'It's postmarked Devon. Sent about a month ago.'

Wesley stared at the envelope with the neatly printed Marbella address. Then he opened it and found a hand-written letter inside along with a page torn from a newspaper. He read the letter first; the address at the top was Woodside Cottage, followed by a phone number. And it was signed Paulette.

The handwriting was rather childlike and it took him a little time to decipher it.

Dear Merlin,

I'm so sorry I haven't been able to get out there to see you this year but I couldn't leave Mother. How I long for some sunshine and to see you again. When I saw you in that bar it seemed it was MEANT. I can't believe it's three years ago now. I always raise a glass of something Spanish on our anniversary. I've cut this from the local paper. Look carefully – see anyone familiar? I've also come across something very interesting and it's earning me a small fortune. Aren't I clever? Or did I just have a good teacher? Anyway, it means I can afford to come out to see you soon. I'll let you know my plans. I can't wait.

All my love,
Paulette

Wesley stared at it. This suggested that Paulette had started the whole business, whatever it was. She'd boasted about it, and Merlin had decided to come over to take his cut. Wesley saw that the cutting was from the front page of the *Tradmouth Echo*, dated a month ago, and when he scanned the page he spotted a familiar face: Simon Corcoran handing a large cheque to a representative of the Morbay Hospital League of Friends. Perhaps, Wesley thought, he'd misjudged the man. However, even the worst of gangsters were said to have their softer side and be good to their mothers.

At the foot of the page was another face Wesley recognised. A miserable Jayden Ross beneath the headline MORBAY MAN CONVICTED OF SHOPLIFTING and a brief account of the charges. Sometimes local newspapers were desperate for stories.

He turned the page over. On the back there was a photograph of a Rotary Club dinner with the mayor as guest of honour surrounded by a smiling group, the men in dinner suits looking like a head waiters' convention, and the women in cocktail frocks. Below this was the usual assortment of small-town news: a report of a local accountant being fined for drink-driving beside a picture of a middle-aged man with a hangdog expression, and at the top of the page a piece about the naming of the committee for next year's Tradmouth in Bloom flower competition with a photograph of a bunch of smug local worthies.

'Can I keep this?' he asked.

'Be my guest. You can have his dirty pants as well.'

'You don't seem upset by his death.'

'Would you be if you were me?'

'Probably not.' He was reluctant to ask the next question

but he had to do it. 'Where were you last Wednesday evening?'

She smiled. 'At home with a friend. We watched a film, ordered a Thai takeaway and shared a bottle of wine.'

'Will he confirm this?'

'My friend's a she.' She winked at him. 'She'll confirm it, no problem.'

'Good.' He wouldn't have liked to think of Roxanne as a murder suspect. After the mistakes she'd made in life he thought she deserved a fresh start, free from suspicion. Free from her past.

He picked up the suitcase from her office and returned on the crowded Tube to Paddington Station. Once he was on the train he tried to call Stephen Newton but again there was no reply.

It was fortunate that photography had become widespread by 1918, the year of the terrible storm that destroyed the village of Sandrock. The TV company's researcher, a permanently harassed lad who scurried to and fro like a beetle, without making eye contact with the archaeological team, had discovered a collection of photographs of the village taken shortly before its demise. The photographer had been an aristocrat who travelled the West Country in search of picturesque working folk to immortalise: ploughmen and blacksmiths; May queens and shepherds. And, in the case of Sandrock, fishermen and their families, mending nets on the beach and returning to shore with their catch.

The researcher's interesting find had emboldened him to speak to Neil. It was the first time Neil had heard the lad talk and he was rather surprised by his strong Liverpool accent, not unlike Gerry Heffernan's. He'd provided copies of the photographs and Neil was planning to go through them at his leisure in the hope of finding new details he could share with Lucy who was busy opening another trench at the east end of the church.

A gazebo had been set up on the edge of the car park so that the finds could be cleaned whatever the weather, and Neil had just taken shelter there to look through the pictures when he heard Lucy's voice. He turned round, feeling like a schoolboy about to come face to face with a girl he'd worshipped from afar. The emotion shocked him.

'What have you got there?' she asked.

'The researcher found them in the history section of the local library. Have a look.'

She took the pictures from him and thumbed through them. Finally she stopped at one and studied it for a while.

'I don't believe this,' she said.

'What?'

Lucy handed him the photograph. 'I've seen pictures of Clara in old family albums and this is definitely her. I wonder what she was doing in Sandrock. Her family was wealthy but she's dressed the same as the other Sandrock kids. It doesn't make sense.'

'It might just be a little girl who looks like her.'

'No, it's her all right. See that small birthmark on her forehead. Wonder who she's with?' She pointed at the child standing next to Clara. This girl was slightly taller with fairer hair, large eyes and a wide, unsmiling mouth.

'Friend? Sister?'

'As far as I know Clara didn't have a sister. But I can see a vague family resemblance.'

'Cousin?'

'A poor relation by the look of it. My mother's more au

fait with family history than I am. I'll ask her.' She peered at the photograph again. 'How old do you think the girls are?'

'About three? Four?'

There was a short silence before she spoke again, quieter this time. 'The same age as the child in the ice house.'

'Let's not jump to conclusions.'

'Before she died Clara was talking about walls collapsing. Could she have meant Sandrock? Before I saw this picture I'd have said that was impossible – but I need to find out what she was doing here.'

'I'll leave it to you then,' said Neil, looking at his watch. Interested as he was in Lucy's family history, he had work to do.

Gerry Heffernan had felt overwhelmed in Wesley's absence, although he'd never have admitted this to anybody, and he was relieved to learn that Wesley was on his way back from London. Since the investigation began he'd tried to conceal the unfamiliar feeling of vulnerability that kept hitting him, especially when Wesley wasn't around. However the last thing he wanted was to be sidelined from the investigation. He wanted to wrap up the case and bring Paulette Reeves' killer to justice.

The fact that Jayden Ross had been remanded in custody was one small triumph, but the lack of progress in Paulette's murder nagged away like an irritating wasp at a picnic; in addition, Simon Corcoran had slipped through their collective fingers for the time being and solid evidence against him was proving elusive. He didn't like Corcoran and he didn't trust him. If he was guilty, he'd prove it. This was another reason not to show weakness: he needed to finish the job.

Wesley had called from the train to ask if Stephen Newton had been in contact. He'd also mentioned a newspaper cutting that had been in Merlin Mitchell's possession, promising to tell him everything when he got back.

In the meantime Gerry wanted to learn more about the origin of Paulette Reeves' mysterious extra income and he reckoned it was worth having a word with her niece, Laura Pullin. Laura had been close to Simon Corcoran and had used her influence with him to get the cottage for Paulette, albeit temporarily. She'd also put cleaning jobs her aunt's way, in spite of her claims that they weren't close. There had been some family feeling there.

When he'd telephoned Laura he'd had the impression she wasn't pleased to hear his voice, although once she got onto the subject of Simon Corcoran she was more forthcoming. She'd claimed she had no idea where Paulette's money came from, adding that she wouldn't be surprised if Corcoran had something to do with it. Gerry suspected that the accusation had been the vengeance of a recently slighted ex.

Somehow he couldn't envisage Corcoran paying an unwanted tenant large sums of cash – unless she had something on him he wanted to keep hidden; something that might give him an added motive for silencing her permanently. Once again he put subjecting Simon Corcoran to an extra dose of police harassment to the top of his mental list of things to do.

Wesley's arrival at six thirty put him in a better mood and after greeting him like a long-lost friend, Gerry immediately ushered him into his office. Wesley was wheeling a large suitcase which he propped up by Gerry's coat stand.

'How did it go?'

Wesley ignored the question and asked again whether Stephen Newton had been in touch. When Gerry answered in the negative he sat in silence for a few moments, frowning.

'You're worried about him?'

'He left a message saying he wanted to speak to me and now I can't get hold of him.'

'Maybe he's just had second thoughts.'

'I hope you're right.'

'So tell me about the lady from Spain. What was she like?'

'She reminded me a bit of Karen Corden. Mitchell latched onto her when she went to work in Marbella: girl arriving in a strange town for the first time and all that sort of thing.'

'Easy target.'

'He gave her a good time for a while then the gilt wore off. She found out he was keeping dubious company and that his showbiz career wasn't as glamorous as she'd thought so she made her escape when a friend offered her a job in London. Only he turned up on her doorstep a couple of weeks ago asking to stay.'

'You don't think she's involved?'

'Highly unlikely.' He handed Gerry the envelope Roxanne Smith had given him. 'It seems that Paulette was boasting that she'd hit on a money-making scheme. I think it might have been a way of impressing him. She said she was planning to come to see him in Spain but it looks like he decided to come here instead. I think her boast backfired when he decided he wanted his cut. Probably not what she'd intended.'

Gerry placed the cutting on the desk in front of him and

took a pair of reading glasses out of his drawer. The glasses were a recent addition to his wardrobe, a small concession to the aging process, but Wesley noticed that he rarely wore them in the main office. He began to study the rest of the page, front and back.

'I see our friend Corcoran's been showing off his generosity. Wonder if the charity knows what a toerag he is.'

'When someone's donating a large cheque, I don't think they ask too many questions.'

'You're quite the cynic today, Wes.' Gerry peered at him over his glasses like an old-fashioned schoolmaster. 'Do you think Paulette was referring to Corcoran when she asked Mitchell if he recognised anyone?'

'It's possible.'

'She knew him but did Mitchell? Would his picture have meant anything to him?'

'He wasn't on the list of names from the holiday camp.'

'He might have met Mitchell somewhere else.'

An idea was forming in Wesley's head. 'Karen mentioned a John who used to hang out with Merlin. Could Simon Corcoran have been using another name? He's about the right age. Any progress on Rob's quest for the missing Johns?'

'Not yet. He's still trying. And our friend Jayden Ross has made the front page for his shoplifting exploits.'

'Well, he's far too young to be our John,' said Wesley. 'Unless Paulette and Merlin knew him some other way. If they met him in Marbella, for instance.'

'We can ask him if he's ever been.'

'I'll arrange it.'

Wesley went and opened the suitcase. 'I don't think there's anything helpful in here.' He wrinkled his nose in disgust as he picked up a sock, holding it between his thumb and forefinger then dropping it back into the case. 'Someone can go through it then it can go to the exhibits store.'

The corners of Gerry's lips twitched upwards. 'Nice job for someone.'

Wesley peered through the glass partition, surveying the outer office. 'Rob seems to have taken over Nick's desk. Looks like he's made himself at home.'

'Seems a hard worker,' commented Gerry.

Wesley watched him for a few seconds. 'He's ambitious.'

'Better watch our backs then,' said Gerry lightly. 'I've told Nick to take another week's gardening leave – not that he's got much of a garden.'

Wesley's eyes were drawn to the pile of old files on top of Gerry's filing cabinet. 'Do you mind if I have a look through the Christopher Savernake case?'

'The what?'

'One of your cold cases.'

'I haven't been through them all yet but be my guest. But haven't we got enough on with these two murders without worrying about another unsolved case?'

'I'm curious, Gerry. Indulge me.'

'Don't I always. Are you going to tell me what's bothering you about it?'

'The couple Pam's got friendly with might be related to the victim so I'd like to read up on the case, that's all.'

'Fair enough.' Gerry looked at his watch. 'Why don't you get off home, Wes. Take the file if you want a bit of bedtime reading.'

Before Wesley left the office, he tried Stephen Newton's

number, again with no luck. For a man who wanted to speak to him, Newton was being very elusive.

The battered Land Rover trundled down the lane with its lights on. It was getting dark early these days and another storm had been forecast for tomorrow. The farmer could see the first signs of it already; the blackening sky and the wind whipping the trees of the small copse in the middle of the field. The cows had taken shelter beneath the trees as soon as they'd returned from milking. Cattle, in his experience, knew a thing or two about meteorology.

He stopped the mud-splattered vehicle by the metal gate and climbed down from the driver's seat, leaving the engine running. There was rain in the air now and he zipped up his old wax jacket against the chill.

He was about to open the gate when he saw something on the ground to his left, lying half under the towering hedgerow. At first he took it for a bundle of rags but when he walked round the vehicle to investigate he saw that the sodden clothes were draped around the body of a man. For a moment he froze in panic; then he took a deep breath and squatted down to feel for a pulse like he'd seen people do on the television.

To his relief he felt something, a faint fluttering against his fingers. But the man's flesh was cold. Something had to be done.

16

11th July 1914

Jane is near her time and only I am allowed to take her food to her room. The other servants know nothing of her condition, although it would surprise me if there is not speculation below stairs. They fall silent whenever I enter the servants' hall, almost as though I were mistress here myself.

17th July 1914

The child is a girl, a pretty child with large blue eyes who cries a great deal. All the servants were sent from the house on the night she was born and only I attended Jane in her labour for Lady Berridge was reluctant to acquaint the doctor and the midwife with the family's shame.

I said I would find a woman in Sandrock to feed the little mite but in the meantime Jane suckles her, her tears falling upon the little bald head, for she does nothing now but weep.

When the child, whom Jane has named Clara, is four weeks old, I offer to take her to my mother, assuring Jane that she will care for the child as her own. Jane weeps as I take the little one from her arms and moves to stop me but Lady Berridge is firm. It is the only way. If Jane is to marry as her mother plans, her secret must never be discovered. No one must ever speak of it.

Lady Berridge will send money for Clara's upkeep but, beyond that, there will be no contact. At her signal I take the child, who is wrapped tightly in its blanket, and I drive myself the ten miles to Sandrock in the dog cart.

By the time I reach my old home it is dark and the baby is silent.

Wesley was eating his evening meal when the call came. Pam heard the ring tone of his mobile phone, a jaunty rendition of Mozart's overture to *The Marriage of Figaro*, and sighed. Another interruption to mess up the quiet evening she was looking forward to after a hard day's teaching.

He saw Rachel's name on the caller display. 'It's work. Sorry,' he said and saw Pam roll her eyes. She carried her empty plate to the dishwasher and left the room. As he answered the call Moriarty jumped up onto the table and began to make for his plate with a typical feline sense of entitlement. Wesley placed the cat gently on the floor before he spoke.

'Rach, what is it?' As he awaited her reply, he turned over all the possibilities in his mind.

'Stephen Newton's turned up,' she said. 'He was found at the side of a lane off the road to Stokeworthy.'

Wesley knew the place; the tiny network of lanes off the Stokeworthy road were single track, walled by towering hedgerows and created for the horse and cart rather than the car. They were so rarely used that weeds grew on the pitted tarmac. 'You're sure it's him?'

'Yes. He had ID on him. The boss thinks he was attacked somewhere else and dumped there.'

'How bad is he?'

'When the farmer found him he was unconscious and the doctors reckon he'd been there a long time, possibly since last night. They didn't know what was wrong with him at first but when they made a thorough examination they found two neat wounds to his chest, so small that they were difficult to see. The doctor I spoke to said they were probably made by a sharp narrow blade which just missed his heart but caused internal bleeding. He's in surgery at the moment.'

'What's the prognosis?'

'Can't be sure. The crime scene team's gone to the location and the boss has come back to the office.' She paused. 'He's looking a bit tired and . . . '

'I'm on my way,' he said. 'Better still, I'll meet you at the hospital in half an hour.'

He realised that he was no longer hungry, so he placed his plate by the cat's bowl, amazed at the feline ability to purr and scoff forbidden food simultaneously. It was Moriarty's lucky day.

Rachel was waiting for him in the hospital foyer. Her engagement ring was back in place and Wesley was surprised that he felt relieved.

'He's still in surgery,' she said when he asked how Newton was doing. 'Nobody's said much yet.'

'Who saw him when he was brought in?

'A Dr Patel in A & E.'

'I've got a question for him,' Wesley said, searching the pocket of his coat for the photograph of the dead Merlin Mitchell. If it was as he suspected, the doctor's verdict might change everything.

Rachel led the way through a pair of swing doors to the admissions department. Even at that relatively early hour it was fairly busy, but quiet compared to what it was like in the tourist season. Rachel located Dr Patel for him; a small, neat Indian man who listened to his question with exaggerated politeness and studied the photograph Wesley handed him.

'You're right, Inspector. This wound looks remarkably similar.'

'So the same weapon could have made it?'

'I can't say for definite without being able to compare the two in the flesh, as it were, but, at first glance, I'd say it was possible.' He paused. 'All I can say is that Mr Newton is extremely lucky to be alive. I think he'd been there quite some time and if he hadn't been found when he was ...' He didn't need to bother finishing the sentence. Wesley knew that, if Newton hadn't been lucky, he would have been investigating another case of murder.

'Going back?' Rachel asked once the doctor had walked away.

'I'd better see how things are going.' He suddenly realised he was hungry. 'I might pick up some fish and chips on the way.'

'Doesn't Pam feed you?'

The sharpness of her words surprised him. 'I was about to eat when you called.'

'Sorry.'

'Set a new date for the wedding yet?' he asked as they walked along the embankment.

'Not yet. There's a lot to organise.'

'You deserve to be happy, Rach.'

She stopped and looked at him. 'So do you.'

'I am.'

'Promise?'

'Promise.'

They walked on in silence, stopping at the chip shop. Wesley felt a little better after his conversation with Rachel; it was as if the unspoken tension that had stood between them like a barrier since that inadvisable kiss in the Manchester hotel room had dissolved. She was marrying Nigel in the spring. He was content with Pam and the children, who needed him, even if they'd soon grow too big and independent to admit it. Any doubts, any niggles of attraction were insignificant compared to that. One day he'd make up for his absences. But not yet, not while he had a killer to catch.

He offered her a chip as they walked by the river and she took it hungrily. The wind was getting up again and the black water was turbulent as a boiling pot.

'Did you see the headline in today's *Tradmouth Echo*?' Rachel said as she helped herself to another chip. '"Brace Yourselves for the Storm Season". The Met Office has issued a warning.'

But Wesley's mind wasn't on the weather. 'Does anyone know why Stephen Newton was in Tradmouth?'

'Not yet.'

'If he was here to visit someone, surely they'll come forward when it's on the news.'

'Unless he came here to meet his attacker.'

'In which case once they find out he's still alive, he'll be in danger. I'll get a guard put on him in hospital. We can't take chances.'

'At least this eliminates him as a suspect.'

'I never thought he was our man.'

When they arrived in the CID office Gerry greeted them and the sight of him pacing up and down, red-faced, made Wesley uncomfortable. Noreen Fitton had given him the unsolved case files so that he could take it easy. Her plan had backfired badly and Wesley felt a little guilty, although in view of Gerry's determination there was nothing much he could do about it.

'Someone's spoken to Jayden Ross. He says he's never been to Marbella and he hasn't even got a passport. Claims he's never been further than Newquay.'

'That's one theory up in smoke then.'

'And we've had a call from an Eddie Villiers. He heard on the radio that Newton's been found wounded.' Wesley could hear the excitement in Gerry's voice. 'He'd arranged to meet Newton but he didn't turn up. Seems they're an item, as they say.'

'I didn't know Newton was gay,' said Rachel.

'I don't think it changes anything.'

'Unless him and Villiers had a lovers' tiff. Or Newton once had an affair with Merlin – he said himself that Merlin wasn't too fussy who he slept with. Or Newton might have been involved with this mysterious John we're looking for. Come to think of it, he was a bit cagey when he mentioned him.'

Wesley didn't answer. Anything was possible. 'What exactly did Villiers say?'

Gerry looked down at the notebook in his hand. 'Newton's

down here staying with him for a few days. Villiers is bar manager at the Marina Hotel and they were both taking time off work to be together, only someone went off sick so Villiers had to do some shifts. They were supposed to meet up when he finished work on Thursday night but Newton never showed up even though his car was still in the hotel car park. He wondered whether to report him missing but he thought it was too soon for it to be taken seriously.'

'We should speak to him.' Wesley looked round the office. With this new development, the team all returned to their posts and most of them looked weary.

'He's already here. I told the lass on the front desk to make him comfortable in one of the empty offices downstairs and give him a cup of tea. I was waiting for you to come back before I spoke to him.'

Wesley and Gerry made their way downstairs in silence and when they reached the front desk the civilian receptionist, a girl with a ponytail who looked as if she hadn't been long out of school, told them where Eddie was waiting. When Wesley had started working in Tradmouth a large and capable desk sergeant had been the reassuring face the public first encountered in times of trouble, but he'd long since retired and times had changed.

Eddie Villiers was a small man in his thirties with a shaved head. He rose to his feet as they entered the room, his eyes anxious. He looked as though he was on the verge of tears.

'How's Steve?' he asked as Wesley shook his hand. 'I've been ringing the hospital but they won't tell me much.'

'Last I heard he was in surgery. We'll let you know as soon as we hear anything.' Eddie's distress was so palpable that Wesley wished he could tell him more, preferably good news. 'When did you last speak to him?'

'He rang an hour and a half before we were due to meet on Thursday night – said he was planning to have a walk around Tradmouth to kill some time then he'd see me in Reception. He never showed up.'

'Is that it?'

Eddie nodded. That was it.

'I think it must have been a homophobic attack,' said Eddie. 'I can't think of any other reason why anyone would want to hurt Steve. He was gentle ... damaged by life. He was accused of a murder once, you know, and it's only recently he's recovered his confidence.'

'We know all about that,' said Gerry. 'And we don't think he was attacked because he was gay.'

Eddie looked sceptical.

'DCI Heffernan's right,' said Wesley. 'We spoke to him a few days ago regarding a murder inquiry and he's been trying to contact me, possibly about something he's remembered. Did he say anything about it to you?'

Eddie hesitated. 'When we went for a drink on Wednesday night he said he'd seen someone he'd known a long time ago but he hadn't had a chance to speak to them.'

'Man or woman?' Wesley asked.

'He didn't say, but it seemed to be preying on his mind. He was quieter than usual.'

'Is that all?' said Gerry.

Eddie nodded. 'I'd better go.' He started to make for the door. Then he turned. 'If you knew he was mixed up in something why didn't you protect him? You could have stopped this.'

Wesley was about to protest, to say that they'd had no

reason to suppose that Stephen Newton had been in any danger, but Gerry put a warning hand on his arm as Eddie disappeared.

'He wants someone to blame, that's all,' he said softly. 'Get home.'

'As long as you do the same.'

'It's a deal.'

On Saturdays Pam usually stayed in bed as long as possible, almost as a matter of principle, until the necessity of seeing to the children or feeding the cat forced her downstairs. When Wesley got dressed at seven and said he was going down to the station she gave him a sleepy kiss and turned over.

Before he left the bedroom she reminded him about the Savernakes' party that evening. He knew she was looking forward to it so he resolved to make a special effort, in spite of the fact that he didn't feel particularly comfortable in Jennifer's company, and made a solemn promise to be home in time.

As started to walk to the town centre, the icy wind hit his face and he pulled his collar up for protection. For once the forecast had been right. He was carrying the file on Christopher Savernake's murder in the leather bag slung over his shoulder. Because of the previous night's events he hadn't had a chance to read it but he intended to keep it in his desk drawer in case he had a free moment.

When he reached the station he called the hospital and was told that there had been no change in Stephen Newton's condition. Then he made another call. Examining the living wasn't in Colin Bowman's remit but

Wesley reckoned it would make a pleasant change from corpses. He was relieved when Colin said he was up for it and that he'd meet him at Tradmouth Hospital at two fifteen.

Gerry arrived at eight thirty looking a little dishevelled.

'I've just seen Aunty Noreen,' he said. 'She's getting her knickers in a twist about Newton being gay. Even though I told her the attack might be connected with the murders of Paulette Reeves and Merlin Mitchell she's still insisting it was a homophobic attack.' He suddenly looked anxious. 'I am right, aren't I, Wes? Only she implied I was condoning the persecution of minorities by suggesting it had nothing to do with his sexuality. I know I'm not always the most politically correct of—'

Wesley sighed in exasperation. 'I think you're absolutely right, Gerry. From what Eddie Villiers told us, I'm sure Newton knows something and this was an attempt to silence him which almost succeeded.' He paused. 'And this afternoon I hope to prove it.'

'How?'

'I've asked Colin to compare Newton's stab wounds with the wound that killed Mitchell. I suspect he'll find they match.'

Gerry sat down and his chair gave an ominous creak. 'You do realise that if he confirms the same weapon was used, it means Paulette didn't kill Mitchell.'

'We'll have to start looking at our suspects for both murders all over again.'

'Well, all the evidence pointed to Paulette's guilt.'

'The fact that she visited Mitchell doesn't necessarily mean she killed him.'

'But Mitchell came to Devon to meet her. She sent him a

259

page of the local paper with Simon Corcoran's photograph.' He jabbed a finger at Wesley. 'Now there's a man we need to put more pressure on. He has no alibi for Mitchell's murder and a very dodgy one for Paulette's.'

'You're right, Gerry. I want to know where he was when Newton was attacked.'

'I'll leave that to you, Wes. Bring him in for questioning again and if he starts bleating about police harassment, tough.'

Wesley made to leave. It was time he found out whether any new information had come in overnight.

'Did you get a chance to read that unsolved case file you took home last night?'

'Not yet. Want it back?'

Gerry shook his head. There were more urgent things to attend to.

Wesley's phone started ringing as he was on his way over to his desk and when he answered he was surprised to hear Nick Tarnaby's voice.

'I just thought I'd let you know my mum's back,' he began in a graceless monotone. 'I've spoken to her. Told her about—'

'How did she take the news?'

'She was upset. Bound to be.'

'Did she say anything that might be helpful – know of anyone we should talk to?'

'Not really,' Nick answered. 'She mentioned a woman called Maud Parkin, someone Dorothy used to work with. She said she wanted to contact her to tell her the bad news. Nothing apart from that.'

'Did she say if Paulette or Dorothy ever mentioned the names Merlin Mitchell or Simon Corcoran?'

'No. All she said was that she hadn't had any contact with Dorothy or Paulette since last Christmas – and then it was only a card. When's the boss going to let me come back into work?'

'Sorry, don't know,' Wesley said, suddenly feeling sorry for the man. 'Look, I'll get someone here to ring your mum for a chat but she might be more willing to speak to you so when you talk to her again, mention those names, won't you.' He thought Nick might be glad to do something useful.

It was to be a quick lunch in the pub before Neil returned to Paradise Court. The only difference was that today was Saturday and Lucy had invited her mother. When she told him, he hid his apprehension behind polite noises. In the past when a woman had suggested introducing him to her mother, he'd always made himself scarce.

'She's feeling a bit low after Clara's death so I thought lunch might cheer her up,' Lucy explained as Neil tried to think of an excuse. But he couldn't, so he yielded to the inevitable. After all, what harm could it do?

He hadn't asked Lucy whether she'd had a chance to show the photograph of the two little girls to her mother but now, he thought, he'd be able to ask the question himself. At least it would be something to talk about.

Lucy was already at the Toncliffe Arms when he arrived at midday. The woman sitting with her was in her fifties with blonde bobbed hair and a pleasant, round face. She was wearing a blue cashmere sweater, flared tweed skirt and suede boots: dressed for the weather. He could see the resemblance to Lucy at once, especially the smile. They shook hands and, now that he was faced with the reality, he started to relax, especially when he was instructed to call her Sue. He'd always thought there was something reassuringly friendly about the name.

Once they'd ordered sandwiches, Neil steered the conversation round to Clara, expressing his condolences and reciting the old cliché about her having had a good innings.

'Did Lucy show you that picture the TV company's researcher found?' he asked.

Sue nodded. 'Yes. It's a bit of a mystery. There's no doubt it is Clara – the birthmark proves that – but I can't think what she'd be doing in Sandrock with one of the village children. I'm not being a snob but I wouldn't have thought it was the done thing in those days, would you?'

'You're right. People were far more conscious of social divisions back then.' He paused. 'There's no chance the other little girl was a relative? A cousin who'd fallen on hard times?'

'It's possible, I suppose. Clara always seemed a little secretive about her past. Maybe I'll find out more when I've researched our family tree.' She smiled. 'It's something I've been meaning to get round to for ages but I haven't had time.'

Lucy turned to her mother. 'How are the funeral arrangements going?'

'You know it's next Thursday? Twelve thirty.'

Sue's eyes were suddenly glassy with unshed tears.

'I hate funerals,' she said staring down at her hands. 'The first one I ever went to was my friend's boyfriend's. I can still see his poor parents now. His mother was inconsolable and my friend . . . ' She fell silent.

'What?' said Lucy.

When Sue answered her voice was low, as though she

didn't want to be overheard. 'Soon after the funeral she was arrested for his murder. It was a horrible time. Dreadful.'

'What happened to her?' Neil couldn't resist asking the question.

'She stood trial but the jury found her not guilty. Even so, suspicion always sticks, doesn't it. She gave up her nurse's training and went up north for years but as far as I know she never had another relationship. I don't think she ever recovered from what happened – Christopher dying and then being accused of his murder.'

'Are you still in touch with her?'

'I've got her address but I haven't seen her for years.' She paused. 'It was ridiculous to think Rosalie had anything to do with his death. I think the police were just looking for someone to blame.'

Neil wasn't particularly interested in the trials and tribulations of Sue's old friend. However, he was impatient to ask the question that had been on his mind since he arrived. Tact had stopped him broaching the subject until now but when the sandwiches were brought, he finally summoned the courage.

'Has Lucy told you about the child's skeleton we found in the ice house at Paradise Court?'

There was a flash of alarm in Sue's eyes, there for a split second then gone. 'She did mention something.'

'Paradise Court used to belong to your family. Have you any idea who the child could be?'

Sue looked away and shook her head before turning her attention to the ham sandwich on her plate.

Neil thought the question had upset her. But he might have been imagining things.

*

The team was out doing a house-to-house near the spot where Stephen Newton was found. Gerry observed it should be called a 'farm to farm' or a 'cottage to cottage'. It was a joke Wesley had heard before but he smiled dutifully.

The only useful piece of information that had come in so far was the statement of a farmer who'd been on his way home at around ten o'clock the night before Newton was discovered. He said a big SUV tucked itself into a passing place to let him by. It had been a tight squeeze and he hadn't seen the driver or noticed the registration number but it was dark-coloured with tinted windows. This snippet had caused Gerry considerable excitement. It sounded like Simon Corcoran's car, he said, so they needed to bring him in for questioning as soon as possible.

Wesley gave orders. If he had his way Corcoran's weekend wouldn't be filled with peace and relaxation.

When he returned to his desk he got out the file on Christopher Savernake's death from the drawer. After fetching a coffee from the machine in the corridor he opened the file and spread it out.

Should he ask Bradley Savernake that evening what relation he was to Christopher? It might be tactless but it would brighten up an otherwise dull party. Putting this mischievous thought from his mind he studied the file.

He could find no mention of Bradley; however, there was a reference to a friend of Christopher's called Jonathan Taylor. Jonathan was staying with the Savernakes and when Christopher set off to meet friends at the beach on the day of his death, Jonathan had stayed behind with Christopher's parents because he had a migraine. According to Jonathan's statement, he knew nothing about

Christopher's death. However, he did tell the police that Christopher had been intending to break up with his girl-friend, Rosalie Slater, a local girl who was training to be a nurse at Morbay Hospital.

Wesley went over to Rob Carter who was sitting at Nick Tarnaby's desk surrounded by neat piles of paperwork.

'Have you got that list of Johns I asked you to check?'

Rob produced it immediately from the top of a pile. 'There's only three I haven't managed to trace, and none of the ones I've spoken to so far worked in the kitchens.'

Wesley asked if he could see for himself and as he ran through the names his finger lighted on one in particular; one of the three that didn't have a neat tick beside it to indicate that its owner had been traced and eliminated.

His heart began to beat a little faster as he took the list back to his desk. He wanted to speak to Rosalie but first he had to find her. As he went through the Christopher Savernake file again he came across another name – a newly married friend of Rosalie Slater's who'd given her an alibi of sorts, saying she'd met Rosalie for coffee in Tradmouth an hour before the murder, leaving her later to do some shopping on her own. In the event the police didn't think the alibi was worth much because Rosalie had use of her parents' car so she could have got from Tradmouth to the murder scene in time to kill Christopher. She'd subsequently been charged with murder, even though a jury had later acquitted her, leaving the death of Christopher Savernake an unsolved mystery. As Wesley reread the file he realised why the name of Rosalie's alibi sounded familiar. Her name was Sue Zinara. Neil's new friend was called Lucy Zinara; surely there was a chance that they were related.

While he was waiting for more information to come in it would do no harm to dig a little deeper.

He looked at Rob's list again, at the name John Taylor, untraced, his present whereabouts a mystery. Had John become Jonathan at some point? Taylor was hardly an unusual name but it needed to be followed up.

17

15th August 1914

The outside world rarely disturbs our lives here at Paradise Court but now news has come to us that we are at war. I do not know the true cause of it but Johnson, our butler, spoke of some archduke being murdered in a far-off land.

It seems that we must now hate the German Kaiser and young men march through the village, eyes shining with desire for glory. Stanley, the undergardener, Jane's seducer, is among them, swaggering, scenting blood. I hope he does not return. Lady Berridge tells me that Alfred has volunteered and will be an officer. How I wish I could see him in his uniform. I have not heard from him for many months. He has not even inquired for his daughter.

I report to Lady Berridge that Jane's baby is well and happy in Sandrock. I say that she grows strong and healthy in the good sea air. It is a kindness to paint a false picture of the village with its stench of fish and its storms that rattle the houses and cause the land to slip beneath the foundations as if the hungry sea is greedy for land.

Jane mopes in the garden now that the weather is better. I wonder if she searches for her lover but they say that his regiment will go to France to fight. Alfred is with the same regiment. Perhaps he will show more courage in battle than he did when he chose to yield to his mother's expectations rather than do the right thing by the woman who was to bear his child.

Lady Berridge worries for her daughter and instructs me to keep her company. Yet even though I tore a child from her body and am privy to her most intimate secrets, Jane and I have not become close. She is distant with me, but then she is distant with everyone including her own mother. She lives in a world of dolls and imagination. Even mother-hood has not changed that. I sit and watch as she plays with her doll's house, muttering to herself, taking on the characters of the little figures in the rooms that are a perfect replica of the real thing.

I fetch her food and drink from the kitchens myself. Last night she was most unwell with vomiting, diarrhoea and burning pain. Lady Berridge called for the doctor and he said that she suffers from a gastric fever. My lady is worried that the strains of childbirth are somehow responsible but I assure her that this is impossible. Jane has picked up a chill, that is all.

My lady asks me to take especial care of Jane in her illness. It is gratifying that she trusts me with her most precious jewel.

Colin Bowman arrived on the dot. The patients he'd had to see that morning hadn't been in a position to detain him longer than he'd intended; he always said that it was one of the advantages of dealing with the dead rather than the living.

He came armed with a photograph of the stab wound that killed Merlin Mitchell, along with precise measurements. As he walked into the intensive care unit at Wesley's side, he seemed uncharacteristically quiet; this wasn't the sort of medicine he was used to. Wesley nodded to the constable on duty who was sitting outside Newton's room. The man looked bored and Wesley felt sorry for him.

After speaking to the nurse in charge Wesley led the way to Newton's bed and stood for a while watching the machines. The bleeps sounded regular, which he took as a good sign.

He watched as the nurse adjusted the unconscious man's hospital gown so that Colin could see his wounds. Colin bent over, comparing the neat little incisions on Newton's chest with the photograph in his hand and taking measurements. Wesley could tell he was itching to probe the wounds for depth and angle as he would have done if he'd been examining a corpse. But there was no question of that this time and Wesley hoped there never would be as far as Stephen Newton was concerned.

As Colin went about his business Wesley whispered to the nurse, 'Has he said anything?'

She hesitated before answering. 'He was trying to say something this morning but I couldn't make it out. Sorry.' Wesley asked her to let him know right away if the patient showed any signs of regaining consciousness.

Once Colin had finished he gave Newton's arm a small, reassuring pat, his one concession to the fact that this time his patient was still alive, and turned to Wesley.

'In my opinion the wounds are identical. I think they were made by the same weapon. A very slim blade, possibly something like a paper knife.'

Wesley thanked Colin for his time and watched him hurry away, back to the domain of the dead in the hospital mortuary. He stayed behind for a few minutes, sitting by Newton's bed. He'd heard that you should talk to someone in a coma but he couldn't think of anything to say and he was too embarrassed to come out with trite assurances that they'd catch whoever did it in front of the nurses.

As he was leaving the ward he almost collided with Eddie Villiers. The man was carrying a bunch of chrysanthemums but Wesley hadn't the heart to tell him that hospitals usually frowned on gifts of flowers these days and, besides, in many cultures chrysanthemums were regarded as the flowers of death. He merely smiled and said he was sorry to report that there was no change. He had a word with the constable on duty in case Eddie was mistaken for the killer, possibly with a weapon concealed in the flowers, and took his leave.

Once outside he found that the rain had stopped and the sun was trying to break through the gathering grey clouds, but the chill wind bit through his coat and made his ears ache as he made his way back. When he reached the police station he phoned Neil and waited patiently for him to answer, knowing that he might be up to his knees in some muddy trench.

He got Neil's voicemail but Neil rang back a few moments later while Wesley was climbing the stairs to the CID office. He hadn't been able to reach his phone in time.

Wesley came straight to the point. 'Your friend Lucy – is her mother called Sue by any chance?'

'Yeah. Why, what's she done?'

Wesley didn't fancy going into long explanations. 'I'm trying to trace somebody and I think she might be able to help me.'

After Neil had promised to call Lucy and get back to him with her mother's number, Wesley entered the office where he saw Gerry standing by Rachel's desk, examining something on her computer screen. He spotted Wesley and raised a hand in greeting.

'How's Newton?'

'No change, but at least his condition hasn't deteriorated.'

'What's Colin's verdict?' Both Gerry and Rachel were looking at him with eager anticipation and he realised that the news he had to tell them would change everything.

'It was almost certainly the same type of weapon that killed Merlin Mitchell.'

'So Paulette Reeves might not have killed him?' said Rachel.

'She could have paid him a visit and then the real killer turned up afterwards, possibly using the staircase leading up from the restaurant.'

'We've already checked the staff and the restaurant customers who made reservations.'

'What about the ones who didn't book?'

'Them as well from the credit card payments. Nothing suspicious. But anybody can walk into that place off the street. The stairs are at the end of a corridor leading to the toilets so you wouldn't even have to go through the restaurant.'

'Might be worth double-checking anyway. Someone might have seen something.'

Rachel hurried over to Rob Carter's desk. As she was speaking, Wesley saw disappointment on Carter's face, as though he'd been hoping for a more exciting assignment.

'Paulette might have been killed because she saw the murderer going to Mitchell's room,' said Gerry as they walked back to his office.

Wesley didn't answer. Paulette might have been a blackmailer and a benefit cheat but he'd never really been comfortable with the idea of her committing such a cold-blooded, calculated murder.

'I've had everyone trying to find out who Paulette was blackmailing – if it was blackmail – but we've had no luck,' Gerry said. 'Paul's been trying to get CCTV footage from the banks where the money was paid in but most of it has been wiped. And we've found no witnesses who saw Stephen Newton on the night he was attacked. This killer's either been ruddy clever or ruddy lucky.'

'Luck runs out eventually.' Wesley was trying to play the optimist, something that didn't come easily to him. 'Has Simon Corcoran been brought in yet?'

'Someone's gone round to pick him up. A car similar to his was seen near where Newton was found. I'm sure he's in this up to his neck.'

Wesley sat silently for a moment. He'd allowed himself to be distracted by the Christopher Savernake case when he should have been concentrating on catching their killer. Gerry was probably right: Corcoran was their best bet. However whenever he thought of Mitchell's murder he couldn't quite square it with the Corcoran he knew. Somehow the sleeping pills and the blade slipped into the brain seemed too subtle for him.

'I thought I'd let Rach and Trish have a go at Corcoran this time. He might respond to the feminine touch.'

Gerry's words roused Wesley from his reverie.

'Are we keeping you awake, Wes?'

'Sorry, Gerry. I'm just thinking of this John who used to hang around with Merlin Mitchell at the holiday camp. Karen said Mitchell might have gone off with him.'

Gerry sniffed. 'Think it's relevant?'

Wesley hesitated. Maybe he was letting his imagination

get the better of him, becoming obsessed. 'A Jonathan Taylor was staying with Christopher Savernake at the time of his death and, according to the list from the Bay View Holiday Camp, a John Taylor was working in the kitchens at the time Fiona Carp was killed. Presumably he's the same one Stephen Newton said was friendly with Mitchell. Rob hasn't been able to trace him.'

Gerry rolled his eyes. 'That's not necessarily sinister. People go to live abroad all the time. Merlin Mitchell did. Anyway, there must be thousands of John or Jonathan Taylors about.'

'I'd still like to speak to Rosalie Slater, just in case.'

Gerry looked exasperated, as though Wesley was being deliberately awkward, dreaming up problems where none existed. 'There's absolutely no evidence to link the murder of Fiona Carp to the death of Christopher Savernake. This cold case stuff would be fine if we didn't have two murders and an attempted murder to deal with.'

He was interrupted in mid-flow by Wesley's phone. It was Neil with Sue Zinara's number and Wesley made a note of it knowing that, whatever Gerry's misgivings, he was going to follow this one up.

'One thing's certain, Gerry,' he said after a few moments. 'Our killer's not a stranger to South Devon. He knows the area.'

'Like Simon Corcoran does.'

Wesley couldn't argue with that. 'I just want to follow up this Jonathan Taylor lead. And if it doesn't go anywhere . . . '

Gerry tutted. It wasn't often the two men didn't see eye to eye and it made Wesley uncomfortable. 'OK. But don't be long.'

He left Gerry's office and made his call.

18

20th September 1914

Jane is a little better today and has taken the soup I spoon into her mouth. Lady Berridge smiles to see my devotion and says that she doesn't know what she would do without me.

War still rages in France and Stanley is back on leave. He swaggers in his uniform, every inch the soldier, and is made much of by the female servants who giggle and preen at his every word. It would not surprise me if there was another clandestine birth in nine months' time. He is the sort who turns any situation to his advantage.

He shows no curiosity about Jane, who has kept to her room for the past month. The girl bore his child and yet he displays no interest. I hate him and wish a bullet would find him.

Whenever my lady inquires about the child I tell that I have received news from my mother that all is well.

The news of my Edith is also good. She is a healthy child, though small for her age. I pray for her each night.

*

Simon Corcoran arrived at the station for further questioning, protesting his innocence loudly, but Wesley left Rachel and Trish to deal with him. As Gerry observed, he might respond better to a different approach.

Before Wesley left for Dartmoor he rang the hospital to inquire about Stephen Newton's condition. The attack on Newton suggested a ruthlessness that might spread to others like an infectious disease. Anybody who knew the truth might be at risk – but what that truth was, he could only guess. Of course there was a chance they'd soon be able to prove something against Simon Corcoran; on the other hand, he had a feeling that Rosalie Slater might be able to help him.

He looked at his watch. It was two o'clock already and Pam had told him not to be late for the Savernakes' party. However, the way things were going, he'd probably have to disappoint her.

As he reached the edge of Dartmoor, the clouds began to lower and the fine mist on his windscreen forced him to switch his wipers to intermittent and use his headlights. It wasn't a day to be out but he had little choice if he wanted to discover the truth about Christopher Savernake's death.

The rolling green landscape gradually gave way to something bleaker but equally beautiful: miles of grey-green undulating land punctuated by dry-stone walls, windswept trees and mysterious outcrops of rock. For several miles he saw no other cars and a sense of isolation began to overwhelm him so he was relieved when he reached Rosalie's bungalow. It stood on the edge of a small, stone-built village and Wesley recalled that he'd been on a dig near there in his student days, excavating the remains of a blowing house used in the fourteenth century for smelting the tin that had

275

once made the area wealthy. This could be a harsh place, especially in winter.

The state of the bungalow shocked him. The paintwork, once white, was flaking to reveal greying wood beneath. Some of the window frames were rotten and unlikely to keep out the Dartmoor chill once the weather worsened. The bottoms of the walls were covered in moss and mildewed curtains hung limply at the windows. There was no doorbell so he rapped on the fly-blown frosted glass of the front door.

A light was on in the hallway and he hoped this meant that she was at home. He waited a while then knocked again. This time he saw a dark shape approaching behind the glass and the door opened a cautious inch.

'I'm looking for Rosalie Slater. My name's DI Wesley Peterson from Tradmouth CID. Sue Zinara gave me this address.' As he'd hoped, Sue's name was his open sesame; the door opened wide to reveal a woman who was almost as wide as she was tall. Her long grey hair fell in greasy ringlets and her body was engulfed in a voluminous purple kaftan. Several brightly coloured scarves were draped around her neck and she smelled of patchouli. She invited Wesley in as though she was pleased to see another human being.

'I haven't seen Sue for ages,' she said. Her voice was high-pitched, positively girlish. 'How is she?'

'She's well,' he answered, not wanting to admit that he hadn't actually met the woman.

'Can you tell her I often think about her,' she said with a desperation that hinted at loneliness.

As he looked at her large, candid eyes he thought that she must once have been beautiful. She should have had a better future than this. 'Yes, of course,' he said.

Then her mood suddenly changed. 'Why are you here?' she asked bluntly. Wesley realised that her arrest for murder was bound to have made her wary of any police visit. Stephen Newton had reacted in a similar way. These were two innocent people whose lives had been scarred by suspicion.

'I'd like to talk to you about Christopher Savernake,' he said gently.

She turned her face away.

'Please. I need your help.'

She led the way into a cramped living room, painted an oppressive dark red and cluttered with the detritus of years. He moved a pile of dusty books and sat down on a sofa that was covered by a filthy Indian throw while she settled herself on an armchair opposite and waited for him to speak.

'You were tried for Christopher's murder.'

'Yes.' Wesley could tell that years of pain lay behind that single word. 'I was acquitted. Lack of evidence.'

'Can you tell me what happened?'

'Can't you read a file or something?'

'I want to hear your version.'

There was a long silence, as though she was gathering her thoughts, then she began to speak quietly, reciting the words as if it was a story she'd told time and time again. She had been seeing Christopher for three months and everything had been going well. Of course the Savernakes owned the brewery and lived in a manor house. They were wealthy, virtually a county family, and she was from a family who lived in what could only be described as genteel poverty, her father running a not-too-successful garage. But the social divide hadn't seemed to matter, not to Christopher anyway. She'd known him for a while but they hadn't started going out together until after he'd returned from Europe where he'd spent a gap year before such things were fashionable.

'Did Chris have a brother called Bradley?' Wesley asked.

She looked puzzled. 'He was an only child.'

'Was anyone in the family called Bradley?'

'I remember Chris saying Bradley was a family name.' She bowed her head. 'I don't know which relatives turned up for his funeral because I'd been arrested by then.'

'Christopher had a friend called Jonathan Taylor.'

She nodded. 'He'd met him while he was on some Greek island. He used to go on about how Jonathan had saved his life – Chris got into trouble while he was swimming and Jonathan rescued him.'

Wesley leaned forward. 'Was Jonathan there when Chris died?'

'He was in the house. Chris was going to the beach and Jonathan would have gone with him but he wasn't feeling well.'

'What was his relationship with Chris?'

She considered the question for a few moments, eyes closed in concentration. 'It was almost as if the fact that he'd saved Chris's life made him beholden to him somehow. I think Chris was beginning to resent it. Not that he ever said anything to me.'

'Did you mention this to the police?'

'Yes, but they took no notice. Anyway, Jonathan had an alibi. He was with Christopher's parents at the house when it happened. He had a migraine.'

'How did you get on with Jonathan?'

'Fine.'

'You were friends?'

'Yes. He used to … he used to tell me things. Things

278

Chris said. We got on well.' She pressed her lips together. 'Although he was the one who told the police we'd had an argument.'

'Was that a lie?'

There was a long silence. 'Well, we had been arguing a bit. But what Jonathan said made it sound worse than it was.'

'You think that was deliberate?'

'I don't know. He was upset about his friend. He probably didn't think.'

'Did Jonathan ever mention that he'd worked at the Bay View Holiday Camp in Morbay?'

She shook her head.

'How did he react when Chris died?'

'Like I said, he was really cut up about it. I heard they'd asked him to stay on after the funeral. He once told me he'd been brought up in care and he liked being part of a family.'

Wesley took a while to phrase the next question. 'Is there any chance he could have been responsible for Christopher's death?'

She shook her head vigorously. 'I've already told you. He was up at the house with Chris's parents.'

Wesley felt a stab of disappointment that his embryonic theory had come to nothing. 'Can you describe Jonathan?'

She thought for a moment. 'He was good-looking with long dark hair. Hippy type, I suppose. Softly spoken. Not the sort you'd notice really.'

Wesley sat for a moment. This description was certainly similar to the one Karen Corden gave of the boy who'd been friendly with Merlin Mitchell.

'Do you know what became of him?'

'All I know is that he was still with the Savernakes at the time of my trial. He came to the court with them, his arm linked through Mrs Savernake's. I heard that people were saying he was a great support to them.'

'Do you know what happened to him after the trial?'

'No. I moved away after my release and so did my parents. My mum and dad suffered as well, you see, and they felt they couldn't stay in the area. People were saying that the police wouldn't have let the case come to trial if they weren't sure I was guilty so ... ' A look of deep sadness passed across her face, as if all the joy had gone out of her life and she knew it would never return. 'Because of what happened I lost touch with everyone I knew back then; apart from Sue. She was the only one who believed in my innocence.'

'What about the Savernakes?'

'I never had any more contact with them.'

'May I show you something?' He took the newspaper cutting from Mitchell's luggage out of his pocket and handed it to her. She stared at the photograph of Simon Corcoran for what seemed to Wesley like a long time. Then she turned the page over and Wesley saw recognition in her eyes.

'This could be him,' she said. 'In fact, I'm sure it is.'

Lucy had arranged to meet her mother at Sandton House after digging had finished for the day. It felt wrong to be there without visiting Clara and as she walked down the carpeted corridor, smiling at a uniformed care assistant as she passed, she could almost feel Clara's presence. Hers had been a strong presence in life and shades of it seemed to have lingered after death.

Her mother was waiting for her by the door to Clara's

room, wearing old trousers in preparation for the necessary task of clearing out. Lucy was still wearing her digging clothes but she'd exchanged her muddy boots for trainers for the sake of the carpets.

'I was talking to a policeman friend of your Neil's earlier, name of Inspector Peterson,' Sue began after the women had exchanged a kiss. 'He rang me out of the blue.'

'He's not *my* Neil.'

Sue ignored the protest. From her preoccupied expression, Lucy knew that something about the call from the police was worrying her.

'What did he want?'

She sighed, as if she was carrying some great burden.

'He was asking about that old friend of mine. Rosalie.' She paused. 'The one who stood trial for murder.'

'Why? Is the case being reopened?'

'The inspector didn't say. He wanted her address. I would have called to warn Rosalie but I don't think she's on the phone.' She put her hand on the doorknob. 'We can't put this off any longer.' She pushed the door open and when she flicked the switch the single overhead light brightened the gloom.

'I'll do the wardrobe and you do the drawers,' Lucy said, taking a roll of bin liners from her bag. 'We can take everything home and sort it out there.'

The two women worked silently, gathering together Clara's clothes and dropping them into the black plastic bags. When Lucy looked at her mother she saw that she was crying.

Lucy opened the bottom drawer of the tall chest in the corner. There were nightdresses in there, all folded neatly, all with Clara's name sewn into the neckline like a child's at school. She stuffed them in the nearest bin liner. Then her fingers came into contact with something that had been shoved to the back of the drawer, an old photograph album. She took it out and opened it. There was Clara, aged around eight in a straw hat and the feminine version of a sailor suit: a sweet little girl from a prosperous family. From what she knew about Clara's life, her mother had died when she was a baby, possibly in childbirth, and she had been raised by her grandmother, Lady Berridge. There were pictures of her with an expensively dressed older lady together with a younger woman dressed in grey who looked as if she might be a relative or perhaps a superior servant. The woman in grey had a sharp-featured, intelligent face and in several of the pictures she stood with a protective hand on little Clara's shoulder. Perhaps she was a governess, Lucy thought. In those days, unlike the present, the family would have been able to afford one.

After a token knock, the door opened and Lucy saw the manager standing there, a sympathetic look on her face. She was holding something in her hand.

'I wanted to give you this,' she said, addressing Sue. 'When Clara first came to us she used to hide it in all sorts of places. The cleaners kept finding it stuffed behind cushions in the lounge and dropped behind cupboards. I didn't want it to come to any harm so I've been keeping it in my office. I really should have mentioned it before but I completely forgot. It looks quite old.'

She handed Sue an old book with a tattered leather cover.

'I haven't read it, of course, but I think it might be some sort of diary,' the manager went on, hovering in the doorway as though she wanted Sue to read it there and then to satisfy her own curiosity.

Instead Sue thanked her and put the book to one side.

When the woman had gone Sue picked it up and began to read; after a couple of minutes her face had turned pale.

As soon as Wesley left Rosalie's house, he made an urgent call to Rachel. She was eager to tell him about the interview with Simon Corcoran in which the words 'no comment' had been uttered more than once, but Wesley interrupted her, saying that he needed her to look up some records. Fast.

He switched on his headlights and began the drive back to Tradmouth. It was five thirty and still raining, the damp conditions turning the winding roads into shiny, perilous snail tracks, but he had to get back. He needed answers to the questions whirling in his head. If his suspicions were correct, the killer of Merlin Mitchell and Paulette Reeves was still out there, and Stephen Newton was in grave danger.

As he turned onto the A3122 he felt the car skidding on the wet tarmac. If he was going to reach his destination in one piece, he'd have to slow down.

He found himself stuck behind a coach. There were still some late visitors keen to sample the picturesque delights of Tradmouth, even on a day like this. He counted to ten and breathed deeply, telling himself to be patient. What did a few more minutes matter? Then he realised they might matter quite a lot.

He used his hands-free phone to call the hospital to check on Stephen Newton, who was still unconscious but stable, and gave instructions that nobody, apart from hospital staff and police officers, was to be admitted to his room. Not even Eddie Villiers was allowed to see him. Villiers might kick up a fuss but those were his orders.

The streetlights were on by the time he arrived at the police station and when he burst into the CID office Rachel handed him a sheet of paper. 'I've checked out those things you mentioned. Are you going to let me in on the secret?'

He studied the sheet. Once he'd absorbed the information, he asked where Gerry was.

'With the chief super. He should be back any time. He wasn't looking too well so I suggested he went home. But you know what he's like,' she added meaningfully.

Wesley thanked her and rushed from the office, almost running up the carpeted staircase to the second floor. Gerry needed to know about this and so did Chief Superintendent Fitton.

19

22nd September 1914

Jane's condition is serious; Lady Berridge summons the doctor day and night and he dances attendance with honeyed words, assuring her that Jane suffers from nothing but a gastric attack. It is a weakness in her, he says once he has left the stench of the sickroom, and my lady nods, reassured. With Martha to care for her, she tells him, Jane will soon be restored to health. I smile and say that I will do all in my power to make Jane well again.

This morning she has worsened and my lady has sent one of the maids to the doctor's house in the village. I sit by her bedside, spooning soup into her dry, white lips. I have put a cloth around her neck to catch the fluid as it dribbles from the sides of her mouth and I tell her she must eat to keep up her strength.

Her breathing is shallow and she has the cast of death upon her. I watch and wait like the devoted servant my lady believes me to be.

Pam wondered whether it would be appropriate to take a bottle of Prosecco to Bradley and Jennifer's. If it was somebody she knew better she wouldn't have been pondering this thorny dilemma but she couldn't be sure of the couple's taste, only that it was likely to lean towards the expensive. Perhaps the fancy box of chocolates that had been languishing in the kitchen cupboard for the past few months would be a safer choice. One of the children in her class had given it to her at the end of last term and it had been awaiting a special occasion. Before placing it by the front door she checked the use-by date and was relieved that it still had six months to run.

As the children put on their coats she was surprised by her son's lack of enthusiasm. 'Have you got your things ready, Michael?'

Michael sighed and held up a rucksack.

'You're going to a sleepover, not an exam,' Pam said. She looked at Amelia and saw that she was smirking.

'Are you going to let me in on the joke?'

'Michael doesn't want to stay at Daniel's. He wants to go to Nathaniel's first thing tomorrow morning. His dad said he'd take them to play football.'

'It's OK for you,' Michael snapped. 'Jennifer's always making a fuss of you but I'm stuck with Daniel. He's weird.'

'Don't say things like that,' said Pam quickly, wondering if she was pushing her son towards a friendship with a boy he didn't particularly like. If she'd had to advise a parent about a similar problem in the course of her professional career, she would have told her to step back and think of the child. But the Savernakes were expecting them so there was no backing out now. Besides, Jennifer had called earlier to say she had a special surprise for Amelia, and she told herself that Michael would enjoy it when he got there.

'Well, if I pick you up early in the morning you can still

get to Nathaniel's in time,' she said to her son, keeping her voice bright and positive. She had always thought that teaching was the nearest thing she knew to acting and over the years she'd become an expert. 'Come on, we're late already.'

She paused to look at herself in the hall mirror before putting on her coat. She was wearing the short gold dress Wesley had bought her last Christmas with a pair of thick black tights and patent leather boots, as unlike a harassed, frumpy mummy-teacher as she could manage. Satisfied with what she saw, she buttoned her coat, tucked the chocolates under her arm and ushered the children out of the front door.

The walk only took five minutes but she wished she'd worn a hat. The wind whipped her carefully arranged hair out of style and as she stood on the Savernakes' doorstep with Amelia beaming by her side and Michael sulking behind, she tried to repair some of the damage with a comb she'd found in her pocket.

As Bradley opened the door she fixed a smile to her face and proffered the chocolates.

'Come in, come in. Yolanda should be here soon.'

Pam smiled bravely at the prospect of having to spend another Saturday evening in the company of her head-teacher.

'Mark and Maritia are in the drawing room if you'd like to go through.'

This was better news, she thought as Bradley, the perfect host, stooped to tell the children that Daniel was waiting for them upstairs and that Monique, the au pair, would offer them the refreshments of their choice. Pam saw her children exchange a glance. At least today they seemed to be in agreement about something, which was better than their usual brother–sister bickering.

Pam asked for a Prosecco but Bradley said there wasn't any and joked that she'd have to make do with champagne instead. As she entered the drawing room she looked round. There were several people she'd never seen before, sipping champagne and looking sleekly prosperous. Then she spotted Mark and Maritia in earnest conversation with an elderly man who was holding forth about the state of the Church of England while Mark nodded politely. She strode towards them like a thirsty woman spotting an oasis in the desert, and as soon as Maritia saw her she came to give her a sisterly hug.

'I hear the food'll be coming out soon,' she said softly.

'Where's Jennifer?'

'In the kitchen. I think I'll offer to give her a hand.'

'I'll come with you.'

'Where's Wes?'

Pam rolled her eyes. 'Where do you think?'

'Well if you will marry a policeman ... Think he'll make it?'

'Who knows.'

Maritia lowered her voice to a whisper. 'I think most of these people are friends or business associates of Bradley's. The man who's collared Mark is something to do with the Rotary Club. If any of them talk to me I intend to keep it quiet that I'm a doctor or I'll have them queuing up with their eczema and varicose veins. Don't laugh, it happens.'

Pam followed Maritia to the huge kitchen with its glossy granite worktops, marble floor and scarlet Aga. It made her own kitchen look small and shabby.

They marched over to the breakfast bar where Jennifer

was putting the finishing touches to a plate of kebabs. The serving dishes were silver and Pam noticed that the spoons had hallmarks too and even the succulent kebabs were speared on what appeared to be antique silver meat skewers. The phrase 'how the other half live' bubbled through her mind as Bradley entered and handed her a glass of champagne.

'Need any help, Jennifer?' Maritia asked.

'No, I'm fine, thanks,' Jennifer replied, a note of anxiety in her voice belying the statement. 'One of the girls from the caterers will hand all these round in a minute but do help yourself. By the way, I made the cheese straws, the salmon quiche and the kebabs. Everything else is down to the caterers, I'm afraid.'

Maritia took a cheese straw and made appreciative comments. They melted in the mouth. Could she have another? Pam fancied the look of the kebabs so she picked up one of the skewers by the little ring at the end to find that the meat was tender and delicious. She helped herself to another before sampling a cheese straw. Then the dish was suddenly whipped away from her by a serious-faced girl dressed entirely in black.

'You have brought Amelia?'

Pam was surprised at the intensity behind Jennifer's question. 'Yes. Bradley sent her upstairs to play.'

'She loves the doll's house.' A distant look came over her. 'I bought a new quilt for her bed. The Sleeping Beauty. Do you think she'll like it?'

Pam nodded, noticing a glimmer of unease in Maritia's eyes.

'I've got a little present for her. I'll give it to her later.'

Before Pam could say anything the doorbell rang and

Jennifer rushed from the room to admit her new guests. The thought that the visitor might be Yolanda made Pam take another long sip of champagne.

'She seems very fond of Amelia,' Maritia whispered.

'Yes.' She looked round to make sure she couldn't be overheard. 'She lost her own daughter so ... '

Just at that moment Pam heard a familiar voice, one she hadn't been expecting. 'I need to speak to Mr Bradley Savernake,' it said. 'Is he in?'

Jennifer said something in reply but Pam couldn't make out the words.

'That sounds like Gerry Heffernan,' said Maritia. 'Didn't know he'd been invited.' She started to make for the door and Pam fell in behind her. Where Gerry led, Wesley often followed and she wanted to see him, to find out what was going on.

Maritia was blocking Pam's view of the hall but she heard her say, 'Wes, you've managed to get here. Great.'

A second later Pam was standing by her sister-in-law's side and she could see Bradley talking to Wesley and Gerry, swaying slightly like a man who doesn't know whether to run or stand his corner. She caught Wesley's eye and she saw him touch Gerry's arm. He was coming over to speak to her and when he gave Maritia a meaningful look the three of them retreated to the kitchen.

'What's going on?' Pam kept her voice low.

Wesley looked from his wife to his sister. 'We need to speak to Bradley, but that's all I can say at the moment. We're taking him down to the station so it shouldn't ruin the party. Where are the kids?' There was a note of concern in his voice.

'Upstairs. Jennifer's au pair's looking after them.'

Wesley seemed satisfied with the answer. He squeezed Pam's hand. 'I'll have to go.'

'Do you know what's going on?' Maritia said as they watched Wesley leave.

'I've no idea. But I'm sure it must be a mistake.'

Maritia said nothing and took another sip of champagne.

'Is this wise?' Lucy said as she stroked Neil's naked back.

'What's the matter?'

'I've always avoided getting involved with fellow archaeologists before. Imagine the embarrassment if they turned up on the same dig after you'd split up. Then there's the gossip – you know how people in our job love to gossip.'

'I can be very discreet when I want to be.' He turned over and pushed her hair away from her face.

They kissed and Neil lay back and closed his eyes. The bottle of wine they'd shared earlier was making him sleepy.

Lucy spoke again. 'I found some pictures of Clara when she was little today. It was definitely her in that Sandrock picture.' She hesitated. 'There was some kind of diary too but my mother took that home with her. I think there was something in it she doesn't want me to see.'

Neil was suddenly wide awake. He propped himself up on his elbow and looked at her. 'How do you mean?'

'While she was reading it she looked as though she'd seen a ghost. I asked to see it but she made some excuse.'

Neil kissed her forehead. 'Must be some dark family secret. Maybe your great- great-uncle was Jack the Ripper.'

Lucy, though, had seen her mother's expression and knew that whatever had been in that book, it had been no laughing matter.

*

There are no social manuals to tell you how to behave when your husband has just hauled your hostess's husband off to the police station for questioning. Pam had left with Mark and Maritia not long after Wesley's fleeting visit, because she'd have been embarrassed to stay, and an hour later she'd called him to find out what was happening.

He'd asked her about the children and was relieved to learn that they'd gone home with her in spite of Jennifer's desperate pleas for Amelia to stay and sleep in the room she'd so lovingly prepared for her visit. It was for the best that his family was safely out of the whole sorry situation.

Bradley Savernake had just been brought in to be questioned in the windowless interview room that had been vacated not long before by Simon Corcoran, who had been released on bail pending further inquiries. When Savernake took his seat at the table, Wesley switched on the tape recorder and began, glancing at the plump solicitor sitting by the suspect's side. He recognised him from the Savernakes' party and thought he looked peeved at missing his free champagne and nibbles. Bradley himself looked calm but concerned; the upright citizen helping the police with their inquiries.

'What's your full name?' Wesley began.

'Bradley Savernake.'

'Your *full* name.' Wesley looked the man in the eye.

Savernake held his gaze and cleared his throat. 'I've told you.'

'Where were you born?'

There was a moment of hesitation. 'Morbay.'

'You see, we can't find a record of anybody of that name who fits with your story.'

'Then you haven't looked hard enough.' The answer sounded confident.

Wesley slid the cutting found in Merlin Mitchell's luggage across the table. 'That's you, isn't it? At the right of the group behind your wife.'

Savernake studied the photograph then remarked, 'I didn't know that attending a Rotary Club dinner was against the law.'

'Where were you the Wednesday before last; between seven thirty and nine thirty?'

'I don't remember offhand. My diary's at home'

'Did you kill Merlin Mitchell at the Morbay Palace Hotel?'

'Don't be ridiculous.' His eyes slid to his solicitor, clearly peeved that he'd raised no objection to the line of questioning.

'What about the following Saturday evening?'

'I was at the Tradmouth Castle Hotel at a school fundraising evening. Your wife was there too. Why don't you ask her? I gave her a lift home if you remember.'

'And the Thursday evening just gone?'

'I've recently stepped down as managing director of the family brewery and I went for a drink with my successor and a couple of my former colleagues, again at the Tradmouth Castle Hotel. I left around nine and arrived home about nine twenty. I'd had a drink so I walked. My wife will tell you what time I got in and that I spent the rest of the evening at home.'

Wesley and Gerry looked at each other. On the face of it his alibi for Paulette Reeves' murder seemed solid. However, Colin Bowman had said she might have died any time up until midnight so there was always a chance he could have gone to Woodside Cottage after he'd dropped Pam off that night; and they couldn't be sure what time Stephen Newton had been attacked that Thursday evening so the same thing applied.

'Can I go now?' Savernake said with the confidence of an innocent man. But Gerry hadn't finished.

'We've been looking at a list of people who worked at the Bay View Holiday Camp back in 1979. A John Taylor worked in the kitchens there and a Jonathan Taylor later befriended a young man called Christopher Savernake who was murdered in 1980.'

For the first time Bradley Savernake looked uncomfortable. 'So?'

'Who exactly are you, Mr Savernake?'

20

23rd October 1914

It is the week for death. Word has come that the father of Jane's child, is missing believed dead at some place in Flanders I cannot pronounce. Maisie the kitchenmaid is in tears at the news. It seems Stanley sowed his seed far and wide. He felt no remorse about taking advantage of poor, stupid Jane so I feel no guilt at wishing him dead.

Today Jane too has gone to meet her Maker, in spite of my devoted care. Her condition worsened last night and for many hours she vomited blood and purged her bowels. Her face, white and glistening with sweat, was a pitiful sight and her once-beautiful hair was plastered to her head. I looked after her the whole night and after a while I became accustomed to the stench. I watched as she weakened and when her breathing became shallow I knew she was not long for this world.

Jane made no mention of Clara in her dying hours. I think she has forgotten the child already, which is a blessing in the circumstances. She breathed her last in the early hours and now the house is in deep mourning. Lady Berridge is distraught and I take it upon myself to comfort her. To lose a child is a terrible thing.

I wonder if Lady Berridge will now wish to assume responsibility for her granddaughter. Since a good marriage for Jane is no longer a possibility, she might want to introduce the child to the world as an orphaned relative she has taken in out of the goodness of her heart.

'Jonathan Taylor was staying with the Savernake family at the time their son, Christopher, was murdered,' said Wesley. 'Christopher met him while he was on holiday on a Greek island. Apparently Jonathan saved his life and then proceeded to befriend him, following him back to England.'

There was no answer.

'I've spoken to Christopher's girlfriend at the time – a lady by the name of Rosalie Slater. She told me Jonathan did his best to ingratiate himself with the family. Then after Christopher's death he made himself indispensable, taking their dead son's place. According to records, he took their name by deed poll, even changing his first name to the family name of Bradley, and he became the heir to the family estate and brewery when they died. Do you remember Ms Slater?'

Savernake didn't answer.

'She identified you from this photograph.'

Rosalie Slater had said it looked like the Jonathan she knew but he'd aged a good deal and the picture wasn't clear. When he'd e-mailed the photo to Karen Corden, her verdict had been similar but Wesley wasn't going to let this hint of uncertainty get in the way. 'What was your relationship with Merlin Mitchell?'

'Who?'

'We have a witness who told us that you two were very close at the Bay View Holiday Camp. Did you know he'd killed the little girl?'

'What little girl?' He frowned, puzzled, as if this was all new to him.

'Her name was Fiona Carp and, according to DNA evidence, Mitchell was responsible for her death. How close were you and Mitchell? Were you there when he killed her? Did you help him cover up what he did?'

For the first time Savernake's calm crumbled. He put his head in his hands.

Gerry, who had been sitting quietly, listening to Wesley's questioning, now spoke. 'You might as well get it off your chest. We've got witnesses and records to prove our story and we can bring Rosalie Slater in to identify you if necessary. Maybe if you give us your version, we can help you.'

The silence lasted for thirty seconds or so then, in spite of the solicitor's warning hand on his sleeve, Savernake began to speak. 'I changed my name to please Chris's parents. It was all their idea. When Chris died they begged me to stay on and I took Chris's place because it was a comfort to them. I'd been brought up in care so it was the first time I'd had a proper family.'

'So your real name is Jonathan Taylor?'

He nodded. 'It's John but I changed it to Jonathan because I thought it sounded better.'

'Did you kill Christopher Savernake?'

He hesitated for a moment. 'I'd saved his life in Corfu. Why would I kill him? It was Rosalie. He'd been about to end their relationship and she lost her temper. She'd always had a violent temper, according to Chris. She should have gone to prison for what she did.'

'She says otherwise. And there are no witnesses to back up your claim that he was going to finish with her.'

'The police knew it was her. They just didn't have enough evidence to convince the jury.'

'She told us she heard you arguing with Chris. She said he was sick of you hanging around.'

'That's absolutely ridiculous.'

'He wanted rid of you but you didn't want to lose your meal ticket, did you?'

'That's not true. If anyone had a volatile relationship it was Chris and Rosalie. She was possessive. Paranoid if he so much as spoke to another girl,' he said with new boldness. 'Besides, I was at the house with his parents when he died. Chris said he was going out to the beach and I'd planned to go with him but I had a migraine so I didn't feel up to it. A witness came forward to say a car similar to hers was seen in Belsham before it happened. My guess is that she was waiting for him at the gates when he drove out. He must have stopped to speak to her and ... ' He buried his head in his hands as though he found the memory unbearable.

'When did you last see Merlin Mitchell?' Wesley asked.

'I don't remember.'

'Did you go with him to Europe after the murder of Fiona Carp?'

No answer.

'According to Rosalie, Chris said Jonathan had been trying to get away from a friend he was with in Corfu because he was getting on his nerves. I think that annoying friend of yours was Merlin Mitchell.' Wesley wasn't sure he was on solid ground here but thought it was worth a try.

There was a long silence before Bradley spoke. 'Merlin wanted to get away from the holiday camp.' He stared at his hands as though speaking was an effort. 'I knew he'd been stealing from the chalets and I just thought things had got too hot for him. Honestly, I had no idea he'd killed that kid. One of the chefs was arrested. Steve. I remember him saying that the kid had been following him around, making a nuisance of herself.'

'You knew Steve Newton well?' Gerry asked.

'I worked in the kitchens with him. We saw each other every day and got on OK but I wouldn't say we were bosom buddies.'

'He's in intensive care at Tradmouth Hospital.' Wesley watched Bradley's face carefully but saw no reaction. No shock. No questions. 'Someone stabbed him and left him for dead in a lane near Stokeworthy. You have a dark-coloured SUV with tinted windows. I saw it when you dropped my wife off at our house.'

'So?'

'A similar car was seen near where he was found.'

'It wasn't mine. It couldn't have been.'

Gerry ignored his protests. 'Did he recognise you and threaten to wreck the life you'd stolen for yourself? Did you need to shut him up?'

'No.'

'When Mitchell turned up in Morbay it must have been the final straw. He threatened everything you'd built up: the nice family, the big house, the successful business. Was he going to tell people you'd been his lover? That you'd been accomplice to a thief and a con man? That would have gone down well with Jennifer and your friends in the Rotary Club, wouldn't it? Was he threatening to say you'd had a part in Fiona's murder? Or had he found out about Christopher? Did he suspect you'd killed him to take his place? You must have a lot on your conscience, Bradley or whatever you call yourself. Why don't you share it with us?'

Wesley wondered whether Gerry had pushed things too far. He had no concrete proof for half his allegations but he'd only voiced the suspicions that had been swirling in Wesley's own mind.

'I didn't kill Chris. He was my best friend. Rosalie Slater killed him and the bitch got away with it.'

Wesley took over. 'Then there's Merlin Mitchell's former lady friend Paulette Reeves – or Paulette Jenkins as she used to be. Remember her?'

The answer was a slight nod.

'She sent Merlin a photo from the newspaper – you smiling and raising a glass with your friends from the Rotary Club. She was blackmailing you, wasn't she?'

The solicitor, unhelpfully, reminded him that he didn't have to say anything and he remained silent for a few seconds, as though he was considering his options. Eventually he spoke. 'OK, I admit that Paulette was blackmailing me and I was paying money into her bank account, but I never harmed her.'

'How did she find you?'

'She came to our house as a cleaner for the agency we use. I was horrified when we recognised each other. I'd put that life behind me,' he said, looking Wesley in the eye. 'I'd become a different person. But even if the truth about my past came out, it would hardly have been worth killing for, would it. I panicked at the time and paid that dreadful woman but I was thinking of calling her bluff.'

'Then she alerted Merlin Mitchell.'

'I had no idea about that, honestly.'

When Wesley announced for the benefit of the tape that the interview was over for the time being, Savernake again protested his innocence.

He almost had Wesley convinced.

It was Sunday morning. Pam had hardly spoken since he'd arrived home at eleven the previous night, almost as if she held him personally responsible for the disruption to her evening.

One person unfazed by the situation was Michael, who had avoided staying overnight with Daniel Savernake, something he deemed rather a triumph. As Wesley prepared to leave the house his son was getting ready for a football session with his friend Nathaniel and he asked Wesley if he could go to watch them play. When Wesley made his apologies, explaining things gently in case the events of the previous night had upset him, Michael seemed to take it philosophically.

Bradley Savernake had spent the night in a cell, sleeping, or attempting to sleep, on a blue plastic mattress. But Wesley found it hard to pity him when he thought of Stephen Newton sprouting tubes and fighting for his life in the nearby hospital.

However, he couldn't help feeling sorry for Jennifer. Although he doubted the wisdom of Pam continuing her burgeoning friendship with the woman, he feared that she might display some of her mother's stubbornness if he advised against it. He'd need to tread carefully to avoid professional embarrassment.

When he arrived in the CID office Rachel greeted him. 'I hear your whole family was there last night when Savernake was arrested.'

'I'll have to have a word about the company they keep,' he answered, half joking.

Gerry was already in his room and although he looked tired, he had the eager look of a man who was anticipating excitement in the hours ahead.

'According to the custody sergeant our friend's spent a comfortable night,' Gerry said as Wesley approached his desk. 'Pam OK?'

'Yes, but I think my sister and her husband were a bit shocked.'

'Your Mark should be used to sinners in his job, repentant and otherwise.'

'Not when they invite him round for drinks and canapés with the great and the good of Tradmouth.'

'They're usually the worst,' said Gerry with a grin. 'I want another word with Savernake but I was waiting until you arrived.'

'What are we doing about Simon Corcoran? Think he's out of the frame?'

Gerry frowned. 'I'd like to do him for something, even if it's only the way he treats his tenants, but it might not be easy if he's been crafty enough to stay on the right side of the law. I still think he's a possible for Paulette's murder though.'

Wesley nodded. 'We can always bring him in for more questioning if necessary. I'd like Rachel to go up to Dartmoor to have another word with Rosalie Slater later. It might be worth making sure Bradley's alibi for Christopher Savernake's death is as solid as everyone assumed at the time.'

'Fine by me,' said Gerry.

'That particular death was a bit to convenient for Bradley, if you ask me. *Cui bono?*'

'You what, Wes?'

'Who benefits?'

'But Christopher's parents vouched for him. He can't have done it.'

'He might have said he had a migraine, gone up to his room and then sneaked out without them knowing.'

'Well, if we could hold him on suspicion it'd do wonders for our clear-up rate and make Aunty Noreen a very happy bunny.'

'I did some research into the deaths of Christopher's parents last night. The father died after falling downstairs three years after Christopher was killed and his wife died two years later. Gastric problems.'

'It's worth looking into, don't you think?'

Gerry's phone rang and he had a brief, monosyllabic conversation.

'Bradley Savernake wants to see us,' he said. 'Maybe he's about to confess.'

Lucy had slipped home to see her mother for an hour after breakfast and when she returned to Neil's room in the guesthouse she found him going through the historical records he'd printed out when he'd first taken on responsibility for the Paradise Court dig. There were context sheets and drawings strewn all over the bedside cabinet and the dressing table too. With two sites to worry about, he felt he needed to keep up to speed with everything that was going on. He'd told her he'd been having a recurring nightmare where the cameras at the Sandrock dig were focused on him, awaiting his pearls of archaeological wisdom, and when he looked down he found that he was completely naked, his dignity protected only by a muddy trowel.

'What's the matter?' he asked as she appeared.

She sat down heavily on the unmade bed, surprised and rather gratified that he'd picked up on her mood. 'I don't know what's come over my mother.'

'What do you mean?'

'That old diary I told you about – she won't let me see it. She's threatening to burn it.'

'Why?' Neil said, so astonished at the thought of Sue Zinara flinging an old book on the fire that the word came out as a squeak.

'No idea.'

'You'll have to stop her.'

'I would have taken it there and then but she's hidden it.' Lucy shook her head. 'Whatever's in it must be really bad.'

'I want to make a statement.'

'We're all ears, Mr Savernake.' Gerry glanced at the tape recorder to make sure it was operating as it should. The last thing he wanted was for the case to fail on a technicality.

Savernake's solicitor, dragged from his lie-in with the Sunday papers, looked worried. He held a whispered conversation with his client that Wesley couldn't quite make out. Then he sat back, as though his work was done.

'Fire away,' said Gerry. He tilted his chair, balancing it precariously on the two back legs, a habit of his that made Wesley nervous.

'I admit that Paulette Reeves was blackmailing me and that Merlin Mitchell contacted me asking for more money to keep quiet. I can't say I'm sorry they're both dead. They were like vampires, they'd have sucked me dry.'

'I can imagine,' said Wesley, playing nice cop. 'Did you kill them?'

'No. And I can prove it. I've remembered where I was the Wednesday before last at the time you mentioned.'

'Where?'

'I was with someone. I went to his house around seven and ended up staying till after ten thirty.'

'Who were you with?'

Savernake smiled triumphantly as though he was enjoying this chance to get one over on the police. 'As a matter of fact it was the vicar of Belsham – the Reverend Mark Fitzgerald.'

21

1st November 1914 – All Souls' Day

The mirrors are covered and everything is draped in black. The servants move about with bowed heads, silent as ghosts.

Maisie's eyes are red and swollen with crying; whether her tears are for Stanley or for Jane, I do not know. Lady Berridge cannot bear me to leave her side. She does not cry. She cannot. Instead she stares at nothing, eyes wide as if she is seeing a vision of hell itself. She does not suggest that Jane's child, Clara, returns to Paradise Court but I know she will in time and when that time arrives I must think what to do.

However, at present she has no wish to be reminded of that unfortunate incident in her daughter's life. As long as the child is well and she can send money for her upkeep, she asks nothing more. I smile and nod as though I understand perfectly.

Lady Berridge says that she does not know what she would do without me and begs me to choose some of the fine clothes that still hang in Jane's wardrobe as she wishes me to wear them. Jane and I were of a size and she says it would give her comfort to see me in them.

*

In medieval times, Wesley recalled, people believed that lives were governed by a wheel of fortune, spun at random by the goddess Fortuna, veering from poverty to riches then down again to the bottom of the wheel. Bradley Savernake – or John Taylor – had started with nothing and, by his own wiles, he had risen in the world, only to face the dramatic fall of being arrested for murder.

But now Wesley's own brother-in-law, Mark, had given him an unimpeachable alibi for Merlin Mitchell's murder so he'd been released. Mark had confirmed that Savernake's story was true and his words still buzzed in Wesley's head.

'Bradley Savernake couldn't possibly have killed that man because he was with me at the time. He came round to the vicarage to go over the plans for his daughter Sally's memorial. I made pasta and Bradley ate with me and Maritia because Jennifer was out at some charity meeting. We talked for a while and he left the vicarage to go home around ten thirty.'

He was absolutely sure of the date because it was the evening of old Mrs Munning's funeral. He'd only just got back from the wake when Bradley rang the doorbell.

That was it. Bradley Savernake couldn't have killed Merlin Mitchell, which meant he was probably innocent of Paulette Reeves' murder and the attack on Stephen Newton as well. It looked as though they'd arrested the wrong man.

Gerry thought they should bring Simon Corcoran in again and pile more pressure on him. His picture had been on the cutting Paulette had sent to Merlin Mitchell so the whole John Taylor thing might have been a distraction. Paulette's death had solved a lot of problems for her landlord and he'd certainly been near Woodside Cottage that night.

It was possible, Gerry thought, that Reeves and Mitchell were blackmailing Corcoran too: a man with fingers in all sorts of dubious pies was bound to have a lot to hide. However, Wesley pointed out that Corcoran had no reason to attack Stephen Newton. Gerry's response was that the incident might not be connected after all. CS Fitton might be right when she said it was a homophobic attack; the fact that similar weapons were used might just be a coincidence.

Wesley said nothing. Although he agreed that Corcoran should be brought in again first thing the following morning, he felt uneasy about Gerry's new theory.

Their one recent success had been the arrest of Jayden Ross, who was now awaiting trial for the burglaries. Everything else was unfinished and this offended Wesley's innate sense of order.

As he trawled through his paperwork, he had the familiar nagging feeling that he was missing something obvious, that something was out of place.

Wesley had set off for work early on Monday morning and as Pam watched him leave she hoped he'd be home at a reasonable time even though long experience told her that this was as unlikely as a lottery win.

Following the dramatic events of the weekend she wondered whether to contact Jennifer. It was hardly Jennifer's fault if her husband had been questioned on suspicion of murder and she was starting to feel awkward about her doubts and her embarrassment, telling herself that she should have been a better friend. But even after Wesley had told her that Bradley had been released without charge, she'd delayed making the call.

She'd just fed the cat and called the children down for breakfast when the phone rang and she answered it with an abrupt hello. The last thing she needed when she was getting ready for the day was a delay to her well-planned routine.

When she heard Jennifer's voice on the other end of the line, tentative and slightly shaky, she felt a pang of guilt so strong it was as if she'd been punched in the stomach.

'How are you?' It was an unoriginal question but, in the circumstances, she could think of nothing else.

'All right. They let Brad go as soon as his alibi was confirmed but the whole thing's been very unpleasant.'

Pam stayed silent. She was a police officer's wife talking to the wife of a man who had recently been arrested for murder and she could think of no suitable response.

'I hope we can still be friends, Pam.' Jennifer sounded unsure of herself, as if she was half expecting rejection.

But Pam's innate kindness meant that she had to offer reassurance. 'Of course,' she said with more sincerity than she felt. She looked at her watch. If she didn't move, she'd be late.

'Can we meet up?'

Pam hesitated. 'Why not?'

'Are you free after you finish work? I need to talk to someone about what happened. Bradley's gone to the brewery for a meeting and you've no idea how isolated I feel. I do miss Amelia as well. I never had the chance to give her the present.'

The woman sounded as if she was on the verge of tears so there was nothing Pam could do but agree to meet her after school and then go for a cup of tea somewhere with Amelia in tow. She was reluctant to invite her into the house again, realising that, from now on, Bradley's arrest by Wesley would form an invisible barrier between them. It would be there each time they met, even if it was never spoken of.

After breakfast she watched Michael disappear down the road on his way to catch the school bus before shepherding Amelia into the back of the car. At least her day would be busy so she wouldn't have much time to think about it.

The rain was clearing just as Neil reached Sandrock. The director had arrived there early today and Neil noticed that he was looking tired; no doubt he'd been back to London for the weekend. Late nights and booze – all right for some.

Filming was scheduled to end that day but the dig would continue until the site was closed down the following weekend. As soon as the filming was over the trenches would be fenced off, allowing the public access to the site to watch them work. Following Health and Safety regulations was important because some people were idiots. Public access had been Lucy's idea as she was keen on community involvement. He liked that about her; he liked most things about her, come to that.

That Monday morning Neil was satisfied that all the necessary arrangements had been made and the thought that he wouldn't have to put up with the TV crew for much longer lifted his spirits even more.

With the public expected, he was planning to spend the next few days at Sandrock as the Paradise Court dig was proceeding well and Dave was quite capable of taking charge in his absence. The builders had already moved in to renovate the ice house. The little skeleton had been taken off to Tradmouth mortuary; sometimes he lay awake at night wondering where it would be buried. He felt an almost parental interest in the small, forgotten person and these protective feelings surprised him. Although he wanted to know the child's identity he feared that if it had a name it would seem even more real.

The wind was getting up now, flapping the tarpaulins that had been placed over the trenches overnight for protection. He looked on as the diggers began to shift them and saw Lucy helping in trench two, struggling with the covering that seemed to have gained a life of its own in the breeze. When she saw him watching she shouted to him to give her a hand, her voice rousing him from his reverie. Once work had started he crouched down next to her and began to trowel the soil away from a medieval tile. They hadn't spent the previous night together as Lucy had wanted to be with her mother and he'd been perturbed to find how much he'd missed her.

'Have you managed to get that book from Sue yet?' he asked.

'Not yet. But at least she's not talking about burning it now.' She scraped away a bit more earth, releasing a corner of the tile from its earthy prison, before speaking again. 'It's not like her to go in for high drama. Besides, it's Clara we're talking about. I know she was a bit gaga towards the end but I remember her as a sweet old thing. I'm sure she can't have done anything bad.'

'Perhaps your mum just needs time,' Neil said.

He heard loud swearing and when he looked up he saw

311

that the wind had snatched a sheet of thick tracing paper from the hands of a young man who was recording the trench, drawing each feature with great care. Neil watched as it danced across the site and fluttered down to the rooftops of the ruined village before being blown into the air and out towards the sea.

'The forecast for today says it'll be stormy later,' said Lucy.

At first the nurse didn't notice that Stephen Newton was trying to open his eyes. She was recording the readings from the bleeping machine by his bed on her clipboard when she heard a faint moan, like the elusive gasp of a ghost.

As she turned she saw his eyelids flicker.

Since Bradley Savernake's release the team had been subdued, working in silence, checking and double-checking statements and timings. Even though Simon Corcoran had been questioned again, the interview had become a monotonous litany of denials ending with the words 'prove it or release me', so when Gerry emerged from his office and called for attention everyone looked up from their tasks, glad of any kind of break.

'Good news. Stephen Newton's come round.'

There was a murmur of appreciative conversation. Rachel was about to speak but Wesley got the question in first. 'Has he said anything yet?'

'Not yet. Fancy a trip to the hospital, Wes? No doubt the nurses will be mounting guard like mother hens but we might manage to ask him a question or two before they chuck us out by our ears.'

Before they left Wesley turned to Rachel. 'Can you give Eddie Villiers a call? He might already be at the hospital but if he isn't he should be told.'

He was glad that Eddie was about to receive some reassurance.

Twenty minutes later they arrived on the Intensive Care ward only to be told that Newton had been transferred to High Dependency. Wesley knew this was a move in the right direction.

The constable on duty at the door to Newton's room was looking alert and rose from his seat as soon as he saw them.

'Morning, sir. He's regained consciousness but the nurse told me it's hit and miss. He still spends most of the time asleep.'

'Let's hope we've timed it well then,' said Gerry, his voice carrying down the corridor. If Newton was dozing now, he wouldn't be for long. A nurse bustled up, giving the DCI a stern look. When he explained why they were there she made a show of examining the watch pinned to the front of her tunic and told them they had five minutes, max. The patient needed rest. And they weren't to get him agitated.

Wesley took a deep breath before entering the room. Stephen Newton was lying on the bed, still attached to an array of tubes and monitors but probably fewer than before.

'Hello, Stephen. All right if we sit down?' Gerry said in a voice guaranteed to wake the drowsiest of patients.

The tactic worked. Newton's eyelids trembled then opened slowly.

'You remember DI Peterson here, don't you? He visited

you in Exeter. I'm DCI Heffernan. Good to hear you're on the mend. We've called Eddie to let him know you're awake. He'll probably be here soon to hold your hand.'

The man's mouth began to move. He was trying to say something and Wesley couldn't quite make out the word but thought it might have been 'thanks'.

Wesley had been hanging behind Gerry, reluctant to approach the bed. All his immediate family were doctors but he'd had no appetite for blood and pain so he'd studied archaeology instead, preferring dry bones to the unpredictability of living bodies. Now though he forced himself to step closer because he needed answers.

'Stephen, can you remember what happened?' he said gently. 'We need to know who did this to you. Can you help us?'

For a while Newton's eyes closed and Wesley wondered whether he'd heard the question. He waited a minute or so then asked again.

'Who attacked you, Stephen? Was it someone you recognised?'

The lips moved again and Wesley bent close, like a priest about to hear a dying man's confession.

He listened carefully, trying to block out the clatter of a trolley from the corridor outside the room, and at first he couldn't make out what Newton was trying to say. Then he thought he recognised a word, albeit an unexpected one. He asked the question for the third time, thinking that perhaps the sick man had misheard or that the drugs he'd been given were clouding his brain, but the answer was the same.

Wesley placed his hand on the man's bare arm: it felt hot and clammy to the touch. 'Thank you,' he whispered.

314

Stephen Newton hadn't actually named his attacker. He hadn't had to. Now Wesley understood everything.

Pam had finished seeing the children in her class off into the care of their waiting parents, grandparents and child-minders and after making sure that her classroom was as she hoped to find it the next morning and transferring her marking into her bag, she looked at her watch. Three forty-five. Amelia would be waiting for her in the school's small reception area, amidst the bright paintings and the autumn craft displays that Yolanda hoped would impress any school inspector who happened to wander onto the premises.

Teaching at the school her children attended had always been convenient. Until last summer, she'd had two to round up at the end of the day but now Michael had moved on to the grammar school there was only Amelia to worry about. She picked up her bag of school books, slung her handbag onto her shoulder and set off down the corridor to meet her daughter, suddenly remembering that Jennifer had suggested meeting after school. She slowed her pace, hoping that the woman wouldn't be waiting for her outside. If she saw her now she wouldn't know what to say.

When she reached the reception area she looked round. Normally Amelia would be sitting on one of the little wooden chairs reading a book from the library corner; but she wasn't there.

Pam called out her name, quietly at first, then louder. When there was no answer she ran to the staff room, her heart thumping. Some of her colleagues were there, drinking tea or thumbing through photocopied worksheets. They all looked up as if they sensed something was wrong.

'Has anybody seen Amelia?'

It was the reception class teacher who spoke. 'I saw her a few minutes ago. She went off with Bradley Savernake's wife – I recognised her from the social evening. She said she'd arranged with you to pick her up or I would have come to find you.' The poor young woman sounded both apologetic and horrified, as if she feared that she'd allowed something dreadful to happen. 'Amelia seemed happy,' she added feebly.

Pam turned and ran down the corridor towards the school entrance. If she was quick she might catch them.

22

12th June 1917

It is more than two years since I wrote down my thoughts in this diary.
I have had a lot to occupy me in that time. A whole new life to become
accustomed to. My lady wishes me to call her Mother. It seemed strange
at first but I have grown used to it. I have little to do with the servants
now and I know they gossip about me. It is something I must learn to
cope with.

I sometimes wonder how my own mother would feel if she knew my
situation, but, as my lady has such need of me, I see her rarely. My last
visit to Sandrock was in the spring and I was most gratified to see that
my Edith grows into a strong and healthy little girl, so like her father,
Alfred, whose bones, so my lady tells me, lie now in some French field.
My lady never inquires about Clara, who is a pretty little thing with
large eyes and an appealing face. Perhaps she has forgotten the existence
of her granddaughter as she has become very forgetful of late. Grief, I
understand, affects some people in that way.

War still rages and there are few families who have not been
blighted by violent death. When it began they said it would be over by

Christmas and yet now nobody can see an end to the slaughter. In such times death becomes commonplace.

I went into the walled garden earlier to gather flowers for the drawing room and I thought there was somebody in the shrubbery near the gate. But I might have been mistaken.

Wesley received the call as he was walking back from the hospital with Gerry.

'I think Jennifer's taken Amelia and I've no idea where they've gone,' Pam said as soon as he answered.

'Taken her?' Those two words made the world freeze around him. He halted and Gerry almost cannoned into him. 'Are you sure? Has she left a message on your phone?'

He was hardly aware that he'd raised his voice, hardly aware of anything except the scenarios playing in his head.

'No. I've tried ringing her number but there's no answer. She called me this morning and suggested that we meet after work. I had the impression she wanted someone to talk to so I said yes.'

She sounded anxious but there was no real panic in her voice. However he knew that if he revealed what he had just learned from Stephen Newton she'd lose control. And that would help nobody.

For a few seconds he couldn't speak; he felt numb, as though somebody had pumped his body with some creeping chemical, but he had to stay calm. Professional. He told Pam to keep trying Jennifer's number and his fingers felt clumsy as he ended the call.

'What's up?' Gerry's voice almost made him jump.

'Jennifer Savernake's picked Amelia up from school.'

'How come?'

'She asked Pam if they could meet after school but instead of waiting for Pam she just took off with Amelia. She's been fussing over her, inviting her to stay the night, offering to take her out and buy her presents. Pam said it was because she'd lost her own daughter and I was starting to feel uneasy about it but Pam . . . '

Gerry put a comforting hand on his shoulder. 'Hindsight's a wonderful thing, Wes. Any idea where they might have gone?'

'No.'

'Think.'

At first the only thoughts swirling around his head were guilt and regret. What kind of a father was he if he couldn't even protect his own daughter? What kind of a policeman was he if he couldn't see the truth when it was so close to home?

Then he felt a glimmer of hope. 'She might have taken her back to her house.'

'I'll send a patrol car round. And I'll ask all patrols to look out for her car. And Bradley's big SUV – we don't know which one she's using.'

Wesley shut his eyes while Gerry made the calls. Amelia had been going on about a number of places recently. She was a chatterbox, always curious, always talking about something. But where would Jennifer take her?

'I have to get out there and look for her,' he said when Gerry had finished.

'You'd be better staying at the station and waiting.'

Wesley opened his mouth to protest but no words came out.

As they reached the CID office Wesley's mobile rang again; it was Pam asking for news and telling him that Michael was safe at his friend Nathaniel's house. Wesley could only repeat Gerry's advice and reassurances. All patrols were on the lookout for them and a car was being sent to Jennifer's address. During the call he managed to sound calm, hiding the turmoil inside. He hadn't been aware that his acting abilities were that good.

A sensation of paralysing helplessness made him feel sick as Gerry stood at the front of the incident room and told the team what had happened. The reaction was horrified silence followed by a flurry of activity as calls were made. It was ten agonising minutes before the patrol reported that there was nobody in at the Savernake house, news that struck Wesley like a physical blow. He could see the concerned, pitying looks of the team as they glanced towards him then away again, but he didn't want their sympathy. He wanted to be out doing something.

After what seemed like an age Trish took another call and announced that a red Mercedes registered to Jennifer Savernake had been spotted on the coast road running between Bereton Ley and the sea, not far from the memorial to the American troops who'd lost their lives near there during the D-Day landing practices. A patrol car was following at a distance.

This was enough for Wesley. He couldn't wait any longer. He was going to follow and would keep in touch with the patrol car to see where she was heading.

Gerry started to make for the door, mumbling something about not letting him go alone. But Wesley told him to stay put. He knew that pointing out that Gerry was still supposed to be on light duties wouldn't go down well so instead he told him it would be best if he stayed to coordinate things. He'd take someone else.

As he was leaving Rachel hurried up to him. 'I'm coming with you,' she said in a voice that brooked no argument. Their eyes met and she touched his hand. 'We'll find her,' she said softly.

Rachel was a good choice. Together they headed out of the door.

As soon as filming finished that lunchtime the film crew vanished in a little convoy of SUVs and vans. Off to make another archaeological team's lives a misery, Neil observed with a cynicism that made Lucy smile.

The safety barriers had now been erected in anticipation of the site being open to visitors. But today wasn't a good day for it. The wind that had been blowing since the previous night was strengthening ahead of the storm that had been forecast.

It was almost five o'clock and Lucy doubted whether any members of the public would be arriving now, so she ordered everyone to clear up, secure everything against the weather and go home.

Rachel pressed the phone to her ear. 'What do you mean?'

As Wesley took his eyes off the road for a second and saw her anxious expression panic welled up inside him again. He heard her lower her voice and repeat the question, replying with a sarcastic, 'Great,' before suggesting that whoever it was on the other end of the line go back and look.

'What is it?' Something was wrong and he wished she'd just get it over with and tell him.

There was a short delay before she answered. 'The patrol

car's lost her. They were following her but they didn't want to get too close. She must have turned off somewhere. Sorry.'

Wesley tried to tell himself that it was just a setback but it was no use. A murderer had his daughter. And by now she must be desperate.

23

3rd October 1917

There have been no male servants at Paradise Court since they went off to fight and now the last of the women have left too; three to aid the war effort and the old cook because the heavy work was too much for her. I have engaged three girls to replace the maids and a cook from a house in Neston that was shut up following its master's death. They call me madam and take me for a relative of my lady's. I do not correct them in their assumption.

At my lady's request I wear Jane's clothes. She speaks of having new ones made. If it gives her pleasure and comfort to treat me thus, it would be cruel to disagree.

I think often of Edith. How I long for her to be with me and be raised as a lady, as is her due as her father's daughter. But my lady needs all my attention. She is my mother now.

14th October 1917

There has been another storm, this time worse than the last. I hear from my sister that two houses in Sandrock have collapsed and are in danger of falling into the sea. The occupants were rescued by their neighbours but I fear for Edith's safety and that of Jane's daughter, Clara.

My lady still suspects nothing of Edith's existence. Perhaps if I tell her that she is some relative of mine, orphaned by the storms, she will allow her to come and live here with me. If so, perhaps Clara and her grandmother will be united again.

I must plan what I will say.

Neil touched Lucy's arm. 'Time to go?'

'I want to double-check the tarpaulins first,' she said.

'I'll give you a hand.'

Everyone else had left for the night and digging would resume tomorrow, weather permitting. Neil had dug in all sorts of weathers but a full-blown gale would be a first. Still, if necessary the team could retreat to the shelter of the nearby barn that was serving as the site headquarters until the worst was over.

'Doesn't bode well for our public outreach,' Lucy said. 'Can't see us getting many visitors.'

'It's been in the local paper,' Neil said, trying to inject an upbeat note.

Fortunately the interior of the ruined church where the trenches lay open was sheltered from the wind by what remained of the standing walls, although that wouldn't afford much protection in a violent storm. With Lucy's help he ensured that the tarpaulins the team had hauled across the open trenches were secure and weighed down. He just hoped their efforts would hold.

'You're not going to your mother's tonight, are you?' he asked when they'd finished. He took hold of both her hands and looked at her sadly, hoping she'd take pity on him and the answer would be no.

'I don't like to leave her on her own.'

In his opinion she was fussing over her mother too much. Clara had been a hundred so her death had hardly been unexpected. However, there was the question of the book that had upset her so much. Perhaps that was why Lucy was worried about her mother's mental state. He hardly liked to ask so he said nothing.

They walked away from the site, arms linked, making for the car park.

All of a sudden Lucy stopped and pointed towards the ruins of the village. 'There's someone on the viewing platform.'

'Bloody hell. There's a kid as well. They should be careful in this wind.'

'Think we should have a word?'

A voice carried over the wind, a child's voice saying she wanted to go home. The adult had the child by the hand and was pulling her roughly off the platform and down the little path that led into the village. For safety reasons the path was blocked off and hung with dire warnings of danger.

'I'm going to see what's going on,' said Neil.

Lucy clutched at his arm. 'Be careful.'

Neil took no notice. He half walked, half ran down the path towards the platform, the wind stinging his face, and when he reached it he steadied himself on the guard rail. Lucy had followed him, her eyes searching the ruins beneath them for signs of movement. After a while she shouted, pointing at one of the cottages. 'There they are.'

He heard the child's voice again, there for a second then swallowed by the wind. He left the platform and began to follow.

'You're not going down there?' Lucy shouted.

'Some people need saving from their own stupidity. Stay there.'

When he reached the gate he saw that it was open and that the chain holding it shut had rusted, rendering it useless. Someone had cocked up badly on the maintenance front.

He found himself on a rough path between the remains of two rows of cottages, their glassless windows dark like empty eyes. When he stopped and listened he could hear nothing above the sound of the wind whistling around the half-demolished walls. Then he shouted, 'You shouldn't be here. It's dangerous.'

At first there was no answer and no signs of movement. Then a pretty child with dark skin and jet-black wavy hair, wearing a bright red coat, emerged from the doorway of the cottage at the end of the row.

As soon as Neil recognised her his first impulse was to rush over, scoop her up in his arms and carry her to safety. But he forced himself to remain calm and called out, trying to keep the panic he felt out of his voice. 'Amelia. It's Uncle Neil. Come on, let's get out of here.' The child looked at him with huge brown eyes and when she didn't move he held out his hand. 'Let's go up to the top where it's safe. Just walk towards me. Don't be scared. Where's your mum?'

She didn't answer. He knew the person she'd been with wasn't Pam, who would have had more sense than to bring her daughter here, but he couldn't think who else Amelia was likely to be with.

The child took a step towards him, turning her head a little as if she was uncertain of something.

'Come on, love. I'll give your dad a call, eh.'

Amelia nodded eagerly but when she didn't move Neil sensed she was frightened of something other than the precarious ruins.

He started to approach her when the woman emerged from behind a half-tumbled wall, her eyes wild. She grabbed Amelia and held her tightly, her arm around her chest. With dawning horror it struck Neil how easily that arm could creep up to her throat. 'Stay where you are and give me that phone,' the woman shouted. 'Throw it over here.'

Neil had no choice. He did as he was told.

The moment Wesley stopped the car and turned off the ignition his phone rang. It was Pam, demanding information, her voice on the edge of hysteria. She'd been ordered to stay at home in case Jennifer returned with Amelia but waiting was shredding her nerves while all kinds of dire possibilities flitted through her mind.

He did his best to calm her, pointing out that, as Jennifer obviously loved Amelia, she wouldn't let her come to any harm. She probably just wanted to spend time with her. As he spoke, Rachel listened in silence, knowing that Wesley needed to believe his own words. The alternative was too dreadful to contemplate.

'I need to think,' he said when the call ended.

'Is there anywhere round here that she's likely to go?' Rachel was trying to sound strong and capable but she was starting to feel helpless. She didn't know Jennifer Savernake and had no idea why she'd decided to take Amelia Peterson. Each possibility that flashed through her mind seemed more alarming than the last but she prayed she was wrong about all of them.

Wesley closed his eyes. For a few moments he looked as though he was asleep. Then his eyes flicked open again, bright with realisation. 'Amelia's been going on about visiting the aquarium in Plymouth. Jennifer promised to take her there.'

'We're nowhere near the Plymouth road.'

He knew Rachel was right. 'There is another possibility. She said she wanted to see the ruined village where Neil's working. It's not far away so she could be headed there.' He turned the engine on again.

'Shouldn't we wait for the patrols to report in? If we set off in the wrong direction . . . '

'I can't sit here and do nothing. Try Neil's number, will you. He might still be there.'

Rachel did as she was asked but there was no reply.

Wesley set off and headed down the darkening lane.

The light was fading and the chill wind was penetrating Neil's coat. If he was cold, little Amelia must be feeling worse.

'What shall we do?' Lucy whispered. She had been unable to resist following him and now she was standing a few feet behind, her eyes fixed on the two figures. The woman was holding the little girl firmly and she was starting to back away down the remnants of the village street, dragging the child with her.

'You still got your phone?' Neil hissed.

'It's in my car.'

Neil swore under his breath. 'Go back and call the police.'

His words were swallowed by a strong gust of wind that almost knocked him off his feet as the sea roared like an engine below. There was a crash somewhere behind them that sounded like an explosion and when Lucy swung round she saw that her path was blocked by fallen masonry from the swaying first floor of one of the cottages.

She could see an alleyway to her right but in all likelihood it too was impassable. However, it was worth a try. She began to sidle towards the gap in the crumbling buildings, only to hear the woman's voice barking an order.

'Don't move.'

As Lucy obeyed she heard a sob. The child had started to cry with fear.

'What do you want?' Neil shouted.

The woman answered after a few seconds' silence. 'We need to get away. We want to go somewhere where we can be together.'

Her reply gave him new hope. If he could keep her talking he might be able to reason with her. 'Can't you see Amelia's scared? You don't want to harm her, do you?'

The woman looked surprised that this man in soil-stained clothes knew the child's name. 'She wants to see the ruins.'

'Well, she's seen them now. There's a storm brewing so if I were you, I'd get her out of here.'

The woman tightened her grip on Amelia's red coat, hugging the girl to her like a thing of comfort.

'I want to go with Uncle Neil,' Amelia sobbed.

'No you don't. We came to see the village. Then we're going away somewhere nice.'

'Why don't you let me show Amelia round? You'd like that, wouldn't you, Amelia?'

When Neil held out his hand Amelia began to wriggle to free herself but the woman glared at him, her face a mask of hatred, like a bad actress attempting to play a mother protecting her young. As she dragged the child into a doorless building, out of sight, he heard more masonry crash. He turned his head and saw Lucy clambering over the collapsed wall, trying to reach the car and her phone, but Neil knew he had to stay there and try to protect his friend's daughter as best he could.

He started to creep forward towards the ruined house. He could hear Amelia crying and though the woman was talking to her in a soothing voice he sensed that things could change in an instant.

He edged towards the doorway and stood still for a while, contemplating his next move. He could hear the woman singing softly to Amelia. It sounded like a nursery rhyme. Even he knew that Amelia was far too old for nursery rhymes.

Then he heard an ominous rumble followed by a crash. Back in 1918 the earth below half the village had tumbled into the sea and since then more of the cliff had eroded, causing landslides at regular intervals. He felt the earth beneath his feet shake a little and knew he had to do something.

'Hello,' he called out.

The crooning stopped and all he could hear was the wind and the relentless waves churning below them.

'This place is collapsing,' he shouted. 'We've got to get out.'

There was no reply and no movement.

'Bring Amelia out. We can take her up to the car park. You'll both be safe there. The police aren't here.'

He heard the sound of scuffling footsteps; he held his breath and stepped back.

The woman appeared from the doorway, holding Amelia's hand tightly. The little girl was looking at him with wide, pleading eyes and he knew he couldn't let her down. He held out his hand to her but when she reached to take it the woman saw what was happening and hauled her back.

'Let's go somewhere safe,' he said, forcing himself to smile at Amelia reassuringly.

The woman wavered, then took a step forward. His tactic had worked. Once they were out of the danger zone he'd decide what to do next.

He was leading the way, stepping gingerly over the rubble, when he heard a police car siren. He swore under his breath and spun round to see the woman hauling Amelia roughly back into the ruined house. He heard the child scream. Then the earth trembled again.

24

4th January 1918

He has been watching me and tonight he chooses his moment, spring-ing from the bushes when I walk in the garden at dusk as is my habit. He grabs my arm. It hurts. He puts his face close to mine and I can feel his stubbly chin against my cheek and smell his sour breath.

'You look quite the lady,' he says.

'You're dead,' I reply.

Stanley, once so bold, grins like a death's-head and I see that his teeth are brown and crooked. He is thin as though he hasn't eaten for a long time.

'Missing believed dead,' he corrects me. 'I got away. I would have been a fool to stay there and die.'

'You're a deserter,' I say, suddenly afraid.

He reaches out his filthy hand and grips my chin between his fin-gers. They feel like pincers.

'I saw a chance and took it.' He pulls me towards him. 'I know your little secret. Captain Toncliffe told me when he was dying. His guts were hanging out and he was bleeding like a pig but he was

thinking of you. Sweet.' His mouth forms a malevolent grin. 'What would my lady say if she knew about your little bastard, eh?'

'You haven't asked about Jane,' I say to distract him. He drops his hand and stands as if frozen by some spell. 'She's dead,' I say. The words are sharp. I have no desire to spare the feelings of a brute.

He turns away from me and begins to walk. He does not ask about the child he fathered. When he is a few feet away he faces me again. 'I know what you are and what you're up to,' he says, then starts to move towards the gate. I ask him where he'll go but he does not reply.

Lucy had managed to reach the top and when Wesley arrived she was waiting there to direct him to the right place. He left her with Rachel and went to the ruins alone, clambering over the wreckage of a collapsed cottage, his heart pounding and his trousers filthy with dust and mud. He found Neil standing, stunned, in the ruined street, his face pale, drained of blood.

'They're in there. I tried to—'

Wesley wasn't listening. He darted forward until he reached the empty doorway where he could see Jennifer standing in what remained of the house, hugging Amelia close. A mother with a precious child.

As soon as Amelia saw him she yelled, 'Daddy!' and tried to break away but Jennifer Savernake grasped her with clawing fingers, so tight it must have hurt.

'Jennifer, let Amelia go now,' Wesley shouted over the wind, his heart racing. 'Can't you see she's terrified?'

Jennifer shook her head vigorously and clamped the little girl tighter in her clinging arms, her desperate, tear-filled eyes searching for an escape route as if she'd just realised her situation was hopeless.

Without warning the ground beneath their feet shook

again, more violently this time. Wesley heard a crash as a wall collapsed nearby. The land was slipping away, sliding into the sea as it had done all those years ago.

Instinct made him lunge forward and Neil, a few feet behind him, did the same. They were heading into danger but all he cared about was saving Amelia. He could hear her screaming, a desperate sound that pierced his heart, then suddenly he realised that she had vanished, as had the back wall of the cottage. It had tumbled down the cliff along with half the floor and he could see Jennifer lying flat on her stomach, her head over the place where the ground had fallen away. But there was no sign of Amelia.

Wesley thought he must have screamed but the wind swallowed the sound. He dashed towards Jennifer, his feet leaden and slow, clumsy with panic. Somehow he reached her and saw Amelia dangling over the edge of the fallen earth, nothing between her and the roaring sea far below. She was crying helplessly and clinging to Jennifer's out-stretched hands.

Wesley's next action was automatic – he grabbed his daughter's arm and hauled her upwards. Jennifer was no longer important; the only thing that mattered was saving Amelia.

With one final pull he succeeded and suddenly realised that he and Jennifer had been working together to effect the rescue. Wesley swept Amelia up and carried her to safety, handing her to Neil who set off for the viewing platform at a trot with the child in his arms.

Wesley turned back to Jennifer, who was squatting on the edge now, staring ahead, tears streaming down her cheeks, seemingly unaware of her surroundings. He watched her for a few seconds, the woman who'd almost killed his daughter. There were no witnesses now so it would be easy to say she'd jumped. One little push and she'd topple into oblivion.

Lucy came to Neil's room that evening and they lay entwined in each other's arms, hardly speaking. The events of that day had stunned them both but at least Amelia was now back home after a quick check-up at the hospital. She was safe, and that was the most important thing.

'I can't understand why she did it,' Lucy said as she poured a glass of wine.

'Wes told me she'd lost her own daughter a few years ago and she became obsessed by Amelia. Simple as that.'

'I suppose it's understandable – sort of. I take it she's been arrested for abduction.'

Neil hesitated. 'That and . . . I don't know the details but Wesley said she's being charged with murder – something to do with those cases he was involved in: the man in the hotel and the woman who was murdered near Whitely, the one who kept her old mum in a freezer.'

Lucy sat up. 'Are you saying that woman killed them?' Her eyes widened at the thought she'd just survived an encounter with a murderer.

Neil didn't answer. Just at that moment he wanted to forget all about it. In his head he could still hear the dreadful crashing of the cliff as it fell into the hungry sea below. It could so easily have ended in tragedy but they'd been lucky and got out of there alive. He was glad when Lucy changed the subject.

'I slipped back to Mum's house to get changed after we left Sandrock. She was out so . . . I found the book.'

'You pinched it?'

'It was hidden at the back of a drawer. I've brought it with me but I'd better put it back before she notices it's gone.'

Neil put a hand out and stroked her hair. 'Let's hope she doesn't look for it tonight then. I take it you're staying?'

'I'm sure Mum can manage by herself for once.' She slipped out of bed and fetched the book from her shoulder bag on the chair in the corner of the room. Neil saw that it was old and battered but, in his experience, old, battered books were often the most interesting. Unselfconscious of her nakedness, she sat down on the edge of the bed and began to turn the pages.

'Well?' he said after a minute had passed.

She was so engrossed that she didn't reply. He watched the expressions pass across her face. Interest turned to fascination which, eventually, turned to worry. After a while Neil couldn't contain his curiosity. He asked her what was in it but again she didn't answer.

She continued to turn the pages, faster now, as though she was devouring every word.

Years of digging disappointing trenches which promised much but contained little of interest had trained Neil in the art of patience but after fifteen minutes he was reaching his limit.

He was relieved when she closed the book and handed it to him, her face giving nothing away.

He read. And when he reached the end he knew the identity of the child in the ice house.

25

1st February 1918

A man has been found in a ditch a hundred yards from the gates of Paradise Court. It seems that he has been dead some weeks and his body froze in the recent bitter cold and snow. The constable called this morning to ask if he was known to anybody in the house. I deny all knowledge and my lady takes my lead.

The constable says that his skull was caved in and I suggest that perhaps he had a fall on the ice. I say it is a tragedy but that we know nothing.

Lady Berridge is most unwell and I see to her every need. Long gone are the days when she held court among her young men, all of whom are now dead; their gilded lives curtailed by shells and bullets and their noble ends announced on black-edged cards sent by their unhappy relatives. There is so much death and I wonder what will arise, phoenix-like, from the ashes of such destruction.

After luncheon I take the trap and drive to Sandrock because my lady desires to bring Clara home to live with her at Paradise Court at last. I have informed the servants of her arrival and I am to hire a nurserymaid.

5th February 1918

I am home in Sandrock but it does not feel like home. After Paradise Court the small stone cottage perched on the side of the cliff above the churning sea seems like a hovel. There is a single room downstairs with a blackened range and rag rugs strewn on the cold stone floor, two rooms upstairs and a privy outside in the little yard. I can see where two cottages at the end of the little street have fallen into the sea and I wonder if my mother's house is in danger.

My sister greets me warily and my mother rocks by the range, her head nodding in sleep. There is no sign that any comforts have been purchased with the money Lady Berridge sends for Clara's keep and I find myself wondering what my sister has done with it. She tells me that when her sweetheart, George, returns from the war she will marry. I do not say that many won't return. My own brother, Nathan, is missing in action and I know he is dead, although I do not say as much. The certainty would kill what was left of my poor mother's spirit.

Edith and Clara are playing with wooden dolls at my mother's feet and I watch them but they are so intent on their play that they do not seem to see me. Edith is not as tall as Clara now and I think she is small for her age and delicate. I can see Alfred in her and for a moment my eyes sting with tears, for she hardly knows me. To her I am a barely recognised aunt who descends into her world from time to time like some distant angel and then flies off again. How I long for it to be different this time. When I say this to my sister, she turns her head away.

The wind is getting up. Now only men too old to serve in the war take the boats out and, out of long experience, they read the weather and know to stay ashore. I go out into the cold and watch them drag their boats up the shingle beach well out of harm's way.

The storm is coming. I put Mother's blanket over her knees and shudder.

*

Wesley had spoken briefly to Pam when she'd arrived at Sandrock to take Amelia to the hospital to be checked out. She'd been distant at first, numb with shock at the thought of what might have been. Then he'd held her in his arms, wiping away her tears of raw relief, and Amelia had clung to them both. When she'd taken their daughter off into the darkness he wished he could have gone with them. But he knew he couldn't leave. He needed to know, to understand why Jennifer Savernake had done what she did.

Gerry was firm about one thing: he wouldn't allow Wesley to conduct the interview. The DCI would do that himself, along with Rachel, and Wesley could watch from the little observation room next to interview room two. He could stay behind the two-way mirror while they probed until they got at the truth.

He tried to forget his split second of madness in that ruined house. That brief moment when thoughts of vengeance had overwhelmed all his beliefs and long-held principles. His momentary loss of control had frightened him and as he sat watching the interview he did his best to put it out of his mind.

In Wesley's opinion Jennifer Savernake had always dressed elegantly. Now though the blue paper crime-scene suit she was wearing reduced her to the same sartorial level as that of all those other female suspects he'd interviewed in the course of his career. The well-cut blonde hair fell limply and the immaculate make-up had been wrecked by the wind and damp. She appeared to have aged ten years since they'd brought her in.

She sat there next to her solicitor. She hadn't chosen Bradley's, the man who usually dealt with Savernake's Brewery's legal business. Perhaps she hadn't wanted him to witness her shame but Wesley thought that, if she'd been innocent, she would have wanted people she knew to fight her corner. The solicitor with her was a stranger from an Exeter practice. He was a small man of indeterminate age with a bald head and a sympathetic expression more appropriate to a doctor breaking bad news than a member of the legal profession. Wesley saw him watching Jennifer warily, as though he feared she might do something foolish.

Gerry began the questioning. In spite of the late hour he looked alert enough. 'Stephen Newton's identified his attacker.'

Jennifer said nothing.

'He told us he saw your husband in Tradmouth. He recognised him from when they worked together years ago and he followed him to your house where they had a lengthy conversation. Your husband kept denying that he was John Taylor and, according to Mr Newton, he seemed upset, which isn't surprising if someone from a past you'd rather forget turns up out of the blue.' He paused. 'We asked Mr Newton if your husband had attacked him but he told us he hadn't. He said it was a woman, the same woman he'd seen at Bradley's house. He described you.'

Wesley held his breath, waiting for an answer, but when none came Gerry continued. 'Bradley's past's been catching up with him recently, hasn't it? First of all one of the women from the cleaning agency turns out to be the ex-girlfriend of a man he was involved with many years ago. Then, lo and behold, she gets in touch with her ex and tells him that Bradley – once known to them both as John – is now worth a fortune and ripe for a spot of blackmail. Have you always known about your husband's past or did it come as a surprise?' Gerry looked at her quizzically, awaiting her reaction.

She sat staring ahead and Wesley fixed his eyes on her face. He saw the solicitor whisper something in her ear but she turned her head away as if what he'd just said was unwelcome.

Then she spoke. 'I'd been going through some bank statements and I found that money was going out of our account with no explanation – large sums in cash. When I asked Brad about it he broke down and told me something had happened long before I knew him. And he said that terrible woman had recognised him.'

'Did he tell you about the Bay View Holiday Camp?' It was the first time Rachel had spoken. Wesley saw Jennifer give her a long stare, as if she was trying to imprint all her features on her memory.

'Yes.'

'Why don't you tell us what he said,' said Gerry, sounding almost avuncular.

She looked uncertain at first, then she swallowed hard and began to speak. 'Bradley's mother was an alcoholic. She abandoned him when he was five and he was brought up in care. He left his foster home at the age of sixteen and drifted from one dead-end job to another before he started working at that holiday camp and met Merlin Mitchell.' She hesitated. 'Bradley said he was a horrible man ... he described him as evil.'

'In what way?' Rachel asked.

'He stole and cheated but he had this charm that attracted people to him. Charisma, Bradley called it. He got away with all sorts – even murder. And he liked to control people.'

'Did Bradley know that Mitchell had killed a child? Her name was Fiona Carp.'

Wesley, his face close to the glass, was listening intently.

'Not at first. He said he wondered at the time but Mitchell convinced him he was innocent. And he had an alibi.'

'Paulette Reeves supplied the alibi but she was besotted with Mitchell. He could have persuaded her to say anything.'

'It wasn't until they'd gone abroad after it happened that Mitchell told Bradley the truth. He told him the kid found him stealing from a chalet and when she started to scream and threaten to tell the police, Mitchell lost it and strangled her to keep her quiet. He told Bradley he hadn't meant to do it.'

'What did Bradley tell you about his relationship with Mitchell?'

There was a long period of silence as she studied her hands with great concentration. This was a sensitive subject, Wesley guessed, something she'd rather not face. She finally spoke in a low whisper and Gerry had to ask her to speak up for the tape.

'They had a sexual relationship,' she began. 'And after the child was killed Mitchell persuaded Bradley to go abroad with him. He went round the Greek islands sponging and stealing, using Bradley as his accomplice. In the end Brad hated it. He wanted to get away but he didn't know how. Then he met a boy called Christopher Savernake and he started giving Mitchell the slip to meet him. I don't think there was anything sexual in it. Bradley just saw in Christopher a way of escaping from Mitchell, and Christopher was everything he wanted to be. He came from a wealthy family and Brad wanted his life – not only the money but the close family he'd never had. Anyway, one day Chris got into difficulties when they were swimming and Bradley saved his life.'

'What happened?' said Gerry, glancing at the two-way mirror.

Wesley held his breath, waiting for the reply.

'Merlin Mitchell was pressuring Brad to get money out of Chris but Brad had other ideas. He'd told Chris his "friend" was becoming a pain and he wanted to get away from him and return to England only he had nowhere to live. Chris was going home and Brad asked if he could go with him. Brad had saved his life, you see, so Chris couldn't deny him anything. They left for the airport without Mitchell knowing.'

'And came back here to Devon?' Rachel said.

'He wanted to make a fresh start and Christopher insisted that he move in with the Savernakes. He'd saved his life after all.' She bowed her head. 'Then Christopher was killed and the Savernakes came to rely on Bradley. He took the place of their only son, which I can understand.' She looked at Gerry with pleading eyes. 'I wouldn't have hurt Amelia. It's the anniversary of my daughter's death today and I just needed her near me.'

Tears began to spill down her cheeks making pale tracks in her make-up. Wesley watched her, feeling for the first time a small twinge of sympathy until he remembered what she'd put him and Pam through. Sometimes forgiveness was the hardest thing.

'Tell Pam and Wesley I'm sorry,' she said, taking a tissue from her pocket to wipe the tears away. 'I'd never have harmed her.' She looked up, suddenly hopeful. 'I never had a chance to give her the present. It's a bracelet. It's in my bag. Can you . . . ?'

Gerry shot another look at the mirror. 'Let's get back to what happened between Bradley and the Savernakes.'

Jennifer took a few moments to compose herself before she spoke again. 'The Savernakes came to regard Brad as their son – he even took the family name by deed poll. When they brought him into the family business he did really well, so by the time Mr Savernake died, he was ready to take over.'

'And when both parents died Bradley inherited everything – the house and the business.'

She nodded. 'He had a lot of new ideas and the business has gone from strength to strength. That's why he's been able to sell the company and take a back seat.' The tears began to form again. 'We had so many plans for the future.'

'You're not his first wife, are you?' Rachel asked. The question was blunt, almost critical.

Jennifer squirmed in her seat. 'No,' she said, looking intently at the table. 'Brad married a girl from Exeter who came to work in the brewery lab. She died when Daniel was a toddler. It was tragic. After Daniel was born she had trouble with depression. She fell from a cliff near Littlebury.'

'Suicide?' Rachel asked.

'There was an open verdict. It could have been an accident. That's what we've always told Danny.'

'How did you meet him?'

'At a function – a charity my parents used to be involved with.'

'Are your mum and dad still alive?' said Gerry.

'No.' She bowed her head. 'They were killed when their light aircraft crashed on the way to Cheltenham races.'

'Did you meet Bradley before or after his first wife died?'

'Shortly before but Bradley kept in touch. I think me losing my parents and him losing his wife forged a bond between us. We married and I had Sally, but a few days after her second birthday she died of meningitis.' She winced as though she was in pain. 'We sold Belsham Manor, the Savernakes' old house, because there were too many bad memories there.' A shadow passed across her face. 'Sally died in that house. I couldn't stay there.'

At the mention of Belsham Manor a small worm of memory wriggled at the back of Wesley's mind. Before he could capture the elusive thought, Rachel spoke again.

'But, apart from losing your daughter, you had everything: wealthy husband, beautiful house.' Her voice was so soft it was barely audible. 'Your inheritance, the proceeds from the sale of Belsham Manor and the brewery.'

Jennifer gave her a sad smile. 'None of it could make up for losing Sally.' The smile vanished. 'Then that horrible woman started demanding money. She threatened to make it public that Brad had been a rent boy and a thief. She was going to say that he'd drugged Christopher Savernake's drink so that he could pretend to save him and that he'd killed Christopher in order to take his place. She said he'd be charged with murder – that we'd lose everything. She said Daniel would be taken away from us. I couldn't let that happen.'

'So you killed her?'

There was a long silence and Wesley saw her bow her head like a penitent.

'Why don't you tell us what happened?'

'Merlin Mitchell contacted Bradley and said he wanted to meet him. To talk about his obligations was how he put it, but Brad knew what he meant. Mitchell had joined forces with that woman and they were going to bleed us dry.'

'Couldn't Bradley have threatened to tell the police how Mitchell killed Fiona Carp?' Gerry asked.

Jennifer shook her head. 'He tried that but Mitchell just turned it round. He said that if Brad tried that one, he'd just say Brad did it. He'd say he confessed to it when they were abroad then ran off. He was going to make himself look the innocent and say he kept quiet because he felt sorry for Brad because he was so young. It would have been his word against Brad's and Brad said he could be very convincing. I had to act. I couldn't let them ruin us.'

'What did you do?' Gerry asked.

'While Brad went to see the vicar about Sally's memorial in Belsham church I went to see Mitchell. I took a weapon and some of my pills with me. I had to keep him talking while they took effect so I pretended to . . . ' She shuddered. 'He didn't see me as a threat. He even suggested that I had sex with him, said he'd let us off a few payments. He was a disgusting man.'

'You went in by the restaurant door?'

'How did you know?'

'Why didn't you go through the main entrance?'

'I didn't want to walk through Reception and I knew that there's a passageway to the toilets and the back stairs. We've been to functions there, you see.'

'What about Paulette Reeves?'

'I called at her cottage, hoping to reason with her.'

Wesley saw Gerry catch Rachel's eye. She looked as sceptical as he felt.

'When?'

'After I'd been to that school do at the Tradmouth Castle Hotel. Must have been just before midnight.'

'You dropped Mrs Peterson off first?'

'Yes.' She smiled. 'I really like Pam. I hoped she'd let me share in Amelia's life: take her out, give her treats.'

The words brought the memories back and Wesley knew that if he'd been in that interview room he would have found it hard to control his emotions. But instead he took a deep, calming breath and listened. Gerry and Rachel were doing well. They were getting to the truth.

'Let's get back to the night you killed Paulette Reeves,' said Rachel. 'What happened?'

'She followed me out and started to attack me so I picked up a tree branch and lashed out. It wasn't planned.'

Gerry rolled his eyes. 'Don't play games with us. She wasn't killed with a branch. What did you use?'

'OK, it was that thing you use to change car tyres. Not sure what it's called.'

'So you must have taken it from the car. It was premeditated.'

She didn't answer.

'Stephen Newton wasn't threatening your husband, was he?'

'Not like the others but he knew Bradley's real identity so I couldn't take the risk.' She looked at Gerry with pleading eyes. 'You have to understand.'

'I'm trying to. You admit trying to kill Mr Newton?'

'He came to the house. We managed to get rid of him and as he was leaving I drove out in the car and offered him a lift. He kept asking questions and calling Bradley "John". He said he had to get back to Tradmouth to meet someone but . . .'

'You stabbed him.'

347

'Yes. Then I drove around for a while wondering what to do. I ended up in an isolated lane.'

'Where you pushed him out of the car and left him for dead.'

She stared ahead. 'He was groaning at first but then he went quiet. I thought he'd die.'

'Where's the weapon you used? We're organising a thorough search of your house but it might save time if you told us.'

A smile crept onto her lips. 'It's part of the Savernake family silver, from a set of silver meat skewers. Georgian.' Without warning she began to laugh, a mirthless, bitter sound. 'Pam and that vicar's wife were eating kebabs off them a couple of evenings ago. That's rather funny, don't you think.'

Wesley felt anger rise up in his throat like bile. How could she laugh after what she'd done to Stephen Newton? To Amelia?

The laughter continued, tinkling at first as if someone had just made an unfunny joke. Then it became hysterical. And as Wesley stood there, fists clenched, watching unseen, the laughter turned to tears.

While he'd been watching the interview with Jennifer Savernake Wesley had turned his phone to silent and when he left the observation room he discovered he'd received three missed calls from Neil Watson. There were many formalities to be dealt with in the aftermath of Jennifer's confession so he resolved to call him back later. Gerry sometimes talked longingly about a far-off past when crime didn't generate so much paperwork, but Wesley was too young to remember that golden age.

After the interview was over the anger he'd felt had slowly lifted. She'd face justice now. It was over. The Savernake house was being searched and the search team had been instructed to pay particular attention to the Savernakes' fine collection of Georgian silver meat skewers.

He wondered whether to tell Pam and Maritia that they might possibly have been eating off a weapon that had killed one man and seriously injured another but he felt it might not be wise. On the other hand, the nature of the weapon would eventually be made public at the trial and Pam would probably ask why she hadn't been told. He smiled to himself. If this was the only dilemma in his life, he was a lucky man.

When Gerry entered the CID office there was a distant look in his eyes, as though his thoughts were far away. Wesley stood up to greet him, asking how Jennifer was.

'As you'd expect, Wes,' was the reply. 'Don't know how she'll get on prison but that's not our problem. Tell you what, will you go up to the house and see how the search is getting on.' He paused. 'And have a word with Bradley while you're there. We need him to come in and make a full statement and as he knows you . . . ' He didn't have to finish the sentence. Wesley understood.

He walked up to the Savernake house, his head bent against the prevailing wind. On the way he saw the words STORM CAUSES CHAOS AT RUINED VILLAGE. CHILD SAVED scrawled on a sign outside a newsagent's shop. The sight made him shudder and hurry on, worrying about his forthcoming meeting. What do you say to a man whose wife has just been charged with murder?

When he arrived, he found Savernake in his study on the first floor. He had retreated there while the search was in progress and he looked almost relieved to see Wesley, offering him a coffee with an eagerness that suggested desperation. Wesley accepted and followed him down to the kitchen. It was a socially awkward situation, so Wesley asked the first question that came into his head.

'How's Daniel?'

'He's gone to school. I thought it was best to keep everything as normal as possible.' He looked up at Wesley with appealing eyes. 'When I told Jennifer the truth about my past and how that woman was blackmailing me there was no way I imagined that she'd react like that. She's been fragile since Sally's death but ... '

'If you'd known would you have stopped her?'

'Of course.' Somehow the answer sounded unconvincing. 'Will Stephen Newton be OK?'

'Yes.'

'I don't know why she had to hurt him. He didn't pose any threat to me. Not like the others.'

'She probably panicked when he recognised you.'

Savernake poured boiling water into the cafetière. 'I'm glad he's recovering.' He stared at the coffee grounds as they settled at the bottom. 'How's Amelia?'

'She's all right.'

'I'm so sorry about what happened. I should have seen it coming and got Jenny to see someone. She needed help. I understand that now.' He paused. 'How's she bearing up?'

'She'll be seen by a psychiatrist. She'll be looked after. You'll visit her?'

He nodded but his expression was uncertain. Wesley wondered whether the man would abandon the woman who'd killed for him or whether he'd bathe in the sympathy that he could generate if he set his mind to it. Poor Bradley – he was the one whose unbalanced wife killed those people. He wondered what kind of man Bradley Savernake – or rather Jonathan Taylor – really was. But the case was closed. Jennifer Savernake had confessed and there were no more questions to ask.

Savernake poured the coffee and they drank in silence, as though the man had run out of things to say. As soon as his cup was empty, Wesley heard his name being called and excused himself. Once out in the hall, he found a uniformed constable standing by the dining-room door, eager to break the news that a set of silver skewers had been found in the sideboard drawer. The constable looked so pleased with himself that Wesley felt obliged to tell him he'd done well and to get the things bagged up for forensic examination.

He felt uncomfortable about leaving Savernake alone in the house with the uniformed intruders but he told himself firmly that he wasn't a clergyman or a social worker and it wasn't his duty to comfort those in trouble. He'd done his job and now others had to face the consequences. Nevertheless as he made his way back down the hill into the town he thought he might call Mark and ask him to go round and have a word.

As the police station came into view Gerry rang him with news which made him feel worse. Rosalie Slater, the woman who'd stood trial for Christopher Savernake's murder, had been found dead in her cottage on Dartmoor. And she had left a note addressed to Wesley.

The information about Rosalie's death had been vague but, no doubt, he'd learn more when he read the note which was being brought down to Tradmouth in a patrol car.

Bradley Savernake was still in his head. Over the years life had dealt him some terrible blows. Then he had risen in the world and had become heir to his adoptive family only for tragedy to strike again when he had lost his first wife to suspected suicide, his daughter to illness and his second wife had become a killer. In the absence of Rosalie's mysterious note to distract him, he needed something else to think about. He remembered that Neil had been trying to reach him so he gave him a call to see what he wanted.

'I've been trying to get hold of you all morning,' Neil said accusingly as soon as he answered.

'We've charged the woman who abducted Amelia with murder,' Wesley said.

There was a shocked silence on the other end of the line before Neil spoke again. 'Amelia all right?'

'She seems fine. I think she's enjoying being the centre of attention. Children are very resilient, so Pam keeps telling me. What's going on at Sandrock?'

'Luckily the church where we're digging is a bit inland so it's not in immediate danger but the safety people have been swarming round all morning sealing off the part of the village that collapsed last night. The public access to the dig's been cancelled, which is a shame. And I'm still busy at Paradise Court. In fact that's what I wanted to talk to you about. Can we meet? Late lunch?'

Food had been the last thing on Wesley's mind and he suddenly realised that he hadn't eaten. He told Neil he'd meet him in Bereton in twenty minutes and picked up a pool car in the station car park.

When he reached the village he parked outside the Bereton Arms and inside he found Neil ordering a pint at the bar. After Wesley ordered a shandy and a sandwich they settled in a quiet corner by a window overlooking Bereton's old chantry chapel. Neil took a sip of Savernake's Best Bitter and smacked his lips appreciatively.

'So what did you want to tell me?' Wesley asked.

Neil took out a sheaf of A4 papers stapled together at the corner and handed it to Wesley. 'This is a copy of a notebook Lucy's mum found when she was clearing out her great-grandmother's things in the nursing home. You should read it, especially the end. It's a confession to murder.'

'Was this over seventy years ago?'

'Yes, but . . . '

He pushed the papers back to Neil. 'Then it's not my problem.'

Neil looked disappointed. 'Don't you want to know who killed the child in the ice house?'

'Normally I would, yes. But I've been up to my eyes in paperwork.' He saw the disappointment on Neil's face and took the papers back. 'Oh, all right then. Who was it and why?'

'You'll have to read it. Lucy and her mum are in shock.'

Wesley had only reached the third page when his phone rang. It was the station. The officer with Rosalie's note had arrived and if Wesley wanted to see him, he'd have to come back to the station sharpish. Wesley drained his glass and took a final bite of his tuna sandwich.

'Got to go. I'll take this with me if that's OK,' he said, stuffing the papers into his pocket.

Neil raised a hand in farewell. He'd done his bit. 'Might see you later,' he said.

But Wesley was already making for the door.

*

Wesley's name was printed neatly on the envelope and the young constable who'd brought it over stood watching as he tore it open with shaking hands and pulled out three sheets of cheap lined paper. If she'd left a note it meant she must have killed herself and the thought of her despair disturbed him.

He read the note through, his heart pounding. Then he read it again just to be sure he hadn't missed anything. It was a confession: Rosalie Slater had killed Christopher Savernake after all but, because of a lack of evidence, the jury at her trial had concluded that the case hadn't been proved beyond reasonable doubt. Rosalie had lived burdened by guilt ever since. And Wesley's visit had acted like a stick probing a wound that had never really healed.

At the time of Christopher's death the lies had come easily but even though she hadn't faced the justice of the law, she'd paid in years of loneliness and misery for her terrible impulsive sin. Wesley put the letter down and stared into space, taking in the words and the pain and guilt behind them. He'd never really believed she'd been responsible for the murder: perhaps he was losing his touch. He could see Rachel, head down over her paperwork. Rosalie had fooled her as well and that made him feel slightly better.

'How did she die?' he asked the constable who was standing there awkwardly, shifting from foot to foot.

'The doctor says it was probably an overdose. The PM's being done in Exeter.' He swallowed. 'From the state of her place, I'd say she didn't have a happy life.'

Wesley gave him a sad smile. 'I know. I've seen it.' He wondered whether to let him in on the contents of the note but decided against it. 'Thanks for bringing this. It clears up a few loose ends.'

He watched the young man leave, fastening his coat against the cold that would hit him as soon as he stepped outside. Then he took the letter across to where Rachel was sitting and perched himself on the corner of the desk.

'This is Rosalie Slater's suicide note.'

'She seemed depressed when we saw her. I feel bad that we didn't do something; put her in touch with someone who could help her.'

He pushed the letter in front of her. 'Before you start beating yourself up over it, read this.'

She scanned the pages. 'So she did kill Christopher Savernake.'

'Yes, but a clever barrister could have reduced the charge to manslaughter. Have you read the second page?'

She nodded.

'What do you think?'

'Just because someone plants an idea in your head, it doesn't mean you have to act on it.'

Wesley took the letter back to Gerry's office. Rosalie's confession had raised some intriguing possibilities; questions that needed to be answered.

Somehow he had the feeling that their investigation wasn't quite over yet.

26

10th February 1918

I would have returned to Paradise Court with the child yesterday but the rain lashes down as the wind tears through the street and sets the waves roaring in the sea beneath the village. The weather is mad; as mad as war. The sea crashes on the shore and the old men and boys, the only ones not away at war, haul the smaller boats up onto the street for safety.

I must stay another night in this hell and I watch as my sister prepares my mother for bed. I see that the left side of her body is now paralysed and her mouth is dragged down at the left corner. I wonder why my sister did not write to Paradise Court to tell me of her illness. Then I look down at my fine leather boots and know that I am no longer a part of this.

I hug Edith to me, fearing that she will be frightened by the storm, and when she wriggles away to play her game with Clara I feel suddenly alone. I am a fish taken from the sea. I do not belong here anymore and my sister has become my daughter's mother. But it was from my own choice. As soon as I met Alfred I knew what I desired from life.

The fire has gone out and I am cold.

12th February 1918

I have been dozing by the fire and I am awoken by a terrible sound as if the house is collapsing around me. I hug the rough blanket that keeps me warm and I think of Edith upstairs in the bed she shares with Clara. As I lunge for the little wooden staircase in the corner of the room I can hear my sister screaming, 'Get everyone out!'

The house shakes as though the earth itself is crumbling beneath it. I call out my sister's name, then my mother's. My sister calls down to me to come up for the children for Mother is cold and dead. I crawl up the stairs on my hands and knees, clinging to the splintery wood as the earth shudders.

I hear a child's cry and I call to my sister but she does not answer. The house trembles again and plaster falls from the ceiling like snow. It is dark and I feel my way to the room where Edith and Clara sleep in their old iron bed. In the light of the moon I can see their small shapes huddled beneath the quilt and I hear wordless, terrified sobs. The room is crumbling. I must get them out.

My daughter reaches out to me, clinging to my sleeve, and I whisper words of comfort in her ear. Then Clara starts clawing at me and I almost drop Edith. I try to lift her but I know I cannot carry them both. I tell Clara in a clear voice to follow me but she wails and clings like a limpet while my Edith is still and compliant in my arms. I call to my sister for help but hear no reply.

There is a crash. Then another like thunder from below and the house shifts again. Holding Edith tightly, I take Clara's hand in mine and make for the neighbouring room where I see my sister on the floor, a great rafter lying across her body. I know she is dead.

As I stagger from the house I see others around me, emerging from their homes dazed as if they have witnessed the terrors of hell itself. Carrying Edith and leading the sobbing Clara by the hand I stumble away towards the church where I meet the vicar running towards me. He asks what can be done for the unfortunate souls in the village. I tell him that my mother and sister are dead.

As the buildings crash into the hungry waves I struggle against the wind and driving rain, covering my daughter with my shawl so that she will not catch cold and dragging Clara after me. She is howling now. I shout at her to keep up and when I let go of her hand the crying stops and she follows me like a desperate little dog following its master. We pass the church where many have taken shelter but a man shouts to me that there is no room so I head for the Toncliffe Arms, named for the family of Edith's father. I make for the stable where my pony and trap are kept and spend a few hours resting with the girls in the warming straw, the animal nuzzling us as if we were its foals. The girls sleep soundly but the howling of the wind keeps me awake and I plan what I must do next.

In the early hours of the morning we set off for Paradise Court while the storm still rages, bending the leafless trees and snatching the roofs off barns. I tell the girls to huddle down in the back but Clara cries and throws off the shawl I have put over them to keep them warm.

Our way is blocked by fallen branches and when I jump down and move them Clara too tries to alight, despite my stern instructions to stay in safety. My Edith is a good and obedient child and I wonder whether Clara has inherited her mother Jane's wayward nature. I scoop Clara up in my arms and place her on the seat beside me yet still she wails. I drive on until we reach Paradise Court, where I take the back drive and see the ice house on my left. A great tree sways next to it, creaking ominously. Clara lets out a howl and climbs down from the trap, having no sense of danger. When I stop and grab her she sinks her sharp little teeth into my arm.

13th February 1918

Lady Berridge stands by the portico of Paradise Court, clinging to a pillar as she watches the trap approaching up the drive. Edith sits beside me, her thumb in her mouth. She wears her nightgown because all her clothes are gone with my former home which is now half tumbled into the sea.

My lady hugs Edith, her tears mingling with the rain that wets the child's hair. She calls her Clara, for I have always kept Edith's existence a close secret and, since Alfred's death in France, there is nobody to tell her that I once gave birth to a daughter so all will be as I intend. When my daughter tells her that her name is Edith, I explain that it is a name my mother gave her but from now on she will be Clara and she shall be raised a lady. I say she is precocious for her age, as clever as a child a year her senior. The grandmother glows with pride, tears glistening in her eyes. She says she is like Jane and I force myself to agree, although I remind myself that my lady is indeed her great-aunt, Edith's father being her nephew. There is a blood tie there.

A week had passed since the night of the storm and Amelia had fully recovered from her ordeal. Pam, however, was still subdued and she confided to Wesley that she'd lost confidence in her own judgement. He'd held her in his arms and told her that nobody could have foreseen what would happen, but however much he reassured her he knew she'd still keep blaming herself.

She'd said little when Neil spent Saturday night with them, discussing what he'd discovered about the child in the ice house. Wesley could see parallels between the way Martha had inveigled her way into the family at Paradise Court and the way John Taylor had wormed his way into the lives of the Savernakes. Perhaps he was letting his imagination run away with him but, reading Martha's journal, he had sensed the same ruthlessness, the same desire for social elevation, the same cunning manipulation.

Neil had come alone. Lucy, he said, was spending time with her mother, who still hadn't recovered from discovering the truth about her ancestress. Wesley wondered whether anything would come of Neil's new relationship. He'd seen so many women come and go in his friend's life but maybe Lucy Zinara would be different. Time would tell.

As far as Gerry Heffernan was concerned, the whole business of Jennifer Savernake's involvement in the recent murders was cleared up. And Rosalie Slater's suicide note had answered most of the questions posed by Christopher Savernake's untimely death.

After meeting Sue Zinara in Tradmouth that day, Rosalie had told her she was going home; but instead she'd driven to Belsham Manor and waited at the gates. She'd been told that Christopher was planning to go out to meet friends at the beach, including a girl she suspected of being a rival for his affections, and when his car appeared she'd stepped out to block his way in the rarely used lane. When he'd left his car to speak to her she'd tried to discuss their future. She'd heard he was planning to finish their relationship and, being insecure, had believed it. Someone had played on those insecurities and planted the seeds of murder in her mind.

Rosalie had always been highly strung and had a violent temper. She and Christopher had quarrelled several times about her possessiveness and on the day of his death she'd pushed him hard in her frustration and he'd fallen against the gatepost, hitting his head and falling unconscious.

Terrified and hysterical, she'd run to the very person who'd placed those worms of doubt in her mind and he'd persuaded her that she had to keep quiet. It would be best if she didn't call an ambulance – that would only draw attention to the terrible thing she'd done.

In her letter she'd named the whisperer of doubts, the person who'd told her Chris's plans that day and suggested she challenge him, telling her how Chris had been saying things about her and was planning to end their romance. And she'd believed every word, every piece of well-meant advice, because, after all, Jonathan knew Chris better than anyone. He'd saved his life once so that made them sort of brothers.

Wesley thought for a while. There was something he could try – it was a long shot but worth checking. Nick Tarnaby had provided his mother's phone number and Wesley rummaged through his desk to find it, doing a quick calculation to make sure that the time in Perth, Western Australia wasn't too antisocial for a call. When a woman answered he introduced himself as a colleague of Nick's and expressed his condolences on the deaths of her half-sister and her stepmother. She said the news had been a shock but as he asked his questions she became effusive, as if she was glad of the chance to talk about it. And he listened carefully to what she had to say.

He hadn't been sure whether the big house where Dorothy worked had been Belsham Manor, then the home of the Savernake family, but now he discovered that his gamble had paid off. Dorothy had indeed been employed as a domestic help by George and Mary Savernake at the time their son Christopher died and, to Wesley, this opened up a whole new set of possibilities – or it would have done if Dorothy hadn't been dead and unavailable for questioning.

Wesley's hopes were raised further when he mentioned the name Maud Parkin, the woman Nick had said Dorothy used to work with. He knew his luck was in when Nick's mother confirmed that Maud had been housekeeper at Belsham Manor when Dorothy had been there. Maud Parkin, a nice woman, she said, had moved into a retirement home in Newton Abbot some years ago. She'd written to tell her the sad news already. Did Wesley want her address?

After Wesley had written down the address and thanked her for her help, he took another look at the file on Christopher's death, only to find that Maud hadn't been at Belsham Manor when it happened because she'd been on holiday. Then for a moment doubts began to bubble up in his mind and he asked himself whether the Savernake connection was really relevant now that Bradley's innocence had been vouched for by his own brother-in-law. But somehow he couldn't resist digging further. He needed to banish the niggling feeling that there were too many coincidences; a feeling that was keeping him awake at night as the possibilities paraded through his head.

However he felt rather pleased with himself for making the connection from Nick's casual remark, and he was anxious to find out what Maud would have to say about those far-off days at Belsham Manor.

He made a phone call to the retirement home before asking Rachel if she was free to go with him to Newton Abbot.

Wesley and Rachel met Maud Parkin in the dining room of the Abbot's Lane Retirement Home. The room smelled faintly of boiled cabbage but it was the only place in the

362

building where privacy was guaranteed. Maud herself was a small round woman in her nineties with snowy curls and clouded eyes, and although she was wheelchair-bound and half blind, her memory was still sharp. She'd worked as housekeeper to George and Mary Savernake and she was only too keen to talk, as though she'd bottled up her thoughts on Christopher's death over the years and was glad of the chance to unburden herself at last.

Jonathan Taylor, she said, was such a nice lad and he'd been a tower of strength to Mr and Mrs Savernake after their loss. If it hadn't been for him, things would have been much worse. He'd become a son to them. Such a charming boy.

Wesley and Rachel listened for ten minutes while she extolled Jonathan's virtues and told them how he'd taken the family name and inherited everything on his adoptive parents' deaths. Maud had left Belsham Manor after George Savernake's death because Jonathan said that, with the household reduced to just himself and Mary, there was no need for a housekeeper. Maud had been intending to retire anyway, so she wasn't too put out about her redundancy and she'd still taken an interest in the family, attending Mary's funeral when she died. Only three years later Jonathan's new wife died tragically leaving him widowed with a small son. Then came his second marriage to a lovely girl from a very well-to-do family and the death of his little daughter, Sally. That poor man, she observed, has been so unlucky.

After she'd finished speaking, Wesley asked the question that had been on his mind since their arrival and when Maud answered, a picture began to emerge of a clever and subtle manipulator, cunning as the serpent in paradise. It was going to be hard to prove but Wesley thought he knew how he could do it.

Over the next few days Wesley obtained a couple of inquest reports, showing them to Colin Bowman to check whether his suspicions were feasible. Several nights later he met his brother-in-law Mark in Belsham churchyard, along with a team of officers and forensic specialists.

He'd never attended an exhumation before and he stood at the side of an open grave lit by floodlights, the scent of dank earth in his nostrils, watching with numb fascination while Mark intoned prayers for the dead. The whole scene seemed surreal, like something from a bad horror film, and Wesley prayed that the sorry spectacle would provide the proof he needed so badly.

Three days later the results of the postmortem on the body of Mary Savernake landed on his desk. He read the report through carefully before taking it to Gerry.

'I think you'd better read this,' Wesley said as he placed the report on Gerry's desk.

Gerry put on his reading glasses and squinted at the page. Once he'd taken it in he filled his cheeks with air and blew out slowly. 'So a quantity of arsenic was present in Mrs Savernake's body. After all this time it's going to be hard to prove who was responsible in a court of law.'

'George Savernake died after falling down the stairs at Belsham Manor. An accident with no witnesses. What if it wasn't an accident? And Bradley's first wife threw herself off a cliff, supposedly suffering from some kind of depression. Then six months later he goes and marries Jennifer, a woman who's just inherited a fortune. Rather indecent haste if you ask me.'

'I don't see how we can prove anything either way after all these years,' said Gerry.

Wesley ignored his misgivings. 'After George's death Jonathan told Maud Parkin, the housekeeper, that her services were no longer required.'

'Maybe they weren't.'

'Or he didn't want a witness to what he was planning to do. After Christopher was killed, the deaths of George and Mary put Jonathan in sole charge of Belsham Manor and Savernake's Brewery. He had every reason to want them dead.' He leaned over the desk. 'Don't you see, Gerry, this was his first mistake. George and Mary Savernake were two inconvenient people he couldn't persuade someone else to get rid of – or, in the case of his first wife, to commit suicide.'

'Jennifer Savernake didn't need much persuading to eliminate anyone who was threatening her family,' Gerry pointed out.

Wesley shook his head. 'I've never been comfortable about her getting the idea out of the blue. After losing her daughter she was unstable and vulnerable. I think her husband played on that just as he'd played on Rosalie's insecurity about her relationship with Christopher. You've read Rosalie's letter. It was in Bradley's interest that Christopher should die so that he could take his place so I think he set it all up.' He smiled. 'He exploited Rosalie's jealousy by suggesting that Chris fancied someone else and he told her exactly where Chris would be. He even stopped her calling an ambulance.'

'There was no guarantee she'd kill him.'

'If it hadn't worked he would have tried again, whispered more poison into her ear until she acted. Or maybe he'd have thought of some other way. He was clever . . . and he was patient.'

'You think he killed George and Mary?'

'After they changed their wills he probably got sick of waiting for his inheritance so he decided to hurry things on a bit. He let Maud Parkin, the housekeeper, go just when Mary Savernake would have needed the extra support.' He paused. 'Arsenic always used to be known as the Inheritor's Powder.'

'Where did he get hold of it?'

'Arsenic was incredibly common at one time: it was used in tonics and beauty treatments as well as to control pests and flies; Victorian homes were awash with the stuff. Belsham Manor was a rambling old place owned by the same family for centuries, so he could easily have come across some in a forgotten attic or cellar. Still, unless we get a confession we'll never know.'

'But there were postmortems on the Savernakes. Surely—'

'Mary Savernake had been prone to gastric attacks for a while and her doctor put her death down to a continuation of her old trouble.'

'Is the doctor still alive? Have you asked him about it?'

'Unfortunately he died ten years ago but he'd recorded Mary's death as due to natural causes and, as you know, it isn't routine to test for poison at a postmortem unless the death as regarded as suspicious. Most people assume arsenic poisoning belongs to another era so I doubt if the doctor would have considered it anyway. And I bet Bradley played the grieving son to perfection.'

'What made you think of arsenic?'

Wesley looked down modestly. 'An old diary belonging to

a friend of Neil's gave me the idea.' He hesitated. 'I wish we knew what really happened in Corfu when he was supposed to have rescued Christopher Savernake from drowning. If I was a betting man, I'd lay odds on the whole thing having been a set-up so he could worm his way into Christopher's life. Paulette Reeves might have been right when she said he drugged his drink. He'd watched Merlin Mitchell. He'd learned from a master.'

Gerry grunted, a sound Wesley interpreted as agreement.

There was a long silence before Wesley spoke again. 'One possibility's struck me. What if he deliberately encouraged Jennifer to befriend Pam so he could keep track of the investigation?' He didn't wait for an answer. 'Are you coming with me?'

'Where?'

'Where do you think?'

'Are you sure about this, Wes?'

Wesley had another look at Mary Savernake's latest post-mortem report. 'Yes, I'm sure.'

Gerry shook his head and exhaled. 'In that case I'll leave it to you. I think I've been overdoing it so I'll stay here and hold the fort.' He smiled. 'Besides, I think this is one arrest you deserve to make. Why don't you take Rach?'

When Wesley and Rachel arrived at the Savernake house half an hour later it took some time for the door to open and when it did Wesley was surprised to see Laura Pullin standing there in a cleaner's tabard, duster in hand. He noticed that Rachel was staring at her; like him, she was probably wondering what this woman was doing cleaning the house of her aunt's killer.

'We're here to see Mr Savernake. Is he in?'

Laura looked from one to the other, her mouth slightly open. 'I'm surprised you haven't heard. He's gone abroad and asked Simon's company to let the house. Fully furnished.' Her cheeks coloured at the mention of Simon Corcoran's name and Wesley guessed that there'd been a reconciliation. 'I'm short-staffed at the moment so I'm having to help out.'

Wesley was surprised when Simon Corcoran appeared behind her.

'Mr Corcoran. Didn't expect to see you here.'

'Just looking after my client's investment,' the man said smugly, putting a hand on Laura's shoulder. 'If you want to speak to me again, I'll need to phone my solicitor.'

'It's not you we want to see this time,' said Wesley, trying to keep the note of regret out of his voice. 'Do you know where Mr Savernake's gone?'

'France somewhere, I think,' Corcoran said casually. 'Or it could be Spain. Or maybe it's Portugal.'

'He said he wanted his son to have a fresh start after what happened,' Laura chipped in. 'I know his wife wasn't the lad's real mum but . . .'

'You'll have a forwarding address for him?'

Corcoran shook his head. 'He's made arrangements for the rent to be paid into a Swiss bank. It was a sudden decision but you can't really blame him for wanting to leave it all behind, can you? Now if that's all, I've got work to do.'

As they were walking back to the car Rachel put her hand on Wesley's.

'Not your fault,' she said softly.

27

12th March 1918

I care for my child, careful to call her Clara, and my lady now treats her as a granddaughter. It is what I longed for, what I committed the ultimate sin for.

I have not been near the ice house since that dreadful night. The place where the real Clara lies is ruined and untouched and for a while I feared that my lady would order its restoration and that Clara's body would be discovered. However, I went to great pains to point out that the ice house is no longer of use so it is hardly worth the trouble and expense of repair. She listens to my advice and says she does not know what she would do without me.

I had not intended her to die when we set out on that dreadful journey from Sandrock but I realised as I entered the grounds of Paradise Court that I had little choice if my plans were to be fulfilled. The death of a young child is something that scars the soul and I suffer for it now with nightmares about the terrible thing I had to do to secure for my Edith the future she deserves.

My lady treated me almost as a second daughter and only Jane stood in my way. My lady has no inkling that Jane's demise was not an act of God. They call arsenic the Inheritor's Powder but it can also serve as the Interloper's Powder. After Jane's death I took her place but another dilemma presented itself when Jane's lover, the deserter Stanley, returned. I had to act before he could discover my secret and left his body in a ditch so that he was taken for a tramp and given a pauper's burial. Nobody looks for a man all believe is already dead.

From the start I had it in mind to swap the girls' identities, to beg my lady to give her granddaughter a home after Jane's death, allowing Edith to take her place. Being loath to kill a child, I hoped that I could accomplish my plan by leaving Clara in Sandrock to be reared as a village child. But on the night of the storm, with my mother and sister dead, it was necessary for me to act. When we reached Paradise Court Clara was crying and struggling against me and, in my attempt to calm her, I covered her mouth with my hand and when I withdrew it she was still and lifeless. I knew that my Edith had seen but she is young and she will forget. Then I heard the tree swaying and creaking, about to fall on the ice house, so I placed her body in there, escaping just before the tree crashed down and crushed the little building, reducing the entrance to rubble. There she rests, hidden from the world for ever for nobody pays any attention to such a sad ruin.

Lady Berridge called her solicitor to the house yesterday and she has made a will leaving me a substantial sum and naming my daughter as heir to her fortune. I pray I will not have to act again but there is always a chance that a face from my past may reappear to betray me and my lady's suspicions might be aroused should she ever learn that I have a daughter. I recall the sharp-faced Daisy from those days in the freezing attic at Sandton House. I will never return to those cold days again.

'Is that your son?'
    'Yes.'

The woman with the Dior sunglasses and the bleached blonde hair made a show of looking round. 'Where's your wife?'

The man's face clouded, as if the question had exposed a deep well of raw grief. 'She died a year ago. Cancer.'

The woman sat up in her sunlounger and began to flap an apology, all sympathy. 'Oh I'm so sorry. Forgive me. It must be difficult for you with . . . ' She nodded towards the boy with the pasty flesh who was preparing to jump into the swimming pool, seemingly without a care in the world. 'I'm a widow myself. I spend half the year here. I find it helps, getting away.' She picked up her glass of sangria.

For a while they sat in adjacent sunloungers, sipping their drinks, before the woman broke the silence.

'I'm Carla Van Husan, by the way. I have a villa nearby but I love this spa. You get such a nice sort of person here. Very *sympathique*,' she added in a faux French accent that sounded vaguely ridiculous. After a few moments she leaned towards him, giving him a good view of her sun-wrinkled cleavage. 'I was thinking, would you like to come up to my villa tonight for something to eat? Bring your son, of course.'

The man smiled, showing a perfect set of teeth. 'That's very kind of you. I don't know anybody here yet.'

The woman giggled and took off her sunglasses to reveal a network of deep lines around her eyes. 'I'm sorry, I don't know your name.'

The man held out his hand. 'Jon. Jon Taylor. Pleased to meet you.'

'Likewise.'

Historical Note

By all accounts the summer of 1913 was glorious. The sun shone for weeks on end in a clear blue sky and all was right with the world – until war was declared a year later on 4th August 1914 and all the comfortable certainties of post-Edwardian British society vanished. The First World War was a catalyst for massive social change. Not only were the lives of a whole generation of young men snuffed out on the battlefields of Europe but, in their absence, the women left behind were obliged to aid the war effort by taking on all those vital jobs necessary to keep the country running.

Before 1914 it was common for women to be employed in domestic service but, as women's opportunities increased during wartime and afterwards, the number who chose domestic work in private households plummeted. War was to change the strict social structure of the country for ever.

But for one small Devon community, war wasn't the only problem they had to face at that time. My fictional village of Sandrock is based loosely on the village of Hallsands on the

South Devon coast. On the night of 26th January 1917, Hallsands fell into the sea during a terrible storm and terrified families – mostly women and children as the men had gone off to war – had to watch helplessly while their homes collapsed around them. Twenty-five families found themselves homeless although fortunately (unlike in my fictional Sandrock) there were no casualties.

As I've been writing *The Death Season*, the south-west of England has once again been battered by violent storms, just as it was on that fateful night in 1917. However, back then it wasn't only nature that was to blame for the destruction of Hallsands. Sadly, the greed of man had a hand in it too.

Hallsands was a fishing village with around 150 inhabitants occupying thirty-nine houses. It had a shop with a post office, an inn with stables, a piggery, a mission room that was used as a community centre and a chapel, and most of the men made their living from the sea. But this little community was to be devastated by the demands of big business.

In 1886 the government approved plans to extend the naval dockyard at Devonport some twenty-five miles away and the lucrative contract was awarded to Sir John Jackson, who was involved in politics and whose company grew rich on public contracts. Jackson needed access to large quantities of shingle to meet his building requirements so he applied to dredge the area around Hallsands. The villagers protested, predicting that the beach would begin to fall, and, even though their MP, Frank Mildmay, began a campaign to stop the dredging and compensate the victims, Sir John Jackson used his considerable influence (and, allegedly, bribery and other illegal measures) to ensure that it continued. Mildmay described the process: 'The greater part of the shingle was taken between high and low water mark, so that the dredgers sucked the very beach itself.'

The beach did indeed fall and eventually the government revoked Jackson's licence. But by then it was too late and houses began to collapse. Jackson finally agreed to a meagre settlement and work began on a new sea wall. This wall was to hold until a combination of high tides and south-easterly gales overcame the sea defences and destroyed the village. The people of Hallsands lost their homes and in 1918 only £6,000 was offered to the village in full settlement. However, in that same year Sir John Jackson's luck ran out when a parliamentary inquiry found him guilty of overcharging the nation on war contracts. He died in disgrace a year later.

As for ice houses, James I commissioned the construction of the first modern ice house in Greenwich Park in 1619 (there were medieval versions known as ice pits but none is known to have survived). Ice houses are subterranean structures, strong and well insulated, and the ice stored in them was usually obtained from a nearby pond or lake and used for the preservation of food. These small brick-lined buildings, with a drain hole in the base so that slow-melting ice could drain away, became widespread in the eighteenth century to service well-to-do estates and manor houses. Once the preserve of royalty, they became a status symbol, albeit a useful one, for the gentry and the wealthy. In the nineteenth century vast quantities of ice were imported from America and Norway for the ice houses of Britain. However, the invention of the refrigerator in the later part of that century put an end to the trade and to the ice house itself.

The structures lay forgotten and abandoned, although some were reinstated as useful storage areas and air-raid shelters in the Second World War. Many, of course, have fallen into ruin over the years, but some that are still intact have once again found use as garden stores, wine cellars and even bat roosts. And, who knows, with modern ecological concerns, those lucky enough to have them might one day be able to ditch their fridges and freezers and return them to their original use.